Mercury Rising

☿

I0769772

C.R. BATCHELLOR

First edition McDermottBooks 2025

ISBN 979-8-9857085-2-3 (ebook)
ISBN 979-8-9857085-3-0 (print)

Table of Contents

1.

Firing from Cold

12th October 1875, Chale Bridge

WITHOUT WARNING, THE straining spanner slipped. A clang echoed across the great space of the fitting shop, followed immediately by a livid Greek oath and then a clatter.

Sucking fresh blood from where her knuckles had barked on the valve chest, Harriet Colton glared at the intractable nut and then stooped to retrieve the spanner from the uneven flags.

"Would you like me to get that, miss?" asked Blakes timorously. He had good reason to tread softly; Harriet had been irascible since she'd arrived that morning.

"It would be a kindness, Blakes." Still furious with the obstinate fastening and her inability to shift it, she handed off the spanner and stepped out of his way.

She watched him work for a while but then realised her presence was making him nervous. Perhaps it was better to delegate to the apprentice the whole matter? No one liked having their shoulder breathed over while they worked, and Father was of the firm opinion that responsibility catalysed learning.

"We need the entire assembly removed to exchange the steam feeds," she reminded him. "Get what you can done tonight, and then finish it off in the morning."

Blakes touched his cap and looked eager. "Right you are, miss."

Harriet strode towards the door to the machining shop but paused to consider the great locomotive, her new-forged metal gleaming in the wan sunlight that filtered in through the grimy skylights, a small bevy of fitters swarming upon her like anxious flies.

Construction was well advanced, yet she remained but the function within the form. Born of a generous imagination, she had frames and driving wheels, boiler and firebox, and even cylinders and driving gear but as yet no cab nor fairings nor copper-work nor any of the miscellanea befitting a locomotive ready for the road. Indeed, she appeared almost *dishabille*, swaddled in underclothes of grey lagging and with all her inner mysteries on display. In Harriet's imagination, however, she was already beautiful and complete, running free over the broad straight metal rails of England.

Her name was *Mercury*, swift messenger of the gods, for speed was at her heart. She was by far the greatest locomotive that Colton and Holm had ever built, and when completed, Harriet knew she would be the finest in the Empire.

Harriet and her father had worked on her now for most of a year. More truthfully, Father had, and she had when she could; even though she had been struggling for her diploma at the Stephenson Institute in Newcastle, they had corresponded almost every day—thick letters crowded with sketches and suggestions, problems and solutions, pressures and dimensions detailing every aspect of *Mercury*'s design.

Mercury was an extraordinarily bold conception, a slap in

the face to the pedestrian progress of locomotive evolution, and her design had thrown up far more obstacles than either of them anticipated. In Newcastle, Harriet spent a sizable amount of her free time studying learned journals in the Institute's prodigious library, seeking precedents. She found few recorded, but those she did find were disturbing, questioning many of the traditional engineering rules that had served everything that previously had emerged from Pennydale Works.

They had striven to include the latest discoveries, but in the face of the unknown, Father's confidence had clearly wavered. He had engaged in her absence a *slip-sticker*—an engineer more at home with paper than bright metal, and who rarely ventured out into the fitting shop.

Gazing at the flat hats and grease-stained overalls of the workmen busy upon *Mercury*, Harriet's expression soured. It was this Mr Staley who forced their labour, insistent on a late change to the steam feeds. Getting out the old feeds was going to be a trial, let alone trying to manoeuvre in the larger bore ones on which Staley had insisted.

Everything about *Mercury* was a tight fit, even upon the forgiving seven-foot gauge of the Empire. Thank God, the miserable four-foot... (Harriet frowned)...—something narrow gauge had been sent packing by Lord Clifton well before she'd been born! Of course, he'd been simply Isambard Kingdom Brunel then.

She reflected on her current mood. Staley's presence irked her. No, it *undermined* her. She'd worked four long, hard years to get her engineering diploma, the first rung in establishing herself in her chosen vocation. Such a thing had been undreamt of in her father's day, when reputation came solely with doing and doing well. In that, Harriet had perfect confidence.

Yet the world was changing. Once, the *scientific* gentlemen had picked over the trail left by the engineers, pontificating to one another, diverting curiosities for the most part ignored. Under Her Majesty, however, the world had rapidly grown more complex, and practical men stumbled where once they had strode. The scientific gentlemen had caught up then and threatened not to be dabblers but the coming masters, and now anyone wishing to establish a reputation had first to learn a new litany of intangible theorems and convoluted equations. Harriet had struggled with it, finding it dry and utterly abstracted from the real business of bringing forth from ingot steel a living thing, yet she had refused to surrender, determined to prove herself.

Giddy with triumph, she returned to Pennydale bearing the precious certificate, only to find this slip-sticker had quietly usurped her place at Father's side. Moreover, where she struggled, Mr Staley effortlessly accomplished, making calculus cavort to the dance-hall ballads that he whistled when absorbed.

"Aye, Miss Harriet."

Harriet turned around at the sound of a familiar and much-loved voice. "Benjamin," she said warmly.

Old Benjamin had always been an anchor in her life, outshone only by her father. He was the longest serving employee of Pennydale Works and already a master fitter when Father had bought his partnership with the late Sir Rupert Holm. When first brought to the works with her doting father, she'd escaped Nurse, rushing off into an exciting world of steam, noise, and spinning metal, and it had been Benjamin, already a grandfather, who had caught her. Father had told her much later that as Benjamin carried her back, her arms about his neck, she looked oddly at home.

On subsequent visits, dodging through drifting steam and the clang of hammers with Nurse giving chase and scolding her, Harriet had sought him out. She'd settle down then, fascinated by whatever he was doing, and he'd indulge her, explaining in his gruff northern accent what this was and why it was, and the girl-child would listen gravely.

Soon she was helping him, struggling to pass him spanners and files and running errands to the stores, wearing overalls of her own, small Harriet-sized ones Mrs Benjamin had run up, which weathered the grease and swarf far better than crinoline and lace. Harriet always accepted Nurse's scrubbing brush stoically at the end of the day, yet even at that early age, Mother's stony disapproval of her chosen playground was clear. She learnt to live with that, knowing that as long as the schoolroom permitted, Father would never go down the hill without her.

Harriet drove her first locomotive—*Bassey*, the light saddle-tank used within the works—at the age of eight. Then she'd had to stand on a box to reach the regulator, and Benjamin had to steady her. Now she had her main line ticket.

When she was eleven, Benjamin helped her *build* her first locomotive, a three-inch-gauge tank engine that she and Father had steamed over a track laid along the terrace; she'd never seen her father quite so happy before.

By then of course, it would have been wholly indecent for her to wear overalls, and she'd graduated to a jacket and ankle-length skirt of hardwearing serge. She wore almost the same today, and now her locomotives ran not the length of the terrace, but of the realm.

White of hair and beard, and stooping slightly, Benjamin had to be in his seventies, yet his grey eyes still twinkled in his time-weathered face. He was past eligible for the small annuity with which the company rewarded their older workers, yet he never asked to be let go, nor would Father ever make him.

"It's gone six, Miss Harriet," he chided gently. "They'll be looking for you up hill."

"Goodness, is it that late already? I shall be late once again."

"Happens young Thorneycroft's waiting with a steamer to give you a hurl up road."

She broke into an affectionate grin. "You always look after me."

"Chance that I do," the old man said. "Now off with you, miss, and mind you give your father my respects."

"I will, Benjamin. Goodnight."

"Aye, goodnight, Miss Harriet."

Wiping her hands on a ditty rag, Harriet hurried down the dim corridors towards the works entrance. Gaslight spilled from an open door along with a self-absorbed tune, and she paused and looked in.

Mr Staley was seated behind a broad desk that faced the door. The desk was covered in a hodgepodge of books, old and new, large and small; a foolscap daybook, the open page half filled with his flowing, confident handwriting; and various engineering schematics of *Mercury*—boiler and firebox by the look of them. Staley was frowning at a slide rule, but detecting Harriet at the door, he looked up.

On learning her father had engaged a slip-stick, Harriet had pictured her usurper as a younger version of her lecturers, ill-dressed in neglected tweeds, with a thin reedy voice, a high pale forehead, thinning torn-at hair, a crazed beard, and peering out perhaps through metal-rimmed spectacles. Meeting Staley for the first time had therefore given Harriet rather a jolt. Her lecturers were to a man either emaciated or portly, but Staley was neither. Rather, he was broad of shoulder yet not coarse and burly.

Neatly barbered and with a frank, honest face, he had assessed Harriet gravely, and it made her shiver slightly and wonder at the thoughts that lay behind those eggshell blue eyes. *It is a pleasure to meet you, Miss Colton,* he'd said with a half bow, his voice rich and measured, and the last shred of Harriet's predetermined image had died.

Now he was gazing again at her, his expression polite but enquiring, and she felt oddly nervous.

"We should be ready to mount the new steam feeds tomorrow, Mr Staley," she said.

"Excellent, Miss Colton," he said with enthusiasm. "I am sure they will answer most favourably in the forthcoming trial."

"I pray that they do, sir." She bit down the temptation to add *considering all the time and effort they're causing us,* then said, "Goodnight, Mr Staley."

He nodded deferentially. "Goodnight, Miss Colton."

CONGRATULATING HERSELF ON remaining civil, Harriet bustled out into the yard. The sun was settling upon Horse Moor, bathing her in old gold as she strode to the waiting steamer. It was a simple affair, lacking any protection against the elements. A tall boiler was set vertically behind the driving bench and bore a stubby black chimney from which a thin trail of smoke drifted. The remainder of the steamer was given over to flat planking suitable to fetch and carry for the works. A bored youth sat on the end of the driving bench, swinging his heels. On seeing her, he dropped to the ground and touched his cap.

"Miss Harriet."

"Good evening, Thorneycroft."

She accepted his hand to clamber aboard and then claimed the tiller wheel. By the time Thorneycroft was aboard, Harriet had the handbrake spun off. She checked the cut-off lever and then, cognisant that she was already late, opened the regulator with reckless abandon. With a sigh and a sudden staccato beat, the steamer leapt forward. As Thorneycroft extracted himself from the coal bunker, Harriet spun the tiller wheel, sending the steamer lurching through the main gate and onto the Kearby road towards Chale Bridge, the once small village that had expanded with the works.

Soon they crested the bridge over the small River Penny, and Harriet let on the steam brake prior to swinging the steamer into the lane opposite The Wheelwrights public house. She opened the regulator then, and the steamer stormed the rough cobbles, skittering between crowded terraces of works housing. A group of grubby children scattered.

The terraces ended, and they were lurching through ruts between the lively waters of the Penny and dense woodland already gloomy with the setting of the sun. The lane led up into Pennydale itself, but Harriet soon turned from it and onto the drive leading up to Pennydale House. They passed the lodge, and then the chuff and clatter of the driving gear grew laboured as the drive steepened, curving gently under mature oaks. Eventually the cover opened up to reveal the east aspect of the house, pleasingly proportioned and unembellished. Harriet took the steamer behind the house and slewed it around outside the stable block, showering gravel. Bolsover, the butler, appeared as she spun on the handbrake, and she accepted his hand to alight.

"Thank you, Bolsover." She turned to the somewhat shaken Thorneycroft, still gripping the driving bench. "It would be prudent to light the lamps before returning. And inform Mr Foscote her nearside cylinder needs repacking."

Thorneycroft touched his cap. "I will, Miss Harriet. Goodnight, Miss Harriet."

But Harriet was already striding for the kitchen entrance. She acknowledged the greetings and bobs of the kitchen staff with a wave and then, gathering up her skirts, raced up the servants' stairs to her bedroom. The gas was already lit and Dimity, her maid, awaited her. A simple celadon gown suitable for dinner lay ready on the bed.

Dimity was too inured to Harriet's tardiness to be reproachful. Instead, she did her utmost to speed her mistress to the dining table, ridding her of the heavy skirt and underlying petticoats even while Harriet was scrubbing her hands. She separated Harriet from her jacket and blouse, then set about removing a day's devotion to *Mercury* from her face. It would have been the despair of another maid, but Dimity never complained. She knew what was truly important to her mistress.

"The cylinder glands again, miss?" Dimity dabbed at Harriet's cheek with a cloth.

"Close." Harriet admired her maid's perspicacity. "Valve

sleeves."

"Same grease though." Dimity upended an open bottle of Hoskins' Patent Balsam. "And, begging your pardon, miss, the very devil to get off."

WITH A SATISFIED smile, Royston Staley closed his daybook decisively. Miss Colton's veiled scepticism regarding the necessity of the new pipework had raised a twinge of doubt in his mind. Knowing that this would fester and quite ruin his evening if left unresolved, he'd revisited his calculations one final time. To his relief, they indicated that at speed the existing feeds would rob *Mercury's* cylinders of much valuable steam pressure. They *had* to be replaced.

He gathered together the strewn papers and slid them with his daybook into a desk drawer. He locked it and then consulted his pocket watch. It had been a bequest of his great uncle, so old that the fine silver chasing was all but polished away. It kept excellent time, however, and he was greatly fond of it.

He was later than usual, but it was Wednesday night, and so his supper wouldn't suffer if he paused for a pint or two on the stroll home. Tonight was his housekeeper's spiritualist gathering, and she would have left early, leaving him a cold collation.

He gathered his top hat and Ulster from the peg and walked out into the yard. A few windows remained yellow with gaslight, and an angry, pulsating glow crept around the main workshops from the forge as those bound to the demands of cherry-red steel rather than the sun laboured on.

Nodding to the night watchmen, he strolled through the gate and turned towards the village. Soon he could make out the darker silhouettes of the hills surrounding him. Whilst nothing like the austere majesty of the Pennines, this was not the soft landscape of his native Sussex. Everything was a step harsher here, the rivers rocky and impatient and the landscape prone to crags. Even the vegetation seemed coarser and more resilient, and no doubt the coming winter would show him why.

He was content with his lot, however. His appointment some months past as the sole academic designer at Colton and Holm represented a noteworthy advancement from being one lost amongst many in the sprawling engineering complex of Antrum Ellis and Partners, the credit for his work divided up beyond his reach. Yes, responsibility might weigh heavier here, but with it came the opportunity to establish a reputation.

He corrected himself. Matters might be clearer here, but he was not the sole master of his destiny. That would be Samuel Colton, who *was* Pennydale Works—owner, decision maker, and often abroad in the workshops, offering censure and encouragement. Royston respected the older man, finding him quick of mind, of unrivalled experience, and yet not blind to new developments. Moreover, he treated his workers fairly, and it was reflected in their loyalty.

There was also, of course, the daughter.

When first Colton briefed him on *Mercury*'s design, the two men walking around the carcass of the locomotive-yet-to-be, it had astounded him how much of it Colton credited to his absent daughter. *I would have set the valve chests so,* the older man had said, gesturing, *but Harriet would have none of it. She wanted them this way. See how it simplifies the link mechanism? So much more reliable, and so much kinder on the shed fitters.* They'd then moved on, Colton explaining and dividing the achievement.

Royston began to appreciate how the daughter must have inherited the same natural affinity with engines as her father, and possibly even more so. That in itself was a little intimidating, but then he'd learnt that she was in Newcastle, completing her *Dip Eng* at the august Stephenson Institute. What would she think of him when she saw that the one gracing his office wall bore the humble seal of the Birmingham School of Mechanics!

There was also the idea of a woman engineer to absorb. Women had begun to enter the professions ever since the State Opening of Parliament in 1869 when, much to the consternation of Gladstone, Her Majesty Queen Victoria had diverted from her prepared speech.

"We are fifty years of age," she told the gathered peers and Members of Parliament, "and have ruled the Kingdom for over thirty years *(Cries of 'God bless you, Your Majesty')*. It is our solemn duty, and the Kingdom has faith in us to discharge it justly and fairly. *(Cries of hear! hear!)*. Why is it then that we are entrusted in this most exacting office, when others of our sex are excluded from any vocation other than of a purely domestic nature? *(A singular cry of hear! hear! from aged Lord Tylson, deaf as a post these last twenty years)*. Our government shall therefore introduce a bill that will ensure women have equal access to education and the professions, that they may better serve the Kingdom and Empire."

She then returned to the clauses her prime minister had been expecting.

However much they may have wished otherwise, it was

difficult for Parliament to act contrary to the clear desire of the monarch, and thus early the next year, Her Majesty signed into law the Bill of Entitlement. The Society of Professional Gentlewomen was convened soon after, and Her Majesty, after an appropriate delay, graced it with her patronage.

Now, apparently, there were the first women doctors, women lawyers, women in the banks of the City, yet Royston had never heard of a woman engineer. It wasn't that he disapproved—that would have shown disloyalty to the Crown—but the prospect of having a woman as his peer and working with her was disorientating and made him a little nervous.

He'd tried to imagine Harriet Colton. Would she be like her mother Lady Alicia, tall and proud and aquiline, or her father, heavier set, and with a broad face, fond of expressing feeling? Her younger sister Bianca was blessed with her mother's irreproachable figure but with the imposing height tempered, whilst her parents' features had conspired to make her so fair of face as to appear doll-like. Indeed, her beauty was so perfect that he found it daunting. That was probably for the best: Cultivating the acquaintance of the eligible daughter of one's employer was rarely wise.

When finally they were introduced, Royston found Harriet Colton to be nothing like her sister. She didn't shy from his gaze as Bianca had but instead returned it steadily, her hazel eyes almost on a level with his own. Her clothing—unrestricting, durable, and much laundered—made it difficult to accurately gauge her build, yet she was certainly not as slender as her mother or sister. She had her father's hair, a soft russet and always worn in a bun. Her face was also quite like her father's yet softer and pleasing to his eye—

disquietingly so.

As the days had followed, he discovered that she had much of her father's personality, albeit with a prickly edge. This was particularly noticeable when he went over with her the shortcomings in *Mercury*'s design that his calculations indicated. She hadn't been sharp with him, but by the way she pointed out how everything embodied in *Mercury* had served in others' designs quite satisfactorily, it was plain she doubted his findings.

He'd tried to explain that he didn't doubt her, that it was how all the parts worked together that mattered, but that only made her defensive. He could understand that; this had been her project first. Yet now it was his, and he wanted it to succeed. The argument continued and was only settled with her father's arbitration.

Royston found himself at the centre of Chale Bridge, where the main road running north from Kearby turned sharply to cross the metals of the London and Northern and meet the bridge that gave the village its name. On the far bank, just past the (unimaginatively named) Bridge End Cottage that Royston leased, the road swung north again towards the market town of Newton-Le-Helm.

Where Royston stood must once have been the village green, nestled between the venerable church of St Catherine's and the inn. Now it was a cobbled square and the once-maypole a smoke-blackened statue of Lord Palmerston. The green might be gone, but, fourteenth century and timbered, The Just Swan had survived, and the windows of its snug glowed invitingly.

Smiling, Royston strolled towards its doorway, low and misshapen with age, already anticipating the crisp taste of a pint of Braces' Albion Ale.

HARRIET WAS LATE down to dinner but, thanks to Dimity's efforts, not abominably so. The rest of the family were, however, already seated, and she received a reproachful look from her mother. Bolsover stood impassively behind her chair and eased it under her as she sat.

The gas lamps were unlit. Instead, on the table, two ornate silver-and-glass candelabra, one the Winged Victory and the other a blind Lady Justice, glimmered in the warm light of their beeswax candles.

"I apologise for being unpunctual, Father," she said. "The valve assemblies were disobliging, and I completely lost track of time."

"They're away?"

"Not quite yet, alas. But they should be in the forenoon."

Her father nodded, but as Cook served him with soup, he wore a troubled frown.

"We have lost but a few days," Harriet said softly.

"I know, but Sunday was the ninth of October; we have less than six months left."

Harriet nodded unhappily. She was quite aware of the calendar and how much closer the ninth of April had crept. It would be Lord Clifton's seventieth birthday and the culmination of his Grand Challenge. It was a competition simply stated: to design and build a locomotive that could draw a train from Bristol to London in the shortest possible time. The prestigious prize was the exclusive contract to construct a whole class of locomotives founded on the winning prototype (which Harriet hoped fervently stood half built in the fitting shop down in the valley) as well as concomitant renown.

"We're close to testing her under steam," said Harriet.

"But we've yet to resolve how to even fire her," said her father. "I have set Mr Staley to making estimations."

That explained the selection of schematics Staley had been consulting earlier. "I can't believe it will be *that* onerous."

"I hope not. I—"

Mother cleared her throat; she did not approve when the works dominated dinner conversation.

Father gave her a feeble, guilty smile in return. "Perhaps this is better left until later, Harriet."

"Yes, Father."

For a while there was silence, broken only by the clink of silver on china.

"I visited Mrs Worthington this afternoon, Samuel," said Mother.

"And how is she?"

"No better, I fear. Indeed, she looked most frail. She tells me her doctors are at their wits' end."

"I have never known her hale. It is as if illness agrees with her."

"Now, Samuel, you are being quite uncharitable."

"Perhaps I am, and for that I apologise, my dear."

Mother accepted his regret with a nod. "She tells me that her niece Bella has made a most suitable match with a Mr Carrot from Derby. An unfortunate name, but by all accounts he is quite successful."

"In what line of business?"

Mother looked a little confused by the question. "I am sure Mrs Worthington did not say."

Father's interest returned to his soup.

"We also received an invitation to the charity ball," Mother continued.

"I don't recall such a thing, my dear."

"Oh, *Samuel*," sighed Mother. "The one at Tharrington Hall, of course. Lady Mallow is *most* insistent we attend."

Dabbing at his lips with his napkin, Father grunted sceptically.

"It is for a most worthy cause," said Mother warningly.

"There never seems to be a lack of those."

"But still it is our duty to attend. Our position in society demands it." As the daughter of an earl, Mother was ever cognisant of the family's position in society.

"Aye, and I see it as *my* duty to ensure no one in Chale Bridge goes hungry or hasn't a roof over their head unless they brought it upon themselves. Charity begins at home."

"Our presence will be expected. We cannot hide ourselves away from society."

When Father didn't answer, Mother grew politely chiding. "Come, Samuel. Poor Bianca is greatly anticipating attending. I'm sure Harriet is too."

Harriet wasn't, but she hid it well.

"Oh, Mama!" Bianca squirmed in her chair. "Don't make Father agree solely on my account. I'm sure there will be another ball."

"That is not the point," her mother told her. "You are of an age when you should be moving in the proper social circles. It is all very well accompanying me on my calls as you do, but it is the larger social gatherings that offer the best occasion of meeting eligible young men." She looked at Harriet also, extending to her the same counsel.

Harriet smiled back, masking her thoughts. Mother only

had her best interests at heart, yet frankly she found such events dull and the eligible young men aloof to her or patronising. Indeed, she had decided that marriage and a family of her own would have to wait for fear that they would interfere with establishing her reputation as an engineer.

The soup plates had been cleared away, and Cook had placed before Father a large pie. He cut into crisp, golden pastry, releasing steam and a mouth-watering aroma.

"Don't fuss, Bianca. Your mother shall write back to Lady Mallow to inform her we shall be delighted to attend." Father served a narrow slice of the pie, the gravy lustrous and rich, to his wife, who gazed at him with surprised gratitude. He carved a significantly more generous portion and slid it expertly onto Harriet's plate. "There, Harriet— that'll stick to your ribs!"

"*Samuel!*" exclaimed Lady Alicia.

But Father was unrepentant. He carved another small portion for Bianca and then an indulgent one for himself. "I have some news for you also, my dear, and it's rather appropriate given the conversation."

"Oh yes?" Lady Alicia paused over the vegetables.

"Aye. We've house guests next Wednesday, some rather important ones."

"Indeed?"

Father looked a little smug. "Aye—the Marquess of Harlow and his agent."

His wife stared at him. "*Next* Wednesday?"

"I believe that's what I said," said Father calmly.

"But there is so much to arrange!"

"You've a week, my dear," he said gently. "And it's pre-dominantly a business matter. There's no obligation to invite others."

Lady Alicia snorted. "It would be highly thoughtless as well, given the lack of notice."

"Then it's fortunate that invitations are not required." Father shrugged, indicating the matter was settled.

After a short silence, Bianca said, "Mama, I do not believe I know of Lord Harlow."

Mother didn't answer immediately, and Harriet found that intriguing.

"He has extensive estates in Yorkshire," said Father, "and the coal under them yields a most handsome revenue. And that's before one considers his interests in cotton and the railways."

"That makes him sound rather old," said Bianca with disappointment. "And married."

Again Mother snorted. "Would that he were."

"He's neither, Bianca," Father informed her. "Why, he can be barely into his thirties. He acceded to the title rather unexpectedly due, I believe, to a hunting accident."

"Oh!" said Bianca brightly, but her eagerness was short-lived. "But a marquess is so... elevated."

"And is he not of somewhat... notorious character?" Harriet frowned. "I believe I read... somewhere... of various scandals."

Mother sighed. "I do wish, Harriet, you would not read the scurrilous ha'penny rags the men bring into the works."

"I don't..." Harriet felt chagrined. "Not very often."

"It is but odious rumour-mongering then?" asked Bianca.

Lady Alicia sighed again. "I wish that it were, Bianca, but I have heard the same from my acquaintances. Lord Harlow is known to be quite dissolute. Most believe it is because he came into his inheritance while an imprudent youth. When in his presence, you must always keep in mind his... *character.*"

"Yes, Mama," said Bianca meekly.

The remainder of the meal passed in relative silence, but by Mother's expression, she was mentally cataloguing what had to be done prior to Lord Harlow's visit—and also what *should* be done, especially in regard to Bianca.

AFTERWARDS FATHER RETIRED to the small library, and Harriet followed thoughtfully. Father did not seem surprised and waved her to the second of the armchairs that stood before a fireplace fashioned in red marble, with intricately carved garlands of wisteria framing the glowing coals.

"A glass of something?"

"I think that I might," said Harriet. "Port wine perhaps."

He went to the table in the corner, and there was the clink of glass. He returned, handing Harriet a liberally filled schooner before settling back comfortably into his usual place, an equally generous whisky beside him.

"So, the firing?" he suggested.

"To be honest, Father, I'm more curious why we're entertaining Lord Harlow next week."

Father nodded. "I'd rather not be doing that at all," he admitted, "but needs must."

"Pardon?"

"It's *Mercury*, Harriet. I'd hoped we could bear her development ourselves, but business hasn't been so good of late. It's mostly the smaller railways that place orders with us, but they're slowly being taken over by the larger companies who have their own locomotive works; they don't need us."

"I thought we were taking in forging work as well?"

"We are, and it's helping, but *Mercury* is a great drain on the coffers. She needs a patron."

"Lord Harlow."

Father nodded. "If I can convince him," he said grimly. "He's no fool though; he puts his money where it brings the best return."

"And how will he get a return with *Mercury*?"

"I'm going to suggest a share of the profits we make from building her class."

"That assumes we win."

Father's expression grew sober. "I think we either win, Harriet, or be done with locomotives altogether. There's no future for Colton and Holm building traditional classes—the larger works can always do that cheaper. To stay in this business, we need to specialise."

Harriet sipped her port, rolling its rich flavour in her mouth. "In high-speed locomotives?"

Father nodded. "First the *Mercury* class, and then from what we learn, subsequent classes. If we do this right, the larger works won't be able to compete. They won't have the experience."

"But we have to win first."

"Aye, and for that we need *Mercury* complete, and that means we need Lord Harlow. Personally, I can live with the man's dubious principles if it means I can keep building locomotives."

"I also. Quite frankly, I'm surprised that once he'd ruined one girl's reputation, he could find one other in society so stupid as to let him bed her, let alone two."

Father laughed. "Don't let your mother hear you speak so plain, Harriet. She would be quite appalled."

"But it's true, Father," persisted Harriet hotly. "The scandal must have dominated parlours across the realm. A young lady could not help but know how dishonourable were his intentions."

"Your sister belies your argument," said Father with a quiet smile. "Yet they may have known and succumbed all the same." For long seconds, he hesitated. "Matters between men and women are not always as simple as you would have them be, Harriet."

"But surely—"

"I think that's enough, Harriet, if you please," said Father firmly.

Understanding he feared she'd stray into impropriety, Harriet relented.

ROYSTON WAS ALSO sitting by the fire, but alone, and the fireplace was smaller and plainer, the ornamental bosses and urns cast simply in iron. A plate bearing the remnants of his supper sat on a table beside him. The table also bore a cut-glass oil lamp, which was tastefully appointed with a glass teardrop shade.

Royston was reading. The small book he held was not, however, a treatise on mathematics or engineering, nor was it one of the classical authors that graced his bookshelf. Royston was in fact reading a popular work, a frivolous tale of pirates, heroes, and lost treasure. He did so unashamedly, having found such reading an ideal way to push from his mind the problems and worries of the day. This was a traditional adventure of privateers under full sails and of broadsides and cutlasses. He had tried a modernised adventure but found it quite unsatisfactory. The engineer in him soon re-emerged, questioning the plausibility of its submersible steam galleons and underwater cannon. No, for relaxation and clearing his head, these sailing adventures were quite the best.

He consulted his watch and then closed his book, finished his ale, and put the grate upon the fire. It was late, and there was plenty awaiting him at the works in the morning.

2.

Raising Steam

B OOTS APPROACHED, AND so brisk and irate were the click of their nails on the sandstone flags that they made Royston pause and look up, pen hovering in his hand. Miss Colton stalked into his office, errant strands of hair flying free, her skin glowing and her eyes smouldering. At the sight, Royston was reminded strongly of an untamed woman in a forbidding place years past, yet in Miss Colton's case he quite properly diagnosed anger.

"What appears to be the matter, Miss Colton?"

"The confounded steam feeds you designed, Mr Staley." She was fuming, breathing heavily. "That's the matter. The centre feeds are too big."

Royston snorted. "Impossible. I checked the clearances most diligently."

"They might fit most perfectly, Mr Staley," she said sarcastically, "but they are most perfectly useless unless we can persuade them into their required position."

"That should not present a problem, Miss Colton. It was considered."

"I would deem a boiler support quite a problem," she retorted. "We have been trying for an hour, and I tell you the feed will not go in."

Royston stood and went to a side table piled with drawings. He shuffled through them and slid one out and onto the top of the stack. "That is anomalous," he said, consulting the drawing. "I assure you there should be a good six inches leeway throughout the manoeuvre."

"And I can assure you that there is not. Perhaps you would like to see for yourself?"

"Indeed."

Rolling up the drawing, he followed Miss Colton out into the fitting shop. Two of the three nearside steam feeds were in place, but the third, a convoluted and substantial piece of pipework, stuck out at an angle from *Mercury*, its weight borne by a sling from the overhead crane. Several men were clustered about the centre cylinder, pointing and peering at where the errant feed was caught in the locomotive.

Royston clambered up onto the staging, and the fitters respectfully dispersed. He pushed his head around the bulk of the cylinder and looked at where the feeder had jammed. He frowned. He'd designed it to slide in *so* and then angle back and into position. It was clear, however, that that couldn't happen because of the heavy support Miss Colton had cited. He consulted the drawing again.

"The boiler flange is misaligned," he declared.

Lifting her heavy skirts, Miss Colton climbed up beside him and snatched the drawing away. She peered at it. "This is out of date," she said. "We added an extra flange to give the framing more rigidity."

"Then why wasn't the drawing corrected?"

"No doubt the master was, but this is a copy. You should have checked it against the master before trusting it."

Now Royston felt angry, but mostly with himself. He

stifled a curse, sensitive to a lady being present.

"Or perhaps for once you could have come out and checked on *Mercury* herself," she added tartly.

It was the most imperfect moment to heap on additional criticism. "I am a *designer*, Miss Colton, not a *fitter*."

He saw the injury in her eyes and knew himself a boor. "I apologise; that was uncalled for."

"I started as an apprentice to the fitters, Mr Staley, and I consider it the most sound grounding from which to have become a designer," she said, yet not as coldly as he deserved. "Perhaps you would be the better for it."

"Perhaps I would, Miss Colton." Royston bowed slightly. "We would not be facing this problem had it been the case."

To his surprise, she laughed. "A fitter is not *infallible*, sir."

"I am relieved to hear it." He paused. "Having been the agent in this misfortune, I feel a duty to help rectify it. That is, if you would allow my help. I assure you that I have *some* practical knowledge."

She nodded. "A handsome offer, and willingly accepted." Turning, she called to one of the men. "Blakes! Find Mr Staley some overalls."

"Yes, Miss Harriet."

STALEY REAPPEARED A little later, wearing requisitioned boots and with his fine broadcloth replaced by cheap stuff overalls. He set to work willingly, lending his strength to coaxing the steam feeder loose. He and Harriet then examined the problem from opposing sides of the cylinder.

"We cannot displace the support," said Staley.

Harriet agreed. "It's riveted soundly into the frames. Even if we did free it, we'd probably have to lift the entire boiler and firebox before we could move it."

Staley nodded and then tapped the cylinder, looking questioningly at Harriet.

Knowing just how much work that would entail, she pulled a face. "Only as a means of last resort, sir."

They each looked at the steam feed dangling from the crane and then back at the cramped space.

"I'd suggest we cut in a union near the elbow," said Harriet, "but I'm not sure there's enough space for it, nor would I relish trying to bolt it up."

"I thought of that originally. You're quite correct; there isn't enough space—not unless one dimensions the union most imprudently."

"I prefer not to contemplate a steam feed rupturing," said Harriet.

"Nor I."

They stared in silence, and then Staley looked again at the steam feed hanging in the dusty sunlight. "How deep is the inspection pit?" he asked softly, referring to the trench between *Mercury*'s wheels that allowed work on her underneath to proceed in relative comfort.

With Staley's gentle prompt, all at once Harriet saw how it could be done. "A clear fathom." She then studied the steam feed, narrowing her eyes. "A more pertinent question is whether it is wide enough."

Extricating herself from *Mercury*, she jumped off the staging and called the men together.

IT WAS IMPRESSIVE how fast Miss Colton could arrange things. Within minutes, the fitting shop had become one of carpentry as the steam feed was laid down and a simple facsimile of it was sawed and nailed from cheap deal planking. This was then carried to the steps leading down underneath *Mercury* and insinuated beneath her. It took several attempts to find which end had to go down first and in what orientation, but finally they managed to twist the wooden arrangement under *Mercury* so that the right end went through the right gap the right way around.

Royston was glad they'd experimented with the wooden version, because manipulating the real steam feed proved exacting and onerous. It weighed several hundredweight and took most of the men to haul and shove it around beneath the locomotive. With Miss Colton directing, they lifted the steam feed by main force up behind the cylinder, Royston sweating with the rest until Benjamin, the elderly workman for whom Miss Colton clearly had a deep respect, managed to secure it into the crane's sling. Then it was easier, but by no means easy, and at one stage the delicate business dissolved into repeatedly hammering at the obstinate pipe with a baulk of wood. It promoted a great sense of relief when Miss Colton, who had returned above, called down that it had finally slipped into place.

Royston crawled out from the oily darkness and, wiping his brow, stood back to admire their achievement. Already the steam feed was being bolted into place between its more tractable sisters.

Miss Colton came over. "My thanks. I feared we would never get it into place."

"There is still the offside one."

She seemed unperturbed. "Unless in a fit of madness you challenged symmetry, we will have it done soon after the men's tea break—which I fear I have kept from them overlong." She appraised him for a moment. "You look like you could do with a cup also."

"It would not be unwelcome," he admitted.

FATHER FOUND THEM in the works canteen, sharing a table a little aside from the rest of the men and sipping tea from generous-sized utilitarian cups. He noted Staley's overalls and raised an eyebrow at his daughter.

"Putting him to work, eh, Harriet?"

"I was assisting in resolving an issue, sir," said Staley quickly. "One rather of my own devising, I fear."

"The steam feeds?"

"We had a little trouble fitting the centre set, Father. Mr Staley's assistance was most welcome," said Harriet, the image of him wrestling his recalcitrant creation into submission returning unbidden. "It is resolved now."

"That's glad news," said Father, "and here's some more." He laid that day's *Birmingham Post* between them. It had been folded to a specific article, and Harriet and Staley twisted on their stools to read.

"Crewe has withdrawn also!" exclaimed Harriet. "That was the last of the big railway works in the competition."

"Aye, none of them had the taste for it, it seems."

Staley was still reading. "They claim that it was unduly affecting their other responsibilities," he said with a hint of scepticism.

"You think it a graceful deception, Mr Staley?" asked Harriet.

"It is not unlikely. Did not Wolverton *and* St Rollox excuse themselves with much the same words?"

"You have an alternative hypothesis, Mr Staley?" asked Father.

Staley hesitated. "I'd be more inclined to hazard they assigned so many to the task that nothing was achieved. Novelty is rarely treated kindly in large shops."

Father's expression suggested he agreed wholeheartedly. "Nor is the pressure of the calendar."

"That also cannot be denied. There is a certain... momentum to large organisations," suggested Staley. "So this leaves just... *Mercury* and two others?"

Father nodded. "And all from independent works."

"I think Lord Clifton will approve," said Harriet. "I am so grateful Swindon choose not to join the challenge. It would have been rather unsporting, given it was *his* works."

"In truth, Sir Daniel Gooch's, but the point stands," said Father. He turned to Staley. "Mr Staley, Lady Alicia requests your presence at dinner Wednesday next, when the marquess visits."

"Did Mother really, or do you want another voice to sway the marquess?" asked Harriet mischievously.

"The latter can't go amiss, Harriet, but it was the former," replied Father. "Indeed your mother was rather insistent; she's anxious over the *balance* of the table."

"I would be honoured, sir," said Staley, "to serve both causes."

ALTHOUGH NO ANNOUNCEMENT had been made, everyone down to the youngest apprentice knew that someone was visiting Pennydale Works and that the visitor was important. Mr Samuel; Mr Bracewaite, the works' general manager; and young Mr Staley were all in their finest suits and tall polished top hats. Miss Harriet also had foregone her usual work dress. Today she wore an ankle-length charcoal grey skirt, discreetly bustled, and a close-fitting velvet jacket of similar hue, buttoned in silver to her neck.

The members of the small group were restless, and their restlessness conveyed itself to the workforce watching discreetly from windows as their betters paced the yard in ones and twos, their attention wandering often to the Kearby road.

Royston consulted his faithful hunter. The marquess was now at least an hour overdue. It was worrisome, but he allowed that the marquess was an important person and there must be a plethora of other matters with a greater claim on his time than Colton and Holm.

He was just about to rejoin Colton and the general manager when they all heard the rapid chuff of a steamer approaching from the south. The beat of the exhaust slowed, and then in through the yard gates swung…

…a most astonishing conveyance, one so extravagant that to call it a steamer would be an insult.

Borne on broad pneumatic tyres after Mr Thompson's patent and painted a rich peacock blue, it had a long, rakish boiler banded with intricate silver scrollwork and bronze rivets, a theme that continued in the coachwork but with the addition of leaded panels of stained glass, great Gothic lanterns, and about the roof a frieze of orbs and strawberry leaves, silver and gold, alluding to the coronet accorded to its occupant.

On the driving bench perched two servants liveried in the same peacock blue who, after they had brought the steamer to a halt, hastened to set out a small set of steps below the door in the coachwork, a door that marked the marquess's achievement, the shield of which was trellised silver and blue and bore an incensed creature thrown together from snippets of fox and greyhound, horse and lion… and even eagle and elephant. *Argent a trellis azure cloué argent, an enfiled rampant reguardant proper*, mused Royston idly.

From the unbelievable vehicle, two men descended. It was immediately clear who was the agent and who was the master for one was utterly eclipsed by the other.

The aspect one noticed first of The Most Honourable The Marquess of Harlow was his hair, which was an abundance of curls the colour of bleached gold. Next was his height, for he towered over those who awaited him, and then his build, which was slight—far more so than the stories of his dissolute life would credit. Finally, there was his face. Again this showed no signs of excess but hung in exquisite balance between the untainted beauty of youth and that of a handsome gentleman in his prime. He disdained a hat, but wore a silver-grey suit of impeccable workmanship with an iridescent blue Paisley waistcoat and affected a slim ebony walking stick topped with a silver coronet. In utter contrast, the soberly frock-coated agent was short and had a thin, weasel-like face upon which muttonchop whiskers had crawled and there died. The marquess appeared bemused, and the agent critical.

"Lord Harlow." Colton bowed deep.

"Mr Colton?" replied the marquess condescendingly. "I am most pleased to make your acquaintance. This is my *aide-de-camp*, Mr Hackett."

"Thomas Hackett, sir," said Hackett, shaking Colton's hand. "Delighted."

"My daughter, Miss Colton," said Colton then, "and my collaborator in *Mercury*'s design."

"Bolts and things?" murmured the marquess. "Most certainly a peculiar hobby for a lady."

Royston grimaced inwardly and noticed the hesitation in Miss Colton's respectful curtsy. They had repeated sharing afternoon tea in the canteen, and from their conversations, he was quite certain how seriously she viewed her calling.

Yet when Miss Colton rose, her features were calm—perhaps a little too calm. "But a most rewarding one, Lord Harlow," she said.

After Colton had introduced the general manager and finally Royston, he led the party through to where *Mercury* awaited them.

"*Three* driven wheels, sir!" said Hackett, astonished. "And each with its own cylinder?"

"The arrangement greatly improves the area bearing on the rail," explained Colton.

"And a single cylinder delivering the same impetus would be quite unmanageable within the gauge," added his daughter.

Hackett seemed to accept that. "But surely there is an issue in coordinating the motion."

"All the valve gear is driven from the centre set of driver

wheels," explained Miss Colton, "and the relative timing of the cylinders ensures even impetus."

Hackett nodded thoughtfully.

They continued the inspection, with Hackett questioning *Mercury*'s progenitors closely on all details resolved and as yet unresolved. By the end of it, however, the only comment the marquess uttered was, tapping *Mercury*'s sole bar with his stick, a bemused, "It is a very *large* locomotive."

The marquess and his agent then went into a brief huddle, after which the marquess asked in a bored tone, "Would you oblige me with an inspection of the remainder of your manufactory?"

His aura of boredom persisted as they passed through the assembly shop with its line of locomotives, each nearer to completion than its neighbour. It was likewise in the machining shop, where even bright swarf curling from a blur of spinning steel failed to move him. He wrinkled his noble nose at the heavy fumes emanating from the paint shop and was done with it. The forge alone stirred him from ennui, captivating him with the spectacle of the hydraulic press inexorably descended upon the glowing steel and the violent explosion of sparks as it coerced the metal to the imaginations of man.

The tour complete and Hackett's final question answered, Colton departed with his guests for Pennydale House.

Royston and Miss Colton drifted to Royston's office. "What did you make of our esteemed visitor, Mr Staley?" she asked, toying irritably with the tight neck of her jacket.

The jacket clearly irked her, yet Royston much preferred it to the coarse cousin she usually wore. The velvet, he mused, recommended her form most attractively.

"Sir?" she asked again, jolting him from his thoughts.

"I do apologise, Miss Colton. I was considering my response," he said hurriedly, and then did. "To be candid, I don't believe my lord gives a jot for *Mercury* or anything else in the works."

His admission brought a smile to her face. "That is my belief also," she said. "Hackett, however…"

"Yes, indeed. I was uncomfortably reminded this afternoon of the schoolroom," he told her. "I think we may safely conclude that Lord Harlow leans quite heavily upon Mr Hackett's counsel."

"I wonder what that counsel will be in our case."

Royston slowly shook his head. "In truth, Miss Colton, I do not know."

THE MARQUESS SEEMED to make a habit of unpunctuality, for everyone but him was assembled for dinner, and Harriet's stomach was threatening to grow uncouth. Father and Sir Geoffrey Mallow in dinner attire were conversing, with Father looking only slightly the more awkward of the two. Mother and Lady Mary Mallow, resplendent in long gowns of fuchsia and peach, were equally engaged in conversation with Cecily, Lady Mallow's daughter of sixteen years, who was wearing white and hovering self-consciously close to her mother. Mr Staley had arrived a little after the Mallows, and Bianca, magnificent in pink silk, had immediately welcomed him.

Harriet of course had been left to entertain Hackett, but

thankfully the agent seemed to have exhausted himself in the works and was taciturn. Finding herself spared the duties of small talk, Harriet's attention drifted to Staley. She had been rather surprised to discover he possessed such fine clothing. Nor was it newly acquired she was sure, for he wore it with practiced ease. Did that arise from self-awareness of how well his attire became him? It surely did, emphasising the broadness of his chest, and…

Troubled, Harriet looked quickly away and dived for refuge in a renewed attempt to make conversation with the grim Mr Hackett.

She was saved from too long an ordeal, for not more than a few minutes later, Bolsover announced, in stentorian tones, the marquess. Immediately, the peer's presence dominated the room. He also wore dinner attire, yet not the sober black of the other gentlemen but a rich cream accented with jade.

Father shepherded the Mallows forward and introduced them.

"I am most happy to meet you, Lord Harlow," effused Sir Geoffrey. "And may I congratulate you on your remarkable win at the Whitsun Meeting at Newmarket.

"On Charybdis? Yes, it was rather jolly," replied the marquess, preoccupied, yet allowing his hand to be shaken.

"Jolly, sir? It was excellent horsemanship. I confess I won a handsome wager on the back of your victory."

"Delighted, delighted," said the marquess, "as I am to meet your lovely ladies." He beamed somewhat distractedly at Lady Mallow and her daughter and kissed in turn their gloved hands. He then glided across the room, bearing directly down on Harriet's sister.

"My younger daughter, Miss Bianca Colton," said Father, trailing in the peer's wake.

"Miss Bianca, I would underwrite a hundred of your father's infernal engines," declared the marquess, "at the merest whim of a lady of such flawless beauty as yourself."

Bianca, rising from her curtsy, blushed sweetly but was plainly tongue-tied.

"Your most humble servant," murmured the marquess, claiming her hand and kissing it lingeringly.

Bianca's colour deepened. Standing beside her, Staley looked at a complete loss.

"I believe," said Harriet's mother firmly, "we may now seat ourselves for dinner."

HARRIET WAS SEATED at her father's left hand. Seated beside her, to her dismay, was Hackett. Beyond him were Cecily Mallow and then Sir Geoffrey. Mother was of course overseeing the far end of the table, with to her left Bianca, and then Staley, Lady Mallow, and finally the marquess, across from Harriet and at Father's right hand.

She noted without surprise that the arrangement placed both Cecily and Bianca as far from the marquess as socially permissible. For a moment she'd wondered if he would have the poor grace to overrule his hostess's wishes, but he did not.

Instead, he talked with some animation to Lady Mallow, describing the extent of his estate at Kimstanton Castle. She seemed pleased to receive the attention, even if his gaze sometimes slipped past her. Privately, Harriet wondered if his boasts were meant for Lady Mallow at all. He barely paid Harriet any attention, and given his earlier attitude, Harriet was glad of it.

Father was not much favoured either. As he should, he did attempt to engage the marquess in conversation, but he met with little more success than Harriet had achieved with the peer's agent. Asking about the marquess's other interests, Father received a vague reply of "Mills, I believe, and railways. Then there's some mines, and, oh, that filthy place in Scotland."

"The Saracen Ironworks," supplied Hackett promptly and went on to catalogue for Father a list of the marquess's other concerns spread all about the realm.

"You seem most diversified, Lord Harlow," said Father.

"What? Oh yes, a little here and a little there."

Staley had become the unwitting centre of conversation at the further end of the table, being quizzed as to his past by Sir Geoffrey. Sir Geoffrey asked after his family, and Staley allowed that his parents were both in good health, as was his younger brother who was serving Her Majesty in the Navy. When asked where he'd been raised, he said Sussex. Sir Geoffrey said he heard the hunting in Sussex was excellent. Staley thought it might be, although he'd only ridden to hounds close to Horsham, where his parents maintained a house just off the Carfax, and was modest over his prowess in the saddle. Sir Geoffrey enquired of his father's interests, and Staley said he had a successful trading house in the City, dealing mostly with English china and Continental furniture. Asked why then he had become an engineer, Staley put it down to previous generations being influential in the once-flourishing Sussex ironworks. "I have iron in my blood," he said.

Since Father was attentive to the marquess, and Hackett was eating in silence, Harriet continued to listen to the more distant conversation, favouring it over that of the marquess. Sir Geoffrey was seeking Staley's opinion of the annual burning of the Pope in effigy in Lewes. Unsure of his ground, Staley was diplomatic, playing it down as simply an old custom. Yet customs, he argued, should be honoured since they commemorated a history that had led to the British Empire, supreme in the world.

"Even customs in poor taste, Mr Staley?" Mother enquired.

"Even then," allowed Staley, "although carefully." Anxious to divert attention from himself, he attempted to draw Cecily Mallow into the conversation by asking of her ambitions.

"Yes, Miss Mallow," interjected the marquess unexpectedly, another glass of Father's finest claret in his hand. "Are you not inspired by Miss Colton's fancy with spanners?"

"I am certain I am by no means as clever as Miss Colton, my lord," offered Cecily timorously.

"Come now; it is not the time to be modest," said the marquess. "Her Majesty is calling on all young women to push to the fore."

Harriet opened her mouth to protest, but Staley spoke first. "Forgive me if I dissent, Lord Harlow, but I believe Her Majesty's wish is that women *may* enter the professions, not that they *should*."

Harriet gazed at Royston with admiration. He had all but said what she had intended.

"Semantics, sir," said the marquess, with a negligent wave of his hand. "I was simply putting forward Miss Colton to the young lady as an exemplary model."

Harriet frowned at the marquess's abrupt *volte-face.* What had become of her "peculiar hobby?" Her "fancy with spanners?" She preferred his disdain to his duplicity.

THE INDIVIDUAL TERRINES of Pennydale trout had been cleared away, and they were being served a medley of game, carved before being brought to table. Royston was congratulating himself on avoiding the centre of attention, for now the conversation had swung to free-ranging exchanges between Sir Geoffrey, Lady Alicia, and the marquess on the comings and goings of the realm's famous and influential. The others also made occasional contributions, but Royston, not *au fait* with the latest gossip, found himself retreating into his own thoughts.

He had expected the general manager to be present and wondered why this was not so. Surely Bracewaite had more claim to this seat at table than Royston. He could only imagine Bracewaite had some prior engagement, but what could be more important than this? Perhaps he entertained some customer? Yes, that was probably so.

He glanced surreptitiously across the table to where Miss Colton sat, framed between the candelabra of Lady Justice and the soaring centrepiece of Britannia, lit by their warm light. How well she looked in a gown! On arrival, it had been Miss Colton, not her radiant younger sister, who had immediately claimed his eye. The bun was gone, and her fine russet hair was woven into a more complicated hairstyle, with curls that discreetly flattered her rounded face. She wore a deep crimson gown with a matching shawl about her shoulders. The shawl disguised yet did not hide her bare arms, against which those of the other ladies appeared frail. They suited her, thought Royston, emphasising the fire that burnt within her. Indeed, there was an odd frisson of exhilaration in knowing her so strong. Her gown, cut fashionably low, did not only reveal her shoulders, and that encouraged conjecture not at all helped by the juxtaposition of Lady Justice, classically bared, in the same tableau.

Just then, Hackett took advantage of a lull in the conversation to address Colton.

"I am curious, sir, of your opinion of the competition you face."

Colton considered the question carefully. "Of the two, I have the greater respect for Owen Perkins."

"The Methyr manufactory? Pray give your reasons, sir."

"They have greater experience of railway locomotives, and those they deliver always answer well. Aye, I warrant Pace, Eston, and Gyllson also built locomotives, but these have always been experimental in nature."

"Indeed does not Professor Gyllson occupy the chair of Mechanics at Durham University?" Royston interjected.

"He does, sir, but the connection does not seem to favour their designs. To my knowledge, none has been a complete success. They're either unreliable or have an unhealthy appetite for coal or are simply no better than more conventional designs."

Hackett nodded. "I have heard the same said."

"Owen Perkins is of course a threat, Father, but not to my mind a great one," opined Miss Colton. "Their strength is in tank engines, most often for service as bankers and upon branch lines."

"Whereas from what I observed this afternoon, Colton and Holm appear to be in the business of light goods engines," said Hackett. "Forgive me, Miss Colton, but I consider those almost as remote from the exacting needs of a high-speed express locomotive as the tank engines you denigrate."

"We build express locomotives also, sir." Miss Colton bristled. "None happen to be on our books at present."

"Harriet is correct, Mr Hackett," said Colton, "and we have never received a bad word upon their performance. But approach the railway companies themselves, sir; I am sure their opinions will not have changed."

"You think I distrust your word, sir?" asked Hackett.

Colton laughed. "Oh, by no means! But speak to the penny-pushers, sir. Speak to the fitters. Speak to the enginemen. Let *them* tell you why they favour Colton and Holm."

Oh nicely done, sir, thought Royston.

Lady Alicia then steered the conversation to subjects that excluded no one, and so it remained through the balance of the courses. The party rose, and the marquess, his agent, and Colton retired towards the library. Royston noticed Miss Colton move to follow, but her father denied her with the smallest perceptible shake of his head. Miss Colton turned then, and from her face as she stalked off, it was clear she was not pleased. Her younger sister then offered her arm for Royston to claim, and honour-bound, Royston did so and conducted her warily after the others to the withdrawing room.

HARRIET SETTLED INTO an armchair. As a rule the family favoured the more intimate parlour of an evening, but although she spent little time in the withdrawing room, she could not dispute it to be the more handsome. It was south-facing and spacious yet agreeably appointed with small tables, pot plants, *chaise-longues*, and armchairs. In one corner stood a pianoforte, and the walls were dotted with oil paintings and fine prints, predominantly of landscapes both local and of the Empire. The gas was lit, the cream-and-gold curtains were drawn against the night, and a bright fire burnt in an ornately filigreed fireplace.

She was not in the best spirits. First there was the matter of the marquess's condescending attitude, and now Father had shut her out from the business discussion that no doubt was in progress in the library. It was his right of course; the company was his, and he had claim to her obedience both as his subordinate and his daughter. That dual role was not always an easy one, being both ambiguous and on occasion conflicted.

She watched as Mr Staley guided Bianca to a *chaise-longue*. Her sister then insisted that he occupy the adjacent chair. Harriet sighed. Bianca's behaviour was not helping her mood. Her sister was being most forward and quite dominating the company of Staley; it was a surprise that Mother had not discretely intervened.

"I am certain I do not know how long the marquess and Samuel shall be," said Mother then to those present. "I fear we must entertain ourselves. Lady Mallow, can I beg you to play? You are so accomplished."

The gentlemen in the library missed Lady Mallow's playing, which was misfortunate for she was exceedingly capable on the pianoforte. She played Mozart and then some Strauss. She then coerced her reluctant daughter into joining her. Even with Lady Mallow's accompaniment, the library was then the better place to be. Cecily Mallow had a thin voice and a penchant for stretching up—and then hopping desperately—for notes just out of reach. Harriet affected an attentive mask.

As the poor put-upon girl lurched through ruts in the melody, Staley stood and drifted around the room, examining the paintings. He paused at the writing table that Mother had brought into her marriage from Selforth Abbey, seat of her father, the Earl of Neme, and which Harriet knew she loved but didn't dare use. When Cecily Mallow's voice took a final stumble and died, he was still examining the table.

"A Joubert, Lady Alicia?" he asked Mother, reverently stroking its red and gold japanning.

Mother was delighted. "Why yes, Mr Staley!"

"Of around… 1760?"

"Admirably close, sir. 1758," she said, replacing the Mallows at the pianoforte.

"It is a most handsome piece, Lady Alicia."

"I am *so* glad to have it appreciated, Mr Staley." She beamed.

At that moment, the marquess swept in. "I do so apologise for having to absent myself from your delightful company." He claimed Staley's chair. "Business, alas," he told Bianca, leaning closer. "So dreary, Miss Bianca, and so cruel to keep me from your presence."

"So good of you to rejoin us so promptly, my lord,"

Mother said a touch too brightly. "I had quite resigned myself to you being detained indefinitely."

"I hope I have not missed too much, Lady Alicia. Have you played? I do hope not—I would quite inconsolable if you have."

Mother accepted the compliment with a courteous nod and then, as her husband and Hackett arrived, addressed the keys. She played one of her favourite pieces, a short Beethoven sonata, then asked her younger daughter to play and called on Staley to turn the music for her.

"No, no—I shall undertake that duty," said the marquess, striding forward. "I quite insist."

Staley had no option but to withdraw with grace.

Bianca played as well as Mother and had a fine clear voice, but Harriet wouldn't be called upon to play. The largest tantrums of her childhood had been over music lessons, and to her eternal shame, she had even bitten one unfortunate tutor.

Bianca played an old and sad French love song, singing it in its native tongue and entrancing the gathering.

Mother looked then for further volunteers. "Mr Hackett, do you play or sing?"

"I use my singing voice solely to praise God, Lady Alicia, and beg his forgiveness on every occasion," replied the agent without an iota of humour.

"Ah then…" Mother's eyes scanned the room. "Perhaps Lord Harlow?"

The marquess bowed. "For you, Lady Alicia, anything."

He settled himself behind the pianoforte and favoured them all with a foppish smile. "I believe I shall play 'Joshua before Jericho.'"

"I am unaware of such a piece," said Mother. "Pray, who is it by?"

The marquess smiled. "I must take the vanity of its composition upon myself." He then adjusted his seat, looked down at the keys, and flexed his fingers. The company waited curiously, although Harriet noted Hackett easing discretely into the background.

The piece began with a bright, complex melody played astoundingly quickly to which the marquess began adding glissandos of lower notes. Now were added great crashing waves of bass into which, fugue-like, the melody was turned about and rewoven. The marquess's bemused foppishness was all gone now, and his face was stern, his eyes sharp, and his movements as energised as his music.

Caught with them all in the strident maelstrom of notes, Harriet could well imagine the walls of the biblical city collapsing and the hopelessness of the occupants within—the panicky high melody emerging briefly above the punishing lower registers. The piece then became martially triumphant (although blocks were still tumbling upon the few surviving Canaanites) and then drew up into a towering finale.

There was a shocked silence in which Harriet wondered why smoke wasn't drifting from the abused pianoforte, and then Staley began to applaud. The others, coming out of their daze, joined in.

"You are so kind," said the marquess with a modest bow. "Of course, it sounds far grander played on my instrument at Kimstanton. It's a… a what, Hackett?"

"A Tannhäuser-Trapp Steam Pandemonium, my lord," said Hackett, emerging from the recesses of the room. "The Leviathan model."

"It sounds magnificent," stated Sir Geoffrey, still a little glassy-eyed.

Hackett nodded. "The local villages attest so," he said,

"although it was quite troublesome to install. It required twelve fathoms of excavation to find bedrock."

"Does anyone else care to…" hazarded Mother, clearly resigning herself to trying to fill the broad, empty wake behind "Joshua Before Jericho."

"I believe that I would," Staley said unexpectedly. "If that is acceptable."

Mother looked relieved. "By all means, Mr Staley."

Staley went to the pianoforte. "I confess that I do not play, but I am content to sing unaccompanied."

After the marquess's performance, Harriet could only admire Staley's courage.

Staley waved down offers of assistance from Mother and Lady Mallow. "Thank you, but no. I fear the tune is rather obscure, being an old folk song of my native Sussex." He then hesitated. "'The Iris of Midhurst' is an *old* song, and a touch *risqué* by today's standards, but not one I believe will bring great offence to the company present."

In an unwavering baritone, he began to sing a galloping lay of a miller's son enamoured of the squire's daughter, the chorus of which was so infectious that he had them joining in upon its second appearance. The song *was* ribald, but teasingly so, with similes that slid past unnoticed unless one was looking for them. (Harriet *was*, and several times had to stifle her shocked mirth for fear of embarrassing herself.)

After various thwarted attempts, through a most witty conceit, the miller's son finally outwitted the squire, true love won through, and everyone—including to her surprise dour Mr Hackett—was joining in on the last rollicking chorus.

Staley accepted their plaudits modesty and then examined his hunter. "With that, I fear I must be leaving."

"Surely not yet, Mr Staley," protested Mother.

"I'm afraid so, Lady Alicia. The hour is late, and I have responsibilities in the morning."

Harriet saw an excuse she could borrow. "I also, Mother. I think I should retire."

"Aye, *Mercury* needs you both," said Father, catching her glance, and that settled matters.

SHE AND STALEY withdrew with good-nights to the company, but paused in the hall where their paths divided.

"You have a fine voice, sir."

Staley smiled. "Thank you, Miss Colton."

He has an honest smile, she decided.

"Harriet, please," she said. "Miss Colton sounds so formal."

He nodded, accepting the honour. "Harriet."

"Do you have means home, Mr Staley?"

"I am content to walk. It is not overfar and the night is dry."

"I will see you in the morning then, sir."

"Indeed you will. Goodnight, Harriet."

"Goodnight, Mr Staley."

She watched the butler help Staley into his Ulster, hand him his hat, and see him to the door, and then she ascended the stairs. Walking pensively to her bedroom, she noticed a shadow out of place. She turned and peered.

"Tollman? What on earth are you doing there?"

Father's driver rose from a chair and touched his forelock. "In case one of me lord's party becomes lost int' strange house at night and requires assistance, Miss Harriet," he told her. "It were Mr Bolsover's idea."

"Was it now?" said Harriet. "How very… thoughtful."

3.

Setting the Road

OUT IN THE sobering pitch-black cold, Royston picked his way down the steps from the terrace and then strode under it towards the drive. He heard music from the withdrawing room and judged the player to be Lady Alicia again. Her sonata had to compete, however, with the sigh and creak of the trees, for while he had tarried in the light and warmth, the wind had risen. He realised by how much when he left the shelter of the house and met its full strength. Clutching at his hat, he thought it a half gale, or soon to be, and out of the north, a harbinger of the coming winter.

He set a good pace until he was amongst the oaks and in the lee of the hill, but then Royston began to amble, pleasantly full of rich food and fine wine. At first he was content to be out walking on such a dramatic night, sharing it solely with the falling leaves—cavorting ghosts in the darkness—but gradually the novelty paled and his thoughts returned to the evening.

All things considered, it had been a most pleasant engagement. Miss Mallow's performance had stung, yet he'd felt sorry for her and displeased by a mother who would insist upon her daughter's humiliation. Sir Geoffrey had been harmless, and Hackett damnably inscrutable, but the marquess he had not taken to at all.

The man was all puff and no substance, a popinjay whose dress, horseracing, and melodramatic music all betrayed an obsession with self-aggrandisement. To Royston's mind a peer of the realm, particularly of Lord Harlow's elevated rank, should set a fine and sober example for lesser men. The man was not even passing gracious unless it served his own ends. Three times he had pushed himself upon the younger Miss Colton and three times pushed Royston out of the way. It was not that Royston had *intentions* towards the younger Miss Colton. No, what grated was the diabolical lack of manners.

No, if Royston held any *intentions*, they would be regarding not the younger daughter but the older. He was aware he was fast becoming an admirer of the elder Miss Colton for her skill, perseverance, and sharp wit. Moreover, he found her very attractive—particularly so tonight, when there hadn't been the practical constraints of the workplace to suppress her true beauty. Royston smiled then, remembering how he now had license to call her Harriet. That warmed him more than the fine dinner. Surnames were so… impersonal, and clumsy in endearments.

Walking now into Chale Bridge, he chuckled at his own presumption—especially when he hadn't asked, and she hadn't suggested, that she call him Royston. He could not deny he was attracted to Harriet, but it was too soon to be thinking of endearments. He had no idea, for example, how she viewed him. She was more affable with him now than when they'd first been introduced, but that hardly meant he'd be accepted as an appropriate suitor! Then of course she was his employer's daughter; that alone recommended circumspection.

Under wildly swinging shop signs and past several chimney pots smashed to shards, Royston pushed his way against the storm up the Kearby road. He took temporary shelter against the churchyard wall and there pushed his hat inside his Ulster, preferring it crumpled to lost.

He was in relative shelter until the level crossing, where he was buffeted by fierce gusts coursing down between the station's empty platforms. Then facing the exposed bridge across the Chale, he walked steadily out onto it, a wary hand on its girders and leaning into the crosswind. He paused midstream and, grasping the ironwork in both hands, turned into the storm to enjoy the simple exhilaration of letting the wind push at him and tease at his hair. And this was only a half gale, barely fifty miles per hour in the gusts. Imagine how more rousing it would be to stand on *Mercury*'s buffer beam when she was at full sprint! His thoughts then took an odd twist. Imagine... *being* her, forcing her way through the air just as he had forced his way up the Kearby road.

Deep in thought, he turned sidelong to the wind and then back. He then leant forward over the rail, gauging the wind's push in that position and cogitating. He was just experimenting with splitting the wind before him with his hands when he was aware of light upon the riveted girders and then upon him also. He straightened up to see a cluster of four lanterns approaching and belatedly upon the wind the chuff of a steamer. It drew to a halt beside him, and then a bulls-eye lantern was pointing in his face, blinding him.

"Is everything all right, sir?" asked a suspicious voice from the driving bench.

"Perfectly, Constable," Royston replied, guessing from the voice and the familiar square silhouette of the steamer (having fled more than once from the scene of a prank in Birmingham) that he was being addressed by a member of Her Majesty's Constabulary.

"Sergeant, sir," said the voice wearily. "Not been spurned by a lady or some such, like?"

"Of course not, Sergeant," said Royston scornfully, and then he realised… "Good Lord, man, you don't think I was contemplating my own destruction!"

"I'm not paid to think, sir. That's for me betters to do. All I know is that on wild nights, lone folk on bridges cause *paperwork.*"

"I can assure you, Sergeant, that I was merely conducting an impromptu scientific experiment."

"At night, like?" the voice said dubiously.

"The concept had only this minute struck me."

There was a pause. "Maybe you should get yourself home, like… sir."

"That I will, Sergeant."

"Goodnight, sir."

"Goodnight, Sergeant."

The steamer began to move off.

"Coo! I reckon he's one of them *savants*, Sarge." Royston caught a different voice in the wind.

"You might well be right, lad. Queer as a bottle o' chips, they be."

STALEY WAS HUMMING distractedly to himself, consulting tables and his slide rule. He didn't seem to have registered

Harriet's arrival, and she found surprising contentment in watching him work for a while. Fearful of being discovered lingering overlong, she was just about to tap on his door when he took up his pen, added another figure to an already lengthy column, and stood up.

"My apologies, Harriet, for not acknowledging your presence sooner, but it is uncommonly easy to lose one's concentration when engaged upon valve timings."

"Indeed I feel it is I who should apologise for interrupting you, sir." Harriet realised he had known she was there all the time and felt heat rise in her cheeks. "But Father sends his respects and was curious whether you wished to attend the trial?"

"The trial? Is it that time already?"

"Past that time, in truth. We've been having a few issues."

"I will, of course, attend." Staley reached for his coat.

Harriet rubbed at her eye. She was feeling stretched a little thin today, having arrived at the works well before dawn to supervise little *Bassey* shunting great *Mercury*, shrouded with tarpaulins, from the fitting shop to the test shop, after which she'd struggled to adapt the apparatus to assess something far larger than ever it had been meant to.

Her gaze landed on some curious little models sitting by Staley's stack of drawings. She went over and examined them. They were made from off-cuts of rod and brazed tinplate and unsophisticated. One was clearly meant to be *Mercury* and others block-like carriages, but one or two were quite odd. One sported a prow like that of a ship, whilst in another the boiler barrel had been given a rounded nose that lent it a disconcerting insinuation of *maleness*. (Harriet sighed inwardly. As if the world had not enough of *that* symbolism!)

"Toys, Mr Staley?" asked Harriet, picking up the miniature *Mercury* and examining it closely. To her disappointment, not all the wheels turned.

"Hmm? Oh those." He frowned upon them with plain frustration.

"They seem very robust," she offered in consolation, perceiving him disappointed with his workmanship. "Whoever is to receive them shall not break them easily."

Royston did not reply but simply shook his head in dissatisfaction.

SET APART FROM the rest of the work, the test shop was smaller than the fitting shop, and with *Mercury* dominating it, it seemed positively cramped. She stood over another pit, not on rails but with a massive steel roller under each of her three sets of driving wheels. Behind the locomotive, a stout pillar emerged from the floor upon which a demonic head had been cast. From its maw protruded a heavy beam, the other end of which was bolted to the rear of *Mercury*'s frames.

More than the beam fettered *Mercury*. Her firebox was unfinished, and so on one side of her was a thick lagged pipe, her umbilical to the works' boilers. On her other side she was bound to a series of plinths by lesser pipes, push rods, and a spider's web of wires and pulleys.

"Ah, Harriet—Staley—we're about ready," said Father from behind the plinths, each of which were fashioned to the Doric order, fluted columns supporting an entablature upon which were mounted dark mahogany panels busy with instruments and controls and decorated with fittings of polished bronze.

Harriet slid beside him and examined a large gauge wrought in glass and bronze. "*Still* under thirteen atmospheres!" she decried, noting where the etch-work hand pointed.

"Aye, I would have liked better, but the boiler-men are hard pressed to give us that," Father told her.

Staley joined them and was examining each of the panels in turn, nodding thoughtfully as he recognised the controls and gauges and lingering over the recording drums with their watchful angels, each of which hid a delicate pen poised to record some aspect of *Mercury*. "She will not run long on one boiler's worth, I fear."

"No indeed, sir," replied Father. "We shall have to be content with a series of runs and see how she answers under different conditions."

THE TESTS CONSUMED the remainder of the day and into the evening. They pitted *Mercury* against the resistance of the rollers first at walking pace, when her driving gear moved with a ponderous yet pleasing unity, each shaft and rod fulfilling its role in delicate harmony with the remainder. Each subsequent run they tested her harder and faster, the recording pens dancing as she strained against the pillar, her exhaust steam filling the rafters and then descending until those who attended her moved indistinctly within a graveyard fog. Now they had to wait between runs, watching the pressure gauge creep back up. Finally, Colton declared the last run.

"Now Harriet, show us what she is truly capable of," he said with a glance at his daughter.

Harriet smiled, the ring of scallop-shaded gaslights above the plinths casting her features into delicate relief. She turned to *Mercury*. "One-quarter cut-off, if you please, Benjamin, and we shall have the regulator full open this time. The roller resistance is upon the second mark?" Receiving a confirming nod, she glanced about her. "Are we all ready?"

They nodded, some with apprehension.

"Carry on, Benjamin," she said calmly.

Royston saw *Mercury*'s wheels begin to turn, and suddenly it was mayhem, the floor shaking with the locomotive's fury at being chained down, her motion a relentless blur, her whole, terrifying power manifest too close, the howl of the roller-brakes and the thunder of her exhaust putting even "Joshua Before Jericho" to shame.

Muggy steam engulfed them all, but in less than a minute, *Mercury* was tiring, and soon her driving wheels were crawling wearily, her boiler spent.

His ears ringing, Royston glanced across at Harriet. Her eyes were bright, her colour high, and her full lips distractingly parted.

"Oh, my," she murmured, gazing raptly at *Mercury*.

"One hundred and forty-seven miles an hour," pronounced Colton with satisfaction, rising from one of the recording drums. "And an initial drawbar pull of nearly thirty tons!"

"That is *most* agreeable," his daughter responded. "Do

you not think so, Mr Staley?"

Royston wiped the clammy caress of the steam from his face. "Yes, Miss Colton." With Harriet's father present, he reverted to formality. He didn't want her family to suspect his feelings for her. "That is certainly encouraging—under the circumstances."

She looked mildly puzzled but then was drawn away by arrangements for *Mercury* to be returned to the fitting shop.

He waited for her to be done, content to marvel at her confidence and the respect she was accorded. He then escorted her back across the darkened works to the main buildings.

"You seemed unimpressed by the last run, sir," she said guardedly, stepping with him over various sets of rails. "Did not you *feel* her power?"

"Most certainly I did," he said. "It was truly astounding. There cannot be a locomotive in the entire Empire that can match her."

That mollified her. "Yet you seem reserved. Is it over whether we can maintain steam?"

He considered that and shook his head. "I believe her firebox is well appointed for the task, although I admit stoking will prove a challenge."

"How so, sir?"

"I estimate *Mercury* may consume several hundred-weight of coal a *minute*."

She was silent for a few moments. "That is beyond the capabilities of human sinew."

"I have watched the boiler-men at their work, and I concur."

She weighed the new challenge in silence.

"That, however, is not at the root of my concern."

"Oh? And what is, Mr Staley?"

"My uncertainty as to how many tons of force the air will present, resisting *Mercury*'s passage."

She glanced at him sharply. "Tons, sir?"

"Tons, madam. Have you not been out in a gale and had the wind try to knock you down?"

"Why, certainly."

"I also," he said. "At speed, *Mercury* will face a gale of her own making—greater than a gale in truth; more the legendary hurricane of the Carribee."

"Several times the force," mused Harriet as they arrived at his office, "yet surely negligible to the drag of her train."

"Perhaps not, alas. The force is not proportional to speed but to the *square* of the speed. If a gale exerts against me a good fraction of my weight, then a hurricane would take me with it. And the wind is a *pressure*; it scales to the area of the object."

"And *Mercury* is far broader and taller than you," she observed with quiet amusement.

It was an odd comparison. Royston, not sure what to make of it, let it pass. "Quite. I believe the pressure of the wind will ultimately determine *Mercury*'s maximum speed. It is essential we estimate it in some way."

She moved to the drawing table. "Ah, *that* is why you constructed these," she said, indicating the models sitting there.

"Quite so," he acknowledged, joining her. "I realised there was little that could be done to *Mercury*'s cross-section, and so I began to conjecture ways to ease her passage." He picked up the prow-nosed model and showed it to her. "Just as ships are designed to slice through the water. Indeed, I considered using water as the test medium. It is over eight hundred times denser than air, and the resistance would be multiplied commensurately."

She took the model from him. "But how would you change the rate of flow?"

"I'd imagined some arrangement in the Penny, with weirs and such."

"That sounds pleasantly diverse," she said, smiling. "I will look forward to it."

He knew his own smile was tempered. "Alas, of late I have lost some confidence in the approach."

"Whyever so, sir?"

"Air is compressible, and water is not. I am sure that must affect the results. Unfortunately the calculations swiftly grow too complex for me to ascertain how."

She thought on that. "So you would have the testing in air?"

"There would be a great deal less uncertainty," he said. "Although I confess I am at a loss as to how to achieve the necessary speeds." He smiled. "Short of dropping the models from a very, very great height."

She smiled with him but then stood silent, thoughtfully turning the ship-like model over in her hands. "I believe I can see a way."

"Really?" he said with sudden hope.

She nodded. "It is only an idea though. It requires deliberation."

"Even so, I am greatly encouraged."

THE NEXT DAY Colton himself came to Royston's office, with Harriet following. Respectfully, Royston made to stand, but Colton waved him back into his chair.

"Harriet tells me you're concerned over how hard *Mercury* will have to push against the air," he said.

Royston nodded. "I believe the problem could be sizable, sir. You see—"

Colton raised his hand. "There is no need, Staley. You have convinced my daughter, and that is conviction enough for me. What I'm worried about is what it implies to the overall design. The time has passed for major changes."

"We should need none, sir. Everything should be of an entirely cosmetic nature. An outer casing of sheet metal, perhaps, and braced to convey the pressure upon it to the existing arrangements."

Harriet nodded. "And we can determine the extent of the bracing once we understand the forces entailed, Father. We may also have to adapt the carriages in some way." She looked at Royston. "A ship's side is generally kept smooth."

He acknowledged the point with a small bow.

"It appears a modest effort to improve our chances," pronounced Colton. "So in this you both have my blessing." He looked then at Royston's models and sighed. "*Mercury* may end up looking quite outlandish."

"Outlandish is, however, apt, sir, since we *are* venturing into another land," said Royston. "Consider: The fastest locomotives today, lightly loaded, barely reach one hundred miles an hour, and that passing brief. We are contemplating significantly higher speeds and a full load, sustained all the way from Bristol to London."

"Aye, I know that, sir," said Colton. "I think it is because I take pride in how handsome our locomotives appear upon delivery, and now you tell me I must conceal that beauty."

Somehow Royston managed to stop his gaze flickering to the man's daughter, modest in hardwearing serge. "Needs must, sir," he said, trying not to think of a crimson gown.

Colton nodded. "The world changes," he admitted. "Now if you will excuse me, I have to attend to the locomotives of *this* land."

Royston bowed.

Once the father was gone, the daughter turned to him. "I was wondering if you would care to take an excursion with me on Monday, Mr Staley. One that has bearing on the stoking, and perhaps also the wind tests."

"I would be delighted, Harriet."

"You would be prudent to affect overalls though," she warned him, a twinkle in her eye.

"Why, pray?"

"Because I have a letter of introduction to the manager at Newton Main."

He frowned. "A colliery?"

"Why, of course," she said. "Where else could one learn more about moving coal?"

THE FIRST DAY of November dawned grey and cold, with Horse Moor lost in cloud. At half past nine, Royston stepped out of the offices, a little nervous to be venturing in public in overalls. Harriet was across the yard, fussing over the boiler on a works steamer. She stood as he approached.

"Are you ready, Mr Staley?" She rubbed her hands

against the chill.

"I believe so."

"I hope you don't mind, but I sent Thorneycroft away. It seemed profligate to take him from the works for a day when you and I can perfectly handle the steamer."

"I trust your judgement, Harriet," Royston said, "and place myself at your service."

"Would you drive, sir?" she asked, donning woollen gloves.

"Ah, that is a skill I lack," he admitted. His father had had little time for road steamers, and he not the allowance nor then the income to aspire to owning his own.

"Really?" She lifted an eyebrow. "That is indeed a failing, sir, and one we must remedy."

But not remedy immediately, Royston realised, for she slid behind the tiller wheel. Whilst she carefully tucked a blanket about her legs, he clambered aboard.

Harriet eased open the regulator, and with a slight lurch, the steamer started to move. She spun the tiller wheel, and they slowly rolled through the works gates and out onto the Kearby road.

Royston found being on the hard driving bench of an open streamer novel and slightly unsettling. All his allied experience had been driving carriages with an attentive pair in front of him or riding inside a steam omnibus. Now there was nothing but the road itself before him, and the familiar cadence of hooves and jingle of harness replaced by a less cheery clatter and chuff from somewhere below.

Harriet drove carefully through Chale Bridge and didn't need to reach for the whistle cord; steamers were common enough that those on foot knew to get out of the way, and the few horses standing patiently with carriers' carts merely snorted.

Once over the Chale, however, she opened the regulator. Soon they were rattling along at twenty miles an hour, and Royston tucked his hands into his pockets and wished he'd brought a hat. The steamer lurched into a rut occasionally, but he found he could brace himself quite satisfactorily against the footboard, and Harriet showed great skill at avoiding the worst of the road.

The road had turned north, following the valley of the Chale, and cattle paused in their grazing to watch them clatter past. Then on the far side of the river, where ran the London and Northern, a goods engine pulling a rake of coal empties caught up with them and then overhauled, its exhaust beat deep and measured against the frantic chuff of the steamer.

"I wonder how much longer we will see that, Mr Staley," commented Harriet.

He looked at her and frowned. "A train, madam?"

"A train *passing* us, sir," she said, taking playful delight at his confusion. Her smile was so infectious that he found he couldn't be offended.

"Ah. Then for some time, I'd hazard," he said. "Steamers may be improving, but the state of the roads will always ensure rail remains supreme."

The steamer gave an opportune wallow, underscoring his argument.

"I would not be so sure, sir," she said firmly. "There is great interest in improving the major highways for steaming, and it comes with substantial patronage."

He was oddly pleased to have her challenge his generalisation. "But how would you attract the capital for such undertakings? Where would be the return?" he asked. "Not by a re-emergence of the turnpike trusts, surely?"

"They were universally reviled," she readily agreed. "Truly I do not know, but I know the steamer lobby has the railways troubled."

"Even though the improvements, if ever enacted, would take many years, Harriet?"

"Even so. The railways have already seen a decline in receipts due to commuter omnibuses." She kept eyes on the road ahead. "Hence their abortive attempts to have punitive restrictions placed on steamers."

"The Red Flag Act?" Gazing at her, he was glad now that he was not at the wheel with the road laying first claim to his attention.

"That and its equally onerous and doomed brethren. Had they lobbied Parliament before 1870, Father thinks they might have had a chance." She shrugged. "But they left it too late; the steamer lobby had grown too strong."

"Yet the railways will always be competitive," he said. "Surely individual steamers can never hope to achieve the economies of rail?" He was enjoying their conversation, and that she had devoted some thought to its subject only attracted him more to her.

"I give you that for the conveyance of goods, sir, but that accounts for barely half a railway's revenue. It is the *passenger* fares that are at risk." She paused for a few seconds, her face pensive. "I do believe that Lord Clifton's Challenge is not at all as self-indulgent as he would have us think, Mr Staley. Indeed, I believe he is being most shrewd."

"Good heavens!" Royston exclaimed. "Why, of course. Steamers could never offer such speedy passage as taking the train behind the likes of *Mercury*!"

Harriet smiled grimly. "Have no doubt that they will *try*, Mr Staley. And have no doubt that it will lead to the most appalling carnage."

Royston thought on that, and he could not find it in himself to disagree.

NEWTON MAIN COLLIERY stood on the edge of a plateau above the market town, its twin squat headstocks an unsightly local landmark. As the steamer climbed up to it, more buildings came in sight, dominated by the winding house. About the colliery, sheep grazed upon the scrubby upland.

Mr Whinstone, an under-manager, hearty and balding, received Harriet cordially and seemed delighted to escape his usual tasks for the distraction of showing visitors around the colliery. It was a noisy and dirty place, busy with tubs and coal wagons, clanking machinery, and the near-continual thrum of the headstock sheaves as they spun to the surface the morning shift, cage upon cage of weary miners, their eyes startling white in their coal-encrusted faces.

The visitors were shown the pit bank, where full tubs came off the cage, then were emptied and returned underground. They followed the coal along a clanking coal walker to the cacophony of the washers, where the coal was washed clean of stones, lifted to be sized upon great shaking tables, and finally passed slowly before long lines of surly boys who picked out any residual stones. All the time, the under-manager attempted to convey by gesture what was going on (it was far too noisy to converse). Harriet caught Royston's arm several times and pointed at some detail of the machinery that moved the coal about. She also made copious notes in a small book with a quick but untidy hand.

When they left the din of the washers, Harriet asked to see the ventilation arrangements. Mr Whinstone showed them the housing for the prodigious fan that drew the foul air from the mine and described what could not be seen.

Royston asked over the roar of the fan how much air it drew and what was the power of the pristinely maintained steam engine that drove it.

The under-manager was quick to answer. "One hundred and forty thousand cubic feet per minute, sir, at a water gauge of three inches," he shouted proudly, "and the *Lady Beatrice* is of ninety horses, indicated."

BACK IN THE colliery yard, they thanked Mr Whinstone for his time, Staley spun a shilling to the boy who had been watching the steamer, and Harriet drove them through the colliery gates and eased the steamer down the hill towards Newton-Le-Helm.

"Might we stop in town for a spot of lunch, Harriet?" suggested Staley.

"That would be most excellent, sir."

"I fear we shall not be welcome in any establishment of class, however."

It was true; although neither of them had touched the coal, the coal had touched them.

Harriet laughed. "I am quite willing to lunch in one with

fewer pretensions, Mr Staley, as long as it is respectable."

They found an inn off the town square, The Silent Fox, and ate in the public bar, which had plain deal tables and stools and, for decoration, shrill handbills advertising forthcoming prize fights. There was, however, a good warming fire, flavourful ham and potatoes, a rich porter, and a friendly if bemused welcome.

"Do you mind if I ask you a question, Mr Staley?"

He dabbed at his lips with his handkerchief. "Not at all, Harriet."

"Forgive me if I am forward, but I am curious as to why you chose to attend the School of Mechanics in Birmingham?"

"Rather than one of the great houses?"

"You read me well, sir," she said. "You appear most able, and your family is by all accounts, ah… well-to-do." She blushed slightly; discussing relative prosperity was never good manners.

"It is a poor mystery, I am afraid," he said. "An Old Boy of my public school endowed a scholarship to Birmingham, which I was fortunate enough to secure. It allowed me to pursue my education without having to ask for my father's financial support."

"Are you… estranged from your father?"

He laughed. "Good heavens, no. It was all to do with my pride. In fact, Father insisted I accept a modest allowance that I might not live a pauper. That, I suspect, had to do with *his* pride."

She smiled. "A prideful family, sir."

"Yes, I do believe we are," he said. "Is that a bad thing?"

"No, indeed—in moderation it is a virtue."

"Your example reflects that," he said courteously, his

blue eyes upon her, and honest. "And that of your father. I am very glad that fortune led me to Colton and Holm."

"We also, sir." She averted her eyes, again feeling heat in her face—not from his compliments, but knowing her response was personal as well as professional.

THEY FINISHED THEIR meal discussing how they might adapt what they had seen at Newton Main to *Mercury*, and then Staley went to the bar to pay.

"Do not forget to render the account for reimbursement," she told him. "We are about the business of the company."

"I will not," he told her, offering his hand for her to rise. "Although it seems almost deceitful for a meal so pleasant."

HALFWAY TO CHALE Bridge, Harriet eased the steamer to a stop. Staley looked at her, curious.

"I believe it is time for you to drive, Mr Staley, and for me to instruct," she told him.

Staley looked uncomfortable. "Pardon me if I seem reluctant, Harriet, but is this wise?"

"The road is flat and straight and quite empty," she replied. "I can think of no better time."

"Then I put myself in your hands."

He slipped to the ground and walked about the nose of the steamer, and she slid across to allow him the tiller wheel.

Staley would of course know the mechanics of the steamer, and so she concerned herself with pointing out which lever connected to which function.

"I must sit close to you, Mr Staley, in case I must intervene," she said.

He nodded. "That sounds eminently prudent, madam, given my lack of experience."

"No cut-off to begin, sir, and gently with the regulator," she said, sliding closer so that she could kick at the foot-bar of the steam brake if he did not, yet leaving a small gap for propriety.

They moved off with rather a lurch, and then the steamer drifted wildly through the ruts as Staley came to terms with the tiller wheel, and Harriet found herself pressed up against him, clinging to the bench back behind him and laughing with him at their ungainly progress. Even when the steamer steadied, she could not bring herself to move away. He felt comforting and strong against her, and she could feel his body heat through her clothing. It was unexpectedly agreeable, so much so that she told her conscience she could ward off familiarity or catastrophe, but not both.

"You drive well, sir," she said.

"We are not yet in the ditch," Staley agreed. "The time to worry is when the road offers me a genuine challenge—such as a corner."

Yet he negotiated several of these and a small hill without putting them through the hedge.

A beech coppice approached that pressed the road against the base of a steep rock-strewn hillside. In its lee, he brought the steamer to a halt and spun on the handbrake.

He turned then and looked her directly in the eyes, his expression oddly serious. Harriet had a sudden awareness of how isolated was this spot in the road, and in it a gentleman had her alone.

No, not *a* gentleman; *this* gentleman. Helpless in his gaze, her heart beat fast, an odd nervous lightness invaded her soul, and she forgot to breathe. If he made to kiss her, she was suddenly unsure she would resist.

"We are near to Chale Bridge, Harriet," he said. "It would not do for us to be seen so familiar."

Bewildered by the emotion that had swept over her, Harriet knew she was blushing now and prayed he interpreted it as overwrought respectability distressed. "But it is quite innocent, Mr Staley," she protested, wondering privately whether it was and whether she wanted it to be so.

"I would not have your reputation put at risk, madam," he said, and slid to the ground.

"You are most considerate, sir," she said, and took the wheel. She drove the remainder of the way to the works with more care than usual, still troubled by her reaction.

ROYSTON WAS WHISTLING "Incautious Claire," a scurrilous pothouse ballad that had been popular in Birmingham, the words of which would never be sung in respectable company. Beside him lay the plans of *Mercury*'s firebox, and he had all morning been sketching stoking contrivances, but none completely satisfied him. He thought he had the problem of getting coal from the tender to the engine solved and even how to drive the endless chains across the coupling between tender and locomotive, but how to make sure the fuel was deposited evenly across the fire bars had so far outwitted him.

Just then Harriet appeared at the door, looking excited.

"Good news, Mr Staley! Father received a letter this morning from Lord Harlow; he's agreed to sponsor *Mercury* to the tune of six thousand pounds!"

Although pleased, Royston was also distrustful of the marquess. "What conditions does he place on the monies?"

She frowned. "A share in the profits of her class—I thought Father explained that to you."

"He did, although I rather expected my lord to insist upon something more, such as having *Mercury* renamed."

"Not the *Marquess of Harlow?*" she suggested darkly.

"Heavens, no," he assured her. "The *Most Commendable And Illustrious Lord Harlow* at the very least. It is providential that she has the boiler length to bear it."

"Mr Staley! You are most disrespectful," she said, but with a smile.

He cocked a wry eyebrow at her. "Or, perchance, I am my lord's most dedicated admirer?"

She laughed. "No, you are right. His rank cannot completely excuse his vanity and conceit."

She then came to see what he was working on yet maintained more of a distance than was her norm. Royston put it down to the previous day and that the familiarity of the steamer had in hindsight been judged imprudent. She looked through his sketches and offered a few suggestions, and then Royston explained the issues upon which the work had run aground.

"You are right, sir," she said. "The solution is not at all

obvious."

"Particularly as it must work within the existing design," he said. "I… I would welcome your assistance."

She looked at him, appeared to hesitate, but then her face showed resolve. "You shall have it. First, however, I must make sure the men know what is expected of them."

She left him for a short while and then returned and took the chair he had placed upon the other side of his desk. By lunchtime, working together and parrying ideas, they had a design that appeared plausible and in some aspects satisfyingly ingenious.

They rose from the desk, and Royston put on his jacket. In doing so, he felt something thin and unyielding in its inner pocket and remembered the envelope that had been awaiting his return to Chale Bridge Cottage the previous evening.

"Ah, Harriet? There is another matter—quite trifling, I assure you—upon which I would value your opinion."

"Indeed? Pray tell."

"I have received an invitation to the Mallows' ball this forthcoming Friday," he said. "I confess it was rather unexpected, having only just been introduced to Sir Geoffrey and the Mallows."

Miss Harriet furrowed her brow. "It is a charity event, sir," she said carefully. "The more that attend, the better the cause is served—although I confess to have quite forgotten the cause."

"The County Foundlings and Waifs Workhouse," Royston informed her. "A new roof, apparently. It seems most laudable, given winter is coming on. And of course it is Guy Fawkes Night, so there are likely to be pyrotechnic diversions."

"Almost certainly," she mused.

She remained distracted, but Royston plunged on hopefully. "My only reservation over accepting the invitation is that I will be surrounded by strangers. Might I ask if the Coltons are also attending?"

"Pardon?"

"Is your family attending?"

"Oh, most certainly, sir."

"*All* the family?" he asked, seeking assurance she would be present.

"All the family, sir," she confirmed, but she did not look happy.

MOTHER WAS ALONE before the parlour fire, embroidering. She looked up as Harriet entered and, seeing her daughter unwashed and in works attire, gave a small exasperated sigh.

"I shall go and attend to my appearance momentarily, Mother," Harriet promised. "But would you be so kind as to answer me a question?"

"If I can, my dear."

"Did you write to Lady Mallow and ask her to invite Mr Staley to the ball?"

Mother regarded her serenely. "I hardly see that as being your business, Harriet."

"Did you?"

"You are displaying rather poor manners, but yes, I did."

Harriet looked away and breathed a convoluted curse.

"Why, pray, should I not have suggested Mr Staley

might like to attend?" asked Mother. "It is a most worthy—"

"Please, Mother, do not patronise me. Your objective is quite transparent."

"It is? And what might it be?"

"You plot a match for Bianca. You are pushing her and Mr Staley together."

"Now you are being tiresome," said Mother archly. "I am certainly not pushing them together. If, however, they continue to meet in a social context, then perhaps a romantic interest will arise."

"But why Mr Staley, Mother?"

"I would have thought that obvious. He is of good family and sound character. Moreover, he appears adroit in your father's profession."

It took Harriet a few moments to perceive the implication of the latter observation. "You would have him succeed Father at the head of Colton and Holm?"

"Your father could groom him to that duty, yes." Mother then grew steadfast. "I do not care to consider your father's demise, Harriet, but it is our moral duty to safeguard the future."

"I quite believe that Father will leave the business to me."

"Don't be foolish," Mother said dismissively. "It may now be considered acceptable for you to engage in engineering, but the business simply would not flourish in your hands, and your father must know that." She saw Harriet's outrage and smiled benevolently. "It is not your *ability*, my dear, but the *opinion* of others. Commerce is the province of gentlemen; that shall not readily change."

"If you truly believe that, should you not be plotting a match for me?" said Harriet coldly. "For I far more represent the company than my sister."

Mother regarded her sympathetically. "I have considered it, my dear, but even though I sometimes pretend it is not so, I accept that you have decided on a different course."

"What do you mean, Mother?"

"You are wed to your… *profession*, Harriet." The concept clearly disturbed Mother, raised in simpler times.

Harriet was stunned. "You actually believe it to be one or the other? A profession or a family?"

"Is that not so? Do not deceive yourself: A family would demand of you at least what the works does at present. One can either excel at one or be indifferent in both."

"Gentlemen appear to combine the two quite adequately."

"That is different and you know it. A man supports his family through his industry. Upon the wife falls the burden of maintaining the household and nurturing his children. Consider Mr Staley. Is he content to work with you?"

"It would seem so."

Mother nodded. "That is because he accepts that you have dedicated yourself to that cause. You may be sure, however, that he does not view you as a suitable match for the very same reason."

"So you believe Bianca is viewed as suitable?"

"Unless the man is a complete fool." Mother snorted. "Bianca is most accomplished in all the necessary social graces."

"You imply that you think her my better."

"As you well know, I do not believe in favourites. But in the matter of securing the future, then yes, your sister has the advantage on you."

Harriet shook her head irritably. "I don't see why you

are so determined that a professional lady cannot also have a family. I fully intend to, once I have established myself!"

"Do not build up false hopes, my dear," said Mother. "I would not have you grow bitter."

"It is not a false hope!" insisted Harriet hotly. "Consider Her Majesty. Does she not combine most skilfully her responsibilities of monarch *and* mother?"

"Circumstances gave Her Majesty no choice, Harriet, and if to persuade me you have to claim yourself the equal of Her Majesty, then do you not see your cause is lost?" She returned to her embroidery. "I shall see you at dinner, my dear."

A civilised person does not storm out of another's presence, certainly not that of one's mother. Harriet left with decorum, but *so* wanted to slam the door.

WITH DIMITY FUSSING over her hair, Harriet gazed at her glum reflection in the looking glass. She had meant everything she had said to her mother, but some of Mother's observations could not be easily refuted. Of course Mr Staley would prefer Bianca. Had he not specifically enquired whether Bianca would attend the ball? Bianca was charming and coy and, yes, beautiful, whereas she was... plain old solid Harriet. How so ingloriously ill-timed it was that Mr Staley found favour in her heart!

"Problems with *Mercury*, miss?" asked Dimity quietly, her reflection sympathetic.

There—everyone thought of Harriet as an engineer and

not a woman. Swiftly, she admonished herself. Her own attitude informed Dimity's assumption; why would her maid suspect anything to have changed?

"No, not *Mercury*, Dimity." She sighed.

"Is it something then that would be helped by sharing, miss?" suggested Dimity softly.

Dimity and she were closer than was the norm between mistress and maid, all because of Newcastle. Dimity had accompanied Harriet north, and they had shared a small set of rooms in that gaunt brick building above the Tyne leased by the Society of Professional Gentlewomen for their unmarried members. Harriet had studied, and Dimity had attended to all their other needs. It was an unusual arrangement for them both, and the years there had weakened the mutual reserve that had stood between them ever since Harriet turned sixteen and Mother insisted Harriet have a maid of her own.

"Dearest Dimity, but I cannot see that it would."

<h1 style="text-align:center">4.</h1>

The Report of Detonators

THARRINGTON HALL, SEAT of Sir Geoffrey and Lady Mallow, lay some seven miles to the east of Chale Bridge, and although Royston took pleasure in walking, that was a little far even for him, especially when formally attired. Accordingly, he had engaged a hackney to convey him to the ball.

A circular lawn lay before the Hall, about which ran a drive tonight busy with gigs, carriages, and the occasional steamer. Faint strains of music floated on the November night from the Hall itself, a neat three-storied building in the Provincial Neo-Renaissance style, whose lower windows were warm with candlelight. Before the door, Royston paid off his driver and, adding a generous tip, reminded him to return for him at the end of the evening. He then ventured within. The music was coming from a spacious room whose doors were thrown open. Glancing in, Royston saw a modest orchestra playing light airs.

Having disposed of his Ulster and hat, he drifted through the public rooms, assaying local society. It was a curious mix: gentleman farmers in their Sunday best, their buxom spouses almost spilling from their gowns, elderly ladies in gowns once fine and fashionable, and gentlemen who had clearly come upon affluence in this new world of industry and were using themselves and their invariably younger wives to advertise the fact.

"Ah, Staley," called a voice.

Royston turned and found Sir Geoffrey addressing him. With him were a well-do-do farmer and an older gentleman in dress uniform and florid of face.

"Sir Geoffrey." Staley bowed. "So kind of you to extend an invitation to me for tonight."

Sir Geoffrey acknowledged the courtesy with a modest gesture. "Now, I recall you soundly refuting Lord Harlow over the Act of Entitlement."

"A mere correction, Sir Geoffrey; nothing more."

That too was dismissed. "We were discussing the ramifications of the Act. Perhaps you could favour us with your opinion."

"Upon what aspect, sir?"

"Colonel Prestbury is of the belief that Her Majesty's armed forces will have to admit women."

"And how does one maintain discipline then, sir?" interjected the colonel. "Damnably difficult, if not impossible."

"I believe," said Royston carefully, "it would not be a popular profession for ladies, even if it was open to them. Moreover, the atrocities perpetrated against us by our barbaric foes argue for the *status quo*. As a nation, we would not have our womenfolk endangered, and surely they too would agree."

"But what of politics?" suggested the wind-burned farmer.

"That is quite another matter," said Royston. "Mr...?"

"Ramsgate, sir. Most pleased to meet you."

"I—"

"Good Lord, sir! You would see women in government?" interjected the colonel hotly.

"In the fullness of time, Colonel, I rather see that as inevitable. Is democracy so precious that we can afford it for only half our people? Besides, women already influence politics through their husbands, do they not?"

"Me lady wife is certainly free with her opinions," vouched Ramsgate with a chortle.

"Then is it such a great step to extend to them the ballot?" asked Royston.

"You are a dangerous reformist, sir," muttered the colonel. "You threaten much that has made Britain great."

"I rather think myself a pragmatist, sir," said Royston. "And would we have achieved anything without the support of the gentler sex?"

Fortuitously, he spotted Miss Bianca Colton through the circulating figures and used her presence to extricate himself from the argument. "Now if you will excuse me, Sir Geoffrey, Colonel, Mr Ramsgate, I see someone I should greet."

Royston threaded his way across the room to the Colton family. Lady Alicia wore a gold gown with lavish skirts, and the younger Miss Colton was dazzling in a bright blue gown with a great deal of intricate lace trim, but his attention was on Harriet, beautifully turned out in a simple green gown that emphasised most splendidly her form, with a simple gold pendant that drew his eyes to the creamy white skin exposed by the gown.

"Lady Alicia, you are looking agreeably well," said Royston. "And you are looking particularly fine tonight, Miss Colton, and you also Miss Bianca." He acknowledged the father with a respectful nod.

"I am quite certain that Bianca would like some refreshment, Mr Staley," said Lady Alicia. "Would you be so kind as to assist her?"

"Delighted, my lady," said Royston, dismayed to have the wrong sister claim his arm and draw him away. Indeed Miss Bianca seemed reluctant to let him free, insisting they watch from the window as shadowy figures lit the towering bonfire upon the rear lawn. Fighting the urge to whistle, Royston tried feverishly to conceive of a way to hand her back to her parents and claim Harriet, but everything he thought of risked a slight upon the younger sister and the concomitant displeasure of his employer.

Then the matter was unexpectedly resolved.

"Sir Geoffrey." A voice rang clear even across the crowded room. "I do so beg your pardon for intruding, but I was in the area and heard of your little patriotic celebration. Neither heaven nor earth could stop me then from calling upon you!"

Royston turned and Miss Bianca with him. Standing beside Sir Geoffrey, his attire so bright with silver, red, and gold that he was almost a firework all by himself, stood the Marquess of Harlow.

"Your presence honours us all, my lord," said Sir Geoffrey, bowing low.

Lord Harlow returned the bow graciously and then turned, scanning the room until his eyes fell upon Royston— or rather, his companion. The marquess immediately sliced a wake through the curious and overawed to claim her hand.

"Miss Bianca, I cannot express my good fortune that Lady Luck has consented we renew our acquaintance." He kissed her hand with more than courtesy. "You are looking so divine this evening that surely you but visit from the court of Venus!"

"Lord Harlow," murmured Miss Bianca, delighted. "You flatter me overmuch, I fear."

"Nonsense, my dear," said the marquess, guiding her away.

Royston, a little bewildered, watched Venus' ambassador and Firework move towards the refreshments, and then he went in search of Harriet.

AFTER THE SLOW carriage drive from Pennydale House (her mother viewing steamers as not a genteel means of transport and worthy of palpitations), Harriet was refreshing herself in the ladies cloakroom, and so the first that she learnt of the marquess's unexpected arrival was when several young ladies rushed in.

"It *really* is him, Belinda," one of them exclaimed, her dark curls bobbing with excitement. "Is he not *so* dashing?"

Harriet exchanged a bemused look with Cecily Mallow, who happened also to be there.

"And a marquess!" exclaimed another as she critically examined herself in the mirror and teased at her hair. "He owns half of Yorkshire!"

Now Harriet realised who was the subject of the excitement, and she was reminded sharply of her father's counsel regarding attachments and the fallibility they brought.

"I must dance with him," said the third. She lifted her petticoats and unhooked a small air pump from a garter.

"Quickly, Belinda, pump me up!" she said, fumbling higher and producing a thin, gutta-percha tube.

Harriet sighed. The golden age of industry had brought many beneficial innovations to society; the pneumatic bustle was in her opinion not one of them.

Belinda complied but after a few strokes of the pump frowned. "You seem quite inflated already, Cora."

Cora examined her profile. "No, it cannot be! More, Belinda—Lord Harlow must notice me!"

Belinda bent to the task.

Completing their toilet, Harriet and Cecily Mallow ceded the cloakroom to the young ladies' quest for cosmetic perfection. Harriet had just closed the door behind them when there was a sharp report from within the cloakroom and a shrill, thwarted yelp. Cecily giggled outrageously, and Harriet could not help but grin.

They returned to the withdrawing room, and Harriet looked for her parents.

"Ah, there you are, Harriet," said Staley, appearing from amongst the small crowd and smiling.

"I understand that we have been graced with Lord Harlow's presence, Mr Staley."

"Indeed. Quite unexpectedly, from what I can ascertain."

"Does Father know?"

"I believe he must, for Lady Alicia is watching my lord most assiduously."

"Oh, has Lord Harlow claimed my sister's attention?"

"Most certainly, and from the moment he arrived. They are with the refreshments." He offered her his arm, which after a moment's hesitation, she accepted.

As HE GUIDED Harriet to the refreshments room, they passed Colonel Prestbury. Royston nodded, but the colonel glowered at him.

"You appear to have made an enemy, sir," murmured Harriet.

"So it seems." He sighed and outlined the earlier conversation.

She nodded approvingly, which warmed Royston. "But did he not harangue you over England falling beneath the Prussian Crown?"

Royston frowned. "He did not, madam."

"That is remarkable."

Royston remained mystified. "I'm afraid I don't quite…"

"Who is the heir apparent, sir?"

"His Royal Highness the Prince of Wales, of course."

"But who is the firstborn of Her Majesty, sir?"

"Oh! The Princess Royal."

"Who is now Crown Princess of Prussia," said Harriet and sighed. "Many think that the Act of Entitlement may force a reform of the Laws of Succession, which if enacted with Entitlement would, as matters stand, place Victoria II on the throne and not Edward VII."

"But surely that would be little different than Her Majesty's marriage to the late Prince Consort?" argued Royston.

"Except the Prince Consort was merely the Duke of Saxony; he was never destined to be King of Prussia."

"Yes… Yes, I can see how that might entice disquiet in certain quarters."

"Indeed it does, sir."

They arrived at the refreshments, where Lady Alicia approached, looking uncommonly vexed.

"Ah, Mr Staley, you are looking after Harriet," she said. "How courteous of you."

He felt Harriet's hand tighten on his arm. "It is my pleasure, my lady," he murmured.

"I am afraid Lord Harlow is quite monopolising poor Bianca," said Lady Alicia, with a glance across to where the inimitable marquess was sitting, talking animatedly with her younger daughter, a glass of port wine in his hand.

"I am sure she will realise that, my lady, and take steps." It seemed poor consolation even as Royston said it, and Lady Alicia did not appear comforted.

Lady Mallow then swept into the room, with servants bearing bundles of coats. "My lord, Lady Alicia, ladies and gentlemen, we are ready for the pyrotechnic entertainment," she announced brightly.

Royston assisted Harriet into her velvet cloak, a deeper green than her gown. He then claimed his Ulster.

The conservatory doors were thrown open to the rear garden and the party moved outside with excited murmurs, their faces lit by the bonfire and by guttering pitch torches set in the lawn in the still, cold air. Servants passed amongst them, offering small pewter goblets of mulled wine to keep out the chill. Royston took one for Harriet and another for himself.

To one side of the bonfire were erected various wooden trellises bearing a diverse collection of shellacked paper tubes. Sir Geoffrey, his face lit by the flambeau he bore, addressed the company.

"My lord, Lady Alicia, Lady Mallow, ladies and gentlemen. We are gathered to celebrate the deliverance of the Crown from those that would see it cast down. Not only do we remember the attempt by odious traitors upon the life of James I, but we are reminded of the diverse attempts on the life of our present Majesty. Let us all pray that her reign shall be long and peaceful. God save the Queen!"

"God save the Queen!" they all responded.

With the affirmation of loyalty, the fireworks began. Rockets soared into the night and exploded in brilliant cascades of red and blue. Fountains of colour burst from grebes and Saxons, pinwheels spun spitting Chinese fire, tourbillions chased their fiery tails and rose into the night, and the sudden detonation of squibs and maroons provoked shrieks of excited alarm from the ladies. Through it all, Harriet clutched his arm, her face animated and delighted beneath the hood of her cloak. Royston found the arrangement most agreeable.

A last rocket wobbled into the night and burst asunder, dispensing intensely brilliant stars of silver and gold that floated below small parachutes. Promoting many an exclamation of delight, they drifted down, winking out one by one. The last one died, and after a few moments, the whole party clapped enthusiastically.

Just as everyone's thoughts were turning to the warmth that awaited them indoors, the marquess stepped out in front of them all. He had declined to wear a coat, and the firelight gleamed on cloth of gold and flashed from a wealth of silver buttons. Royston looked around for Miss Bianca and saw her returning, no doubt gratefully, to her mother's side.

"I BEG THE indulgence of the company," Lord Harlow piped, "but I happened to have with me a pyrotechnic contrivance of my own devising which I would offer humbly for your entertainment." He waved his hand in a vague summons.

Two figures walked into the circle of firelight, carrying between them a wooden box, heavy and plain and passing ominous. They placed it before the trellises, now blackened and scorched. One of the figures approached the marquess bearing a slow match, and Royston realised it was the agent Hackett, the firelight unflattering and rendering his narrow features sinister.

"Would my lord"—he offered his master the slow match—"care to put fire to the mechanism himself?"

"No, no," said the marquess, reclaiming Miss Bianca's hand. "Carry on."

Hackett looked disheartened but returned dutifully to the box. The other man was nowhere to be seen. The agent bent over the box for a few moments, and then it suddenly erupted in a cascade of red and gold sparks, Hackett positively sprinting away into the darkness.

Now amongst the mist of fire, the box was angrily spitting out brilliant embers that spun and squealed and then proceeded to add heavier ordinance dispensed with loud pops and whooshes and which exploded in blue stars at a disturbingly low altitude.

Royston began to grow alarmed; the box had started to act like a horse beginning to bolt, growing wild and furious. It belched a wave of green sparks and something like pinwheels, but unrestrained. Several larger objects shot from it, leaving fiery trails; one exploded in brilliant red in the sky, another in the herbaceous border beside a terrified Hackett, and a third streaked low over the audience's heads, hit the Hall, and there detonated.

Then the box seemed to lose all sense of order, casting out sprays of vivid colours in odd directions and objects that groaned and exploded barely above it. Suddenly—instantly—there was a great multi-hued blinding flash and a deafening report that rocked the very ground.

Royston instinctively drew Harriet protectively against his chest, and she clutched at him in terror. Various people were screaming, but their cries were thin in his ringing ears. The wooden trellises had vanished, glowing logs from the bonfire were strewn across the lawn, and small fires dotted the landscaping. Where the box had sat, there was simply a smouldering hole.

The marquess was clapping his hands in childish delight and barely seemed to register when a fragment of blazing planking spun out of the sky and stuck, dagger-like, in the grass before his feet.

"Is everyone quite all right?" asked Sir Geoffrey.

Everyone looked at each other, and it appeared that they had all survived. Harriet, clearly embarrassed for having been terrified, self-consciously released Royston, and that brought a flicker of loss.

"Then I think we should return inside," said Sir Geoffrey. "I am sure the ladies will wish to sit down quietly and recover from my lord's... ah... astonishing artefact."

Many of the ladies did, although Harriet exhibited greater fortitude. "I fear, Mr Staley," she said, accepting a glass of wine from him, "that against your current experiences you will find our future social gatherings quite dull."

"Not at all, Harriet. I find the company most engaging, notwithstanding my lord's presence." He lowered his voice for her ears alone and added, "and his theatrics."

In the adjoining withdrawing room, the small orchestra had embarked upon a lively waltz. Miss Bianca on his arm, the marquess swept past, ignoring them both. Royston turned to his companion.

"Do you dance, Harriet?"

"Tolerably well, Mr Staley."

"May I have the honour?"

She nodded.

IN FACT, IN contrast to her childhood frustration with music lessons, Harriet enjoyed dancing. That she was rarely invited to dance at these events only made them the more infuriating.

Staley proved to be a satisfying, competent partner in the waltz and the quickstep that followed. He held her not with the indifferent loose clasp that other gentlemen affected but with his hand firm and steady upon her waist. Nor did his attention drift in boredom away from her. It seduced Harriet into forgetting her mother's dismissal of Staley ever being attracted to her, and her heart grew gay with the music and his proximity. She knew she was smiling, and she wished it were permissible for him to hold her closer.

They paused then, to take refreshment, and stood sipping wine and watching the other couples. Prominent among them, like the sun amongst the planets, was the marquess with her sister.

"I am quite determined, Harriet, to find a copy of *Burke's Peerage*," Staley said unexpectedly.

"Whyever so, sir?"

"I am curious"—he favoured her with a wry smile—"to whether my lord has an elder sister."

It took her a moment to work out why this mattered, and then she recalled their early conversation on succession. For a moment she was amused, and then her humour soured. Staley really didn't like the marquess at all. And why should he, when the marquess was again monopolising Bianca? She was then suddenly miserable. Her mother was right; Staley would be interested in Bianca and not her. She didn't hate him for it though, just hated her circumstances. Staley was a *good* man and gallant—see how he danced with Harriet when others ignored her?

Staley drained his wine. "Would you dance again, Harriet?"

"I think not, sir. I would attend to my mother."

"Oh. Yes, of course. Perhaps later then?"

"Perhaps, sir."

She went and sat beside Mother, who was catching up on local social developments with Lady Mallow. She listened with half an ear, her heart heavy and tender. See, now Staley was being gallant to young Cecily Mallow, who even in her pretty cerise gown was being passed over by all the other gentlemen. She watched the two of them begin to dance, remembered his hand upon her waist, and wanted to go home.

THE HACKNEY ROCKED and lurched back through the night towards Chale Bridge. Inside, Staley had wedged himself into a corner. He could hear the driver talking intermittently with his horse, but it barely grazed upon his thoughts.

He very much regretted his quip over a reformed succession and the marquess falling foul of it. He should have thought it through better. The Act of Entitlement and all that might mean to the future was dear to Harriet's heart. No wonder belittling it for a cheap stab at the marquess had upset her—no wonder she had excused herself. Later in the evening, he'd asked her for another dance, hoping by then he would have been forgiven, but she'd declined with cool politeness, claiming that she was tired. How long would she punish him for his insensitivity?

It was a decidedly bad development. Of late he'd convinced himself that she viewed him favourably and perhaps—just perhaps—might welcome his advances. It was a perilous supposition though. He remembered a particular moment on their return from Newton Main Colliery, when he'd stopped to return the controls to her. He had turned to her. Her skin was cheery from the cold, and she looked so wondrously beautiful. On that bleak stretch of road, hidden from prying eyes and safe from spiteful tongues, the impulse to cradle her head and softly kiss her had been so hard to resist, particularly when his hopes had him read encouragement in her hazel eyes.

Royston sighed. If only he could be sure of her heart as he was of his own. He wished that he had dalliances in his past that might offer guidance, but there had been none. It wasn't that he was awkward around the gentler sex; he had polished his skills in polite conversation and dancing at any number of social gatherings around Horsham. The problem was that that had been all they were: social. Certainly a number of ladies had caught his eye, but none had proved more than courteous to him in return.

Rocked by the road, Royston stared into the dark countryside, watching the silhouettes of trees pass. It all reminded him of the Forest of Dean, even without a moon. There had been one that night, and it had been full.

Reverend Dory lectured in the history of industry at Birmingham, a subject new to the curriculum and in itself largely recent also. Dory was young and radiated a fresh-scrubbed enthusiasm for what was his consuming hobby. It was he who organised the expedition to the Forest of Dean, having chosen the area because of the primitive industry that had flourished there since England was Anglia and under Roman rule. It was an opportunity to see the interrelations of iron ore mining, smelting, rolling, and tinning in one contained area.

Dory took six of them with him, all in their first year in Birmingham. A good friend of his from seminary days lived in the area, and he arranged that they could camp in the field adjoining the friend's vicarage.

Even as they entered the forest, Royston had realised that they were intruding, for those they passed glared at the outsiders' carriages with a fierce suspicion. The foresters attracted equal attention from the students, for they were dressed in crude leather waistcoats fastened with unfinished wooden buttons and toggles and worn over undyed woollen clothing. On their heads were formless caps, again of leather.

"The natives look altogether *primitive*," said Garson, city raised and brash. The villages were as undistinguished as the foresters themselves—simple windowless hovels for the most part, although some modern buildings had been thrown up.

The landscape was also strange to Royston. It was as if a quart of features had been squeezed into a gill pot. The valleys were narrow and twisting with steep wooded sides. One was not sure what to expect around the next corner. Sometimes it was simply more forest, but equally, hidden until the last moment, it could reveal a busy manufactory or mine.

They also passed rudimentary tunnels cut into the hillside. Dory explained these were each worked by a handful of "free-miners," for it was a forester's right to take coal from the ground beneath the forest. Apparently, the Freeminers even had their own small government to resolve disputes over prospects! It was without doubt a world apart from the bustle of Birmingham, yet barely sixty miles separated the two.

His fellow students found the area and its inhabitants backward and absurd, yet Royston, raised where each village was important to itself, could tell that under the homespun clothing there was pride in being of the forest. Their isolation and independence may have let the rest of the realm leave them behind, but they were ignorant, not simple. Having made this insight, he felt rather ashamed of his companions' snide observations.

They spent the latter half of that late May afternoon visiting a small tin-plate works. Watching the repetitive and unrewarded labour and choking upon the fumes of the acid used on the sheet iron prior to it being dipped into molten tin, Royston was left acutely depressed by the lot of his fellow man.

Afterwards they went to the vicarage, struggled with the tents, and then shared a plain supper at the kitchen table. Garson then announced he was up for a constitutional, and two others immediately voiced the same accord. As they left together, Royston was privately amused. He'd seen what was almost certainly a pot-shop as they passed through the local village. Given their habits, he was as certain they were off to investigate.

An hour or more later he was still at the kitchen table, reading by candlelight, when Dory came looking for him. "Have Garson, Trent, and Watlins returned, Staley?"

"Not yet, sir."

"Oh dear." Dory touched his clerical collar unhappily. "I fear they may have become lost."

"I will go look for them immediately, sir." Royston put aside his book. Better he "find" them than Dory!

It must have been less than a mile from the village as the crow flies, but since the valley containing the vicarage all but reversed direction before reaching the village, by road it was almost a two-mile walk. It was, however, a fine night for walking. The air was temperate, the sky clear, and the road bathed in silver moonlight. Moreover, his exercise would be rewarded with a mug of ale before persuading the miscreants to return.

With a few hundred yards remaining to the low cluster of buildings, Royston heard the sounds of a scuffle. More than a scuffle indeed, given the crashing, cries, and cursing. Immediately, he loped forward, keeping to the deep shadows of the trees.

It was as he had feared; the outsiders had got into an

altercation with the natives, and they were losing. It was hard to be certain in the thin moonlight, but it looked like Garson was already down, leaving the other two to fend off twice their number. Royston swore silently; Trent and Watlins were poised like boxers and were no doubt trying to fight honourably, but he'd been in enough scraps around Horsham to know that Queensberry rules were only honourable when both sides obeyed them, and tonight this was not the case. Quietly, he picked up a heavy branch and eased through the shadows towards the fight.

The two on Trent, the lighter of the students yet standing, leapt forward, intent on overwhelming his guard with the ferocity of the attack. Trent landed a punch on one but took a swinging blow from the other. He staggered, but before the two could press home their advantage, Royston rushed from the shadows. He struck the larger one a great blow on the head with his branch, dropping him immediately. Exploiting the element of surprise to the utmost, Royston drove the end of the branch into the midriff of the other. The fellow's wind left him explosively, and he doubled up most satisfactorily, but Royston lost his branch in the process. He hooked the man's legs from under him and shoved him down by his companion, who was now lying very still.

About to go to the assistance of Watlins, Royston was momentarily distracted. On the road towards the village stood another figure. Silent and monk-like, the figure watched the fight, its face hidden in the shadows of a cowl. But then he knew a sudden rush of inexplicable dread. He dodged blindly, and a boot—iron-toed by the harm it wrought—caught him hard at the knee.

Royston cried out in pain, but the boot had missed its

intended target. His attacker, another burly lad in a miasma of ale fumes, stormed in against Royston, a great fist swinging. Royston dodged again, and the blow glanced off a shoulder. Royston drove his fist up hard, catching the fellow under the chin. To Royston's dismay, not a lot happened except his knuckles howled with pain. Thick, calloused hands caught him by the neck, squeezing. Royston rained blows on the man, but he seemed invulnerable to pain. He heard a terrible cry, but didn't know whether it was friend or foe.

Just as Royston's limbs were growing sluggish and dis-embodied and his vision thick with strange, swimming constellations of stars, suddenly there were arms about his assailant's neck dragging him back, and a fist flashed in catching the man square on his chin. The hands at this neck slipped, and Royston staggered backwards, watching the world as if it was a dream. Then his vision cleared, and he saw Watlins and Trent struggling with the one who had tried to throttle him and making little headway. Royston locked his hands together, rushed forward, and dealt the brute a heavy overhand blow on the neck. Even that seemed to be brushed off, yet the man did turn then and set off at an untidy lope for the village, shaking Watlins off as a dog shakes off water.

"Let him go," gasped Royston. He took stock. The one he'd winded was creeping cautiously away, and the one he'd pole-axed was stirring also. Royston was glad of that; he feared he might have killed him. The last of the four locals was sitting unhappily in the road, nursing his nose, whilst the monk had vanished entirely.

They hauled Garson to his feet. He'd sustained a cut above the eye, his clothing was torn, and he was wavering as if punch-drunk, but at least he could stand.

"We had better be quit of this locale before fellow-me-lad rouses reinforcements," counselled Royston. "What on earth did you do to provoke the altercation?"

"Nothing," protested Trent.

"Nothing much," muttered Watlins, as he and Trent, supporting Garson from each side, urged him away.

"Define *nothing much*," suggested Royston coldly, limping after them, his wounded knee complaining at the pace.

"There was this minx in the pot-shop," explained Trent. "She took a fancy to Garson and was most forward towards him."

Royston sighed. "And no doubt he returned her interest in kind," he suggested.

"'Course I did," slurred Garson. He sniggered, and then coughed fitfully.

"Apart from her, the atmosphere was decidedly icy," said Trent. "So after a while we left. Those dullards followed and assaulted us."

"Of course they did," said Royston angrily. "They're not simpletons, Trent, just backward. The last thing they'd welcome would be strangers with airs taking interest in their womenfolk."

"Blame Garson," said Watlins sourly.

Royston to his shame was lagging behind them. "It would be prudent to get clean away before blame is apportioned," he said. "You three go ahead, and don't slow down."

"What about you?" Watlins asked, concerned. "You're not going so well on that leg, Staley. What if they catch you?"

"They won't," promised Royston. "I'm going to cut up

over the hill. They won't be looking for me up there, and I can take my time."

"Have a care you don't fall in one of their infernal coal pits," said Watlins.

Royston nodded. It was sound advice.

"What should we tell the Reverend?" asked Trent.

"Tell him everything; I can't see how dissembling will serve you," said Royston unsympathetically, limping into the shadow of the trees. "Now make best speed; I'll see you later."

Once under the trees, the ground began to rise immediately. Royston set a very gentle pace, to favour his knee and to make as little noise as possible. There were also the shafts to worry about, which the foresters dug wherever took their fancy. The agony in his leg settled to a throbbing ache, and now that the excitement was over, his neck and shoulder complained also. But if he kept this slow pace, he was confident of reaching his destination.

The hill steepened, and he moved with greater caution, pausing once or twice against a tree trunk to rest his leg. The night was extremely peaceful. Moonlight filtering through the leaves cast muted patterns upon the leaf mould, and Royston could hear the sounds of the sleeping forest: the sudden flutter of wings in some tree, the chuckle of a distant stream, owls screeching to one another across the valley, and some animal snuffling about its business—most likely a badger.

Royston continued to climb, and then the slope eased as he neared its crest. There he happened upon where a tree had fallen, leaving a gap in the canopy open to the sky. The fallen trunk lay stark and black in the silver light. About it, exploiting the tree's demise, grew weeds and bracken.

Preferring the shadows, he skirted around it. He was just at the other side when he had a peculiar notion that he was being watched. He turned, somehow knowing what he would see.

At the centre of the rare patch of moonlight stood the monk. Royston's first thought was that he was on the verge of being ambushed, but the woods seemed empty. He thought the monk would call the locals down upon him, yet although undoubtedly sensible to Royston's presence, the figure remained silent. Royston then had a terrible thought. No one at the road had appeared to register the monk's presence. Was that because only Royston could see it? Was this a wraith, perhaps a mute harbinger of his forthcoming doom?

The figure began to walk slowly towards him, and Royston knew dread. He was on the point of taking to his heels when the figure pushed away the cowl, and dark tresses fell to frame the face of a young woman. He immediately knew she was no ghost, and yet, under a full moon, in a forest so ancient as to have seen pagan rites, where superstition was rampant and the greatest trees bore names, she did not seem completely of this world either.

Unsure of what to do—perhaps already bewitched— Royston stepped out of the shadows and watched her approach, her long untamed hair moving as she did, her narrow features accentuated by the moonlight, her silvered lips slightly parted, and her eyes, locked with his own, dark and impenetrable.

She moved up close to him, and he was as silent as her. It was as if this fey glade denied speech, if indeed she had left him capable of that. Still holding his gaze, she reached up, drew his head down, and crushed her lips resolutely upon his. He made a silent cry of pure astonishment, and immediately her tongue was inside his mouth, spirited and pugnacious. For a moment he was stunned, and then he responded in kind, his hands closing upon her waist, instinctively pulling her against him. So soon—so unaware of the propriety of the living world—she took his hand within her rough woollen cloak and to her meagre bosom. He kneaded her softness which, shielded only by a layer of poor cambric, responded with astonishing impudence.

A fever was taking her, setting her writhing against him, her breathing pained. She had infected him also, for his blood pumped furiously as he feasted upon the license she allowed so carelessly. She slumped then. No, her hand was holding their lips together as she drew him down with her onto the forest floor where all sense was lost. For all that there was precious little to her, she was wondrous strong, and before he knew it, stones were digging into his back, his knee bright with pain, and she was astride him, her nimble fingers busy with his trousers. Having stripped his clothing from what had grown impossibly stiff, she drew up her skirt, revealing not petticoats but her thin thighs, blanched in the moonlight. Her hand was between them now, and it guided him to the tickle of hair and wetness. She then settled on him determinedly, driving him into the torrid, liquid clasp of her body.

She was still for a moment, and then, fixing him with her almost closed eyes, her expression stern, she began to ride him as if he were a horse at trot, taking his sensitive flesh repeatedly into her, her breath growing rapid and sibilant. The sensations were intolerable, and suddenly his pleasure was upon him, and he screwed up his eyes as he emptied his seed into her. She bucked upon him, once and once more, then let slip a short, triumphant cry, the first sound he had heard her make.

The fever past, suddenly aware of the hard ground sucking away his warmth, Royston gazed up into the shadows of her face, hopelessly disoriented. She stood then, drawing herself off what was now lethargic, and then stole away into the darkness. Royston looked after her, a question on his lips, but she was already gone, and only her carnal scent lingered. He never saw her again. He did not even know her name.

He staggered his way back to the vicarage, and there, exhausted, weathered Dory's anxious, fluttering concern before finally being allowed to his tent. He did not sleep though, for a great dread gripped him. In that primitive rite upon the hillside, had the fey woman tricked from him something more precious than his seed? His youth? His fortune? His soul?

Even when they were quit of the forest, the fear of the unworldly proved persistent, and it took several dirty, noisy weeks of the modern world to wash it from him. That night did, however, change one manner permanently, and that was how he viewed the women of low reputation that loitered in Birmingham's public houses. Previously, their worldliness had piqued his curiosity, but even after a good night's roistering with his fellow students, he'd never quite summoned the nerve to approach one of them. After the expedition to the Forest of Dean, the curiosity was gone and pride asserted itself. He did not want a woman's desire if it was founded on the specie in his pocket. The girl in the forest had plainly chosen him, and although the reason would ever remain a mystery, it was surely nobler than pecuniary gain.

Now there was Harriet, and he felt for her as he had not for any other woman. There was a longing for her, softer and stronger than desire alone. Yet how could he discover whether she would welcome his suit or whether he grandly deluded himself? He knew social pleasantries and the tempest of carnal satiation, but between these extremes was a great void offering nothing to further his affection for her. Guessing wrong had appalling consequences. At least in his present circumstances it would be so. If he advanced himself upon his employer's daughter and was unwelcome, he could well be dismissed from his post without references. Without references, he would not even be able to sink back into obscurity at Antrum Ellis and Partners. Indeed, he had no idea what options would be available to him!

It was better not to think about it, and he would be a fool of the highest order to bring upon himself such a fall from grace. He had no option but to show reserve towards Harriet. *Miss Colton.*

Yet what if *Mercury* did win the Grand Challenge? As her sole academic designer, Royston could easily secure alternative employment with or without Samuel Colton's recommendation. If *Mercury* bested her competitors, he could un-gag his heart and with impunity press his suit to Miss Harriet Colton, and if she refused him, then only his heart would be ruined.

In that hackney in some dark Derbyshire lane, Royston realised he was wagering upon *Mercury* not only his reputation, but also his happiness.

5.

Trespasser on Line

"Harriet?" called Staley cautiously.

Harriet was sitting on *Mercury*'s fire bars, protected from their chill touch by a folded wagon sheet. She looked up from holding a pair of measuring callipers to a bracket mounted above the fire bars, one of the many that had been put in to support the final section of the coal walker.

There was an oil lamp beside her, and she lifted it towards the firebox door. It illuminated Staley's face, for he squatted just outside on the footplate. "What is it?"

"Your father sends his compliments and asks that we attend him in his office."

"Now, sir?"

"That was his request," replied Staley. "The matter is of some urgency it seems."

Harriet sighed and stood as decorously as was possible in the circumstances. Balancing against the firebox roof, she picked her way carefully across the fire bars towards the firebox door and then ducked down for the undignified crawl out onto the footplate, Staley withdrawing to give her room.

On this instance her egress was even less composed than

usual, for she caught her head on a protruding lip of iron. With a spirited curse, she scrambled out into the dim daylight and stood, furiously rubbing her head. Staley was staring at her, scandalised. With a sudden sick sensation, she realised he understood Greek.

"I am so dreadfully sorry," she stammered, mortified and blushing furiously. "It is a bad habit I have acquired."

"I… I suppose it is understandable," he said. "You gave yourself quite a knock."

"Even so," she said sadly.

Staley snorted. "The men are at times most profane. It must be hard not to be led on by their example, particularly when one injures oneself." He then smiled. "But to use Greek is a shrewd deceit."

"I thank you… I think." Harriet rubbed at where the iron had struck her.

Staley looked at her with concern. "You had better let me see that."

She submitted to his inspection and felt his fingers gentle in her hair. Having him so close was difficult and pleasant both. Mother had been pushing forward with her machinations, and in recent weeks Staley had been invited once to dinner and twice to Sunday tea. On each occasion, he had been seated beside Bianca, and Harriet had to watch, melancholy in her heart. Although she would never deny her sister happiness, she'd been secretly heartened that, though it must vex Mother, nothing appeared to be developing between Bianca and Staley beyond polite conversation.

"*Ow!*"

"Sorry." Staley withdrew his fingers. "It appears though to be just a graze. There's no blood."

"That is a thankfulness." She accepted his hand to alight from the footplate and down onto the staging. Behind *Mercury* stood the skeleton of her tender-to-be, and beyond that, a railway carriage supported on jacks, missing its wheels and with raw metal betraying new journal boxes and substantive brake reservoirs.

"Did you know, Harriet," ventured Staley as they walked towards the offices, "that whilst credited with a great civilisation, the Greeks were in private… rather aberrant?"

Harriet blushed softly. "I have happened upon strange references that even a gentle soul can interpret no other way, sir."

"Quite." He lowered his voice. "Yet even with the greatest will, I hazard the ancients would have found *your* proposal quite impossible."

Now Harriet truly blushed.

FATHER HAD A large office on the second floor with a wide bay window overlooking the yard. The room was dominated with dark bookshelves of ledgers and correspondence, upon each of which stood handsome models of every class Colton and Holm had ever produced. Yet only one model, its apple-green livery spotless, was honoured with space upon Father's broad leather-topped desk, and that was the tank engine Harriet had made as a girl. It always pleased Harriet to see it there; it reminded her of how much her father thought of her.

Father was not alone. Old Benjamin stood by the window, his cap clasped respectfully in his hands. Rain battered against the panes, the drops heavy and verging on sleet. With December only days away, that would not be unusual.

"Ah, Harriet, Staley." Father was seated behind the desk. "Close the door, if you would."

Staley did so quietly.

Father nodded to Benjamin. "Tell them what you told me, Ben, if you please."

Benjamin turned to the newcomers. "Miss Harriet, Mr Staley, it's about young Evans, like."

Harriet frowned. "Evan Evans, you mean? What about him?"

"Well, I'm not sure there's anything to it," said Benjamin, "but happens I've been finding him in odd places recently."

"How do you mean?"

"Like hanging about drawing shop near close o' day, or in model shop where he has no business."

"I hope you sent him on his way with a stiff word, Benjamin," said Harriet.

"I did that, Miss Harriet. But..." The old man looked to Father, his expression uncomfortable.

"Ben fears, and I fully agree with him, that Evans may serve two masters," said Father.

"You mean... he's *a spy*?"

"Quite possibly, Harriet," said Father calmly.

"Who for?"

"That Evans is Welsh recommends Owen Perkins," said Father, "but it could equally be our Durham friends."

"But this is quite unacceptable, Father!" exclaimed Harriet, deeply hurt. When her outburst did not animate her father, she looked to Staley for support, but he only looked saddened. "Well, is it not?" she added hotly to them all.

"These things happen, Miss Colton," said Staley gently. "We had a most disagreeable example at my old works."

"But we would never consider such a thing," Harriet said haughtily.

"That is not the question, Harriet," said Father. "The question is what are we going to do about it."

"Dismiss him of course," said Harriet. "Send him packing back to Merthyr."

"If we do that, they will only try again, forewarned to make the infiltrator that much harder to detect."

"Staley's right, Harriet," said Father. "We're better off with the evil we know."

"But how then can we ensure Evans does not make off with *Mercury*'s secrets?" asked Harriet.

"I would recommend keeping him away from *Mercury* all together, sir," said Staley.

"Then he would be sure we were onto him," countered Harriet.

"Not if he thinks he is learning what his masters desire," said Staley with a small smile.

"Aye, you have the way of it, sir," agreed Father. "Ben, would you be so kind as to set up a small shop over in the forge for... special projects."

"That I can, sir. And assign Evans to it?"

"And a few others who can be spared." Father turned to Staley and Harriet. "And I'll be looking to you two to spirit up some designs for them to prototype."

Staley nodded. "Credible innovations."

"You have my thoughts, sir," said Father. "But mixed with non-contentious work if you will; we can't afford to waste too much effort upon this bad business."

He looked at them all then. "Are we agreed?"

They all nodded.

"YOU DO REALISE," said Harriet when the two of them got back to Staley's office, "with this we could quite undo a competitor."

"Have a care." He closed the door gently. "We do not know who might be listening."

"You are right. I apologise for my indiscretion."

"You mean that we could encourage them to introduce a detrimental feature to their locomotive?"

Harriet snorted. "Detrimental, sir? I would have it take them off the road!"

"Would you really, Harriet?" asked Staley softly. "A derailment at the speeds we envision would be a horrific catastrophe."

"I know that, sir, but they deserve no better. Their conduct leaves them without honour. They would profit upon the stolen genius of others!"

"If those who set Evans amongst us had their hands on the regulator, I would agree wholeheartedly with you."

Harriet was chastened. "But that will not be so, will it?" she said in a small voice.

"It would be unlikely. Moreover, I refine my statement, madam: Only those responsible deserve to suffer for the malice they perpetrated."

"How is that different, sir? Lord Clifton has already stipulated that there shall be no passengers on the runs themselves."

"But consider how much attention is being paid to the Grand Challenge. Will not the metals be lined with spectators?"

"Oh my God," whispered Harriet.

Staley was sympathetic. "We must hold ourselves most accountable in what we allow Merthyr or Durham to steal, Miss Harriet."

"If anything were to be set to fail, it must not foul the running," said Harriet thoughtfully.

"Better to my mind is not a failure *per se*, but a more insidious flaw."

"How so, sir?"

He waved a hand, as if summoning an ominous muse. "A contrivance that as the miles pass shall rob their cylinders of steam."

"Or deny its release—a confusion of their motion perhaps?" Harriet quickly warmed to the idea.

"Indeed," agreed Staley, "but clearly most intractable to detection in advance."

"Sir, we set a witch to steal away their locomotive's soul," gloated Harriet.

Staley gave her a most peculiar, fearful look.

"I do apologise, sir," she said, again chastened. "The drama overwhelmed me for a moment."

IT WAS A week of surprises, none exactly pleasant. On the Monday there had been Evans; on the Thursday evening, Mother had left word with Dimity that she wished to see

Harriet as soon as she had made herself respectable (Mother had not actually stated the latter, but it was a healthy assumption). Once clean and gowned in ginger toile, Harriet asked Bolsover of her mother. The butler directed her to the conservatory.

Mother was tending to the various hothouse plants—begonias, cyclamens, and geraniums predominantly—that she prided herself in.

"You asked for me, Mother," said Harriet respectfully.

"Ah yes, Harriet. Do you recall a Mr Barnet from the Stephenson Institute?"

Harriet did. He had been one of her younger professors, albeit that he was already growing a little portly. She had quite liked him, for he was more gregarious than his colleagues and certainly less eccentric and intimidating than, say, "Batty" Thanes who, wearing a startling blue fez on his sparse feral hair, harangued his students with a battledore racquet.

"Yes, Mother. He instructed in the mechanisms of heat. What of him, pray?"

"Your father received a letter from him yesterday."

"That is most unforeseen. Is there some problem with my studies?"

"No," said Mother, laughing as she trimmed away dead leaves with a pair of brass scissors. "Quite the opposite, indeed. In his letter, Mr Barnet confides that he is your most ardent admirer."

Harriet stared at her Mother. "He *does*?"

"Most emphatically, dear. He claims this state has existed since first he met you. Of course, while you were his student, he could do nothing but admire from afar. Most commendable of him, don't you think?"

"I am quite sure I do not know what to think, Mother," professed Harriet truthfully.

"Well, I believe it to show him in a very positive light, Harriet. A lesser man might have exploited his position and placed you in the most awkward dilemma."

"So he might have," murmured Harriet, still at a loss.

"He has asked your Father's permission to approach you. Don't you think that most encouraging?"

"I'm… flattered."

Mother turned and frowned. "You do not *sound* flattered, my dear."

"It comes as a great surprise, Mother."

Mother looked at her doubtfully. "Now, Harriet, you can always refuse him, but I counsel you to be pragmatic about your prospects and give Mr Barnet's interest careful consideration."

Harriet saw the ghost of a previous argument and did not wish to see its rise again. "I will, Mother."

"I am glad." Mother smiled. "Think, Harriet. You could become the first woman professor at the Institute. Would that not be a wondrous thing?"

"You assume that Mr Barnet is not simply looking for a wife."

"Oh, tish! Certainly Mr Barnet wants you to be his wife, but I cannot believe him blind to your ability. Why should he place that light under a bushel?"

"I bow to your greater experience, Mother."

"You worry overmuch. But I am sure Mr Barnet will reassure you on that matter when he writes to you, which he will, now that your father has given his permission."

"I see. Thank you, Mother."

Harriet left then and slowly walked the long corridor to

the parlour. There she sat before the fire and stared into the flames, deep in thought.

SITTING UP IN bed, Harriet watched Dimity bank her bedroom fire for the night.

"Dimity?"

Her maid hung up the shovel and rose. "Yes, miss?"

"Can we talk?"

"Of course." Dimity moved into the glow of the gas lantern by Harriet's bed. "What about?"

Harriet patted the bedcovers. With a smile, Dimity boosted herself up and settled comfortably, her legs under her, just as she had when they'd shared the small rooms in Newcastle and talked into the night.

"What about, miss?" repeated the maid.

Harriet hesitated. "A gentleman has declared an interest in me, Dimity."

"That's grand, miss," said Dimity with soft sincerity. "Who?"

"One of my professors at the Institute. One of the younger ones." Harriet explained about the letter Father had received.

"He acts the gentleman at least," said Dimity carefully.

"I'm sure he is one."

Now Dimity hesitated. "Do you intend to accept him, miss?"

Harriet sighed; that said it all.

"You're not ready for marriage then," said Dimity sympathetically. "Is that the problem?"

"I suppose it is to some degree. I had intended to get established before considering that side of my life... Yet..."

"Oh! Is it that you don't really like him?"

"On the contrary, I did rather, although I never thought of him... romantically."

"That might come, as you get to know him better."

"I suppose it might." Harriet sighed again.

"Miss?" Dimity frowned.

"Dimity, you mustn't tell a soul, but there's another gentleman."

"My, but you're filling your dance-card," teased Dimity gently. "And you're more interested in him?"

Harriet nodded. "I truly hope that was mere conjecture."

"Not really, miss. I've noticed you've been distracted by something of late and thought something might be afoot."

"Am I *that* transparent?" moaned Harriet.

"Gracious no—but you do relax more about me. And didn't you guess about my Tom?"

Harriet smiled. "Indeed I did, Dimity, but then you were all but swooning over him."

Dimity grinned. "Tom was like that, miss. Who is this... other gentleman?"

Harriet glanced at the closed door. "Mr Staley," she whispered.

"Ah," said Dimity. "Most pleasing on the eye is Mr Staley."

"You really think so?"

"Let me put it this way, miss," replied the maid. "If he wasn't well above my station, and you weren't there already, then I'd certainly be trying to catch his attention."

Harriet looked down glumly. "Alas, I'm not as you put it

'there already,' Dimity."

The maid touched Harriet's hand tenderly. "Has he refused you then?"

Harriet drew a breath. "No… I just don't know if he has any affection for me."

"Gentlemen can be very cautious about such things."

"But Mother's trying to bring him and my sister together!" blurted Harriet, letting free all her fears. "And Bianca's so much prettier and… and more womanly than I."

Dimity was silent for a few seconds. "If it's any consolation, miss, no one below stairs thinks Lady Alicia's getting anywhere at that game. The two of 'em just don't seem at all set on each other."

"That is no guarantee it will not happen in time!" Harriet dabbed at her eyes.

"It is if you move first," murmured Dimity.

Harriet looked at her sharply. "What do you mean?"

"All I'm saying, miss, is that if you wait for a gentleman, you can end up waiting a long time."

"Oh no! I could never ask Mr Staley if he has interest in me!"

"Of course not. But you can offer encouragement."

"I can?"

"Certainly, miss."

Harriet digested that. "I am sure I do not know how."

"Just let your feelings show a little. Even a nice smile can work wonders."

"I see." Harriet would have to think on that. But then she creased her brow. "But what about Mr Barnet? What do I do about him?"

"If you're not interested in him, then you should tell him so."

"It is not that easy, Dimity. What if Mr Staley has no interest in me? What then?"

"There'll be other gentlemen."

"How can I be sure of that?"

Dimity sighed. "Well then, can't you hold Mr Barnet off until you know one way or the other about Mr Staley?"

Harriet nodded. "That approach has some potential."

"'Course it does. If Mr Barnet holds any real affection, he will wait. And if he won't… you're better rid of him anyway, to my thinking."

"You may well be right." Harriet smiled fondly at her maid. "Thank you, Dimity."

Dimity patted her mistress' hand. "You've done the same for me, miss."

Harriet nodded and then grinned. "Who knows, if I end up marrying Mr Barnet and setting up household in Newcastle, maybe your Tom will have waited for you."

Dimity rolled her eyes. "Lor', I hope not!"

Harriet blinked in surprise "Pardon?"

"I'm over Tom, miss. I wished him well before we left Newcastle."

"I know, Dimity. I greatly feared at the time I was going to lose you to him."

"There was never a chance of that."

"Surely you hoped he'd ask for your hand?"

Dimity laughed. "If he had, I would have refused him."

"You would have done that to stay in my employ?" asked Harriet, awestruck.

"That's neither here nor there, miss. One day I hope to marry, but not to the likes of Tom."

"But you must have walked out with him for more than half a year."

Dimity thought. "I suppose I did, at that." Seeing Harriet's continuing confusion, the maid tried to explain. "See, miss, Tom was grand to be with of an evening, and he knew how to show a girl some fun, but he's not the sort of man you'd want to be stuck with for the rest of your natural."

"That is a rather... forward attitude."

"Is it, miss? Beginning your pardon, but aren't gentlemen like that all the time, what with their mistresses and such? Two can play at that game, says I."

Harriet giggled. "You can be quite incorrigible, Dimity."

"But ain't I right, miss?"

"I suppose in principle you are, but society judges with inequity. What of your reputation?"

"We were discreet, and I'd have had nothing to do with him if I thought he was one to spread tales. I'm not stupid."

Harriet hesitated but could not deny a dreadful curiosity. "Did you... did you lie with him?"

Dimity smiled and wriggled closer. "By-and-by I did, miss," she breathed.

"Oh, poor you!" murmured Harriet with tender sympathy.

"Poor me, miss," echoed Dimity, her smile broadening.

"You... you enjoyed it?" whispered Harriet, fascinated.

Dimity nodded, the smile lingering. "Tom knew what a girl likes, if you get my drift."

Harriet nodded. She did. Her natural curiosity wasn't limited solely to engineering. A few joshes between the men in the works which they'd never meant her to overhear, augmented by the beasts of the field following their nature, had led to hypothesis and experiment, with unexpectedly agreeable results.

She found it to be an experiment that periodically demanded its results confirmed. Never would she admit to such research though. Yet she feared Dimity suspected, if only because one quiet Newcastle night she'd heard sounds suggesting her maid conducted the same experiment, presuming Harriet asleep, just as Harriet on prior occasions had assumed Dimity asleep.

"Even the act itself, Dimity?" she murmured, an ephemeral Mr Staley at the edge of her thoughts.

Dimity sighed deeply. "Lor' yes, miss! Tom was a right lusty fellow. I quite forgot myself!"

"My!" sighed Harriet, feeling oddly educated.

Dimity beamed at her, and then grew reflective. "Mind you, he were careful, miss. He didn't want me in the family way, like."

"If you had found yourself in that situation, I would not have dismissed you. We would have found some way through it."

"That's most kind of you, miss, but I'm glad it didn't come to that. I wouldn't like to put you against your family, if you see what I mean."

"I do, Dimity."

They looked at each other, the patter of rain steady on the glass beyond the curtains.

"It's late," ventured the maid.

"It is, and I am being most thoughtless keeping you from your bed."

The maid patted Harriet's hand. "That's all right, miss, I enjoyed our conversation."

"So did I."

Dimity slipped off the bed and in doing so returned to the world of that which was expected. She curtsied to Harriet. "Goodnight, miss."

"Goodnight, Dimity."

Dimity left, closing the door carefully behind her. Turning down the valve on the gas lantern, Harriet settled under the covers and stared into the darkness.

Mr Barnet. Mr Staley. Lustful Tyneside Tom.

How was a woman *ever* expected to sleep?

"THE DRYING ENGINE is complete, Mr Staley," announced Harriet from Royston's office door.

Royston looked up. "The drying engine?" he asked, perplexed.

"Come see," she said eagerly, beckoning him with a gloved hand away from his slide rule.

Royston shrugged on his Ulster. Everywhere was damnably cold these days.

Outside, the pounding of the steam-hammer in the forge that pervaded every part of the works grew louder. Harriet led him to one of the outlying buildings on the banks of the Penny. Large doors had been fashioned in each end, and these stood open.

The interior was dominated by a structure of circular cross-section fashioned mostly from wood. From one end at twelve or more feet in diameter, it converged to a length of iron pipe barely a foot in diameter and then diverged again to the same great diameter. At the further end, looking out towards Horse Moor (again lost in cloud) protruded an axle bearing a flat pulley. Beside it, bolted stoutly to the floor, were the frames of a small locomotive, yet only the cylinders, valve gear, and a single set of driving wheels were present, even though the frame was clearly meant to bear a second set. Moreover, the flanges of the driving wheels hung a good foot off the floor. Between them, set centre in the frames, was a large pulley, and a broad belt linked it to the smaller pulley of the wooden assembly.

"There, sir. I promised you a wind-drag machine, and here it is," announced Miss Harriet proudly.

"Ah… drying engine… a wise conceit," said Royston, taking in the strange collection of parts. "And I much admire how you have extemporised the colliery's ventilation engine."

"I must confess to having been quite profligate with our spares on hand," said Miss Harriet, "but it was the most expedient solution."

"What speed does the air take?"

"M. Pitot's apparatus indicates twenty-two inches' difference in water gauge. I deem that to be in excess of two hundred miles an hour!"

"Even *Mercury* will be hard pressed to match that speed."

"You think it suitable?"

He inspected the device more closely. "Eminently so, I believe. I must put construction of models in hand immediately."

"Would you care to operate it, sir?" she asked. "I warn you it is rather boisterous."

"Certainly."

"Come then."

The controls were simple enough. There was a large valve with dolphins chased into its hand-wheel, and a disappointingly plain reversing lever.

"No cut-off to begin, just as the steamer." Harriet stood

beside him.

He set the lever appropriately and grasped the handwheel, pleasantly warm from the standing steam. She then placed her gloved hand over his bare one. "Have a care, sir," she murmured as he suppressed his surprise. "The motion is prone to race; the fan offers little load at low speeds."

He nodded, and eased the valve open. The driving wheels, adrift of a rail, began to slowly turn and then gathered speed. Initially there was just the sound of the valve gear working—the hiss of inlet and the loud chuff as the expended steam was discharged up a pipe penetrating the roof. Yet as the speed increased, there was added the whirr of the fan hidden within the woodwork.

Harriet moved the reversing lever two notches and put her hand upon his again, indicating he could increase the steam flow. This time he found a quiet pleasure in her unexpected touch. She now pointed to the diverging water levels in a manometer as the whirr of the fan became a sharp whine and then grew to a dull howl. The manometer showed fifteen inches difference... then seventeen... nineteen. Slowing now, it crept to twenty... twenty-one... and then crawled slowly to twenty-two inches.

She grinned at him then and made a motion suggesting he close off the steam. The roar subsided, and soon there was the slowing whine of the fan and the soft chatter as the engine idled over.

"What are your thoughts, Mr Staley?"

"It is most excellent, Harriet. And such a better solution than wading in the Penny."

"Oh, I think that would have been quite amusing all in of itself!" she said. "Although I imagine the water a little chilly at the moment."

"I think that quite an understatement," he said, laughing.

She turned to him then. "We have not continued your steamer instruction, have we, Mr Staley?"

"We have not, madam," he allowed.

"It must be a month or more?"

Staley consulted his memory. "Quite certainly."

"Goodness, I have quite neglected you. A lesson is well overdue." She smiled at him warmly. "Indeed, perhaps we can find reason for another excursion? I most enjoyed our last one to Newton-Le-Helm."

"I also." He bowed. "And I would be most honoured to receive further instruction from you."

Her smile grew brighter. "Then you shall have it, sir."

AFTER HAVING BEEN distressingly correct towards Royston since the night of the ball, Harriet appeared to have finally forgiven his insensitivity. He received more of her pretty smiles, and when they were poring over diagrams, puzzling over why some assembly had decided not to take its place in *Mercury*'s gathering complexity, she once again chose to be at his elbow rather than at the far side of the desk. Royston began to grow a little more confident about his prospects.

Harriet also came up with a coasting valve design that Royston thought most elegant. That is, until she pointed out that once it grew good and hot, the more the valve operated, the more likely it was to jam open and vent the steam line. Royston suggested they add a thin rod running past the valve on the centreline of the steam feed just to pique the curiosity of those who might see it, to which Miss Harriet agreed. They then sent the plans off to the special projects shop, and Evans, for prototyping.

That week they paid host to a visit from *Mercury*'s sponsor. The marquess's resplendent steamer did not, however, appear; instead, the marquess's agent arrived by an early-morning down train, offering the regrets and apologies of his master, who had a pressing engagement elsewhere.

Hackett inspected *Mercury* carefully, commenting on the steam braking arrangements, and the other ancillary but crucial functions that the great locomotive was gathering. He was particularly probing over the mechanical stoking contrivance, now almost complete.

After the inspection, they partook of luncheon at The Just Swan, who delighted them with a most acceptable meal. Colton had reserved a room off the main lounge so that he, Hackett, Harriet, Bracewaite, and Royston could converse in private.

As his second glass of Braces' Special Ale grew low, Hackett professed himself quite satisfied with their progress and ready to convey this opinion to his master. There was a general sense of relief, but then the conversation took an unusual turn.

"Might I enquire if Colton and Holm have ever considered manufacturing road steamers?" the agent asked Colton.

"No, sir," said Colton. "There's scant profit in that game unless you send a hundred or more of them out the gates every week."

The agent nodded. "That is my belief also, sir," he said, "but I would hazard there might be ample reward in producing small numbers of *racing* steamers."

"Racing steamers, sir?" queried Colton.

Oddly, it was the general manager who spoke up. "It's a recent pastime of privileged young gentlemen, Samuel," he said. "It's very much like horse racing, but with steamers. Certain young gentlemen are keen to race; more are keen to gamble."

"Lord Harlow, I am sure, would find great pleasure in racing a steamer from the stable of Colton and Holm, sir," said the agent, embarking upon a refreshed glass of Special Ale.

"I remember Lord Harlow races horses," said Harriet. "I had no idea he raced steamers also."

"He will find the sport most exhilarating," said the agent.

"But it can hardly be safe though," said Colton, frowning.

"Most certainly not, Father," said Harriet. "The popular press positively revels in the tragedies."

"Which befall only the inept," opined Hackett. "The marquess is most accomplished in everything that he takes an interest in." He turned to Colton, sober in face and speech. "I believe this to be a very interesting proposition for your company, sir. You should immediately apply your mastery of high speed to producing the *Mercury* of the steam-racing ground. When my master rides it to countless victories, imagine how the racing fraternity will clamour at your gates, offering you their very birthright for a Colton and Holm steam racer!"

Colton was dumbfounded. "Harriet? Staley?"

They looked at each other.

"Clearly minimising the weight is critical," ventured Harriet.

"And keeping it low to aid stability," put in Royston.

"The fire would have to be most furious to sustain pressure."

"Assuming we can efficiently move the heat into the water."

The general manager frowned. "Samuel, I beg caution. *Mercury* must be our priority."

"Aye, you're right, Godfrey," said Colton. He turned to the agent. "It is an interesting proposal, Mr Hackett, but we must concentrate on winning the Grand Challenge first. Surely that would improve our racing pedigree, as it were?"

"Oh, most certainly, sir," agreed the agent. "But I pray that you give the idea your careful consideration. I am certain racing steamers would be a profitable adjunct to your present business. And whilst I cannot pledge Lord Harlow to this manner, I am quite confident he shall be enthusiastic to lend you his racing skills."

"Fairly spoken, sir," said Colton. "And I promise we shall give it the attention it deserves."

THE SMALL PARTY stood on the bitter windswept platform of Chale Bridge Station, watching the Two-Seventeen Up Mixed disappear towards Kearby, bearing Hackett away south. They then turned towards the waiting carriage, Royston and Harriet trailing behind the older gentlemen.

"I fear I am entertaining the most slanderous speculation concerning Mr Hackett," murmured Harriet.

"You are?" breathed Royston. "Could it be that he appears not averse to seeing his master put in harm's way?"

"Why yes, I rather think that to be it. Might Hackett prefer to serve the heir apparent?"

"One does wonder." He hesitated, but decided to continue anyway. "That would be his younger sister, Lady Jessamine."

"Indeed?" mused Harriet. "He must imagine her more malleable than her brother."

"I cannot think of any other reason." Royston paused. "Unless it is a matter of the heart, currently thwarted by Lord Harlow."

Harriet snorted. "What a wild imagination you have, sir!" Then she saw he was smiling. "You jest of course."

"I do. One could hardly imagine a less suitable match."

"And one Lord Harlow would certainly disallow. Oh! Has Lady Jessamine reached her majority?"

"She has."

"Then Lord Harlow *cannot* intervene. Hackett offers for her, and she accepts," she sighed. "It is so easy for the man in such matters."

Royston deliberated, then dared to hint at his own dilemma, veiled in that of another. "It is not always so, Harriet. The man has to consider untoward repercussions. Hackett would be dismissed and probably barred from all respectable employment, and I doubt that Lady Jessamine is wealthy in her own right."

"That is true. Yet to arrange an accident... how tiresomely histrionic that would be!"

"*The Countess and Her Dark Agent; An Exciting Penny-Romance for the Undiscriminating Reader,*" Royston suggested.

She laughed. "Aptly put, sir."

6.

Conflicting Movements

O N MONDAY MORNING beside Harriet's place at the
breakfast table. One look at Mother's delighted face
told her it bore a Newcastle postmark. Harriet felt only mild
trepidation.

She tried to ignore the letter while she ate, but Mother
grew more and more restless.

"Aren't you going to open Mr Barnet's letter, my dear?"
she asked finally.

"I intend to open it tonight, Mother, when I have more
time." Mother looked upon the point of protest, so Harriet
decided to put the matter beyond recall. "Bolsover?" she said
to the butler, indicating the letter. "Have this taken to my
room, please."

"Of course, Miss Harriet," he murmured, then whisked
the offending salver smoothly from the table.

IT WAS AFTER dinner, and Harriet was alone in her bedroom,
unable to delay any longer. She broke the seal on the

envelope and withdrew from it two pages inscribed by a fastidious hand. Moving closer to the gas lantern, she quickly read Mr Barnet's letter.

My Dearest Miss Colton,

Your father has given me his gracious permission to correspond with you, and so this humble letter is, I trust, not unexpected. Nor, I suspect, shall be the matter I lay before you, for I intimated its nature to your father and I am sure he would not have you completely unaware of my intent.

We live in fast-changing times, yet these do not, as the Romantic Movement would have it, bring all manner of ill to mankind. I consider myself most favoured in this light, for had change not occurred, my dearest Miss Colton, I would never have made your acquaintance. How blessed I am that you chose to study at the Institute! To look out and see a rose amongst the weeds (I use the term as a literary simile, and not in general denigration of my students) in my lecture hall gave me great pleasure. I confess to losing my place in my notes several times over your attentive beauty!

My dearest Miss Colton, I declare that I am most attracted to you. I hope that you hold some modicum of affection in your sweet nature for me also, and that we are mutually attracted to each other, as are, as Newton observed, Venus and Jove (I am of course Jove, for I freely admit my hearty appetite [1]). In truth, of course, the planets are much more attracted to the sun. Furthermore, they orbit and never meet. That is certainly not what I have in mind. Venus and Jove must stop orbiting, so that they may be attracted together! But then, dear me, they would fall into the sun. Perhaps we should be akin to opposed electrical charges, attracted as described by M. Coulomb, and demonstrated when an amber rod is briskly stroked with fur.

A great distance currently separates us, my dearest Miss Colton; however, once the students go down after the Michaelmas term and my responsibilities to the Institute are discharged, I am fully determined to journey to Chale Bridge and call upon you. I feel confident that when we are in the same locale, we shall discover just how strong is the attraction we have for each other (just as my metaphor suggests, the mutual affection growing to the inverse square of the separating distance, rising ad infinitum the closer we approach each other).

While positively gladdened at the prospect of renewing your acquaintance, I must digress to enlighten you of my circumstances. Naturally, such prosaic matters do not sway the course of true affection, but a gentlewoman must prefer the assurance that the refined life to which she is accustomed will persist. Of this I gladly pledge, for I am advantaged with a salary of some 120 pounds per annum, which I am sure you will agree is not only sufficient to maintain one's place in society, but indeed generous (for which thanks are due to the numerous benefactors of the Institute for their largesse towards maintaining the realm as the shining beacon of industry to which all the world turns).

I write to you from a pleasant villa upon Carr Hill, which you may recall to be a respectable area south of the river, with two fine churches and one moderate one, as well as all the principal dissenting chapels, and various respectable establishments permitting the most genteel social discourse. In addition there is a school much admired (although the architecture is frankly not uplifting) for the civility of its pupils (the learning is also of a superior quality, and the sexes properly divided).

In the vicinity also is Great Beatings, the elegant seat of Lord Shilbottle, with diverse woods and prospects, and to whom all persons of local renown are frequently invited (I have been included in this company, I can only presume, because of my rôle fostering the Future Leaders of Industry). My own residence is of the Italian persuasion, and handsomely proportioned. In truth it is more than I (and housekeeper, manservant, my little diversions, &c) alone require.

I shall close by assuring you of my devotion to you, my dearest Miss Colton, and how often and fondly I recall the warmth of your person, your radiant beauty, your conductive charm, and how your presence convects a sense of refinement to wherever you may find yourself.

Your humble and most obedient servant,
Thaddeus Barnet, Professor of Heat.

[1] *My intention here was also to convey your beauty. I also find need to admit that Jove is some ten times larger than Venus, and hope you will overlook this exaggeration in order to serve the allusion.*

Harriet put the letter aside, then went to the small decanter by the door and poured herself a generous measure of port wine. She was on her second glass, rereading the letter, when she heard a soft and familiar knock on her door.

"Come, Dimity."

Her maid entered and curtsied. "When were you thinking of retiring, miss?"

Harriet glanced at the mantel above the fire and the clock there, resplendent with eagles that were Teutonic when they weren't involved in the mechanism. "Soon." She looked at the letter, shaking her head slowly.

Dimity was turning down the bed. "I see Mr Barnet weren't slow in writing, miss."

"Indeed not," sighed Harriet.

There was a pause. "Is he… being bothersome?"

"No, not… bothersome," replied Harriet thoughtfully. She turned and proffered Barnet's letter. "Read it for yourself."

Dimity looked uncomfortable. "Are you sure, miss? It's right private, isn't it?"

"I suppose it is," said Harriet, "but truly I desire your opinion."

"Really, miss?"

"Really, Dimity."

The maid reluctantly accepted the papers and moved under the sputtering gas lamp to read.

"Well?" demanded Harriet once the maid was done.

"It's certainly not what I expected."

"He is a diffident man," said Harriet. "Do not judge him by your Tom's *lettres d'amour*."

Dimity snorted. "Him? He never wrote anything to me. I'm not sure he *could* write. No, it's more that Mr Barnet can't seemingly keep a single idea in his head."

"That is very much Mr Barnet," said Harriet. "But what do you see in his letter?"

"That he is of comfortable means?"

"I did not doubt that. But what else?"

The maid scanned the letter again. "Honestly, miss?"

"Honestly, Dimity."

"I'd find out more about his 'little diversions' if I were you." She frowned. "Some men have some pretty queer tastes."

Harriet laughed. "I have reservations about Mr Barnet,

but certainly not of that nature."

"I wouldn't be so sure. That amber rod sounds pretty exotic to me."

"That is a common scientific experiment. I am sure he was quite unaware of… insinuation."

"Then he is truly a rare man." Dimity handed back the letter.

"Perhaps," allowed Harriet. "But you do not see anything else?"

"Not really. What do you see?"

"It is more what I do not see," said Harriet darkly.

"How's that, miss?"

"His letter is all about the local society, as if he expects that to be my new life. Nothing speaks to my career. I am quite convinced he would see me put aside engineering to be a dutiful wife."

"And produce little Barnets for him," noted her maid sympathetically.

"The reference to the school was not lost on me," agreed Harriet, then found herself collecting her thoughts. "It is not that I do not *wish* to have children. I do, yet not at the cost of my profession." She glared at the letter. "I am quite minded to decline him without further ado."

"To be fair to Mr Barnet, he may not be aware of your aspirations."

"Then he knows me not at all," exclaimed Harriet haughtily.

"I cannot argue with that. Decline him now if you wish, but you could still reply asking time in which to consider his proposal. Then you can also make him aware of your expectations of any marriage you would enter into. If he doesn't agree, you'll know to refuse him."

"That would be the wise thing to do, I suppose. He may be quite at ease with a wife with a profession."

"If you're set on marrying at this juncture."

Harriet sighed. "I am not, but it would have the advantage of taking me from Pennydale."

"You wish to leave your home, miss?"

"If Mr Staley marries Bianca, then I am determined not to stay, Dimity. I would want for them every happiness, but not wish to suffer seeing it."

"That's understandable."

Harriet nodded. "Besides, if they marry, Mr Staley will in time take over the works. My situation would then become doubly awkward. If I have to consider seeking alternative employment, it is best done earlier rather than later."

"Or you could set yourself up in business."

"Goodness! What an ambitious goal."

"Aye, but wouldn't it be grand? The Harriet Colton Engineering Company." The maid grinned. "Or maybe just Colton and Daughters, Engineering."

Harriet laughed. "Perhaps in time, Dimity."

Dear Professor Barnet,

Thank you for your letter of the eleventh of December. How unworthy I am of the compliments you shower upon me!

In the years that I spent at the Institute, you were always my favourite professor. It was not always easy being one of the very few women students present, but you always offered a rare sympathetic face. Now you say that, in truth, I was in receipt of more than your kindness. I can forgive you that, sir, for your conduct was always irreproachable. For my part, I have considered you with friendly affection rather than in a romantic light, although

I quite accept this capable of change.

I must also ensure that you are not viewing me under a false light. If I am anything, sir, I am foremost a practical engineer, and this will not change with my domestic circumstances. I am quite resolved to continue in my profession, balancing it against the gentler responsibilities that come with marriage and motherhood.

You write that you would call upon me at the earliest opportunity, but alas that would be dreadfully inconvenient. You would find me quite distracted, and I would not have you mistake that for disinterest. As you must be aware, my father's company has accepted Lord Clifton's Grand Challenge, and I am actively engaged in that business. It quite consumes all my thoughts and more and more of my waking time. Put simply, sir, I am certainly not in a position to offer your romantic considerations the full attention they deserve. Can I therefore beg your indulgence and request that we delay renewing our acquaintance until the Challenge is complete? It is but a few months, sir, and you may be sure that I will view your patience as an encouraging indication of your affection.

Yours very truly,
Harriet Colton

Harriet folded the single sheet of writing paper and sealed it into the envelope. Many failed attempts littered the desk, and yet she was not wholly happy with her final draft. She saw herself deceptive, guilty of offering Barnet false hope.

Her parents already knew she was going to ask Barnet to wait. Father had understood completely and told her she was being wise. His opinion was that the best decisions were made when there was the least clamour from other matters.

Mother had been angry and thought her a fool to jeopardise her prospects, for Barnet would be quite within his rights to look elsewhere for a wife.

Harriet, however, had made her decision, and if Barnet refused the delay, then she would refuse him—without betraying her true feelings—willing to delay and delay Barnet until all hope of Staley was exhausted.

Indeed, she had in gentle ways been trying to coax Staley to her, and although so far her efforts hadn't yielded a grand declaration of his affection, there had been small encouragements here and there.

When they were together, he seemed more engaged with her, especially during their ritual of tea in the works canteen. He offered his hand more readily, even when in truth she had no need of assistance. Yet Harriet had no idea how to coax him further. She found herself wishing for some imminent social event—she who was bored to distraction by social events!—where she could hope to dance with him and, in the permitted familiarity, feel him close, and yearn for him closer.

Harriet shook her head and found herself holding the letter to Barnet, the clock having jumped some minutes as she allowed herself indulgent dreams. With a sigh, she turned to the business of addressing the letter. Was 47 Sebastopol Crescent to be her future? She fervently hoped it would not come to that.

She was just blotting the envelope when there was a knock on the door.

"Come, Dimity." When she heard the door open, she continued. "That is our letter to Mr Barnet, signed and sealed. Might you pass it to Bolsover to take to the post?"

"Of course, miss," said her maid flatly.

Harriet turned. Dimity did not look at all her usual self. Instead, she looked quite troubled. "Heavens! Whatever is the matter, Dimity?"

"Nothing, miss."

"Of course something is the matter. That is quite plain."

"It's not your concern."

"Yet that does not mean I do not wish to help. Is it your family? An illness perhaps?"

"Thank you, but no. All are well at home."

"Yourself then?"

"I am perfectly fit, miss."

"Perhaps… some gentleman?" The last time Harriet recalled Dimity this anxious had been with Tom in the ascendant.

That coaxed a smile from Dimity. "No indeed, miss, more's the pity."

"Is someone being beastly to you then?" hazarded Harriet, fast running out of reasons. "Bolsover? Mrs Plugnal?"

"Certainly not, miss."

Harriet threw up her hands. "Dimity, you are being damnably enigmatic with me!"

Dimity took pity on her mistress. "It's not *my* burden, but another's. But I say again, it is *not your concern*."

Harriet thought on that. "I would know, Dimity, that I might offer advice."

"Believe me, you'd rather not know."

That was too great a declaration for Harriet's curiosity to abide. She rose and, slipping off her house shoes, climbed onto her bed. Looking at her maid, she resolutely patted the bedclothes.

"Miss, I can't," implored Dimity. "Not on this."

"Come, Dimity. You know it will always be our secret."

"I know that." Dimity looked stricken. "But you'll wish that promise unmade."

"Even so, you know that it shall be kept," declared Harriet, patting once more.

With reluctance weighting her steps, Dimity approached, yet woven in her anxiety was shrouded relief.

Harriet waited for her maid to settle. "Well?"

"Are you sure, miss?"

Harriet nodded gravely.

Her maid sighed. "It's Veracity."

Harriet frowned. Veracity? What malign card had Fate dealt Bianca's maid? "Does she find herself... in an awkward situation?"

Dimity offered the ghost of a smile. "Not in the way you're thinking."

Harriet blushed and felt awkward herself. "You must forgive me."

"Oh, I do, miss," said Dimity. "She does have a gentleman, after all."

"She does?" Had everyone found romance but Harriet! Had her profession rendered her *that* unsuitable?

Dimity nodded. "You probably know him from the works."

Harriet looked aside and put up her hand. "Better you not tell me his name."

"As you wish, miss... but I *will* tell you that it isn't Mr Staley."

It was a generous consideration, and Harriet appreciated it. "But what of Veracity?" she asked. "And pray, let us be done with prevarication."

Her maid grew reflective. "I'm not sure how to put this."

"Then tell the whole, unadulterated."

"Well, it's Miss Bianca, miss. She's put Veracity in an impossible position."

Harriet frowned. "How so?"

"Miss Bianca is forcing Veracity to support a great deception."

"What sort of deception?"

"An *affaire*, I'm afraid," said Dimity. "Or so I read it."

Harriet's heart shrivelled to a corrosive husk. Staley was lost to her.

Then, in her moment of bleakest despair, reason came to save her. Why would Bianca embark on a secret *affaire* with Staley when Mother was all but pushing them together? If Staley was thought suitable, why keep it such a great secret? She had to be wrong; she *prayed* she was wrong.

"An *affaire* with whom?" She was barely breathing as she awaited her maid's response.

Dimity took a deep breath. "Lord Harlow."

Harriet almost screamed denial, but remembered herself in time. "*Lord Harlow!*" she hissed.

Dimity looked miserable. "Yes, miss."

"Great heavens," said Harriet, her voice dull with shock.

"Quite, miss. Miss Bianca bound Veracity not to tell a soul, but she had to tell someone like—it was tearing her apart. She's a decent girl at heart, and having to choose between being loyal to her mistress and loyal to the household is more than she can bear."

"She should never face that choice," declared Harriet. "My sister is acting most improperly in this matter. Her conduct is quite unforgivable."

"That's for you to say, miss," observed Dimity. "Us? We have to live with it."

"Not with something of this nature," insisted Harriet.

"You had better tell me all you know."

"Yes, miss." Dimity appeared to collect her thoughts. "So Miss Bianca is fond of visiting the shops in Malbury."

"I have heard her claim them superior," allowed Harriet.

"So whenever she visits Malbury, Veracity goes with her."

"I am quite certain Mother would insist upon it."

"I'm sure Lady Alicia does, miss. So Tollman takes them over in the steamer and goes back for them later in the day."

"He does have other responsibilities."

"Quite so, miss. Anyway, last month they're in Malbury, and they happen to meet Lord Harlow in the High Street."

"*Happen* to meet?" echoed Harriet dubiously.

"Veracity's not that quick, like, but even she thought the surprise a pretence," said Dimity. "My lord proposes a stroll along the river, Miss Bianca accepts, and Veracity follows behind."

"Was anyone with Lord Harlow?"

"No, miss."

"Go on."

"Well, after a while, the two of 'em seat themselves at a bench. Veracity finds one within sight, but not so close as to pry upon their conversation, She is meant to be acting chaperone, see?"

"She acted quite properly. Did they give her any reason for disquiet?"

"Not really. They kissed once or twice, but it was nothing more than friendly, like."

"That is a thankfulness," said Harriet. "But even so, it would not have done for them to be seen together. Lord Harlow is most distinctive and the ha'penny press keen to publicise his indiscretions."

"That's the odd thing, miss. My lord was apparently most soberly dressed. Veracity didn't even recognise him at first."

"At least he showed some sense of caution," muttered Harriet. "Which is more than can be said for my sister."

"She did have Veracity swear not to mention meeting Lord Harlow, miss."

"I rather meant Bianca having anything to do with the man. She has no choice but to weather him at social gatherings, but this *rendezvous* I suspect was mutually planned."

"I tend to agree. The others certainly were."

"Others? How many others?"

"At least three."

"And did the same thing happened each time?"

"It did the next, miss. Veracity has no idea what happened after that."

Harriet gaped at her maid. "She doesn't?"

"No. Miss Bianca goes off with my lord in a carriage—a *drab* carriage, miss—and leaves Veracity in town."

"No!"

"I'm afraid so. Veracity is told to make purchases to Miss Bianca's directions, and later in the day, Lord Harlow's driver picks her up and takes her to this common out of town. There she attends to Miss Bianca's appearance before they're returned to town to meet Tollman."

"And Veracity has to keep silent over the whole matter?"

"That's right," said Dimity, then gazed sadly at Harriet. "What are we going to do, miss?"

"I am certain that I am not sure," admitted Harriet. "We do not even know quite what is going on."

"It looks pretty obvious to me."

"On the face of it, certainly, but we must not rush to condemn my sister."

"I don't condemn her," said Dimity with mild affront. "I should be the last to do so."

"Well, I would condemn her poor judgement," replied Harriet. "My lord has done most poorly in keeping previous liaisons from public consumption. Even so, we should not assume; perhaps Bianca simply enjoys his company."

"So why go off with him?"

"That they may not be observed together. She hardly wants her name dragged through the gutter by faceless slanderers."

"Then if it's so innocuous, miss, why is Veracity not included?"

"Ah… Perhaps they find it awkward to have her loitering close," hazarded Harriet, but that sounded terribly weak. "All I am saying, Dimity, is that I must be very sure of the ground before I dare do anything. You must get every detail from Veracity. I am particularly curious to know exactly where she is taken to meet Bianca."

"Yes, miss. It bodes ill for Veracity's prospects though, doesn't it?"

"She is conflicted, and it is wholly my sister's doing. If this matter becomes public knowledge, then I am sure Veracity will be treated with compassion."

Dimity looked dubious. "If you say so, miss."

ROYSTON WAS IN the model shop and glad of it, for the kiln

used to dry the castings made the place comfortably warm—certainly so compared to the great barns of the fitting shop and assembly shop. On the table were various parts of model locomotives. They were larger than the ones he himself had constructed and fashioned completely from beech wood. To compensate for the relative lightness of the wood, a substantive lead slug would be added later to hold the model upon the tracks inside "the drying engine."

"No, Clacton, it has to be smoother here," he explained to the craftsman who had been assigned to the work, pointing at a sketch.

"I don't see how that can be, Mr Staley," said Clacton. "You have to have spectacle glasses or the driver can't see the road."

"We shall have them," said Royston. "Only they shall stretch from the driver at a fine angle, so as to slip through the air."

Clacton scratched his head. "Well, if you're sure, sir."

"Quite sure, Clacton."

"Oh, there you are, Mr Staley," said a much-liked voice. "I was looking for you."

Royston turned, happy for the interruption. "Is it teatime already, Miss Colton?"

"It is," she declared, warming her hands at the kiln.

Royston remained in Harriet's favour. She had given him a belated steamer lesson from the previous Saturday. This close to the end of the year, how could the day have been anything but cold, grey, and damp, but he quite forgave the dismal weather for having her warmth against him. Alas, their run to Kearby was curtailed, for a band of rain had swept in, making the unprotected steering bench miserable, however pleasant the company. Miss Harriet had driven them back, and with bone-jarring haste, hoping to outrun the weather.

"How goes the drying engine?" she asked quietly as they made their way to the canteen.

"Very well, Harriet. My initial assessments indicate that the wind drag is not as onerous as I had first feared, but it is certainly significant."

"And rises disproportionately to the speed. To its square, you said?"

"I did, and my findings support that hypothesis. If we do not act to reduce the drag, we shall certainly deny *Mercury* the speed she might otherwise achieve."

"Father is determined to do what is necessary."

"It reflects well on him, madam, to not be bound to tradition."

"An unfortunate sentiment for Christmas week, sir," she teased.

"There are traditions and traditions, madam. I certainly would not have Christmas done away with!"

"No indeed. Do I recall you saying you were going to Sussex for the celebration?"

"Your memory serves you correctly. My brother will be home from overseas. For a short while the family will again be complete."

"That will be agreeable. It is a shame that you shall miss the works party, however. It is always jolly."

"Is that not on Thursday evening?"

"It is, sir. I fear you will already be travelling."

"Not a bit of it. I plan to travel on Christmas Eve itself, the Friday. I can attend, if I am welcome."

"Everyone of the works is invited, sir, and all their families. It is Father's way of thanking the men for the year's success. Indeed, no one from the village is turned away, and many of the other concerns in the village also offer contributions. There is always plenty to eat and drink and games for the children and dancing for their elders. Everyone has the most wonderful time."

"By all aspects, an event not to be missed," suggested Royston.

"I am sure it has been one of my favourite parts of Christmas since I was a young girl."

"Then you have me persuaded, madam; I will most certainly attend."

Dear Miss Colton,

Thank you for your gracious reply. I am greatly saddened to read that you desire we delay renewing our acquaintance—or perhaps that should be a fresh acquaintance now that we are no longer teacher and student (by which I mean that you have received your diploma, not that I have relinquished my position at the Institute) but as beautiful lady and hopeful gentleman. I do, however, understand that your first duty is to assist your father in rising to Lord Clifton's Challenge, and thus reluctantly grant your request.

Be assured of my continued devotion.

Your most obedient servant,
Thaddeus Barnet, Professor of Heat.

"Oh dear," said Harriet. "I fear I have quite upset the poor man."

Dimity glanced over her shoulder at the short note. "It's certainly a lot cooler than his last effort, miss," she said. "But at least he agreed."

"There is that, I suppose, but I do wish he had also made

comment on my professed desire to maintain my profession."

"He probably wants to mull that bit over."

"I do not see anything over which to mull. I made my case quite unambiguous."

"Well then, he is either comfortable with the idea, or perhaps he thinks once there's romance, you will meekly become a traditional wife."

"*Meekly*, Dimity?"

Dimity shrugged "Everyone's allowed delusions, miss."

7.

Stoking the Fire

CHALE BRIDGE VILLAGE Hall, a low yet broad wooden structure, lay on the works side of the village, cheek by jowl with The Wheelwrights public house. When Royston arrived, he joined in a positive throng of others—men and women in their high-day finery, with as-yet clean children running excitedly amongst them.

The inside of the hall was already crowded. Above, holly and ribbons hung from the hammer-beams. At one end of the hall a tree rose above the animated company, its boughs decorated with candles and tin ornaments. Beside that, Royston caught the occasional glint of gaslight upon polished brass as the works band prepared for a long and thirsty evening.

People were coming and going through the rear door of the hall, and Royston investigated. Outside, in the small patch of ground squeezed between the hall and the fence guarding the metals of the London and Northern, several fires flickered and blazed in the crisp night. By the mouth-watering smells from the prodigious sides of meat above them, they must have burnt for most of the day. By one of them stood Lady Alicia.

"Ah, Mr Staley. I am so glad you could join us," she said

warmly. She was attired as much for a hunt as for a party, and Royston saw not only a practical compromise but also a purposeful rejection of her exacting standards of fashion.

In a flash, he realised this was to not humiliate the womenfolk of her larger family, that of Colton and Holm. Indeed, the event seemed very much of a family nature. He spotted apprentices drinking while over-men hauling wood for the fires, and even the Colton's butler was out of uniform and looking passing odd.

"Good," said Lady Alicia. "Someone reminded you to bring a tankard. We have plates after a fashion, but drinking receptacles are rather as we find them." She herself clutched what appeared to be a slightly dented christening mug, seemingly more at ease than ever he had seen her.

"Miss Colton was most firm upon the matter," he told her.

"I am glad. Harriet is so practical. But your tankard is empty! Pray remedy that; the barrels are set up yonder."

"I will at once, my lady," he said and bowed.

At the barrels, he was astounded to be served by Samuel Colton himself, who was wearing a tapster's apron.

"Ah, Staley." He claimed Royston's tankard of student days. "You must try Messrs Stallows' Full Reign. The Iron Duck sent a barrel our way."

"Then I indeed shall," declared Royston, amazed that the support of The Iron Duck, the disreputable pothouse on the far side of the village, ever maligned for sucking away the wages of the men, would be welcomed at the entertainment. It was, however, he allowed, not the time of year to be judgemental.

Colton returned the tankard, now brimming. Royston raised it in a toast and took an inch off the contents. He almost coughed.

"Is this *permitted* to be sold as ale, sir?"

"Quite a kick, hasn't it," said Colton. "They only brew it for the Christmas trade."

"Only *dare* brew it, I venture, and I am surprised it is condoned even then. It could quite render a soul insensible through the New Year!" declared Royston, taking a second sample. Once one expected the strength, it was decidedly flavoursome.

Colton laughed. "I am certain for some it does, sir."

Nodding his thanks to his employer, Royston moved back inside, where the band had started playing Christmas airs, but soothingly. There he found Harriet conversing with another lady. Rather than gowns, both appeared to have conspired upon vaguely Gypsy attire of gaily embroidered dark skirts worn with a plain blouse. The unknown lady bore a half tankard, whilst Miss Harriet held a curious chalice depicting the muses of art and science under an ornate rim of interwoven leaves.

"Miss Colton!" he said, "and… actually, I do not believe we have met?"

"Oh!" said Harriet. "Mr Staley, may I introduce Miss Dimity Marsden."

"Most charmed, I am sure, Miss Marsden." said Royston. He swapped grip on his tankard to shake Miss Marsden's hand.

"I also, Mr Staley." Miss Marsden curtsied. "Forgive me, I quite give myself airs."

"Pardon?"

She grinned. "On any other evening, I'm Miss Harriet's maid."

"And tonight you should be enjoying yourself, Dimity,"

said Harriet firmly. "Not feeling you should keep me company."

"I am sure I would be delighted to relieve you of that pleasant duty," offered Royston.

"I leave you in good hands then, miss," said the maid. She curtsied to both of them and disappeared into the crowd.

"She seems a pleasant girl," commented Royston.

"She is, and I am greatly fond of her. She looked after me all through Newcastle, Mr Staley."

"Then we are all indebted to Miss Marsden," declared Royston. "Now can I refresh your... um..."

"It *is* rather outrageous, is it not?" she remarked, examining her chalice, "The Society of Professional Gentlewomen presented it to me when I received my diploma. I am afraid I am being quite disrespectful employing it so."

"I am sure there are some amongst the membership who would most heartily approve," suggested Royston.

"I think you may be right, sir. The society serves an important role, but there are too many members who are too dreadfully serious. Fortunately, not all."

"But does it require refreshing, Harriet?"

"Heavens, no! I am finding it holds rather too great a quantity. I am having to tell myself to be cautious."

Royston considered his tankard, which he found already half drained. "Then perhaps something to eat?"

"That is a fine notion, sir," she said.

He offered his arm.

IT WAS A simple but tasty repast, predominantly generous amounts of good meat and thick slabs of bread, then cakes and puddings from a hundred or more kitchens, all guided by a single will (Royston rather assumed it to be that of Lady Alicia). He forewent the puddings, preferring to burn his fingers upon roast chestnuts for himself and Harriet, the scent of which elicited for him the sweetest childhood memories of being with his father, indulgent on Horsham's streets as the Great Day approached. His tankard had grown empty and then full again, although not of the Full Reign but rather the more honest Albion Ale that had grown to be his taste since he had arrived in Chale Bridge. And now it was empty again.

He was just considering refilling it when a horrible thought struck him.

"Harriet? If everyone is here," he said, "then who is guarding *Mercury*?"

Beside him (they were sharing a bench near one of the fires), she carefully finished the chestnut in her mouth before replying. "Do you think our rivals so despicable as to desecrate the spirit of Christmas?"

"In truth, I believe they might be."

"And so does Father," said Miss Harriet. "And so do I. But have no fears, she is safe. We can never leave the works completely unmanned, even on a night like this."

"Those who remain must be greatly disappointed to miss this entertainment."

"Oh no. There is extra pay, and it is quite voluntary." She then smiled. "Indeed, privy to who favours the work, I can state without doubt that any person who attempts to molest *Mercury* tonight will meet the most dreadful challenge."

"They will?"

"Most assuredly. They will face our dissenting teetotallers, driven to fervour by the sinfulness of this gathering."

He laughed. "That sounds a most horribly protracted doom, Harriet."

"Indeed it does, sir."

AGAIN HE EYED his tankard, and this time acted upon it, coaxing the feebly protesting Harriet to allow him to refresh her chalice.

On his way back from the makeshift bar, Lady Alicia waylaid him.

"Ah, Mr Staley," she said. "The dancing has started, and perfectly no-one is offering my dear Bianca a turn upon the floor."

"Then I shall do so with haste," said Royston, masking his exasperation. "But first I must deliver this, ah, vessel to your other daughter."

"Of course, of course," replied Lady Alicia.

It did not surprise him that everyone was being very cautious over Miss Bianca. He'd seen her amongst the crowd, and although she had also adopted the greater family spirit and wore a simple dress, there was no masking her startling prettiness. Royston was sure she was receiving a plethora of longing glances but, given her station, no one dared approach.

He returned to Harriet and apologetically offered her chalice. "I am afraid Lady Alicia has prevailed upon me to dance with your sister," he told her. "She apparently wishes to dance, yet no one is requesting her pleasure."

"Then you should do as you must, sir."

"I will, but I very much look forward to dancing with you also."

"Then you shall," she declared with a smile. "Would you have me care for your tankard?"

"That would be most thoughtful."

Royston gulped down a good two inches of the tankard's contents, handed it to her, and then went in search of Miss Bianca. Even in the crowded hall, she was not difficult to find for she sat alone on a bench, nursing a christening mug of her own and looking downcast.

"Would you dance, Miss Bianca," he asked with a careful bow.

"I... Yes, I suppose I might," she replied uncertainly. She put aside the mug and accepted his arm to stand.

They joined the couples on the floor, but very soon Royston realised that matters were not in order. This was an undemanding waltz, yet Miss Bianca stumbled once and then a second time, clinging to him to recover her balance and muttering her apologies.

"Is everything all right, Miss Bianca?" he asked, yet already suspecting his partner to be decidedly inebriated.

"I freer—I fear I'm quite light-headed, Mr Straly."

"Then you would prefer some night air rather than the dance, madam," he suggested, guiding her from the floor.

"I think tha' might be a wise idea," she murmured, and seemed glad of his arm as he took her out to the fires. Harriet was still at their bench, the firelight warm in her hair, picking at chestnuts and wincing. She looked a little surprised to see them approach.

"Your sister is a little overwrought from the excitement, Miss Colton," Royston announced diplomatically.

"She is?"

Royston guided Miss Bianca onto the bench beside her sister. She settled gracelessly and hiccupped.

Harriet looked at her with consternation. "How much have you drunk, Bee?"

"Only a few of s'punch, Harry." Miss Bianca said defensively, and then grew alarmed. "Oh! My mug!"

"I shall fetch it," Royston assured her, and went to recover the christening mug. On his way back he sniffed what remained within it. The aroma was sweet and heady. Unseen by Miss Bianca, he pantomimed his discovery to Harriet.

"Oh, confound Mrs Bracewaite and her punch!" muttered Harriet crossly. "She simply has no concept of restraint. And have you eaten anything, Bee?"

Miss Bianca shook her bowed head.

"Bread, Mr Staley, if you please."

"Of course, Miss Colton."

He scavenged some, and brought it back. Harriet thanked him and turned to care for her afflicted sister. He then began to find lingering ghoulish. "I will see you presently, Miss Colton," he said, reclaiming his tankard.

"Indeed you shall, sir," she replied warmly. "I quite believe I owe you several dances for your conduct."

HARRIET FOUND ROYSTON a little later on.

"May I enquire after your sister, Harriet?" he asked.

"She is resting and feeling a little better, thank you, Mr Staley."

"It is easy to be incautious when all are celebrating," he said sympathetically. "I am sure in the past I have been equally incautious."

"As have most, sir," agreed Harriet, but then she frowned. "Yet this evening my sister is of an odd melancholy."

"That can have the same effect as one seeks cheer," suggested Royston. "Is it that the evening was overly anticipated, perhaps?"

"I am sure that is the reason, sir," she said readily. "And another to which we are all fallible."

"Would you dance now, Harriet?"

"I would, sir."

THEY JOINED THE crowded dance area and a spirited polka. This was followed by a more sedate schottische, allowing everyone to catch their breath. As at the Fireworks Ball, Harriet proved as competent a partner as she was a pleasing one. They paused for refreshment, then returned to the floor for a lively waltz and an opportunity to have his hand upon her waist. Harriet seemed to be enjoying herself thoroughly, laughing and smiling with him as they circled the floor.

The band fell silent then, and Old Benjamin called for their attention and offered a toast to Her Majesty, hoping for her to long rule over realm and Empire, another to Samuel

Colton, thanking him for the evening's entertainment and praying for good health to him and his family, and a final toast to the season, and peace and goodwill at every family's hearth. All the sentiments were vigorously supported.

The band then struck up another polka, which had Harriet's Gypsy skirt swirling. There followed a two-step, and then another waltz, but one much more leisurely, during which Harriet allowed him to draw her closer against him.

It was as they slowly progressed about the floor that Royston noticed other couples pausing at a certain spot away from the band, and then moving on. He peered carefully over Harriet's shoulder, then spotted the mistletoe hanging discretely from the beam above. Her softness against him conspired with the conviviality of the ale to forge boldness from temptation, so that the next time that certain spot was close, he eased her to it.

"Mistletoe, Harriet," he murmured, glancing up.

"So it is, Mr Staley," she said, and smiled at him softly.

Emboldened, he eased his head closer and kissed her tenderly upon her lips. Wondrously soft and warm, their press upon his own brought a sudden hesitation in his spirit and exhilaration to his heart.

The moments seemed to stretch, yet all too soon the propriety of the surroundings intervened and had them waltz on. Yet Royston was encouraged; Harriet seemed to be content to be drawn even closer now.

The band set up a galloping pace in their next number, but by the end of that, Lady Alicia was hovering. Royston guided the flushed Harriet over to her mother.

"Pardon my intrusion, Mr Staley."

"I am sure your presence is never an intrusion, Lady Alicia." He bowed.

She favoured him with a brief smile, but then turned to her daughter. "Harriet, we must be leaving."

"Already, Mother?" protested Miss Harriet.

"It is best we go before the largesse promotes complete immoderation. You must have heard your father speak of this," said Lady Alicia. "And it is nearly midnight, dear."

"Truly? I had no idea."

"The carriage is waiting in the yard of the public house."

"I will go there at once, Mother," she said.

Lady Alicia nodded, then sailed off with great purpose upon some task yet unfulfilled.

Harriet sighed. "And I was so enjoying myself."

"I also, Miss Harriet—very much so," Royston assured her, then consulted his hunter, which verified Lady Alicia. "Although I suspect I would soon have to be leaving also. I have an early train in the morning. But may I see you to your carriage?"

"I would like that, sir."

He offered his arm.

THE NIGHT AIR was crisp and refreshing after the torpid, tobacco-smoke-hazed interior, the streets dark and quiet except for a few stray revellers stumbling home.

"When do you return to Pennydale, Mr Staley?" asked Harriet. Oh, she so wanted him to kiss her again! Would he? Or dare she kiss him?

"On the twenty-seventh. I anticipate Father shall prevail upon me to ride to hounds on Boxing Day, although it has been a while since I took the saddle."

"Then do have a care, sir."

Mr Staley laughed. "I fully intend to, Harriet."

They were almost upon the Wheelwrights' yard. If she dared, it had to be now, before they were at the carriage with at least Tollman present. She paused her already lethargic pace and turned to him in the darkness. She sensed him turn also.

"You need not trouble yourself further, sir. I will be perfectly fine from here," she declared. "I do hope, Mr Staley…" An impulsive notion came to her. "No, I would have you Royston, if that is not overly familiar."

His silhouette bowed gently. "I would be greatly honoured, madam."

"Then I do hope, Royston, that you have the most pleasant Christmas, and your family as well."

"I also wish that for you and your family, Harriet."

"Then I bid you goodnight and safe journey, sir," she said and then, risking all, laid a hand on his shoulder, and found his firm lips with her own. He was close, he was warm, and his hand closed upon her side, but then revellers approached, their accents loud and broadened with alcohol. She hastily eased away from him.

"Goodnight, Harriet," he murmured warmly. "I shall see you on the twenty-seventh."

"You shall, sir."

They separated from each other then. Harriet turned to watch him walking away, then moved slowly towards the waiting carriage as if in a dream.

STANDING BEHIND MERCURY on boards thrown across the inspection pit, Harriet grasped the bar coupling as the bulk of the tender crept closer, eclipsing what little light managed to enter the fitting shop on this gloomy morning.

"Two feet," she called, and then with a grunt lifted the heavy forging that it might find the recess awaiting it on the tender. "A foot."

The progress of the tender slowed, yet in the narrow gap between the twenty-odd tons of advancing steel and the far greater mass of *Mercury*, Harriet felt extremely vulnerable. She had insisted on this duty, however, wanting to be the one to officiate the special moment of linking the locomotive and her tender together.

The coupling slid home into the recess, just before the tender pressed into her. "Halt," she called, releasing the bar, her muscles grateful. Wriggling out from the gap, she crawled underneath and, taking up the coupling pin, felt with her fingers into the hole awaiting it, looking for the corresponding hole in the coupling bar. She found it amongst the grease, a narrow crescent to one side.

"Towards her, and dead slow," she requested, reaching around with the coupling pin and locating it in the upper side of the recess. The tender began to creep forward as out of her sight levering bars were applied, and then with a satisfying clunk, the pin dropped home.

"Done," she announced and spun the retaining collar onto the thread of the pin, completing the job by inserting a split pin under the collar and bending each side around the coupling pin with pliers.

There, that would not come adrift in a hurry. In fact, she reflected, crawling out beside the front tender wheel, it might never be undone for the remainder of *Mercury*'s life.

Benjamin helped her to her feet.

"Thank you, Benjamin," she said and then addressed the gathered fitters. "Carstairs, call the tea break, after which we shall attend to the remainder of the arrangements."

The others drifted off towards the canteen, and she went in search of Royston. He was not in his office, nor in the model shop. She then went to the drying engine, but found that unattended and the cylinders cold to the touch. Perplexed, she wandered back towards *Mercury* but then saw him standing in the open doors of the assembly shop. She approached and found that he was considering the front buffer beam of a completed Peak class goods locomotive and appeared deep in thought.

"Good morning, Royston," she said, a little nervous to use his Christian name. This was not, after all, the forgiving darkness after the heady familiarity of the dance but days later, and upon a bleak grey morning.

He turned. "Ah, good morning, Harriet!" he said warmly. "I hope you had a very pleasant Christmas?"

She forgot her nervousness in his smile. "It was most agreeable. And how was yours? And your family?"

"Enjoyable, and thank you, my family are quite well."

"Did you ride?"

"I did indeed. My father considered I gave a good account."

"That is gratifying," she said. "Will you take tea, Royston?"

"I will, but first might I have your thoughts on what may

be a rather foolish notion?"

"Certainly, sir."

He looked at the locomotive. "Does *Mercury* truly *need* a front buffer beam?" he asked. "Her role is not to bank, nor should she draw a train tender-first, nor indeed take a pilot."

"Wind drag, Royston?"

"That and pride, Harriet. It makes an untidy prefix."

"Yet alas a necessary one, sir. Under abnormal circumstances, tender-first working can be unavoidable for lack of a turning-table."

"Hmm."

"There is the matter of breakdown. No locomotive is invulnerable, and when they fail, the recovery engine *must* act as pilot."

"I confess I had not considered that."

"And would you not wish to see two of her class double-heading a heavy express?"

"Now that would be magnificent!" he exclaimed, and then smiled at her. "I concede. Her buffer beam stays."

"You should also not be dismayed by this example, sir. Whilst the height from the rails and the buffer separation is dictated, that does not mean one cannot change its *appearance.*"

Staley nodded thoughtfully.

"To tea, Royston?" she prompted gently when he appeared in reverie with the buffers, coupling hook, and vacuum brake hose before him.

He came out of his trance. "I am sorry, Harriet; of course." He offered his arm.

"I shall not be at the works from tomorrow," she told him as they walked. "Nor will my father."

"A family commitment?"

"Indeed. We traditionally celebrate the New Year with Mother's family at Selforth Abbey. It is quite the family gathering."

"And quite the distance."

"We shall travel by train, sir, changing at York," she told him. "And do you have plans?"

"None of great mention. I expect I shall go into the village. I am sure that I shall find some celebration to join."

"I expect you shall find the various establishments plentifully lively."

"I confess the company in The Just Swan was most welcoming when I was a stranger, and always convivial since, yet..." He glanced at her then, his expression regretful.

"Sir?"

"I would have welcomed another opportunity to dance with you," he confessed, then smiled.

That brought a pleasant glow to Harriet. "I also. I am sure, however, that an opportunity will arise soon in the New Year."

8.

Tapping the Wheels

"WELL, DIMITY?" HARRIET held the vehicle against the gradient with the steam brake. "Is this not just as Veracity described? We have our common land rising to the hilltop, our great tree with a three-sided bench about its bole, and that, I believe, is our narrow lane to the left."

"It seems right, miss," said Dimity, beside her on the driving bench. "A lot more right than the last two places, leastways."

Veracity's grasp of geography had proved negligible to say the least, and in the previous two hours they'd found how often the environs of Malbury offered the opportunity to "turn left at a large house after a farm." Up until now their left turns had only brought disappointment (and, as two women abroad on a streamer, disapproving looks).

Harriet screwed down the handbrake and locked the motion. "Veracity said my sister arrived from the lane?"

"Yes, miss; it's too narrow for my lord's carriage apparently."

"As it is for the steamer." Having checked the sight glass on the boiler, Harriet slid to the ground. "Come."

Dimity climbed down also, but with reluctance. "I'm still not sure about this."

"I see no other option," said Harriet. "I am not about to pry into my sister's correspondence, and questioning her directly will not serve; she is sure to dissemble."

After her sister's cheerless humour at the Christmas party, Harriet feared she had been thrown over by Lord Harlow, but then Bianca appeared quite herself through Christmas.

Then Dimity learnt of another trip to Malbury in the offing and suggested a much simpler diagnosis of Bianca's melancholy: Everyone was having a fine time, but her lord wasn't there. "If so," concluded Dimity sadly, "she's really got it bad, miss."

The lane was narrow and sunken and overhung with dark yew and winter-stark hornbeam as it twisted up and away from the common. A little way up into it, Harriet paused and prodded the ground with her boot. "Marl, just as Veracity has to clean from Bianca's shoes."

"But we knew she came this way anyway," countered Dimity.

"*If* this is the correct lane; the marl encourages me to believe that it is."

After a few more twists and turns, they passed a small, low cottage which they both eyed thoughtfully. A little distance after that, the lane emerged from woodland and ran straight for a time beneath the crest of the hill, pastures to each side of it.

"And my sister's clothing was not sullied?" mused Harriet, gazing along the lane.

"No, miss. Nor in any way disarranged. Veracity tended mostly to tidying her mistress's hair."

"That *suggests* an innocent walk," said Harriet thoughtfully. "Any form of wind could explain the hair."

"Yes, but begging your pardon, I'm not convinced."

"In truth, nor am I," confessed Harriet. "We must inspect that cottage."

"That was what I was thinking too."

They retraced their steps until they stood before the cottage, which was whitewashed and frugally windowed, suggesting it housed a coppicer or herdsman. There was a single door of dark wood, with plant pots clustered on either side, each bearing the dismal remains of summer glory.

"There's not much to it," noted Dimity, "but it could serve."

Harriet nodded and opened the gate.

"Miss?" said her maid in a worried tone.

"How shall we learn anything from out here, Dimity?" Harriet was already upon the path to the dark wooden door.

"But what if my lord is here?"

"I thought you told me the next assignation was not planned until Tuesday?"

"I did, but that doesn't mean he might not be here. What if he's having more than the one *affaire*?"

Harriet grimaced, certain that the marquess was capable of such treachery. More fearful for her sister's well-being than before, she fortified her resolve. "Then perhaps we shall find something that will tell us that."

"I'm still not happy, miss."

"Come now, Dimity. The place is perfectly uninhabited." Harriet pointed to the chimney-pots. "See? No fires are lit."

"But isn't it trespass?"

"We have excellent reasons, to which the law will be sympathetic," said Harriet firmly. "And naturally I take full responsibility for any consequences."

Dimity ventured through the gate. "If you say so, miss."

For all the assurances she'd given her maid, when confronted with the door Harriet decided it wise to knock first. When there was no response, she reached for the doorknob.

"Locked," she said with a sigh.

"You stay here, miss, and I'll see if there's another door." Dimity disappeared around the side of the cottage but returned soon after, shaking her head.

"This is *most* aggravating," said Harriet.

"We're not dead yet." Dimity crouched down by the door, turning over stones and looking under the plant pots.

"You think the key might be hidden?"

"My ma always had one hid, and it certainly don't hurt to—Ha!" The maid snatched at the ground and stood in triumph, bearing aloft a stout iron key.

"Oh, well done!"

Dimity unlocked the door and pushed it open, revealing a gloomy kitchen. They stepped timidly over the threshold, and she closed the door behind them. There was a sink, a range, and a plain table with honest chairs. The table bore a wicker hamper, some heavy bottles, and various glasses and plates.

Dimity crossed to the range and laid her hand upon it. "Stone cold, miss."

"That is reassuring," said Harriet, exploring the hamper. It had once held an assortment of fine food but had been picked over, and what was left was growing mould.

"Champagne, miss," said Dimity, hefting an empty bottle, "and lead crystal."

"The fare quite outshines its surroundings." Harriet turned over a dirty plate to find it to be Wedgwood. She placed it carefully back.

"This must all be from last time, miss."

"I agree. Whosoever has the responsibility for the arrangements has yet to discharge them for Tuesday."

They opened every cupboard and drawer, yet all were poignantly bare.

"We should explore further," declared Harriet, addressing the only other door in the room. She opened it carefully, and they crept through it.

"Oh my," she murmured. Dimity offered a low whistle of astonishment.

The walls were plain whitewash, but the floor was covered in a rich oriental rug. The further wall had a large fireplace, presently dark and cold, before which was an elegant *chaise-longue*. A fine glass garlanded by gilded cherubim stood upon a dressing table, an ottoman beneath it, and other small cabinets stood against the walls. What truly dominated the room, however, was a great canopied bed, rich with gold leaf and ornamentation, its linen in a state of furious disarrangement.

"He has this set up right grand, miss."

"Yet one would never suspect from the outside," replied Harriet, suddenly more wary of the marquess and distrustful of his apparent foolishness.

"Handy he had a place so near Malbury, eh?"

"It is no coincidence, Dimity. I am sure this was all put in place solely to prosecute the *affaire*."

"He must be really earnest about Miss Bianca then."

Harriet shook her head "He is fabulously rich, able to have all this and more for any passing whim." She moved into the room and looked back. "Oh, the gall of the man! He dares boast his accomplishment upon the bed."

Her maid came up beside her and stared in puzzlement.

"He does?"

"The shield upon the headboard, Dimity," said Harriet, pointing. "It is that of his family, the Dallorys."

"*Oh that*," said Dimity slowly. "He's a bit cheeky, ain't he, miss?"

"He is *conceited*. But for once I am glad of it. It leaves no doubt to his erstwhile presence."

"And that means we know everything, miss," offered Dimity. "He was here, Miss Bianca comes from here, and that bed didn't end up like that through sleeping in it, if you get my drift."

"Too clearly I do," said Harriet, trying to suppress her imagination. "Yet, since we are already here, we should investigate further. It would be remiss not to be diligent."

Dimity took upon herself the unsavoury duty of searching the bed, and Harriet hunted about the rest of the room. Some half-burnt log ends remained in the fire, and the ashes looked credibly recent. The *chaise-longue* yielded nothing, and so she moved to the cabinets. All were empty, the last thankfully so since it proved to be a commode.

"Find anything, miss?" Dimity turned her attention from the bed to the dressing table.

"Nothing," said Harriet, joining her.

The maid pulled out the single drawer and then from it drew a gauzy garment. She held it up for inspection. "Night gown, of sorts," she muttered.

"But hardly modest," opined Harriet dubiously. Not only was it diaphanous but also scandalously short. She doubted it even covered the knees.

"I think that's the idea, miss."

"It is of quite splendid lace, however," noted Harriet. "A gift from my lord?"

Dimity carefully replaced the garment. "Possibly—not one she'd want known though."

Harriet looked around for anything they had overlooked and saw nothing, but then Dimity pulled out the ottoman and lifted its seat. Harriet was delighted; she would have quite overlooked that hiding place.

The maid fished inside. "Here's something, miss." She withdrew what appeared to a thin ledger, bound in leather.

"Bring it over to the window."

The leather turned out to be wondrously soft, creamy gold and unadorned except for delicate fleur-de-lis tooling around its edges. The maid opened the cover, and inside there were not pages, but rather a block of paper with various pencils and other accessories arranged about it, all marshalled in little leather loops.

"What a lovely thing, Dimity," breathed Harriet. "I would quite wish its like for myself."

Dimity stroked the leather. "It's rather fine," she allowed. She lifted the cover of the block of paper, then turned the ledger. They gazed upon a sketch of a bucolic landscape, with a great minster rising in the distance. Dimity turned to the next page, a placid river fringed with delicate willows, a small rowing boat being plied through the lily pads.

"I would not have imagined Lord Harlow capable of this," remarked Harriet with slight wonder.

"If it is his work," snorted Dimity, turning the page to reveal a mountainside, with more mountains behind and a very believable storm looming. The next page had a painstakingly devoted study of fruit heaped in a bowl.

"It is not Bianca's doing, of that I am sure, and if it is here," argued Harriet as her maid carefully turned up the sheet of fruit, "then how can it be anything bu—*Oh!*"

Harriet jerked back in shock, but then could not help but return to the pad. "Oh, great heavens," she breathed, gazing down at her sister, who was depicted standing with her long hair loose and lifted by the wind—and wearing not a stitch.

Dimity turned the pad to bring Bianca to her feet. "It's Miss Bianca, isn't it miss?" she said plaintively.

"Alas, a very true likeness," said Harriet reluctantly, "although I have not seen *that* much of my sister for quite a few years."

"It's her figure though, miss," said Dimity contemplatively. "I'd believe it's drawn from life. But what's that queer thing she's standing on?"

"Oh, that," said Harriet dismissively. "It is a scallop shell. My lord pretends after Botticelli's *La Nascita di Venere*, or *The Birth of Venus*."

"Does he now?" muttered Dimity. "Quite the flatterer, isn't he?"

"Most certainly," said Harriet. "Although the original artist had the grace to offer Venus *some* degree of modesty."

"But it's not *dirty*, miss," protested Dimity. "It's artful, like. And she looks happy."

That Harriet could not contest. Bianca's expression was serene yet affectionate.

Dimity turned the page. Again, it was Bianca in all her glory, but now draped languidly upon the *chaise-longue*, her features soft and enticing, as was the errant way she arranged herself.

The maid opened her mouth, but nothing came from it. Harriet was also lost for words, unable to countenance mild-mannered little Bee harbouring such a licentious spirit.

"My lord sketches most attentively," she offered weakly.

Dimity took a sudden gulp of relief. "He certainly does."

She quickly turned the page to Bianca curled on the bed in the lacy nightgown, but the sketch was only half done. Dimity shrugged and turned again.

The *chaise-longue* again, but—

Harriet made a sudden squeak of panic and sharply looked away.

She heard a low throaty chuckle. "So *that's* what's under those flash clothes," murmured her maid.

"Dimity!" protested Harriet, fiercely blushing, yet finding her eyes dragged back to the paper.

"I'm guessing Miss Bianca did this?"

"It is reminiscent of her style," allowed Harriet weakly, wanting to avert her gaze but yet not.

"At least she didn't end up the only one exhibiting her personals," offered Dimity. "I'm glad of that."

"But he's... it's..."

"Yes, miss. No wonder she looks so happy in the earlier sketches."

"Dimity!"

"Sorry, miss." The maid turned to the next page, where the marquess was posed somewhat like Michelangelo's *David*, but with a sultry gaze and holding a wine glass. Moreover, more than one vine leaf would be needed to preserve his modesty, and none were present.

"My lord's a bit skinny for my likes, miss," commented Dimity with a critical frown. "Not much to get a grip on there."

"But is he... um... properly proportioned otherwise?" said Harriet, shocking herself by peering closer.

"Oh, yes, miss. Nothing for a girl to complain about there."

"Truly?" murmured Harriet, her thoughts in confusion.

Dimity glanced at her sympathetically. "Assuming my lord knows when a girl's ready and when she's not, miss. His reputation suggests he would."

Currently the girl to whom the marquess would be attentive was little Bianca; Harriet preferred not to let her thoughts wander that way. Dimity turned the page, but the next page was perfectly white, as were the pages that followed. The maid closed up the pad and the ledger holding it.

"Well, miss, what do we do with this?"

Harriet hesitated. She hated the idea of leaving these images of her sister where they might fall into malicious hands, but to take them away would alert someone to their trespass.

"I fear we have to put it back where we found it," she said sadly.

Dimity nodded and went to replace the ledger in the ottoman.

"What now?" asked the maid.

"I believe we can leave," said Harriet. "I cannot imagine we will find anything else, and to tarry only increases the chance of our discovery."

With a last look around, they quit the cottage and locked up, Dimity secreting the key where she had found it.

"I fear I shall be ill at ease in my sister's company," commented Harriet as they walked back to the steamer.

"Try not to dwell on it," suggested the maid. "We've all got a private side after all."

"I accept that, but I was about to observe that my discomfort with my sister will be as nothing compared to the next time I have to share pleasantries with Lord Harlow!"

That earned her one of Dimity's earthier chuckles.

A SUDDEN MIGHTY roar rattled the windows in Royston's office, and he jumped in panic, the slide rule slipping from his hands. Then a youth lurched in from the corridor, ricocheting off the doorframe.

"Miss Harriet says come at once, sir," he gasped out. "It's *Mercury!*"

Royston leapt to his feet and, crowding past the apprentice, sprinted for the fitting shop. The thunder grew louder, and then he realised it came from *Mercury*'s blow-off valves, thrown full open and rapidly filling the fitting shop with steam. He ran through the fog, hurdling over a heavy hose being dragged by other ghostly figures to the front of the locomotive, and stormed the staging for the footplate.

It was insufferably hot in the cab, waves of heat emanating from the boiler back plate and the dull red glow of the fire escaping about the stationary coal walker sensibly toasting the skin. Harriet was struggling with the offside boiler feed-water injector, whilst Carstairs, the lead fitter, battled the nearside. Royston put his hand on her shoulder.

She looked up, perspiring and terror-stricken. "Injectors will not restart!" she screamed over the noise. "Water level dropping fast!"

He glanced at the sight glasses; they were indeed empty. If the water got too low, then the fire would melt the copper crown of the firebox, and the resulting explosion would not only destroy *Mercury* but also kill everyone within the fitting shop and probably demolish the building.

For all the heat, Royston felt the cold touch of dread—

dread for her, and dread for him. He quickly checked that the damper levers for the fire were closed and then glanced at the steam gauge. It was dropping sedately past 130 pounds, which given the thunder of the escaping steam was an unwanted testament to the effectiveness of the fire.

"Getting water hose on blow-down valve," yelled Harriet. "Works pressure thirty-six pounds."

If the boiler pressure dropped below that before the fire boiled off enough water to expose the firebox, then they had a chance of replenishing the boiler that way. He peered over Harriet at the injector; water was jetting from its overflow instead of being impelled past check valves into the boiler.

"Both stopped?" he yelled.

She nodded. "That one, then this," she yelled back.

He watched as she adjusted the injector's needle setting and cycled the steam and water valves, but to no avail. Water still gushed in the wrong direction. He looked to the steam gauge; it was lethargically passing 120 pounds.

"Half needle, full steam, slow with the water," he yelled, offering only what he'd been taught at Birmingham.

"*Tried*," she yelled back contemptuously. "Does not work."

To humour him, she demonstrated. The overflow spat water, then dribbled, and then dripped. Frowning, Harriet checked the valve positions, then mouthed something that was lost to the din. She scrambled across to the nearside injector, pushed the lead fitter aside, and worked its controls. She then stood up slowly, frowning at that injector also.

Royston looked to the pressure gauge, which was dropping faster now, sure evidence that cold water was surging into the boiler.

Remaining perplexed, Harriet spun shut the blow-off

valves, bringing abrupt silence, into which returned only slowly the hiss of steam and the reassuring if belated song of the injectors.

"Royston," she said, looking shaky, "I do believe I quite abhor steam injectors."

It did not seem the moment to admit that he found them ineffably cunning.

"That they both stopped working suggests not a failure of some sort," suggested Royston as they awaited the water level to rise to the sight glasses.

"Especially now they both have decided to work again," agreed Harriet. "It must be a design flaw. They cannot be generating enough water pressure to push the water through the clack valves."

"If that is so, then as the steam pressure rises, they will fail again. What pressure was it when they failed?"

Harriet wore a guilty frown. "I am uncertain, sir. A little time passed before their malfunction was noticed. *Mercury* steams so hard it does not take long for a simple matter to become grave."

"The pressure had dropped to around 120 pounds when they were minded to restart," he offered.

The water level appeared, and Harriet opened the fire dampers and set the coal walker in motion. Nuggets of steam coal moved slowly past, and into the firebox's glow.

The steam pressure started to slowly rise. At just over 140 pounds, the nearside injector began to gurgle and hiss. Twenty seconds later, the other also ceased to function. Harriet offered something certain to startle Greek ruminants and reached for the handle for the blow-off valves. For a while it was impossible to converse.

She gave instructions to the lead fitter on how to keep

the water level safe as *Mercury*'s fire died down, and then they withdrew to Royston's office.

"Perhaps scaling up our existing injector design was imprudent," said Harriet wearily as Royston found the drawings for the offending unit. "Yet as you said yourself, they must each be capable of delivering two hundred gallons per minute."

"A ton of water, all but," Royston agreed. "Does the existing design serve at 220 pounds, Harriet?"

"Most excellently, sir, and at higher pressures also."

"Then they could be pressed into use."

"But we would need eight where we have two," she contended. "It would be a prodigious family for the fireman to tend."

"We have relieved him of stoking," he reminded her.

"Even so, perhaps some form of mechanical pump would be preferable?" she suggested, growing animated. "If it was directly coupled, steam cylinder to water cylinder, I am sure I could design one that would be delightfully compact. It would be self-acting also." She then grimaced. "Father would hate it of course. He is quite wed to reliability; he perfectly detests adding anything that in failing would bring a Colton and Holm locomotive to a standstill."

"Injectors are usually most reliable." Royston examined the drawing closely but found nothing unconventional. "And I confess I cannot see a reason why those of *Mercury* are proving obstinate."

"And I see no reason they should not." She sneered. "They are infernally paradoxical."

"You understand the theory of course?"

"Perfectly, yet I am suspicious of anything that works for no better reason than that the calculus so ordains. I am afraid that I am a woman that likes matters to be intuitive."

"There is a subtlety to their design," he acknowledged. "It is all in the profile of the delivery nozzle." He traced a finger upon the drawing. "It must be perfectly matched with that of the receiving cone for everything to be brought to delightful harmony."

He looked up to see if she understood, but then came thunder as the pressure in *Mercury*'s boiler was again blown off. Harriet, he noticed, had an extremely high colour.

"Is everything all right, Harriet?"

"Oh yes," she said, and gulped. "It is that *Mercury*'s foot-plate was intolerably hot."

"Alas, it must become more enclosed to reduce wind drag. We must arrange a reasonable draught, or I fear parties may be rendered quite insensible."

"That... That would not do," she managed, not at all herself.

"Are you certain you would not sit down?"

"I think that perhaps I shall, sir."

Worried, he assisted her to his chair. "Should I fetch water?"

"No, I believe that not to be necessary," she said, and then made a commendable effort at rallying. "What... What do you propose, sir?"

"I believe we should prepare alternatives—a pump or a multiplicity of injectors—yet I wish to study the current design. I may discern an efficacious remedy."

"I am convinced that you shall find it, Royston," she said smiling.

He laughed. "You flatter me, madam."

9.

Fog men Required

IN THE THIRD week of the New Year the weather turned bitterly cold, easterly winds bringing icy Russian air over the German Sea. Frost lingered in the fields throughout the day, the ground froze, and even simple spanners had to be warmed before use for fear they would shear clean in half. Yet on the Friday morning as Harriet walked across the tracks to the drying engine, the air seemed somewhat warmer, boding that the bitter snap was over, albeit that the wind was backing to the northeast and freshening.

She discovered Royston warming his hands on the nearside cylinder of the improvised fan engine. As she approached, he turned to her. He smiled, yet there was some ineffable quality to his eyes and in that smile that went beyond welcoming her presence to fiercely encouraging her into his arms. Sudden emotion shivered through her, and she felt her body react shamelessly to the invitation, anticipating a great deal more of his attentions than a simple embrace. Mortified by her reaction, Harriet hurried to the offside cylinder and made a pretence of following his example.

"Good news, Royston," she said, eager to make conversation and have him think nothing was amiss. "I believe this terrible weather may be waning. It feels less bitter outside."

"I cannot be more glad," he replied over the frames, with another smile but thankfully one free of sudden bewitchment. "I confess these last few nights I have resorted to sleeping before my fire. Retiring to bed had very little appeal."

"Have you no fire there, sir?" she said automatically, and immediately wanted to unmake her words. She bent lower over the cylinder, blushing furiously.

"Not alas that will last the entire night."

He appeared not to have noticed the unintended intimation or her discomposure; if he had, he had the decency not to show it. "I myself have been quite smothered by a surfeit of blankets of late, and that with a fire," she said quickly, desperately hoping to show there never had been anything more than innocent enquiry.

Curse the marquess's boudoir and the confounded sketches! A gentle spirit would be scandalised by the undiluted carnality that innocent-looking cottage hid, and she should have been also, yet…

No. Her thoughts slid off that way enough of their own accord; this was certainly not the moment to *encourage* them.

Harriet looked about for distraction, and her eyes fell upon the model standing on the workbench.

"Is that *Mercury's* latest guise, Royston?"

"I believe it to be her *final* guise, in truth," he replied. "I doubt I can improve on it."

She went and peered closer. The model was sleek, with a sloped nose and the cab a subtle taper before the tender. "You have assessed the forces that the wind shielding will impose on the frame?"

"I have. They are not greatly onerous."

"You have extended the wind shield almost to the metals," she noted; the wheels barely protruded below it on the model she held.

"It improved the performance."

"But how then can one attend to the motion?"

"I am aware this is not a practical design, Harriet," he said, coming over, "but it is the form your wonderful drying engine recommends." He picked up the model. "I believe it could be made practical in the right hands, and those hands are yours." He handed it to her.

His appreciation of her ability filled her with precious warmth, pure and joyous; how so much he was *not* Mr Barnet, she thought. "You would have me do the final design?"

"Of course. I only implore that you keep all the arrangements to gain access as smooth as possible."

"You may be sure that I will, sir," she promised, whipping an errant thought back into the fold.

They left the drying engine with Harriet on his arm and the model tucked under her other arm.

Royston paused, and looked up to where dark clouds were rolling in, borne on the wind. "I fear we shall have snow."

"Snow, sir? But surely the weather grows more clement?"

"I do not dispute that it appears so, Harriet, yet do you not smell the snow on the air?"

She sampled the air carefully but found upon it only the fiery business of the forge. "In faith, no."

"But snow we shall have," he assured her firmly.

Harriet laughed sceptically.

YET ROYSTON WAS more right than he could himself have believed. The snow started just as the afternoon shift began. First it was small flurries of the sort that made children hopeful and then disappointed. But then the snow came in earnest, and Harriet had never seen snow quite like it. Looking out from the door of the fitting shed, all she could see was the swirling white of snowflakes, each impossibly large. She could not even make out the forge, and that building was as imposing as the fitting shop and barely a hundred yards away. Moreover, with the ground already frozen, the snow immediately began to settle. Old Benjamin was standing beside her, and he shook his head in disturbed wonder.

"Have you ever seen it coming down like this, Benjamin?"

"Not in all my born years, Miss Harriet," he announced soberly. "It'll do folk mischief, that I warrant."

Soon work was coming to a standstill, the men fixated by the blizzard raging outside, with drifts already forming against anything that offered resistance.

Harriet was in *Mercury*'s cab, tools and parts scattered about her as she reassembled the offside injector, when she heard someone jump upon the staging.

"I am perfectly sure I am not in Sussex, Harriet," Royston enthused.

She turned to find him grinning like a schoolboy at her, his Ulster plastered with snow and his hair also. "Are you sure you are even in Derbyshire anymore, sir?" she replied.

"It seems quite like Siberia."

"Should we then not be conversing in Ruski?" he suggested.

"My Ruski is abominably pitiable," she admitted. "But you were out in it, sir?"

"The drying engine doors were open," he explained. "Everything would have been swallowed by the snow."

"You should have sent a hand."

He grinned again. "I rather coveted the challenge for myself."

She wiped the oil from her hands. "And was it so?"

"Most certainly!" he enthused. "I hope that the doors are not damaged. The windward ones came home with a frightful crash, and the lee side ones needed bullying. And the snow! It is so disorienting. On venturing out I feel I chanced upon the drying engine by luck and returned by equal providence."

Father then clambered up with Benjamin. He looked concerned. "I've passed the word to the foremen to let the men away, Harriet."

"What of those that live distant, Father? I fear for them."

"My instructions are not to allow anyone to try for further than Chale Bridge, and I've called for Good Samaritans to care for those who live beyond. Anyone left we can probably use here."

"What of yourself, sir?" put in Royston. "Pennydale House is somewhat isolated."

"Don't worry for me, sir, nor for my daughter; My lady wife has sent down the carriage horses." He turned to Harriet, and winked. "Up for a ride, lass?"

"Most certainly, Father," she declared. "Since the alternative appears fast becoming wading."

OUT IN THE yard, the driving snow was making the horses fretful, and they sidestepped and snorted, trying hopelessly to keep their tails into the wind. Colton was already mounted, as was a young stable lad. Tollman was holding the bridle of Harriet's horse, and beset by swirling snowflakes, Royston was helping her mount the skittish beast.

He knelt, offering his hands for her boot, which she carefully accepted. Making sure she had a good grip on the saddle, he boosted her up but averted his eyes as she threw her other leg over the saddle and kept his gaze elsewhere until he was sure she would have her clothing modestly arranged. It was not a night to be riding sidesaddle, and he was glad Harriet was more pragmatic than prim.

She was wearing a heavy riding cloak, and looking up at her, he could barely see her face beneath its hood. Claiming her gloved hand from the pommel, he kissed the damp wool. "Take the greatest care getting home, Harriet," he implored. "It would be easy to become disoriented."

She laughed. "It may be for me, but I am certain Andromache knows where her stable lies. But have a care yourself, sir. You have as far to go."

He still held her hand, unwilling to relinquish it, and she continued to offer it to him. "Others will have broken the ground to the village, and my cottage is no distance beyond that."

"Even so, sir," she said with soft concern. "The bridge will be treacherous."

"I assure you that I will be careful, madam," he said. He

kissed the glove again. "Goodbye, Harriet."

"Goodbye, Royston," she replied with tender warmth. "I shall see you in the morning, weather permitting."

He steadied her horse's head while Tollman mounted the last of the carriage horses, and then Royston followed on foot as the small group left the works. Once on the Kearby road, they soon drew ahead, their horses growing blurry and wraith-like in the snow, and then Royston was alone. He trudged on, glad to have their tracks, yet feeling deeply isolated in his own tiny world of white.

After a while, when the blizzard had all but erased the tracks of the horses, his small world steepened, and he realised he had found the Penny bridge. After that he was in the village and the going got easier. The warm glow from the windows of The Just Swan tempted him, and its jovial company of which he had grown fond, but the light was already fading as the storm brought in premature night, and to invite darkness to join the difficult conditions would be madness.

At the level crossing the gates were against him, but beneath the up starter signal the indistinct figure of a fog man waved him across. Using the picket gate, Royston crossed the lines, and then walked the few yards by the metals to the signal, which hung at danger, the bundled-up man carrying a red signal lantern and watching over the detonators he had clipped to the rail.

The man nodded to Royston as he approached.

"Are the trains yet running?" Royston enquired with some astonishment.

"None have passed for several hours, sir, but we cannot be sure; the telegraph's dead. The signalman reckons the snow's brought the wires down somewhere."

Royston looked up and saw the cables drooping heavily, an inch of ice upon them. "I can well believe that."

"Aye, what soul's seen the likes o' this?" the fog man readily agreed. "The signalman has to stay put until he's relieved, but I can't imagine he'll keep us out much longer. Nothing can be moving in this."

"By rail or by road," noted Royston, then nodded a farewell.

"Safe home, sir," the fog man called after Royston as he walked back to the road.

"You also," Royston called back.

Crossing the Chale was not at all the ordeal Harriet had feared. The open latticework had prevented the snow from building up, although the ironwork was thickly glazed with ice. Royston crossed carefully, keeping to the middle of the bridge, the girders to each side hazy in the beating snow. He reached the far side, and a minute or so later was home.

He went about the side of the cottage to the kitchen door and there, after stamping the snow from his boots, went inside. The kitchen was deserted, but there was a comforting glow from the range.

"Mrs Sparrow?" he called, but his housekeeper did not respond.

Only when he had a candle lit did he see the note on the kitchen table. He read through it quickly. Mrs Sparrow was most apologetic, but had decided she had better get home before the weather grew worse. She was sure Mr Staley would understand. She had left him a crock of stew in the range and had banked the fires before she left.

Royston nodded approvingly. Apart from her predilection for spiritualism, his housekeeper was an eminently practical and no-nonsense woman.

He hung his Ulster to dry by the range, placed his boots before it, and then set a large wash pan of water to heat. Under its blanket of snow, the cottage was for the first time in a week decently warm, and he was intent on exploiting the fact.

Sitting at the kitchen table, he consumed two platefuls of the thick, tasty stew, making a mental note to congratulate Mrs Sparrow upon it. Pleasantly full, he stood at the window, sipping a stiff hot toddy and watching the snowflakes spin and dance in the candlelight. He was sure several feet of snow must have fallen by now, and in such a short time. He wondered how much of England was affected, sure that entire counties would be at a standstill for days.

Royston drew the curtains against the winter night and, finishing off the toddy in the process, made preparations to bathe. Stripping to the waist, he knelt on the rug before the tin laundry tub to wash his hair. That done, he stood, made a final check that the curtains were truly closed, and then removed the remainder of his clothing before stepping naked into the tub, there to stand and lave the rest of him.

The water was good and hot, and the soap lathered freely, and it felt good to scrub the grime from his skin, yet the cottage was draughty and did not encourage lingering over his ablutions. Soon he reached for the towel and dried himself off vigorously, then feeling for the first time in days wonderfully clean, swathed his nakedness in a dressing gown. He tidied up after his bath and then peered through the curtains out into the night; thankfully the snow seemed to be falling more lightly. Refreshing his toddy, he took it through to the parlour, there to lounge pleasantly in the heat of the fire and read.

He soon found his glass empty and padded through to

the kitchen for more. He returned to the fire and, nursing the toddy's warmth in his hands, lazily watched the cheerful flames, feeling supremely content. *Mercury* was progressing well, and if his redesign of the injectors proved remedial, they would soon be pitting her under her own steam against the rollers.

That was certainly reason enough for satisfaction, yet much more so was that he was convinced Harriet favoured him. Royston lounged back and allowed his dressing gown to gape, the coals' heat upon his bare skin agreeable. He sipped at the sweetened rum, recalling how her demeanour had softened towards him and how readily she would place her hand upon his to emphasise a point, and of course the shy smiles he received from her. That naturally set him remembering the Christmas party, and of holding her soft against him, and her ready collusion to the familiarity, and of kissing her beneath the mistletoe, and of more import, the kiss returned in the winter darkness.

Half closing his eyes, he conjectured how long that kiss might have lingered had the drunken revellers not intruded. If he had gently encouraged her lips to tarry, he had the intuition that Harriet would not have protested. And if they were *truly* alone, could not lingering kisses erode the vestiges of detachment and invite passion?

Royston had seen Harriet passionate over many matters, but never of course transfixed with passion. That led to speculation over the moment he yearned for, of being in fervent embrace with the woman whom he so deeply adored, reason lost to them both. Naturally, there was a strong stirring within his dressing gown as his body concurred gladly with his thoughts. He smiled wryly, indulgent of his body's tantalising impatience, yet in his mind he remained steadfast to a path of caution.

The Challenge would have to be theirs before he could ask Harriet to be his.

He shifted in the seat to bring more comfort and took a sharp breath as the weft of the dressing gown dragged over that which was prematurely eager. Warm, comfortable, and pleasantly mellow with rum, two immediate pastimes offered themselves. He deliberated for long moments, and then sighed and picked up his book.

"HAVE YOU SEEN the newspaper, Royston?" said Harriet with a glum expression.

"I have not," he admitted. "I fully intended to purchase one this morning on my way through the village, but there were none to be had."

"They arrived with the first train to make it through the drifts." She then laid the *Birmingham Post* on his desk, presenting him with the headlines.

"Appalling Railway Accident," proclaimed the strident type. "Up Flying Scotsman Collides With Coal Train," "Leeds Express Steams Into Wreckage," and "Many Thought Dead."

"Oh, great heavens!" he gasped, then read through the columns below. "*Both* the expresses were ignoring the signals? How can that be?"

Harriet shrugged. "It must be that the weather was so abysmal that neither footplate could see them."

"But that is precisely why fog men are called out."

"The newspaper makes no mention of fog men at all," said Harriet. "I cannot believe they could countenance running trains without them."

"Yet it seems they did," said Royston. "And the second express was still making at least thirty miles an hour when it came into the wreckage."

"It was that second collision that was the more murderous," she said soberly.

"Yet the paper claims the driver was alerted by the explosion of detonators placed after the accident a good distance back."

"Clearly the train lacked continuous braking."

He shook his head sadly. "The Board of Trade will be more than typically scathing."

"Rightly so, sir," said Harriet with conviction. "Continuous brakes deserve to be mandatory." She then paused. "Father believes one of our locomotives may have been involved."

Royston scanned the paper again. "There appears no blame apportioned to the locomotives, Harriet," he offered sympathetically. "It seems to be wholly driver error."

"I agree, but it is never good business to have an association with any accident."

"There will be an enquiry," he declared. "I am sure Colton and Holm will be completely exonerated."

A SUBDUED MOOD settled over the works for the remainder of the day, and even though Royston's modified injector was still running true when *Mercury*'s safety valves lifted at 220 pounds, no one could summon much will to celebrate. Royston did not begrudge the lack of enthusiasm. There had been days like this at Antrum Ellis and Partners over a loss within the greater railway family.

Over the following days, in which the snow melted away, its malevolent work done, more details of the Abbots Ripton accident emerged. Thirty-seven people had been killed; it was reported the weight of ice on the signal wires had pulled the signals from "danger" to a false "clear" and that, with eleven hundred yards warning, the *Leeds Express* had against all efforts failed to be brought to a stand.

A Colton and Holm locomotive had been involved, but it had been drawing the coal train and survived the accident unscathed. Indeed, it had been crucial in summoning assistance.

It was the letters to the papers that invoked the most alarm. Some wrote to complain about the disgraceful braking arrangements on the express trains, yet others denounced the speed modern expresses were run at, with more than one calling for the Grand Challenge to be abandoned. When trains already run at reckless speeds, argued the writers, why hanker for more?

The letters put Harriet in a high temper. "This is pure Luddism," she proclaimed, "perfectly of the same mould as those who would have us believe passengers would suffocate at speeds greater than thirty miles an hour."

"*The Scotsman* had no chance, Harriet, but that the *Leeds Express* was unable to stop in time does suggest it was travelling too fast," said her father, for they had gathered in his office to discuss the adverse press.

"But that was due to its execrable braking, Father," she

countered. "With proper continuous brakes, they could have pulled up with plenty of room to spare. No, these people wish only an end to progress. They would not have Mr Bouch building his fine bridge across the Tay, the longest in the world, nor have us challenging what can and cannot be achieved on the railway. They would have us back in the days of the canal, with commerce strangled."

"They do seem intent on handing the traffic to the roads," mused Royston.

"Yes, that is it!" exclaimed Harriet. "These letters must be the work of the steamer lobby, Father!"

"Aye, most like they are, Harriet," said Colton with a sigh. "I like it as little as you do, lass, but what can we do?"

"You must write a letter of your own, Father," demanded Harriet firmly. "In it, you must stress the braking issue and that we are not only designing for speed, but also for safety. Why, we are providing unprecedented levels of braking upon *Mercury* and her train."

"Might I suggest, sir," said Royston as Colton considered his daughter's proposal, "that you telegraph Merthyr and Durham and suggest a single letter delivered under the seals of all the competitors?"

"Perhaps you should telegraph Lord Clifton, soliciting his support also, Father?" offered Harriet eagerly.

"Aye, fine ideas both," agreed Colton, "and worthy of putting in hand immediately."

"I also think it wise that we include braking experiments on the final trials, sir," said Royston. "I would have us know the least distance from Paddington that we must effect braking to ensure we do not overrun the buffers."

"From the highest speed the trial metals will allow?" queried Colton.

"Naturally, sir. And the fullest brake application."

"This is going to be yet another of your square-of-the-speed affairs, is it not, Mr Staley," ventured Harriet with a sigh.

He smiled at her. "I am afraid so, madam. Just as we struggle to bring *Mercury* to her full potential, so must we struggle to rid her of it."

10.

Booked Through

"Is that all, miss?" asked Dimity, standing by the bedroom door.

Harriet settled under the covers, glad to get to her bed after what had been a particularly wearisome day. She was about to dismiss her maid but then noticed the unease on Dimity's features. "Unless there is something for your part."

"There is, but I wouldn't keep you from your rest."

"Nonsense. If you wish to talk, then by all means we shall."

"Thank you, miss." Dimity approached and settled on the covers beside Harriet, pulling up her legs and smoothing her skirt over them.

"I assume it concerns my sister," said Harriet, lowering her voice.

"And Veracity. It's been over a fortnight since we were in Malbury; have you decided what we are going to do?"

Harriet sighed, unhappy to be reminded of that dilemma. Indeed, she had been trying not to think of it, although Bianca's continuing "shopping excursions" made it difficult to put the matter completely from her mind.

"I am certain I do not know what to do," she said. "Every possibility brings untold distress."

"How's that, miss?"

Harriet thought on that. "If I broach the subject with Bianca, it will bring her fury upon Veracity, for how else could I have found out? And even if I do talk to my sister, I hold little hope that she will heed my advice."

"And what advice would that be?"

"That she end her attachment with Lord Harlow, of course, before she is compromised."

"I agree, miss. She won't do that, not while she still loves him."

"I could take the matter to my mother. She would certainly put an end to the *affaire*, if only by forbidding Bianca from leaving the house."

"Perhaps that would be for the best."

"Would it, Dimity? Veracity would have Mother *and* Bianca furious with her, and it would be exceedingly difficult to stop her being dismissed in bad standing. There is also the possibility that my sister will guess my hand in ending her *affaire* and rightly hate me for it."

"What about your father, miss? He could talk to Lord Harlow, like."

Harriet shook her head. "I would not burden Father with this. And besides, the marquess is *Mercury*'s sponsor. Father could hardly call him to task and hope also for his continued support. Lord Harlow might even demand the return of the funds advanced and ruin the company."

"Then what *can* we do?"

"Nothing, I fear. We must pray that the *affaire* runs its course and ends as discreetly as it is currently being prosecuted."

"My lord hasn't done well there before," warned Dimity.

"I know, but I quite believe he has learned from his mistakes. The present arrangements are unusually subtle for a man such as he."

"There's still a chance someone will get wind of it though."

"We can only hope that they do not," said Harriet firmly.

Dimity appeared to think on that. "I don't like it, miss."

"Nor I, but I cannot see a way to force the matter to a decent close," said Harriet with exasperation. "And Dimity? I have never seen my sister happier than in these past weeks. To be the one to turn that to misery… Why, I would hate myself as much as my sister might hate me!"

"Does that make your mother suspicious?" said the maid. "Miss Bianca walking on air?"

"It is hardly that marked. And if Mother has noticed, she is more likely to conclude that her machinations regarding Mr Staley are succeeding."

Dimity grinned. "She's backing the wrong horse there, if you don't mind me saying."

Harriet blushed. "You think so?" she asked cautiously.

Her maid smiled. "I saw the two of you together at the Christmas celebration, miss. I'd say your luck's in there."

A burst of joy welled in Harriet. "Truly?"

Dimity cocked her head. "Don't you think so?"

Harriet laughed happily. "I confess I do not know what to think. Mr Staley is very attentive and appears to find any familiarity we share pleasing."

"I think you have him persuaded, miss. Now you must wait for him to summon his courage."

Now Harriet knew impatience. "Is it *so* hard for a man to reveal such sentiments?"

"I can't speak personal, like—no man's made an offer for

me—but I've heard it said, miss. Fear of being given the brush-off, like."

"I would *never* reject Mr Staley."

"'Course you wouldn't. But he can't know that, can he?"

"He must suspect."

"But he's got to have doubts. Takes time to get the better of them, those do."

"I suppose." Harriet thought for a while, then looked back at her maid, who was gazing at her with fond patience. "Dimity?"

"Miss?"

"Recently, when with Mr Staley, I sometimes fall prey to… improper notions."

Dimity smiled slyly. "Like becoming a great deal more familiar with him?"

Harriet blushed and nodded. "It is most wicked of me and perfectly inexcusable, but I seem not to be able to help myself."

"Don't worry yourself over it, miss. We all have such thoughts."

"We do?"

"No one's to know, and no one mentions it, but I'm sure it's true all the same," said Dimity. "I certainly have 'em for a man who pleases my eye."

"But it can be perfectly involuntary," confessed Harriet. "Once, Mr Staley simply smiled at me, and suddenly I was… well, quite affected."

"Oh-ho, that is serious."

"It is? Am I abnormal?"

"Lor' no! I meant that you're *very* taken with the gentleman."

"As you were with Tom?"

"Not Tom," said Dimity scornfully. "I was *very* much affected by him, but it wasn't by a look, if you get my drift. But Tom wasn't my first attachment, miss. Eddy was my first, and I had it real bad for him. He could do right mischief to me with just a glance."

"So did he not love you in return?" asked Harriet sympathetically.

"Oh, I'm certain he did, but it didn't come to anything. It was scary and secret and wonderful at the time, but after a while things went off the boil, particularly on his side. We were seeing less and less of each other, and then I entered service and we lost touch completely."

"That's so sad," murmured Harriet.

Dimity shrugged. "It is and it isn't, miss. Looking back, I can't see how I thought it could last; we weren't that far beyond being kids, really."

"Was it Eddy who… claimed your virtue?"

Dimity nodded softly.

"Were you scared?"

The maid pondered that for a few moments. "Nervous certainly, but not scared." Her face grew passive in the gaslight. "I was clumsy and so was he, and it hurt, and I really could have done without the stink of the fish market, but we both wanted it to happen."

"Both of you?"

Dimity grinned. "Oh yes, miss. We were right set on each other, and things had got to where I had no will to resist." She frowned, searching for words. "It felt right."

"Goodness," breathed Harriet. "But did you wish afterwards that you had not succumbed?"

Dimity pursed her lips, as if deciding. "No. It had to happen sometime, like, and soon Eddy and I got a lot less clumsy and I realised what I'd been denying myself."

"Don't you ever worry that no man will now marry you?"

"What, because of those before?"

Harriet nodded.

"Not me, miss. I'd not marry a man that set on his own importance anyway."

Harriet laughed. "There is some truth to that statement."

"See, I don't think of myself as a wicked girl," said Dimity with a serious frown. "I'm choosy who I walk out with—there's only been three since Eddy. Nor did I leap straight into bed with 'em, miss, but waited to make sure they're reliable and discreet. None of them turned into marriage, and with Tom I'm glad of it, but they *might* have. Even so, I'm a happy girl. I enjoyed my time with each one of 'em and don't regret my behaviour at all."

"You are forward, Dimity, but I have never thought you wicked."

"Thank you, miss."

"But now I should send you to your bed; again it is late for both of us."

"Just like Newcastle, eh, miss?" said the maid, sliding from the bed.

"I have very fond memories of our talks then, Dimity."

"Me too, miss. Goodnight, miss."

"Goodnight, Dimity."

Harriet watched Dimity move to the door. "Oh—Dimity?"

"Yes, miss?"

"The fish market? Truly?"

"Close by it, yes. Beggars can't be choosers, miss, not

when you're right scared of getting found out." She grinned. "The smell o' 'em still brings memories. It can leave me quite unsettled in the kitchen, like."

Harriet laughed. "Goodnight, Dimity."

"Goodnight, miss."

ROYSTON STOOD BY the test shop in the cold predawn, mist drifting over his feet from the neighbouring fields, watching *Mercury* move for the first time under her own steam, pulling slowly forward to clear the points that would guide her back to him. He was not alone witnessing this moment; for his part he thought the loss of sleep well-rewarded.

Mercury always seemed impressive within the fitting shop, and now Royston found her as remarkable outside it. Much was due to her sheer size but also evident in her voice—the potent throaty beat of her chimney as each cylinder exhausted in turn—and in the quiet yet supreme self-assurance the locomotive projected.

With the hiss of steam brakes, she came to a halt, waiting for a hand to play pointsman and wave his green lantern. *Mercury*'s whistle sang out—briefly, but deep and vaguely menacing—and as the sound echoed between the buildings, she began to sedately back up, the beat of her exhaust ponderous.

As the locomotive negotiated the first set of points, Royston saw Harriet leaning out from the cab, her hand on the regulator and her fine features composed yet grave. A lump came to his throat. At that very moment he felt so proud of her, that she could bring such a wonderful machine into existence and be mistress of it also.

Mercury slowed as she approached, then slowed more as she passed Royston, the complexity of her driving gear easing slowly over, a delicate motion even when executed by heavy bars slick with oil, each playing its part in transmitting the fury of the steam to the driving wheels. Her tender was now in the shop, and then the locomotive itself was creeping over the rollers until, with a sudden hiss of brakes, she came to a halt, her squat chimney under the larger one piercing the roof.

Royston walked down the locomotive's length, then grabbed her handrails and climbed up into the cab, where Harriet was busily setting the motion out of gear as Carstairs screwed down the handbrake.

"Well," he demanded. "How does she answer?"

Harriet turned to him and grinned broadly. "I quite feared she would put me straight through the paint shop, but truly she is the most well-natured giant, Mr Staley. I simply cannot wait to take her out on the line."

"I am afraid that will be a little while yet, madam," replied Royston.

"Truly, sir, but at least the dates have been set," she replied, crouching to assess the slumbering fire, then checking the sight glasses carefully.

"They have?"

"Most certainly. A significant period of notice must be given when requesting running rights from a railway company. We have been granted them for the first and third Sunday of March."

Royston frowned. "That will only give us three weeks before the Challenge itself."

She nodded, clearly uncomfortable with the timing also. "We can only pray we encounter no major issues during the line trials."

THE MEN WERE already festooning *Mercury* with the same pipes, wires, and rods as at the previous tests, although now of course she had no need of the swaddled umbilical to the works boilers. Royston watched but felt he was loitering and, soon after, superfluous. He therefore left, leaving word to be called if needed.

Once in his office, it being still well before normal hours, he read the newspaper. With their letter, Colton and his competitors had stoked new life in the debate over the merits and demerits of the Challenge, and he noted with satisfaction that opinion had begun to run their way. The paper done with, he went for a hearty if greasy breakfast, sharing the canteen with the forge shift.

Returning to his office afterwards, he suddenly found himself at a complete loss as to what to do. His work with books and slide rule now stood in the test shop awaiting judgement. If problems were encountered, then he would again become useful, but what was he to do until then? He could never abide being indolent.

He supposed he could consider how to improve the prototype for the production class, but he thought *Mercury*'s design to be basically sound. Improvements would only suggest themselves when they knew her foibles.

Perhaps he should go back and watch the preparations

for the trials? He certainly wished to be there when they ran her hard; he only hoped the hammer-blow of her cylinders didn't bring the whole building down upon her. The vibrations would certainly be worse if she had the conventional two cylinders rather than six, but he remembered the first trials, and now she wouldn't be limited by the inadequacy of remote boilers.

Then Royston remembered the challenge Hackett had made to Colton over racing steamers. That would certainly be a complete change from *Mercury*; instead of the issues of extrapolating larger, he'd have to worry about making everything as small and light as possible.

Taking up his daybook, he began to sketch. Soon, however, the sense of being on the periphery of matters became too much to abide. He closed the office door and donned overalls.

Returning to the test shop, he clambered up into *Mercury*'s cab.

"Miss Colton," he said, "would you accept me upon your footplate?"

"With pleasure, Mr Staley," she replied with a warm smile.

THE TRIALS AGAIN began slowly, and Royston found it relatively simple to adjust the strength of the fire to *Mercury*'s work, all the time with an eye on the boiler water level. But as the trials continued into the next day and *Mercury* worked harder, balancing everything became more of a stimulating challenge. The conditions steadily grew more onerous, with the firebox burning brighter and throwing out more heat and *Mercury's* toil louder in the confined test shop. Her exhaust soon lost the steady beat of a conventional engine and instead became more a great growl, husky and deep.

Harriet and he were slouching on the padded tender bench between runs, water-soaked towels wrapped about their necks and glad for the respite. Royston had just been regretting the gap between them when Colton unexpectedly pulled himself up onto the footplate.

"Something's amiss." Colton handed Harriet a sheaf of indicator charts.

His daughter flicked through them. "Oh," she said, worriedly. Royston shared her concern.

"Steam feeds?" she suggested.

"Indeed, it looks like cylinder starvation, but the onset of that should be much higher," said Royston. "The valve timing must be out of synchronisation."

Harriet scoffed. "Come, sir, that would have shown up immediately." She stared hard at the charts. "What if the centrifugal compensator is not increasing the valve throw as it should?"

Royston looked at Colton. "Are all the cylinders exhibiting the same behaviour?"

"Aye, they are," Colton affirmed.

"Steam feed problems would not affect each set equally. It must be the compensator," said Royston. "We had best have its covers off for the next run."

Harriet pushed herself from the seat wearily, smoothing down her skirts.

"No, I can attend to it," he told her. "Indeed, I quite

insist. Your duty is here."

She seemed surprised, but grateful.

Royston gathered a small team of fitters, and they clambered down into the darkness beneath *Mercury*, laden with lamps, stepladders, and tools.

Several feet in diameter, the centrifugal governor was mounted horizontally between the bottom of the boiler and the central drive axle. They set up ladders beneath it, and as *Mercury* creaked and hissed over their heads, dripping hot condensate on them, they worked at loosening the shroud that protected the mechanism.

Once the shroud was off, Royston inspected the arrangement of bronze arms, each tipped with a leaden weight. Everything appeared in order. He tried tugging at an arm but could not shift it. That didn't surprise him greatly; the mechanism was only meant to actuate when the whole assembly was spinning at great speed.

He clambered down. "You men may leave. Give Mr Colton my compliments and ask him to undertake a brief run at the last speed. I will stay and observe the compensator."

They laid down the stepladders and retreated. Royston looked at the drums at each side of him, soon to be in furious motion, and decided it might be prudent to sit down on one of the ladders rather than be shaken from his feet.

"Are you ready, sir?" asked Colton, clinging to *Mercury*'s frame as he peered down between the drive wheels.

"Quite ready, sir," declared Royston.

He heard shouts and responses, and then with a groan, the drive wheels began to slowly turn. He pitched up his lantern and watched the heavy compensator picking up speed in sympathy. Soon in the darkness the concrete beneath Royston was shuddering violently as *Mercury*'s roar competed with the banshee howl of the drum brakes, whilst on all sides spun metal at deadly speeds.

Royston was as thrilled as he was fearful. There was something unbelievably inspiring about witnessing at close quarters so much power unleashed; Royston had a sudden appreciation of Harriet's passion for the practical.

He was not down here for his entertainment though. Setting his teeth against the vibration, he stared at the compensator, now a shimmering blur. That was in order, yet the blur was no larger than the assembly had been at rest... The weighted arms weren't extending at all. He looked then at the bell cranks that conveyed the arms' outward motion upwards to the valve gear, and they confirmed the same story.

Gradually the assault on his senses diminished and *Mercury*'s drive wheels slowed to a stop. Royston stood up cautiously, then walked a little unsteadily out of the inspection pit with his unwelcome news.

IT TOOK A day and a half under *Mercury*'s cold boiler, a set of heavier weights, the replacement of various springs, and several badly cricked necks to resolve the issue with the compensator and allow them to recommence the testing. The compensator now answered perfectly, and they set about experimenting and adjusting, fine tuning the locomotive's power at speed. Finally they were running her as fast as the rollers could tolerate, *Mercury* filling the shed with steam and quaking thunder, and with plentiful more power to give.

Colton brought the trials to a close. "She answers perfectly at 150 miles an hour," he declared, "and I can see nothing on the charts to hold her back from going faster."

Royston and Harriet shared a look of nervous, bright-eyed wonder. The current speed record was 122 miles an hour. To achieve 150 in the Challenge would bring great admiration. To achieve higher would make them ... why, gods in their profession!

THE EUPHORIA PROVED, however, ephemeral. As Harriet drove *Mercury* back to the fitting shop, Royston rode the footplate, savouring the novelty of the great locomotive moving under her own power.

"I wonder," Harriet said thoughtfully as they waited for their road to be set, "how fare our competitors?"

"In terms of what speeds they are achieving?"

"Of course. They must be designing for above the speed record, but by how much?"

"I cannot even speculate," Royston replied. "We would need to place an Evan Evans in both their camps to know the truth, madam."

"Better men than Evan Evans, sir. I am certain he has learned little to our competitors' advantage."

"Let us only hope he is the only one in Pennydale who is in another's pay," he suggested darkly.

She shuddered. "I pray that is so. Nor would I see Colton

and Holm tarnish itself by being a party to skulduggery."

"I would not expect less of you or your father, Harriet." Royston didn't categorise the false information they'd served up to Evans as skulduggery; rather, it was a necessary defensive *response* to skulduggery, and a relatively harmless one at that. "We shall make honest competition, we shall demand of *Mercury* her utmost, and we shall always know that whatever the outcome, we tried our best."

Yet as *Mercury* drew into the fitting shop, Royston looked thoughtfully at her outer cladding standing upon blocks to one side of the shop, part framing and part a shell of smoothed metal. Had the competition realised the wind-drag factor also? *Or might someone have told them?*

HARRIET ATTACKED HER lamb chops with gusto, glad that the trials were complete and a success. Bianca and her mother ate their dinner more delicately, and Father absently, his thoughts elsewhere.

Lady Alicia dabbed at her lips with her napkin.

"Lady Mallow has invited us to a ball, Samuel."

"Another ball at Tharrington Hall, Mama?" echoed Bianca with sudden delight. "What good news!"

Father, however, did not respond but seemed instead entranced with his lamb.

Lady Alicia sighed. "Samuel?" she said with greater emphasis.

"Hmm?" Father emerged from his reverie. "Pardon, my dear?"

"I was just saying that Lady Mallow has invited us to a ball."

"Ah. Another charity event, one presumes," he said warningly.

"Of course, but please do not be tiresome, Samuel," said Mother with mild exasperation. "The needy are not always to be found at home."

"And what cause does it serve, my dear?"

"The County Foundlings and Waifs Workhouse. Yes, I do realise it is again the same cause, but the weight of the new roof apparently caused the foundations to crumble."

Father accepted this in silent disbelief, then returned his attention to his plate. "Civil engineers," he muttered grimly.

"When is the ball, Mama?" asked Bianca.

"On the nineteenth. Its theme is that of Valentine's Day."

"Do you think that Mr Staley shall be invited?" asked Harriet, mustering the idlest curiosity of which she was capable.

"I'd hope so," stated Father. "He seemed to fit in well with the Mallow's usual circle."

"Except with that Army gentleman," suggested Harriet, recalling the antipathy.

"Colonel Prestbury? Oh, don't mind him, Harriet." Father chuckled. "He's not had a good word for anything since the Crimea."

"Now, Samuel," said Lady Alicia reproachfully. "You must not instil in your daughters a poor opinion of Colonel Prestbury. He is an important person within the county and has a splendid reputation."

"I don't doubt it, my dear. I simply find him irascible and irritating."

"He is that, I fear," allowed Lady Alicia sadly. Then she brightened. "Never fear; Lady Mallow is sure to remember to invite Mr Staley." Her warm assurances were for her younger daughter, even though it was the elder who had enquired.

Harriet, however, was pleased for Mother to maintain her delusion of making a match for Bianca. She was quite aware how dismally her prospects with Royston were viewed by her mother and would rather not give her any reason to air those hurtful opinions again—especially since Harriet was feeling quite buoyant over the matter.

"And thankfully we shall be spared Lord Harlow's presence," continued Mother. "It is quite irresponsible to expose respectable young ladies to his kind, whatever their rank. They can be incredibly foolish and might fall under his influence."

With dismay, Harriet saw that her sister was blushing fiercely. That might be condonable, yet the guilt in her face was not. Harriet had to act quickly before Mother noticed. By no means dim-witted, she was sure to infer the true reason and wreck all possibility of a discrete close to Bianca's *affaire*.

"A lady should be free to act as she chooses in such matters," Harriet stated, borrowing Dimity's philosophy and knowing full well the maelstrom she courted.

Mother glared at her, outraged. "What absolute nonsense!" she blustered. "A lady must guard her reputation with the utmost care if she is to be accepted in society."

"Then why are gentlemen not held to the same standards, Mother?" Harriet pushed the point, wanting to give Bianca more time to recover. "They may consort with women, and provided they are neither profligate nor indiscreet, they are held up as ideal marriage material."

"Harriet!" exclaimed Mother. "You are being utterly uncivilised."

Good, the damning look on Bee's face had vanished; instead she was watching the sudden skirmish with astonishment. "Yet my observation is correct, Mother," Harriet said.

"I do not know where you get your ideas," said Mother angrily. "I cannot believe they come from that ladies' society you attend. I am sure Her Majesty would withdraw her patronage if she learnt it to be so!"

"Harriet, this isn't appropriate dinner conversation," said Father gruffly.

Harriet sighed with relief. "Of course, Father. I apologise."

"It is not appropriate conversation at any time," decreed Lady Alicia.

"Let it be, my dear," said Father. "Harriet's observation is awkward, yet nevertheless accurate."

"This is what happens when the concept of Entitlement is taken too far," said Lady Alicia. "Genteel society is threatened."

Harriet itched to respond, but she never had wanted to argue with Mother; she only wanted to protect Bee. Fortunately, Lady Alicia read a sort of victory in Harriet's silence and allowed the matter to drop.

"WHAT POSSESSED YOU, Harriet?" demanded Father in the library after dinner. "Surely you knew that opinion would rile your Mother."

"I'm sorry, Father, but I was having difficulty with her attitude that girls are sheep to be guarded from the wolf. The concept is terribly old-fashioned."

"Its day is not as done as you'd like, and you'd be wise to remember it."

Harriet blushed. "I am not intending to philander."

Father laughed. "I'm glad to hear of it."

"It is more the spirit of the matter. If society turns a blind eye to certain behaviour by gentlemen, they should also do so for a lady. Or the blind eye should not be turned at all."

"You're telling me what I've already heard once to-night," cautioned Father, but then relented. "Whilst I admire your principles, if you expect the world to change at any pace, you'll be setting yourself up for long disappointment."

"I realise that. But no change will happen at all unless people speak up."

"That's true also, Lass. But maybe not to your Mother, eh?"

"Yes, Father."

"Now, I wanted a word about *Mercury*."

Harriet grinned. "I am so pleased with her, Father."

"Aye, I'm proud of her too. But I'm also worried. Too much rides on the Challenge."

"I know that, but I'm confident. Truly I am."

"My worry is with our competition. They're small companies also, and risking much if not all on winning the Challenge. They may become desperate and try desperate tactics."

"We already know that. The spy that was put amongst us, and there may be others we do not know of."

"It might go further than espionage. I'm worried about

sabotage. I'm going to increase the watchmen, particularly around the fitting shop at night."

Harriet nodded. "That seems prudent."

"And before we take her out on any run—and before the Challenge itself—I want you and Mr Staley to go over her inch by inch, looking for anything that might have been interfered with. That goes for anything attached to her drawbar also."

"Yes, Father. We trust Benjamin and Carstairs as well, do we not?"

"Aye, they can assist."

"It shall be as you wish." Harriet took a sip of her port wine.

"Good. Now the other business is who is to be at *Mercury*'s regulator for the Challenge."

Harriet was taken aback. "I assumed it would be me, Father," she said fiercely. "I have experience on the main line, and I know *Mercury* intimately."

"Aye, all that is so," acknowledged Father, "and I expected you to say that, but you do realise the danger, don't you, Harriet? We'll not have a chance to push *Mercury* to her full speed until the Challenge itself, and a catastrophe at those speeds would certainly claim the footplate crew."

"All the more reason that I should be on her footplate. I built *Mercury*; it is hardly right to ask another to risk their life upon her."

"I have more in her construction than you, Harriet. I got us into this business, didn't I?" responded Father. "I am minded to renew my main line ticket."

"Nonsense," snorted Harriet. "The company needs you far more than I, as does the family. You know that is the truth."

Father sighed. "As much as it pains me, you are right."

"Of course I am. You assent to me being at her regulator?"

Father nodded. "I do. We'll need a second driver though, in case you fall ill on the day of the Challenge."

"Benjamin?" she suggested. "He has his main line ticket also. Goodness, he taught me to drive."

Her father thought on that. "I'll not order any man aboard *Mercury*, but I'll ask Ben if he's up for it. He may think he's a little long in the years."

"I think he would be most insulted that you think that, Father."

"No, Harriet, it's whether *he* feels that way. I believe him still sharp."

"Oh… yes, I see."

"And I shall ask Carstairs to stoke for you."

"Or Mr Royston," said Harriet, instantly warming to the idea of having that particular company upon the Challenge. "He managed the boiler very well in the trials, and it is not at all forgiving."

"Then if he agrees, we have a second fireman," said Father. "The Great Western will provide us a guard; it is a stipulation Sir Daniel made in having the Challenge upon his metals. I presume it will be a volunteer."

"We will also need a team of fitters at both Bristol and Paddington."

"That was my thinking also, and they can serve to guard *Mercury*."

Harriet slowly shook her head. "I cannot say I care to consider this darker side."

"Aye, none of us do, Harriet, but I am afraid we have to," said Father unhappily.

11.

Is Line Clear For...?

Harriet accepted Father's hand to alight from the carriage. They were stuck in the logjam of conveyances arriving at Tharrington Hall, but Bianca was eager and Mother indulgent, and it was but a short walk to the door.

It was a breezy night, and Harriet was glad of her cloak as she and Bianca followed their parents, the gravel crunching under the feet, passing between motley barouches, landaus, and phaetons, harnesses jingling as the horses grew impatient.

Father looked back to his daughters.

"Well, Harriet, what do you make of her?" He indicated a small steamer almost lost amongst the parked carriages. It was narrow and low, with a rear boiler sunk into cherry-red coachwork, its chromed chimney rakishly angled back. The driving bench was not a bench at all but a padded leather recliner, complete with antimacassars. The cylinders were set forward and glistened in the carriage lamps. They, the chimney, the coachwork, and even the antimacassars bore the silhouette of a winged horse, caught in full flight.

"It is hardly discreet, Father." Harriet grimaced.

Father laughed. "No indeed, but do you think she will answer?"

Harriet gauged the cylinder diameter and stroke. "Well enough, I imagine, although I would not care to ride her at speed, particularly upon corners."

Father nodded thoughtfully. "Cost a good bit o' tin, I imagine."

"Her form appears arranged purely to exaggerate her price," said Harriet dismissively.

"Aye, like"—Father appeared to remember who else was present and quickly rethought his words—"as not." He looked at the steamer wistfully.

Harriet had a sudden premonition. "Goodness, you are not considering acquiring one yourself?"

How could this machine seduce Father's head? He was usually eminently sensible.

He laughed. "Nay, lass, but you recall Mr Hackett's proposition?"

"Racing steamers? Of course, yet this is not a racing steamer, merely a poor pretence."

"Samuel? Harriet? Please can we go? It is cold," chided Mother.

"I'm sorry, my dear. But of course," said Father.

THEIR OUTERWEAR WAS spirited away by the Mallows' servants, and the Coltons passed into the crowded reception room garlanded in pink crepe and filled mostly with familiar attendees.

"Colton!" A boisterous Sir Geoffrey approached them with Lady Mallow upon his hand. "I declare I have not seen one whit of you these three months, sir."

"It must be that," allowed Father. "I'm afraid I've had far too much on my hands of late."

"Lady Alicia intimated as much." Sir Geoffrey lowered his voice. "The Challenge, eh? It can't be that long now."

"Fifty days exactly, Sir Geoffrey," said Harriet. It was difficult to put from her mind since the number was inscribed in bold chalk upon the fitting shop wall and Benjamin decremented it daily.

Sir Geoffrey acknowledged that with a nod. "A word to the wise, Samuel," he said confidentially, but not so much that Harriet could not overhear. "There's a gentleman and his, ah, lady present tonight who has no love for the railways."

Father glanced at Harriet, his eyes recommending caution, then back to Sir Geoffrey. "Who is this gentleman?"

"A Mr Mordecai Leyland. He recently took up the lease on Renton House; it seemed ill manners not to welcome him into the area."

"Most certainly," agreed Lady Alicia.

"And why does he hold railways in such poor opinion?" enquired Harriet, yet in a discreet tone.

"He has come into means through the construction of steamers, Miss Colton," replied Sir Geoffrey. "You may observe him by the harpsichord, conversing with your Mr Staley."

Wistfully hoping that Mr Royston was truly hers, Harriet looked through the throng and saw him, so impeccably turned out, in animated conversation with a shorter gentleman, pugnacious in manner, with a wiry build and sandy hair so profusely oiled as to catch the candlelight. Under his tail-coat, he wore a bright red cummerbund instead of a waistcoat. Hanging off his arm was a lady in a gown of a similar red that advertised her bosom to all, her raven hair a snide play upon abandon, long locks of fallen hair conjoined with meticulous braids. Harriet guessed which vehicle they had arrived in, and took an instant dislike to them both.

ROYSTON WAS FINDING it increasingly difficult to retain his temper. Not only was Leyland brash and condescending, but also Mrs Leyland had once again set her glass down on the fine polish of the Shudi buff-stopped harpsichord. She insisted on doing so, and clumsily, despite all Royston's disapproving glances.

"Oh come, sir," proclaimed Leyland. "Travel by trains is tiresome—all this changing and so forth—whereas a steamer takes one door-to-door. What could be better?"

"I hardly think it affordable," argued Royston. "The private hire of a steamer for long distance—"

"Who says hire?" cut in Leyland. "Everyone will insist on owning their own machine."

Royston allowed himself to laugh. "Everyone of great means, certainly, but—"

"Not great, sir. As the manufactories grow larger and production increases, so will steamers become within the grasp of even those of quite modest means."

"Good evening, Mr Staley," murmured a soft voice.

Royston turned with gladness. "Ah, good evening, Miss Colton."

She was wearing a gown of soft blue with a low-cut back that permitted the pleasing contrast of her russet locks against her unblemished milky shoulders, as well as enticing conjecture to what lay beneath the fabric. It was a much more beguiling arrangement than that of Mrs Leyland, who clearly considered a man's imagination unreliable.

He turned to the couple beside him. "May I introduce Miss Harriet Colton? Miss Colton, this is Mr and Mrs Mordecai Leyland."

Leyland bowed slightly, Miss Harriet made a diminutive curtsy, and Mrs Leyland reached for her glass.

"Leyland was just espousing how everyone of any means whatsoever will soon own a steamer," said Royston.

"Great heavens! What a frightful prospect."

Leyland frowned. "How so, madam?"

"Purely from the chaos, sir. There would be so many steamers that they could barely move for each other. Indeed, it would be quicker to walk."

Leyland shrugged. "Improvements will of course be necessary to the roads."

"But what of the city streets? Would you have buildings torn down for the sake of steamers?"

"You exaggerate, madam," he said dismissively.

"I am certain I do not."

"And what of freight, sir?" asked Royston. "Would you see that go to the steamers also?"

"Of course. Just as passengers are inconvenienced, so are goods. Steamers would prevent all trans-shipment."

"But at greater cost," countered Harriet. "A steamer cannot match the rails for efficiency."

"The gap will narrow as road steamers grow larger."

"There, and now we have roads clogged with private

steamers and behemoth freight steamers," declared Harriet. "I cannot see how that will be anything but detrimental to the commerce of the realm."

"I have already allowed that the trunk roads will need much improvement," said Leyland.

"But even with your larger steamers, you will still increase the cost of transportation and render us less competitive with other nations," said Harriet.

"My, you're full of opinion, aren't you," murmured Mrs Leyland.

"It is rather more than opinion, Mrs Leyland," suggested Royston. "Miss Colton speaks with authority. She is a professional engineer."

"You are?" said Mrs Leyland, with a sudden superior smirk. "Well, never mind, dear. It's better than nothing."

There was a sudden cold silence.

Then Leyland said, "By that Maxine means to say that—"

"Thank you, sir, but it is quite obvious what was intended," said Harriet evenly, although with colour in her cheeks. "Come, Mr Staley." She turned and strode away.

Royston quickly caught up with her. "I am sorry to have introduced you. I truly have no idea why Leyland would have married such a ghastly creature."

"Do not read overmuch in the presence of a ring." Harriet snorted softly. "And as to why he tolerates her presence... must I employ Greek, sir?"

"No... No, I quite believe it unnecessary," murmured Royston.

THEY REJOINED COLTON and Sir Geoffrey. Lady Alicia and Lady Mallow were conversing with a middle-aged lady in a bath chair.

"I see you were talking to Leyland, Staley," said Colton. "Would you favour me with your opinion of him?"

Royston reflected for a moment. "A zealot for steamers, sir," he opined, "and quite deaf to reason."

"They *are* his livelihood," noted Colton tolerably.

"No, Samuel, I believe Staley has his mark." Sir Geoffrey nodded towards the lady in the bath chair. "He was trying to press a steamer upon Mrs Worthington, and the poor woman suffering from such maladies as one can only imagine."

Lady Alicia joined them. "I hope you are not neglecting poor Bianca, sir," she admonished Royston gently.

"Of course not, Lady Alicia," he said with a bow. "If you would excuse me, Sir Geoffrey, Miss Colton, sir."

With an inward sigh he went about the mother's bidding. As he left, he heard Miss Harriet also murmur her excuses.

IN THE CLOAKROOM, Harriet stared miserably into the looking glass. She might have retained her poise with the Leyland woman, yet the slight had struck cruelly home. Did everyone perceive her as a pitiable soul, so plain that a husband was beyond reach and immersing herself in a profession to try to forget? Her hair was mousy and lacked lustre, her chin manly and unsubtle, and she had not the silken complexion men favoured, for she had sacrificed it to grease and cleanser.

Was that foul woman right and she was cruelly deluding herself about Royston? There was no doubt he enjoyed her company, but were her dreams of his affections just that? Dreams?

At that moment he would be dancing with Bee. She trusted Dimity that there was nothing but politeness there, but what would happen when Lord Harlow threw Bee over? There would be Royston… so kind, clever, witty, handsome… and suitable. Harriet wished her sister no ill but also wished that men were not so swayed by simple beauty. Bee was delicate, flawless in face and form, whereas she was unreasonably tall, Harriet-shaped, and capable of freeing the hold-down bolts of cylinder heads.

Damn Lord Harlow! Harriet would have taken a wager with a Scot that he would be here tonight. Bianca had been so delighted when the ball was announced, and almost insufferably excited through the slow carriage ride from Pennydale House, that Harriet was certain that arrangements had been made.

Perhaps Bee would be disappointed. Perhaps Lord Harlow had vowed to be here and would later offer plausible excuses? After all, what was the attraction of a ball in polite company compared to that mean cottage close by Malbury?

She stared at her reflection. There were matters she might fix, but why bother? She might as well resign herself to an evening of Mother's company and Mrs Worthington's afflictions.

Leaving the cloakroom in a cheerless mood, Harriet went in search of port wine and petitioned the footman to pour generously. Returning to the reception room, she could not help but look in upon those already dancing. Royston's partner wasn't Bee but Cecily Mallow, the latter enjoying the dance with simple delight. He saw her at the door, and immediately his features expressed a fondness that warmed Harriet more than the port wine—and made her content to return to Mother's company.

"LADY ALICIA, SIR Geoffrey, Lady Mallow, ladies and gentlemen," announced the butler. "The Most Honourable The Marquess of Harlow, Earl of Kimstanton, Baron Ravensworth."

Harriet looked up to see my lord beaming genially on the company. He wore a frock coat and trousers of cream and pink brocade, gilded leaves were upon his brow, and he bore a bow and quiver adorned with ribbons. Goose-fletched arrows protruded from the quiver, the feathers stained pink. Soberly dressed, Hackett loitered behind him in the hallway.

"Oh, how *excessively* tiresome," muttered Lady Alicia between gritted teeth.

Lord Harlow advanced upon their host. "Sir Geoffrey." He sketched a bow. "Once again I intrude upon your hospitality, I fear."

"You are most welcome, my lord," allowed Sir Geoffrey, bowing deeply.

"I confess I enjoyed your fireworks diversion so much that I spoke well of it to many. So much so that word you were holding another splendid event reached me at my London Club, espoused by those rueing their lack of invitation. What could I do then but throw myself upon your generosity?"

Sir Geoffrey was overwhelmed. "You honour us by your presence, my lord. And may I congratulate you on your splendid interpretation of the occasion."

"I would have wished for the wings," confessed Lord Harlow, "but my agent thought they would prove intrusive. He did, however, ensure otherwise I had the proper accessories." He reached for the quiver and withdrew an arrow. "Are they not most authentic?"

The broad steel arrowhead glinted blue and deadly in the candlelight.

The marquess dropped it back into the quiver. "Ah, Colton. How fares our big engine?"

"Most satisfactorily, my lord," answered Father. "We shall be conducting full trials very soon."

"Very good, very good," said the marquess. "Did my agent mention the racing steamer notion?"

"He did," replied Father, but then added softly, "but might I make you aware that we have a potential rival here tonight?"

The marquess looked slightly foolish. "Oh, yes, Hackett did mention it. Completely slipped my mind." He leant closer to Father; Harriet struggled to catch his words. "I do think trying my hand at racing steamers would be stimulating and would be delighted to have a part in it."

"We're determined to view that proposal most sympathetically once the Challenge is won," Father assured him.

"Capital, sir!" The marquess turned and bowed. "Lady Alicia, Lady Mallow. I trust you are perfectly well."

"In the most perfect health, my lord," replied Lady Mallow, and Mother acknowledged the same with a gentle nod and slightly fixed smile. "May I introduce Mrs Worthington of Hapton Chase?"

"Delighted," said the marquess. "And your health, madam?"

Mrs Worthington was completely flustered by the arrival of senior nobility. "Most well, my lord. It is kind of you to ask."

"I am gratified to hear it," he replied heartily, and then he noticed Bianca loitering at the edge of the small group. "Ah, and here is my Psyche."

An unfortunate allegory, thought Harriet. If she remembered her mythology correctly, Cupid had treated his wife quite abominably.

"Good evening, my lord," said Bianca shyly.

"Would you dance, my lady?" he asked, with a careful bow.

"If it would please you, my lord."

"Indeed it would." The marquess offered his arm to Bianca and then turned to the company. "If you would all excuse us."

LEAVING THE DANCE floor with Miss Mallow, Royston was surprised to meet the marquess and Miss Bianca in the opposite direction. Royston bowed and Miss Mallow curtsied, and the marquess acknowledged them both with an affable nod.

"Goodness, I am sure Mother did not expect Lord Harlow tonight," murmured Miss Mallow.

"No indeed," said Royston. "But here he is."

Miss Mallow recognised a friend at the refreshments, and that allowed Royston to take his leave of her without awkwardness. He walked back to where he had last seen Miss Harriet and in doing so passed behind Colonel Prestbury, in conversation with the convivial farmer Ramsgate.

"Leyland has me quite convinced over armoured steamers," pronounced the military gentleman.

Curious, Royston paused.

"He were at me over land steamers," admitted Ramsgate "Go anywhere, tow anything?"

"And as a platform for ordinance of course. Imagine—a dreadnought of the battlefield!"

"Heavier than your land steamer then," mused Ramsgate, with a surreptitious wink to Royston.

The colonel didn't see the trap. "I allow they may be somewhat leisurely," he said, "yet quite invincible."

"Completely invisible too," noted Ramsgate. "Good military advantage, that."

Royston read the puzzlement in the colonel's stance. "How do you mean, sir?"

"A neighbour o' mine tried a land steamer. It sank to its frames in the mud. Took 'em a week to dig out. With luck, a land dreadnought would vanish completely."

It was the appropriate moment for Royston to move on.

He discovered Miss Harriet sitting alone and thoughtful. Quite nearby, Colton conversed with Sir Geoffrey and Lady Mallow, but Lady Alicia was nowhere to be seen.

"Would you dance, Miss Colton?" he asked.

"Indeed I would, sir." She replied with a smile that lifted his spirits, which were elevated further when in their first waltz the rapport of the Christmas party so naturally returned.

WHEN ROYSTON WENT to furnish them with refreshments, Harriet happily dived into the cloakroom to make quick repairs to her appearance. From the depths of despondency she'd been thrown up to nervous joy, and all for having Royston close against her, his gaze fond and undivided.

"No, tighter, Belinda!" said a muffled voice from one of the closed doors.

"You look rather… forward already, dear Cora," offered a second voice hesitantly.

"Tighter," insisted the first voice. "I must emphasise my womanliness."

There was then a series of grunts. "There. That is as tight as I dare have you, Cora."

"But have you seen that Leyland woman?" gasped the first voice with some difficulty. "I will be quite drab if I am not at least her equal."

"But you are now… passing wanton," protested Belinda. "Besides, I greatly fear Miss Colton already has completely captivated him, as he has her. Did you not see them dance?"

Harriet frowned into the mirror. She hadn't been paying attention to Bee and Lord Harlow—quite naturally only having eyes for Royston—but that others had so readily noticed the affection between them did not bode well. No, not at all.

Cora was not to be so easily dissuaded. "If you are truly

my friend, Belinda, have me tighter."

There was a pause, a protracted groan of effort, then the sudden sound of fine material sundering, silence, and bitter tears.

"Goodness," cried Belinda in horror. "Oh, gracious! Not only Lord Harlow will stare now, my dear Cora."

Harriet went in urgent search of Cecily Mallow to suggest that a certain party might be thankful of the loan of attire. She then rejoined Royston and, sipping her port wine, moved to where she could watch her sister and the marquess circle the dance floor, the bow and quiver put aside.

Oh heavens, it *was* rather obvious, yet in an odd way delightful. The couple moved as one with unselfconscious harmony, their expressions fond and rapt. All at once she was so happy for Bee, and also dreadfully afraid.

"They dance well," murmured Royston at her shoulder.

"Indeed, sir," returned Harriet absently, noting Mother's tight expression as her eyes tracked the couple. Thank goodness Mother had no inkling of Malbury!

"But not quite as well as you do, Harriet."

Harriet laughed lightly, but blushed all the same. "You flatter me, sir."

"I do not think so," he said, and so perfectly softly and so perfectly intimately that a shudder coursed through her, fortunately insensible to all others.

The small orchestra brought the current dance to a close, and the marquess, with Bianca upon his arm and laughing, came in Harriet's direction in pursuit of refreshment, but then Leyland and his offensive companion imposed themselves in the path.

"Mordecai Leyland at your service, Your Right Honourable Lord," offered Leyland with an obsequious bow.

The marquess appeared baffled. "Delighted… and?"

"I'm Maxine, Your Right Honourable Lord." Mrs Leyland affected something between a bow and a curtsy, then rose slowly, smiling pointedly at the marquess.

"My lady wife, Marquess Harlow," imposed Leyland swiftly.

"Quite," murmured the marquess, apparently bemused. He looked at Leyland for a moment. "But I am quite uncertain as to *how* you are at my service, sir."

"Oh, forgive me, Marquess Harlow," professed Leyland. "I am Leyland of Leyland Steamers. I have been led to understand that you are always interested in lucrative investments."

The marquess made a subtle yet abrupt gesture with his free hand. Harriet realised Hackett should have at that moment materialised beside his master, yet he did not. Maxine must have been truly overawed by my lord's presence for she seemed affected by the most subtle, sinuous convulsions, her lips parted.

"By lucrative, sir, I assume you mean sound?" hazarded the marquess.

"Naturally, my lord," breezed Leyland with a gentle bow. "An investment in expanding my steamer production would bring you ample returns."

"Leyland… Leyland…" The marquess tapped his temple, as if trying to recall something, then made a foppish gesture of delight. "Ah, yes… *Leyland!* Rear axle fractures… two boiler explosions… fifteen dead, forty-one maimed to date… Board of Trade inquiry—"

"We are investigating assiduously," interjected Leyland with sudden anxiety.

"But not so as to threaten… lucrative profits, one trusts,"

offered the marquess absently. Harriet saw him study Maxine. "Your wife appears poorly, sir. Pray attend to her."

Lord Harlow cradled Bee's arm and walked on.

"My lord is perhaps not so thoughtless as he would have others believe," Royston said in Harriet's ear.

"I have suspected the same for some time," she murmured back. "He enjoys distraction, but he is no fool."

"No, indeed." Royston drained his glass. "Would you dance again?"

"Of course." There was a good depth of port wine left in Harriet's glass; she drained it anyway—but with decorum.

WITH ROYSTON'S ARM about her waist, it was unconscionably easy to forget Mother's consternation. Indeed, with her hand upon his broad shoulder, the whole matter of Bee and Lord Harlow slipped from Harriet's mind as she lost herself in Royston's gaze.

The dances passed, and they remained on the floor, moving in the candlelight, barely aware that they shared the world with others. Then came a slow waltz, and Royston's arm was holding her so close, and she found herself drawing upon his shoulder, wanting him closer still—wanting him closer than was even possible.

She glanced up, and his eyes were brimming with fondness, but there was more in their eggshell blue than that. A hint of desire barely bridled, at once frightening and disturbingly alluring. His mere glance had once undone her, but now his gaze did not relent, nor would she have it do so, even as it promised to wreak catastrophe. An anxious, delightful fever consumed her; she was preternaturally aware of her body to even her toes, and that her soul leant too far over a void too deep.

The orchestra brought the waltz to a gentle conclusion, and Royston eased from her as decorum required.

"You look flushed, Harriet," he said softly. "Would you care for refreshment?"

"I… I do not believe so, sir," she said, embarrassed that he would notice and fighting the instinct to avert her gaze lest he realise the true reason for her colour.

"Then perhaps a little air," he suggested. "A respite from the cigar smoke."

"The candles also," she said, grasping at mundane conversation. "Gas lanterns are not perfect, but tonight I am reminded of the fortune that Pennydale House benefits from the village gas."

He offered his arm and led her to one of the glazed doors that let onto the rear garden. He opened it and bowed, indicating she should precede him.

Harriet stepped out into the darkness and heard Royston draw the door closed behind him. He took her arm, placed it upon his, and led her along the gravel path away from the house and leisurely about the garden. The confidence of his arm brought immeasurable calm, for Harriet could not see the ground in front of her.

"More peaceful tonight, Harriet," Royston ventured.

He must be thinking of Guy Fawkes Night and the marquess's contrivance. Harriet found herself wondering idly whether the crater had been filled in.

"Very much so," she said. More peaceful certainly, yet the night was as cold, and she had not a cloak. As they returned towards the house, she started to shiver violently. He must have noticed, for he drew to a halt.

"You must think me terribly remiss," he declared, letting free her hand.

In the twilight of the candlelit windows, she watched him unbutton his tail-coat. Shrugging it off, he faced her and swept it about her shoulders. The material settled on her bare skin, the lining comforting, and warm from his body.

"You are most chivalrous, sir," she said softly, aware of his hands lingering upon her shoulders.

"Albeit belatedly, Harriet," he murmured, close and abruptly nervous. And then he hesitantly eased closer still.

Her heart giving a fitful, joyous leap, Harriet made the same cautious advance, encouraging him. His lips touched hers tentatively, and she pressed back. His hands slid from her shoulders to encircle her waist, and she lifted her arms to the lapels of his waistcoat to draw him to her. In a splendid soaring daze she could feel his lips press ardently upon hers. She welcomed them and his closeness and the forgiving darkness. He continued to kiss her, first firmly and then sensuously, catching her lip between his. That felt implausibly good, and she dared the same, enthusiastic if unskilled. His embrace tightened and then—

Twang!

The reverberant *thonk* sounded frighteningly close by. As sudden laughter rang out, Royston grasped her arm and positively dragged her towards the solid silhouette of the house.

"My go!" exclaimed an excited voice, bright with youth.

Royston drew her protectively against the brickwork and held her there.

"I suspect Cupid's tools have been purloined." She heard

the quaver of fright in her own voice.

"Without a doubt," muttered Royston worriedly. "And I am most distrustful of their competence. It would be prudent to make our entry elsewhere."

He led her around the side of the building and perhaps just in time, for there was another *twang*, and this time the *thonk* was closer still.

They passed by windows and then reached a door through which flickered inviting firelight. Peering through the glass, Harriet saw what was most certainly the library, unlit save for the cheery fire.

"Let us see…" Royston tried the handle; the door yielded to his hand. With a look of small victory, he bowed, ushering her into the library's warmth.

Royston followed Harriet into the library and was not truly aware of closing the door behind him. She had been so wonderful to have in his arms and so welcoming of his advances, her lips soft and eager upon his. Let caution be thrown to the winds! Surely there was no possibility of her rejecting his offer? Light-headed with excitement, he determined he would ask for her hand now—this minute.

There was a single uncomfortable-looking chair by the fire and before it a curious lectern wrought in bronze. It had the form of a bowed, brooding harpy, erroneously voluptuous, its spread wings bearing a heavy open book. Harriet stood by it, warming herself by the coals. As he moved towards her, she turned and slipped his tail-coat from her shoulders. With a heart-rending smile she extended it towards him.

"May I return this, and with it my gratitude, sir?" she murmured, the flickering firelight accentuating her beauty and treacherously emphasising what her gown allowed of her bosom.

His thoughts were too stirred up to find a reply, and instead he came forward and took the coat. Their hands touched, she was gazing into his eyes, and suddenly she was in his arms again, silken and soft, the coat cast across the harpy, bringing it unexpected modesty. Her lips were soft and expressive against his, her embrace firm and unwavering. A hand above her bustle (a contrivance that in all honesty he thought marred her natural perfection), the other higher on the silk, her scent consuming his senses, he realised he'd parted his lips, ready to kiss her as a lover, and wanting them to do much more than kiss. He remembered his resolve then and struggled to shore up his teetering self-control. Before he lost everything to his passion for her, he had to assure her of his intentions. Yes… yes, that was what he must do.

With an effort, he eased back from her yet claimed both her hands between his.

"Harriet," he said, realising his voice was oddly rough.

"What is it, Royston?"

He smiled at her reassuringly as he tried to put into words all the hopes of his heart. "I—"

Damn! Wasn't he meant to be kneeling? He should, and thank goodness the harpy was now veiled and could not demean his noble declaration with its immodest presence.

The door to the library opened with a creak.

"Oh, *here* you are," said Colton.

They quickly released hands.

"Thought I'd find you working on some problem," the older man remarked jovially, ducking under the pink-fletched arrow that stuck from the door's outer panels. "*Mercury* can stand the occasional night off, you know."

"We have not *that* long before the Challenge, Father," said Harriet with a twinge of false brightness.

"Aye, but long enough, lass," said Colton. "But I'm afraid we have to be leaving. Your mother's feeling poorly."

"I hope it is nothing serious, sir." Royston suddenly realised how suspicious it must look that his tail-coat was thrown aside.

"Nothing that won't be cured by getting our Bianca safely home, sir," allowed Colton with a wink.

And away from the influence of Lord Harlow, Royston realised immediately.

Harriet turned to him. "I must go, sir," she said, regret in her eyes.

"Of course," he said with resignation, and then realised Colton might read too much into his bearing. "I am saddened though," he extemporised. "I had hoped you would favour me with another dance."

She smiled. "I would have gladly, sir, but I beg you ask Miss Mallow in my stead. She so loves to dance, and too few honour her."

"I will take you at your word, madam," said Royston. "Goodnight, Miss Colton."

Her smile persisted. "Goodnight, Mr Staley."

AFTER HARRIET AND her father had left, Royston reclaimed his tail-coat and stood by the fire in thought. The moment he'd wanted so much had been lost, but even so, the certainty that Harriet would accept his hand lingered. He only had to find the right moment to ask. Not in the works, he told himself. He had a deep enough respect for romance not to consider that. He would contrive a private moment with her, and then ask. Yes, that was what he would do.

With a spring in his step, he left the library and, to celebrate his good fortune, obliged the footman at the refreshments table to offer him a tot of neat rum (by preference, of Cuban origin). He then honoured Harriet's request by seeking out Miss Mallow, who accepted his request to dance with youthful alacrity.

As he danced with Miss Mallow, he noticed Lord Harlow in conversation with Sir Geoffrey, not appearing to be at all perturbed by the premature departure of Miss Bianca. That aggravated Royston. She was in danger of giving my lord her heart, and he thought of her as a mere diversion.

"You consider Lord Harlow, Mr Staley," said Miss Mallow.

"I do," he said, then looked at her instead. "And must apologise for not giving you my full attention."

"No apology is necessary, sir. Lord Harlow is a *most* curious gentleman."

"I suppose that he is," said Royston carefully.

"I quite like him, Mr Staley. You never know what to expect from him next." Miss Mallow then frowned. "But Mama has a dreadfully poor opinion of him."

"She may believe he should take his rank more seriously," Royston suggested.

"It is more than that, I think. She even made me promise

to try to keep away from him. Why is that? He does not seem a bad person, more … ridiculous."

Lady Mallow should have provided the explanation her daughter demanded, and Royston fervently wished that she had. "There have reputedly been certain blemishes on his reputation in the past," he said carefully.

"Has he broken his word, sir?"

"I think not that perhaps," allowed Royston, "but other conduct."

"You pique my interest, sir," she said with a grin. "Pray tell."

"Ah…" Royston smiled at her, his teeth set. "Ah, courting a series of eligible young ladies with never an intention of offering for any of them."

"Goodness! The scoundrel," said Miss Mallow. "And how discouraging for the ladies concerned. He appears most eligible himself."

"Quite so," said Royston, relieved to have escaped indelicacy.

"Poor Bianca," she said then. "He was quite monopolising her."

"I am sure Miss Bianca is aware of his reputation and tolerates his attention only to maintain accord between Lord Harlow and her father," said Royston, remembering Miss Bianca's expression when dancing and not believing a word of what he said. "There is business between them."

"How admirable of her." She smiled then. "Please do not judge me harshly, for I love both of them, but I have often thought that Miss Bianca would wed before her sister."

Royston smiled to himself, greatly heartened that he might upset Miss Mallow's supposition. "I am sure many have thought the same, yet it will not be through the agency of Lord Harlow."

"No indeed," said Miss Mallow. "I fear I was mistaken and it shall be Miss Colton who weds first. Isn't it a wondrous thing that she has a suitor, and such a distinguished gentleman?"

He thought himself more discreet than that, but... distinguished? "Pardon?"

She smiled, delighted to have him at a disadvantage. "Have you not heard, sir? An eminent professor is utterly enamoured with Miss Colton."

He knew he was staring but could not help himself. "Are you sure of this?"

"Most sure, sir, for I heard Lady Alicia tell Mother. The gentleman lecturers at the institute that Miss Colton attended."

"And is she as enamoured with him as he is of her?"

Miss Mallow frowned. "I rather *assumed* that to be the case. I do know, however, that any engagement must wait upon the Challenge." She then looked at him with concern. "Is something the matter, sir?"

12.

A Rough Road

THE FOLLOWING WEEK, Harriet never seemed to have a moment to pause. Because of *Mercury*'s nature, the Railway Inspectorate had insisted on reviewing her design and inspecting her prior to allowing her out upon the public railway. She and Royston put in many hours preparing everything they could imagine the inspector might demand to see and checked every recommendation the inspectorate had made regarding locomotives the past ten years to ensure *Mercury* would please them.

On that were heaped other pressing matters. Their attention had been focussed on *Mercury*, but now the eight carriages she would draw had thrown up a serious issue. Each of their four dozen axle sets—an axle and its two wheels—had to be perfectly balanced so that at high speed they did not shake the bearings to destruction, and the only way to do that was to spin them up to full revolutions on a test bed.

On Tuesday in one such run, one of the wheels had suddenly failed. In an instant, the finishing shop had been filled with shrapnel and chaos, leaving an apprentice on the flagstones screaming, blood pouring from his leg, and a ragged new egress in the finishing shop wall where the second wheel and axle, hopelessly unbalanced and flying amok, had punched through the brickwork, later to be retrieved from the Penny.

It was highly providential that no one had been killed, and the apprentice appeared likely to recover, but every wheel set had to be condemned. That meant forging from raw steel new wheels and axles with, as Benjamin had solemnly chalked that morning, only forty-seven days left before the Challenge.

Not only were they pressed for time, but also it would mean telegraphic fury from customers whose forge jobs were delayed and yet another furrow upon Father's forehead.

Even when she did find a moment for herself, there was no respite. When the Challenge did not prey upon her, then her hopes for Royston would, for this whole week he had been acting oddly towards her and, what was worse, inconsistent.

He would be distant, and she would scour her memory to how she might have caused offence, and then he would turn effulgent for no reason at all. The natural familiarity that had grown between them had withered also. The touch of hands had become delightfully natural, yet now he seemed to hesitate and deliberate over what he had started to do without thought.

Harriet was confused and a little hurt. In Sir Geoffrey's library, she had been sure Royston was on the point of asking for her hand, and her heart was welling with joyous consent, but then Father had walked in upon them. Was that intrusion the reason Royston had grown circumspect? With good reason, she had to admit; imagine if Father had walked in a minute earlier!

She then recalled something he had said weeks ago, when they'd jested that the agent perhaps pursued an *affaire* with Lady Jessamine. The agent's hands would be tied, Royston had declared, for his employer was the lady's brother.

The moment Harriet had remembered Royston's observation, the parallel with his own circumstances was obvious. He had to be guarded with his feelings for her, in case Father disapproved of the attachment. Harriet did not think that Father would, but she could understand Royston's concern.

Her hopefulness returned, yet she realised it was quite unreasonable to expect him to offer for her in the works where anyone might happen along. Alas, that was also his only opportunity.

"DID YOU READ the report to Parliament upon the Abbots Ripton accident, sir?" she asked Royston in the canteen over their morning mug of tea.

"I did," he said. "A very unhappy business—poor signalling and deficient brakes—but at least no blame was placed upon Colton and Holm."

"That is indeed a comfort. But we can expect the inspector to be most assiduous concerning *Mercury*'s braking arrangements."

"Do you not believe them in order? The train shall use the automatic vacuum brakes they champion throughout, and *Mercury* has her steam brakes as well as the ability to reverse her motion."

"The latter will be the most efficacious of the three, I believe," stated Harriet. "The cylinders advancing *against* the steam provide commensurate resistive effort as traction."

"It will be effective," allowed Royston, "but never *as* efficient. The steam must fill the cylinder even as the cylinder advances."

"I realise that, sir, but pitting even a third of *Mercury*'s efforts against her own impetus will have far greater effect than we can hope from the braking blocks."

"That I can believe," he said. "And we shall prove it or not in the forthcoming trial runs."

"Assuming the Railway Inspectorate passes *Mercury* as worthy."

"Oh, I am sure that they will, Harriet," he said, touching her hand.

The gesture encouraged her. "Do you think we shall be ready by the forthcoming Saturday?" she asked.

"I would imagine so. But why Saturday, pray? The inspection is not until next Tuesday."

"I had an excursion in mind for Saturday and hoped you might accompany me," she said casually. "And it would be quite correct to be absent from the works; our objective relates to Colton and Holm's business, albeit in a speculative manner."

"You intrigue me, madam," he said. "How so?"

"There is to be a small racing steamer meet at Church Houlton that day. I thought it might be profitable to attend and observe."

He nodded. "It might indeed prove elucidating," he agreed, and then smiled. "But isn't that a little underhanded, Harriet?"

"I suppose so, but it is steamers, not another locomotive

company, and after the delight of meeting Mr Leyland at the ball, I have no qualms poaching his livelihood."

"Well said, madam."

"I thought we would take the Horse Moor road. You professed to wish practice upon hills and corners, and that road will provide you with a surfeit."

"I am not sure I 'wished,' Harriet," he said with a chuckle, "but I acknowledge that I am deficit in that area. I accept the challenge and hope not to have us in the ditch."

FROM THE STATE of emotional devastation in which he had returned from Tharrington Hall, Royston had by degrees rallied. On the Sunday he was stricken with helplessness and loss. He could not deny that a professor at the Stephenson Institute would be a fine match for Harriet and knew his prospects to be thoroughly eclipsed. Then he grew angry with her for misleading him. How could she welcome his advances, knowing she already had another's heart?

It had been difficult to face the works on Monday morning, but he had greater responsibilities than his personal happiness that he knew he could not shirk. Harriet greeted him warmly, her attitude towards him unchanged. Why would it not be? She believed him as yet ignorant of her professor.

Yet her gentle familiarity was infectious, as were the soft smiles that had so affected him, and affected him still. He began to believe those smiles genuine and to doubt Miss Mallow. And even if Miss Mallow was right and he had a rival in the North, perhaps her information was woefully out of date. Harriet had not been north since the previous summer; perhaps her affection for the professor had waned? Or perhaps it had been infatuation with his authority, and now, beyond his influence, she realised her foolishness?

Even if she *did* still have feelings for the professor, no-where was it written that he could not compete for her regard. He had the field to himself until at least the day of the Challenge, and he was too proud to see the woman he loved lost to the arms of some wizened academic.

Her invitation to the Saturday excursion served to give them time together far better than it served the company, and reading that to be her intent, it heartened him. If nothing more, it would give him a far better opportunity to assay her feelings for him than with her rushing about the works, her presence demanded by everyone everywhere—and that before the additional stress of the carriage wheel accident. If he found her affection as true as his own for her, then perhaps Saturday might hold the right moment to complete the business Colton interrupted at Tharrington Hall?

SATURDAY DAWNED DULL and sullen and remained the same way, with a sky of unbroken grey hanging low upon the hills. Waiting for Harriet in the village square, Royston wondered whether she would now reconsider crossing the moor to Church Houlton. He also fretted about how he was dressed. His normal work attire he had deemed would be out of place amongst racegoers and could compromise what they might learn of racing steamers. Accordingly, Royston had replaced the sober grey waistcoat with one of jaunty blue and a cravat to match. But was that perhaps too much? Would he stand out just as badly for the opposite reason? He quelled his indecision by reading the morning edition of the *Post*.

A good twenty minutes past the hour appointed, just when Royston was thinking he should walk to the works, a steamer appeared from the Kearby road and rumbled across the cobbles towards him, Harriet upon its driving bench. He was relieved to find that she had also put aside her works clothing, for although she wore a heavy dark velvet cloak, it did not hide all of a bodice of forest green fastened to her neck by japanned tourmaline buttons, nor her rather elaborately trimmed skirt.

"I apologise for being tardy, Royston," she said as he clambered up with her. "There was a misunderstanding and the steamer was not readied."

"That is quite all right, Harriet," he said. "I imagined it must be something of that nature."

"Do you think it shall rain, sir?" she asked, opening the regulator.

He considered the sky. "I am uncertain."

"I am disappointed," she told him, but with a sideways grin. "You foretold our blizzard; I had you quite the psychic of weather."

"Snow is one thing, madam; rain is far more capricious," he said, then added. "I see from the newspaper that Owen Perkins have begun their trials."

"Already? Were there any details of their locomotive?"

"Alas, the report is quite anecdotal: a handsome and

substantive locomotive without nameplates seen running light on the Swansea main line."

"It does sound the reporting of hearsay, sir," she said. "And nothing from Durham?"

"Nothing, madam."

She had them back on the Kearby road, which if his local geography did not fail him meant she still was set upon crossing the moor. That was confirmed when she swung the steamer onto the Pennydale road, He accepted her decision, trusting in her better knowledge of the conditions they would encounter.

A mile or so out from Chale Bridge, she handed off the tiller to him, then fussed with the boiler's pressure gauge as he settled himself. "We have not yet a full head of steam, sir," she cautioned. "Pray go quietly through the dale so that we may not stall on the ascent."

He nodded his assent and started off at a sedate pace along the gentle valley.

"I imagine Pennydale is not looking its best at the moment," he noted, looking at the fields of poor winter grass and the dour brown hillsides.

"You are right. Give it another two months and you shall be astounded by the change. It becomes most picturesque." She snuggled closer. That quite upset his concentration, and the steamer lurched through a pothole. She clutched at him and laughed, and then he realised her arm was now behind him, clasping him firmly at the waist.

"You must show me," he said, willing the arm to linger and wishing he could do the same, "after the Challenge."

"You have my promise on that," she murmured.

The road remained undemanding, with an occasional bridge as the Penny criss-crossed its valley, and Royston could enjoy Harriet's warmth and closeness, and wish it for the rest of his life. Then, however, the valley gave out, and they faced the hillside.

"Take off your cut-off," instructed Miss Harriet, "and temper her speed with the regulator alone. But take the road softly; not only is it steep, but serpentine as well."

Royston followed her instructions, and soon was glad of them, for the road twisted into the gully of every rill descending the flank of Horse Moor; yet it rose fiercely also, and the cylinders' exhaust grew laboured. Occasionally the road would throw itself back on itself, and the steamer would yaw alarmingly as he made to follow suit. Just when he needed no further complication, they rose into the hazy half-world of cloud, and sight and sound grew muted.

"We are almost to the top," encouraged Harriet, her cloak dusted with pinpricks of dew.

"I am glad to hear that," admitted Royston.

She was right of course. The road levelled and then set off across a landscape of dead bracken and boulders, all attenuated by the white.

"Why is this place named Horse Moor?"

She chuckled. "It is not the time to be asking that," she murmured.

"Whyever not?"

"Are you superstitious, Royston?"

Suddenly his thoughts were in the Forest of Dean, and he shivered. "To a degree."

"Then if out there you see the spectre of a horse with ember eyes, you must cover your ears."

"And what precisely would I be protecting myself from?"

"Those who hear its cry fall to a murderous madness, sir."

He considered that. "I grant I harbour some irrational fears, Harriet, but they cannot encompass such an alarmist superstition."

"I would hope the same of mine, but I confess I would not venture upon this road after nightfall."

"Truly, madam?"

"Truly. Nor would anyone of this area."

Royston was shocked, thinking such deep superstition hid only in the villages of Sussex.

"You must not fret, Harriet," he murmured, and found the confidence to put his hand about her also. "I would not let you come to harm."

THE DAMP WAS pervasive and chilling, but Harriet was warmed not only by Royston's closeness but also by her own happiness. She had been right; away from the works, Royston had become his old self, and now they were positively nestling together. His nearness fostered the delicious yearning for greater intimacy, and she found herself entertaining excuses for them to stop so that she alone could occupy his attention. Before a credible pretext came to her, however, the undulations of the road were growing distinctively more down than up.

She sighed silently. "We are coming off the moor now, but fortunately the slope on this side is much more lenient."

"I am glad of that," he said with a wry smile.

"A turn or two of the handbrake until you feel it rub, and then moderate her impetus on the steam brake. If you find you are having to employ the latter overmuch, more handbrake is called for."

He nodded carefully.

Initially he was snatching at the brake and sending them both lurching, but by the time they emerged from the cloud layer, he was growing more considerate of the controls and managed the remainder of the descent with pleasing competence.

The landscape this side of the moors was flat and dreary and even less appealing under the day's drab skies. The road levelled out to twist amongst winter fields, some exposing bare soil and others covered in thin grass churned up by miserable muddy cattle. The road was in an equally poor state, and fearing Royston might through inexperience get them stuck, she requested the tiller.

Even so, and despite her best efforts, the ridged iron wheels spun gobs of sticky mud into the air. Harriet was sad for her cloak but glad that it saved her finer clothing. That morning she'd spent an immoderate time before the glass, selecting what to wear, and was quite pleased with the result. A gown had been out of the question, but she thought the ensemble emphasised her form without seeming deliberate.

A fine tall steeple announced the presence of Church Houlton before the rest of the town came into view. It had no indigenous industry, but stretched out along its principal road was the equal of Chale Bridge. They drove the length of the village. Competing across the cobbles, the timbered Black Bull and the austere brick New Inn marked the centre of Church Houlton. About them were gathered various emporia, but soon the houses were again thinning out. Just beyond the village lay a sweep of uncultivated common land, and there they found the meet. Its modest scale was disappointing.

They found a patch of firm ground for their steamer, attended to it, and then Royston offered his arm and they joined the small crowd that had already gathered. Two small marquees had been erected, but all other shelter from the elements had been improvised from weather sheeting and odd timbers. Posts bearing limp pennants demarked ground already torn up by previous races. The track threaded out amongst the hawthorn and furze and then reappeared far out in the common for a heroic run home. Not all made it that far, for a pair of straining horses was recovering a crippled competitor from the scrubland.

The attendees were a curious mix of labourers and gentlemen, amongst which hawkers of street food circulated. Ladies were not altogether absent, however, so Harriet did not feel utterly conspicuous. Men crowded for ale against a makeshift bar of old splintered doors, and they passed bookmakers offering strident odds on *The Halforth Hurricane*, *Bedlam Reborn*, *Zephyr-cum-Indomitable*, and other intrepidly named contenders, but she and Royston were interested only in the steamers themselves.

At each one, Royston peered with idle curiosity and Harriet feigned polite ennui, but her sharp eyes took in every detail. Many appeared ready for the next race, fires bright and steam hissing from unions, but others were not so ready. Sheared frames were being splinted with wood, bent rods were being hammered straight, and others had their owners flat on the mud under them, claiming attention to their running gear.

"Have pity, sir," demanded Harriet peevishly. "Surely you have seen enough?"

"My lack of consideration, madam, is unforgivable." Royston sketched a noble bow and guided her away.

"For my part," she opined softly once they were a little alone, "I have surely seen enough of patched-up boilers and screwed-down safety valves. Might we go a distance away? A sizable distance perhaps?"

"I think that a very prudent suggestion, Harriet," he returned. "But did you see anything otherwise of note?"

"Nothing. They are all over-cylindered, of course, but that is hardly ingenious. Otherwise they appeared mongrels, constructed of whatever parts came to hand."

"They were a sorry lot, were they not?" he agreed. "I think we need to attend one of the larger meets if we are to truly gauge the competition we might face."

"That is my thought also. I fear I have wasted your time."

"Not at all," he said. "It is pleasant to be away from Chale Bridge, and in such agreeable company."

She felt herself blush softly. "I find that also."

That brought a wonderful fondness to his face. "Do you wish to see them race?"

"I think I do," she allowed. "It might prove entertaining."

The next race was not long in coming. Eight steamers of motley sizes and colours were lined up across where the track was marked wide. Officials wearing blue armbands fussed along the line, ensuring a nicety of sportsmanship, and then all withdrew and one brandished a revolver in the air.

Harriet jumped at the gunshot, and the steamers lurched forward. Six of them did at any rate; the other two sent up cascades of mud as their wheels spun madly and sank to their axles before their drivers could prevent it.

The remaining steamers rushed towards where the track narrowed and then curved sharply for the outward leg. Two crashed into each other, pitching one driver clean out of his machine. Steam roared from sheared pipework, and the two left the course locked together as if in mortal combat.

The remaining four, lurching and bucking, disappeared off into the depths of the common. Harriet heard over the escaping steam a dull report in the distance, but thankfully no immediate sign of a boiler explosion. Presently two steamers hove into view, and then belatedly another.

The contenders rushed the finishing line, pitching alarmingly, but the smaller one got there first and then skidded away, barely stopping before the fencing.

"And to think Lord Harlow wishes to try his hand at this sport," said Harriet with wonder. The spectacle had thrilled but also horrified her.

"I welcome healthy competition, madam," said Royston carefully, "but I am not yet so weary of this world to wish to join my lord."

"I am heartily glad to hear it, sir," she said, laughing.

Royston considered the surroundings. "I imagine that one of the hostelries in town might provide a passable lunch," he suggested. "A better one, I would hazard, than the dubious comestibles on offer hereabouts."

"It also has the advantage of placing us beyond reach of a boiler failure," she said. "Not to mention that I would welcome a good warming fire."

THE BLACK BULL looked comfortingly traditional, but Royston emerged from its dingy atmosphere of stale beer shaking his head. He hadn't liked the look of the saloon and the public bar even a woman of low reputation would shun. Offering his arm to Harriet, he tried their luck at the New Inn. That was anything but traditional. Its saloon, with its heavy curtains, stuffed chairs, ceramic figurines, potted plants, and needlework samplers, had more the aura of a parlour than a bar. Whilst certainly respectable, it gave him the sense that he was a stranger who had walked unannounced into another's house and sat down at their table.

He could not fault the fire though, or the repast of a thick barley soup and silverside sandwiches, smeared with a horseradish that astounded, accompanied by a heady barley wine that was guaranteed to keep the chill away. Harriet, of course, was the most delightful company, and he would not have wished for any other. Heavens, that bodice looked uncommonly well on her!

"Do you believe your father humours Lord Harlow?" he asked.

"Regarding racing steamers?" she said. "Perhaps he does, although he has admitted that Colton and Holm must specialise if it is to survive. We have pinned our colours to *Mercury*, but I do not see why we cannot specialise in two areas."

"I would have to see the zenith of steamer racing before I could judge." He shrugged. "Would you not agree that our winner managed thirty-five miles per hour at best?"

"I do, sir, but you must allow that it was across ground little better than a ploughed field," she said. "I believe that what we witnessed here, to allude to the equine sports, was a steeplechase rather than flat racing."

"Even so," he countered, "a steamer of any sort will never have what the Great Western Railway has claimed of their improved main line."

"Do not delude yourself, sir," she replied. "The sport appears to be attracting great interest and with it persons of significant means. I imagine the premier steam racing tracks will soon be as smooth as a billiard table, with the turns super-elevated commensurate with the speed." She took a sip of her barley wine. "Just as the Great Western has promised us."

"*Touché*, madam," he murmured, and raised his glass to her.

HAVING GAUGED THE state of the road on their way to Church Houlton, Harriet decided it not too great a risk to allow Royston to attempt the return. Especially as nestled against him (whenever the boiler did not demand her attention), she could say when to take care and when to put on steam and have the steamer's impetus carry them through the worst patches.

Eventually the dismal fields were behind them and they were climbing the lesser flank of the moor. Harriet kept quiet then, letting him work through the ascent on his own. As the clouds descended about them, Harriet found him pleasantly proud of his growing competence.

The moor slid by, with the swirling white only allowing ephemeral glimpses of greater moorland, sodden and brown and speckled with sharp grey boulders. They saw not even sheep; the only sound was the chuff and rattle of the steamer, and even that had a mournful deadness to it.

"Royston," she enquired, "would you be terribly offended if I insisted on taking us down into the dale? The descent is not forgiving of error."

"Not at all, Harriet," he responded. "I would fear the consequences were I to attempt it. Would you take her now?"

"I would, sir. The road starts down quite unexpectedly."

ROYSTON DREW THE steamer to a halt beside a rough boulder, patchy with yellow and grey-green lichen. Ahead a thin rill flowed across the stones of the road. He set the handbrake, disengaged the motion, and then made to slide to the ground.

Harriet laughed. "Come now, sir! If you slide this way, I can easily climb past you."

"If you permit it, then of course," he said, certainly unwilling to protest.

Harriet moved to give him room, and he slid along the polished wood, and then she had a hand on the backrest and was swinging a leg past his, her skirt brushing against his knees. Her other hand now gripped the backrest at his right shoulder, and it was then, in the midst of rearrangement, that their gazes met. It made her pause, and her eyes grew pensive. It was scant encouragement, but more than enough for him to lift his arms and steady her, his hands just above her hips.

A few moments passed, each one timeless, and then he cautiously drew her towards him. She acceded, leaning down towards him as he tipped his head up, and her delicate lips met his fleetingly. He returned the subtle invitation, and then their lips met with sudden mutual purpose. Immediately he brought a hand up to cradle her fine, mist-dampened russet hair, holding her lips to him. Hesitating but a moment, she forsook the backrest to clasp his shoulder, bringing them together, her moist, silken lips pressing and catching upon his.

He struggled from under her then, wanting her closer than the moment allowed. She drew herself up, allowing him to rise, and then they turned, one with the other, a private dance in the mists upon a lonely steamer footplate. She then came willingly into his embrace, her arms rising to encircle his neck as their lips hungrily sought each other.

How good—how unspeakably right—it was to have her softness pressed against him once again, her lips eager and nimble upon his own. How easy and natural it was to trace across her perfect lips with his tongue. He felt her shudder then and fleetingly dreaded revulsion, but then gloried as her tongue tentatively hazarded the same impudence. Immediately he sent his tongue questing in response, then unexpectedly met hers about the same purpose. Driven by a sudden undeniable need, he pressed his tongue against her parted lips, and then past them, his arms tightening about her, drawing her loveliness closer still.

HARRIET FOUND HERSELF pressing against Royston, abetting his strong embrace, the damp and the cold driven away by the joy of being so close to him. How little encouragement he had needed! She delighted in the press of his firm lips, and then knew a nervous thrill at the caress of his tongue. Immediately, she had to know his lips also, and then their tongues brushed, and then suddenly he was holding her closer still, his insistence driving her response, taking the sensuous tussle into her mouth. How singularly wonderful that felt; she parted her lips wider in encouragement.

Veiled in the kiss was heady insinuation, his tongue miming a deeper want, and her body not slow in reacting. The nervous, needful warmth spread quickly through her, familiar yet so much more sudden and fierce, and almost immediately coalescing low in her belly. He moved his hands then to within her cloak, one firm on the small of her back and the other stroking luxuriously upwards. It felt good, although Harriet had a sudden worry that he might feel under her bodice. A sudden thrill took her; perhaps that was his precise intent, to assay how to best rid her of it?

As he renewed the kiss and she fought back his tongue into his mouth, careless whether this was a man's prerogative or not, he changed tack, ceasing to stroke her back but rather bringing his hand between them and then upwards. His intent was clear, and Harriet sensed her clothing tighten as her breast swelled in furious anticipation of his attention. His fingers grazed over where they were wanted, and Harriet, her legs feeling curiously undependable, held her breath, wanting not tentative caresses but to be resolutely claimed.

ROYSTON WAS STRUGGLING desperately to maintain any semblance of control. With Miss Harriet blushing prettily, but so eagerly welcoming his advances, his desire for her seethed dangerously high, and the demand of his fiercely straining member was strong. Soon, caution would be cast to the winds and he would take her right here on the open public road. With a shudder, he pulled back from her.

"I apologise most profusely, madam," he said, his voice oddly strained. "I am in danger of taking grave advantage of you."

He saw stark disbelief fill her eyes.

"I fear it is true, Harriet; your beauty moves me beyond reason." Royston took a deep breath. "As it is, I am being most cavalier with your reputation. What if someone happened along the road?"

She stared at him for a few moments, shaking. "Not you *also*, sir?" she said angrily. "What of *your* reputation?" She threw up her hands. "Oh, but that is of no import, for you are a man."

"I…"

"And might I point out that it is *my* reputation to do with as *I* wish, and not yours to hold captive."

"That's not what I meant, madam."

"I sometimes have no idea what you do mean, sir," she replied, her temper simmering dangerously. She shook her head and turned to claim the tiller wheel. "See to the boiler. I would be out of this damp."

HARRIET VENTED HER frustration on the handbrake and reversing lever and then her anger on the regulator, the steamer surging through the rill, scattering stones and water. Royston cried out and clung to keep his footing, but at the moment Harriet did not care a jot if he took a tumble.

His eyes held fondness for her, and his compliments sounded sincere, yet he would not offer for her. He would bring her to a fever of excitement, yet then make polite apology. It was as if he toyed with her to boost his self-esteem. In that, he would be no better than the marquess. She sighed angrily. Were all men such?

CLINGING TO THE driving bench as the steamer descended the steep road, Royston had no idea what he had done wrong. He thought that he had acted honourably, indeed for a moment had entertained that the setting, unconventional as it was, might have been just the place to ask for her hand, but then she'd flown into a temper.

He screwed his eyes closed as Harriet threw the steamer with fierce bravado at a corner that nearly turned the road upon itself, the steep hillside beckoning greedily.

What had she meant that her reputation was hers to do with as she wished? Did she consider him a mere dalliance? That he could be her "Forest of Dean" before respectable marriage into Newcastle society? Had there been others before him? He doubted that greatly; she was willing in his arms, yet not confident. In any case, what right did he have to judge her in that matter? He had hardly fought to preserve his innocence when that strange girl had offered herself to him.

He didn't want to be a dalliance; he wanted Harriet by his side from this day forward, but a glance at her scowl as they sped into the dale told him this was just the wrong moment to entreat that of her.

HARRIET LET THE steamer slow to the lethargic bump and pitch in which it was used to pottering away its days. She was ashamed of her anger, but it had been just the wrong moment for Royston to grow cautious, and she had taken out her body's anguish of abandonment upon him. Hardly fair when his concerns were just. The mist offered false security, masking vision and deadened the sound of anything approaching.

But then Harriet smiled. She knew his fondness for her, and accepted the compliments, and now Royston had admitted in the boldest terms allowable that he yearned to lie with her. That should alarm her, but it did not. Nervous she might allow, yet Dimity's revelations had bolstered her confidence, and the speed and degree by which his closeness had affected her was in fierce harmony with the affection her heart held for him.

Pennydale Lodge passed on the left. "I shall see you

home, Royston."

"Are you sure, Harriet? I am quite content to walk from The Wheelwrights."

"But I insist, sir. It will only add a few minutes to our expedition."

HARRIET DROVE THROUGH Chale Bridge and then past Bridge End Cottage to turn at a farm gate before bringing the steamer to a halt before his cottage. He clambered down and walked about the nose of the vehicle to stand beside her.

"I shall look forward to seeing you tomorrow, Harriet," he said carefully.

"Of course, at church," she replied, then unexpectedly extended her arm, offering him her glove.

He made to claim and kiss it, but in a sudden move she had him by the forearm, tugging him closer as she leant out from the driving bench to kiss him briefly yet with incredible warmth upon the lips. She withdrew, grinning. "Until church, sir."

"Until then, madam," he said, and belatedly remembered he should bow.

Now ever more bewildered, he watched the steamer cross the Chale and, thin smoke trailing, vanish into the village.

HARRIET WOKE WITH a gasp. Her breath fast and shallow, she stared up at the elaborately corniced ceiling, lit faintly by the dying coals in the fireplace. There had been a dream—a most unsettling dream. She remembered Royston standing in the river, holding a wine glass, mildly annoyed that his wooden models kept floating away. She would chase them and bring them back, all the time aware of his state of complete undress and rueing that the river stood above his waist. That she also was naked seemed unremarkable. Then all his models floated away while he and she waltzed together in the river, with him gazing at her with *that* undeniable expression, his firm hands drawing her tighter against him, his lips seeking her own. Then…

Then she'd started awake, hopelessly affected by the illusory Royston.

Harriet did not return to sleep for a little while, just long enough for a truly necessary experiment to yield remarkably positive results.

Oh dear, it was the Sabbath…

13.

Pulling off Signals

ON LEAP YEAR Day, with forty days remaining until the Challenge, Major-General Hutchinson of Her Majesty's Inspectorate of Railways called.

Hutchinson was in his thirties—younger than Royston had expected—but had the sober dedication of a man double his age. The inspector expressed no need to know the technical details of *Mercury* for he assumed her design was sound and the workmanship good. Rather, he was interested in the impact her presence would have on the railway.

He expressed satisfaction with the braking arrangements, although he cautioned that with such generous braking power, care should be taken to avoid locking the wheels completely. Her other arrangements he pronounced in order, and he approved them to proceed to trials upon the public railway, indicating that his intention was to attend. He wished, he said, to satisfy himself of *Mercury*'s behaviour on poor sections of track since, although less than the permanent way could tolerate, her axle weight was unusually high.

The Sunday of the trial arrived. They would not be afforded running rights until two in the afternoon, but in the fitting shop the day began early, with *Mercury* being checked from buffer beam to buffer beam as Colton had instructed. Every steam union readily accessible from beside or below her was checked for tightness, all the pipework was checked for malicious blockage, and each collar and retaining pin in her running gear was inspected, as were the tender connections.

Once Carstairs, Harriet, and he were satisfied they could find no mischief, *Mercury* was bunkered with twelve tons of the finest Welsh steam coal, and her tender tanks, capable of holding twenty-two thousand gallons of water, were filled to overflowing.

At eleven o'clock her fire was lit and the slow process of raising steam began. Outside the fitting shop, *Bassey* puffed back and forth, assembling *Mercury*'s short train. Coupled to her tender and containing the same instruments that had monitored her during her static trials was the works' dynamometer car. Behind that would be three of her carriages, the only ones so far fitted with replacement wheel sets.

By half past one and with the dampers barely open, Royston had the boiler to 150 pounds of steam pressure, and then Harriet carefully backed *Mercury* out into the bright sunlight and onto the traverser. Clanking and grinding, it slid *Mercury* past the assembly shop and her lesser kin to the works' exit roads. There, leaning from the footplate, Harriet eased *Mercury* back against her short train.

Royston spun on the tender brakes, and they waited for the coupling to be made. Harriet wore a heavy workman's jacket, for whilst the day was bright it was also cool, and since *Mercury*'s cab remained but partially enclosed, it could only grow colder with speed, the heat of the boiler back plate notwithstanding.

The previous Sunday after church she had been pensive, but then on Monday she had become as genial to him as if the unfortunate business of Horse Moor had never occurred. Why her moods swung so wildly baffled Royston, yet he was glad to be in her good graces again.

"Excited?" he enquired, rubbing at the safety panes of the sight glasses with a ditty rag and peering at the water level.

She offered him an eager grin. "Of course, sir. Finally we shall truly know what she is capable of."

"I hope you are not intending to ignore the maximum speeds set for the various routes," he said with mock severity. There was a roar of inrushing air as the brake line was opened to allow connection to the carriages, and the needle of the vacuum gauge spun back to atmospheric.

"I will attempt to restrain myself, sir," she said mischievously, "as shall I try to restrain *Mercury*."

"I believe that may be the greater challenge."

"That's you, Miss Colton," called a fitter from the ballast.

"Thank you, Polebrook," she replied and nodded to Royston, who then engaged the large ejector to restore vacuum in the brake line.

Soon a workman waved them forward, and Harriet called for the tender brakes to be released. She reached for the whistle, gave it a short tug, and then drew *Mercury* forward to where a gate separated the works' metals from those of the London and Northern. There a small group awaited them. Benjamin, Carstairs, Major-General Hutchinson, and Colton boarded by the footplate steps, followed by a deputation from the test shop. All but Colton and Benjamin filed through the tender corridor to the dynamometer car.

There was then a delay as the guard assigned to their run, a red-haired youth in London and Northern livery, walked once around the train, ensuring the brake line was properly connected throughout, the tail lamps were properly present, and that *Mercury* bore the correct head code. He then swung up into the cab, greeted the footplate with a broad grin, evidently pleased to have drawn this unusual duty, and disappeared through the tender.

Colton moved to the spectacle glass on Royston's side of the footplate. "I shall call for you, Harriet," said Colton, "whilst Mr Staley handles the firing."

"Thank you, Father," replied Harriet. She saw Royston's confusion. "It is best to have two sets of eyes reading the signals, for fear the driver overlooks one. Usually it falls to the fireman when not otherwise engaged."

"Ah, and I expect I shall be fully engaged in gauging *Mercury*'s appetite."

"Indeed, although I think you shall find her relatively abstemious until we reach Grantham," she said. "We are held until then to no more than fifty miles per hour."

"Were time when fifty was premier express speed," muttered Benjamin.

"I remember that too, Ben," said Colton with a rueful shake of the head.

"We shall soon have the public thinking that one hundred is pedestrian, Father," proclaimed Harriet.

The older men exchanged a peculiar, slightly melancholy look.

Royston glanced at the gauges and then pulled out his hunter. "Five minutes to two," he announced.

"Aye, let's be having the gates open," said Colton.

Benjamin leant from the cab and waved for *Mercury*'s

path to be cleared. Beyond them, at the level crossing by which the works' spur crossed the Kearby road, the waiting railway employees took it as a sign to close the road against traffic.

"Guard's giving us the right-away," said Benjamin, looking back down the train as one of the test shop men appeared with his watch and clipboard and claimed an unobtrusive corner of the tender bench.

"Two o'clock precisely," called Royston presently. Colton, who also had his watch out, nodded in agreement, and then in the distance the tower clock of St Catherine's tolled twice.

"Down outer home *on*," said Harriet in a strong, confident voice.

How many times had she done this before, wondered Royston, as completed locomotives took their test and acceptance runs?

"Up advanced starter *on*," responded Colton. "Whistle off our signal, Harriet."

Mercury spoke, a long deep howl. Royston came to stand behind Colton's shoulder and gazed at the signal by the level crossing, its arm horizontal, set at danger against them. Almost immediately, the arm dropped.

"*Off*," said Colton and Harriet together, the father then murmuring softly, "Take us out, lass."

With a hiss, the steam brakes came off, and Harriet eased open the regulator. *Mercury* crept forward from her home, slowly crossed the Kearby road, and then, with the occasional wheel squealing in protest against the sharp curve of the spur, negotiated the points onto the main line. For a hundred yards she proceeded the wrong way along the down line before being swung across onto the up line.

Harriet waited until the last carriage had negotiated the crossover, then advanced the regulator. Smoothly, *Mercury* accelerated, leaving Pennydale behind. Royston allowed himself a few moments to savour the great locomotive free in her element, the fields and telegraph poles slipping past and the familiar song of the rail joints rising in tempo, then was obliged to tend to the boiler.

"Distant *off*," chimed Harriet and her father together, and then a minute later, "Home *off*."

"Starter *off*," added Colton.

"Starter *off*," concurred his daughter.

Royston was worried by the steam pressure dropping and opened the dampers wider, then started the coal walker sedately. Then his attention was on the water level dropping in the sight glass, and so he engaged the offside injector. Pressure dropped faster, and he opened the dampers, with a concomitant brightening of the glow from the firebox. The steam pressure wavered lower and then began to rise, and then rose fiercely, forcing him to reduce draught, and by then the water level was too high.

Signals were called as *Mercury* rocked on east, and between the competing and connected needs of fuel and draught and water level and pressure, Royston felt like a juggling vaudevillian, assuming the showman juggled knives. It was a world apart from his tables and slide rule, although in his head he juggled the theoretical fuel consumption rates and steam production, trying to anticipate *Mercury's* needs.

He was just congratulating himself on managing to bring matters to a nice state of balance when he heard, over *Mercury's* exhaust beat, the clickity-clack of the rails, and the wind whistling into the cab, an emphatic "Distant *on*."

"Brakes, Mr Staley," called Harriet. "Fifteen inches of vacuum, if you please."

He hurried to comply and was aware of Colton's watchful eye on him. There was a sharp snap as couplings pulled taut, and *Mercury* began to slow. Royston slammed shut the dampers, and then *Mercury* slowed faster as Harriet engaged the locomotive's steam brakes also.

"Home *on*," called Harriet with exasperation. "Ten inches of vacuum, Mr Staley. I thought we were booked through Nottingham, Father?"

"We are," grumbled her father. "We're a 'special' too. An express must be running late."

Mercury came to a halt and lurched slightly. Harriet gave a hard pull on the whistle chain; *Mercury* cried her frustration.

A minute passed, Royston in dismay watching the pressure gauge pass working pressure and climb steadily on, yet the signal remained at danger.

"Rule 55, Father," said Harriet.

"Aye, lass," sighed Colton. "And there I thought I'd ducked my Sunday constitutional for once."

He clambered down onto the track and was stomping away along the rails when, with a roar, *Mercury*'s safety valves lifted. Royston winced, but Harriet appeared oblivious to the sound.

"Rule 55, Harriet?" he ventured, albeit loudly over the escaping steam.

"We have to ensure the signalman does not forget we stand at his signal," she called back.

"Aye, lest the fool puts a heavy express up our ar—rear," added Benjamin.

"In that case I consider it a most admirable rule," pronounced Royston with a shiver.

Just then the signal arm dropped.

"Bring off the train brakes, Mr Staley," Harriet said.

As the ejector drew the vacuum gauge down, she brought *Mercury* forward at a fast walk and soon caught up with her father who scrambled gratefully aboard. She then put on steam, yet the safety valves continued to roar for some time while Royston shamefacedly tried to make amends.

Harriet took *Mercury* sedately through the environs of Nottingham, and from the few glances ahead he allowed himself, Royston could see why. Junctions abounded and the proliferation of signals baffled him; he was astounded at the confidence with which Colton and his daughter rendered judgement upon their import.

"Time Ben and Carstairs took a shift," said Colton once Nottingham was receding, and sent Benjamin to summon Carstairs. When he returned with the lead fitter, with them was Hutchinson.

Royston conveyed to Carstairs how *Mercury* had performed and how he had matters currently arranged and heard Harriet tell Benjamin "in stopping, she is a Pennine, but otherwise as flighty as a new Peak." He saw the older man nod.

Colton elected to remain on the footplate, and so after watching their replacements for a while, Royston and Harriet withdrew. They felt their way through the darkness of the narrow tender corridor and stepped briskly over the sliding plates into the dynamometer car.

Even though the trial proper had yet to begin, the men there were bent over their instruments. There was an urn of tea brewing, and Royston drew mugs for them both from its swan's head spout. Not wishing to distract the test men, they moved to the first carriage. Hutchinson's briefcase lay on a seat in the first compartment, with papers spread around it, and so they took the next one along.

"It is good to be out of the wind, Royston." Harriet claimed a window seat and sipped the tea, her skin soft and rosy in the warm sunlight angling through the window.

"I fear we shall be wishing for it once *Mercury* has her carapace, madam." He took the seat beside her, feeling slightly guilty to affront the first class finery with his overalls. "Even with the louvres that you have added, the footplate may grow fiendishly hot."

She set aside her tea and stripped off her gloves. "I fully believe I would take that over the cold. I have had quite enough of this winter."

"I confess it does seem to have overstayed its welcome," he answered. "So how does *Mercury* answer, Harriet?"

She grinned pleasantly at him. "Most obligingly, sir; she is almost disquietingly willing."

"It is not to be unexpected," he opined. "She is hardly at the trot now, and today will see her barely canter."

"And the firing?" she asked, loosening her jacket.

Royston pulled a face. "I fear my skill as a fireman is nothing compared to your skill at the regulator."

"I hardly think that fair."

"What of the signal?" he protested. "The fire got completely away from me there."

"Come now, sir. That was an unexpected check." She frowned softly. "*Mercury* is not the kindest introduction to the art of firing; a man with many years on the footplate would be challenged by her." Her hand found his on the armrest between them and squeezed gently. "I think you are managing very well. I confess I am quite proud of you."

"You are too kind, madam," he said, delighting at her touch.

They sipped their tea in a comfortable silence for a while, but when Royston glanced at Harriet again, he realised the warmth of the sun and the rocking train had lulled her into a doze. Tenderly, he rescued the mug from her slack fingers, set it safely under the window, and then drained his own mug.

"MR COLTON'S COMPLIMENTS, sir. You and the lady are wanted on the footplate."

Harriet stirred awake to find the young guard at the compartment door. "Where are we, sir?"

"Through Cotham and coming up on Newark Junction, ma'am."

"Excellent." She pushed herself from her seat and stifled a yawn. "Come, Royston. We are about to join the London and Northern main line."

Once back on the footplate, Harriet relieved Benjamin at the regulator, but Carstairs remained at the firing, with Royston being tasked with calling signals for her. When he displayed nervousness, Father reassured him. "If there's several of the same type, Staley, call the highest signal you see. That's always your main line."

Harriet requested brakes, slowing *Mercury* for the junction. They clattered through the points, and she let the locomotive coast through Newark station, but once that lay well behind, with nervous anticipation she advanced the regulator and kept it open.

Mercury surged forward powerfully, and soon the wind was howling into the cab and the telegraph poles were flashing past. It was perfectly exhilarating, but all too soon Father was tapping the speed-gauge pointedly. The twin needles, one off the tender axle for rail speed and other indicating drive wheel speed, were together fast closing on the line speed of one hundred miles an hour. Harriet nodded, and spun on more cut-off to rein back the locomotive.

She had only once brought an engine to this speed, and that had been on a test run of a Peak class, very lightly loaded and at her father's indulgent whim. It had been thrilling, yet the locomotive had truly struggled to reach the magic third digit; by comparison *Mercury* had taken it in her stride and wanted to go faster.

"She rides very well," yelled her father, glad, as this had been a matter upon which Hutchinson, back in his compartment when they passed forward, wished specific confirmation.

Harriet nodded; *Kinder Low* had been leery of the rails at this speed.

Tuxford Station flashed by, and then with a sudden blow to the senses, *Mercury* plunged into Askham Tunnel. After a full minute of thundering, reverberating darkness, she burst out into the sunlight and through Ranskill.

"Coming up on Doncaster," said Father in her ear, and then he went to remind Carstairs of the same, who closed over the dampers and paused the coal walker.

"Distant *on*," yelled Royston.

"Outer distant *on*," confirmed Harriet, closing the regulator. "Twenty inches of vacuum if you please, Carstairs," she called, spinning the reversing wheel as quickly as she could.

"Twenty inches, Miss Harriet."

The wingtips of the *petasos* crept past neutral gear and then into reverse cut-off. When they marked 40 per cent against *Mercury*'s motion, Harriet hauled up the regulator.

The locomotive lurched violently, knocking Father from his feet and pitching the test man from the tender bench.

Harriet swore, furious at her own thoughtlessness. Carstairs swore also, but in English and from pain.

Harriet risked a guilty glance. Father was clambering to his feet. "Is everyone all right?" he asked, dusting himself off. "You, Carstairs?"

The lead fitter had his arm out in the wind. "I put a hand up to save myself, Mr Colton, and burnt myself on the boiler back plate," he said. "My own stupidity; I'll live."

"Inner distant *on*," Royston reminded them, but *Mercury*, her exhaust making an odd coughing noise, was already dropping past seventy.

"Fifteen inches of vacuum," requested Harriet. "And my sincere apologies to all. I did not expect that fierce a reaction."

Father admitted more air to the brake line. "I'm certain none of us did, Harriet. At least she's willing, eh?"

THEY WERE CALLED on at the inner home, and Harriet brought *Mercury* to a stand beneath the signal box. She crossed the footplate and hailed the windows above. The signalman popped his head out.

"Aye, missy," he called, "sure you can handle that monstrous engine, like?"

She sighed. It was not the usual man. "Quite certain, bobby," she said icily, in no mood to be cheeked.

"And what brings you to me box, eh?"

"Special to set back into the Mallow branch, then out onto the Up Main," she responded, knowing full well this information had been telegraphed to him.

"Come up to me advanced starter, missy, and I'll flag you back."

"*So* kind of you, bobby," she said with mocking pleasantness.

HUTCHINSON JOINED THEM on the footplate for the journey south, and Royston fired since Carstairs had injured himself. The high-speed run to Peterborough was thrilling yet uneventful except for the planned emergency stop. They arranged for the guard to choose the moment so that it would be unexpected by all upon the footplate.

The shrill tone of the guard's whistle sounded just as *Mercury* thundered through Corby station at line maximum speed. "Hold on, everyone," yelled Colton over the gale.

"Twenty inches of vacuum," cried Harriet, cranking the cut-off wheel furiously. Royston quickly complied, then hauled closed the fire-pan dampers and stilled the coal walker. He moved back to the brake stanchion and was thrown into it as Harriet engaged the regulator and then the steam brakes. He clung to the cast iron column as *Mercury* decelerated.

"Fifteen inches," called Harriet presently, pushing the regulator lever upwards to pit more of the locomotive's boiler pressure against the cylinders. Royston admitted air, watching the vacuum gauge like a hawk. She then called for full train brakes, and Royston opened the valve wide and left it open.

Mercury came to a juddering halt, and Harriet closed the regulator and spun the cut-off wheel back into forward gear. "Evacuate the train pipe if you please, Mr Staley," she said. "I have us on the steam brake."

The guard came forward as the safety valves lifted. "Right-away, ma'am," he yelled at Harriet over the roar, showing her his green flag for good measure. She nodded and opened the regulator.

Hutchinson went back to the dynamometer car and then returned. "One mile and sixty-seven chains, from the signal to the stop," he told Colton. "Given the initial speed and the weight of the train, I judge that quite satisfactory."

HUTCHINSON LEFT THE train at Peterborough, walking back along the metals to the station ramps, a queer plate-man in his overcoat, starched white collar, bowler hat, and brief-case.

They turned the train again and were standing beneath the junction home, waiting to be readmitted onto the main line, when Harriet beckoned Royston to her. "Come, sir. You shall take a turn at the regulator."

Benjamin frowned. "That's fair against regulations, Miss Harriet. Mr Staley ain't got a ticket."

"Oh, don't fuss so, Benjamin. Who let me drive *Bassey* when her cab front was taller than I was?"

"That were different, Miss Harriet. That were in works," countered Benjamin.

"Tush!" said Harriet dismissively. "The inspector is gone, and Carstairs can keep an eye out for the guard. And I shall be most attendant to Mr Staley's actions."

"If we're at that game then, miss, shouldn't your father have the privilege?"

"Oh, Father!" exclaimed Harriet in dismay. "I am so sorry. Of course you should!"

Colton chuckled, "Nay, Harriet, I'll fire. Staley deserves the chance better than I. I'll have myself a turn presently."

Royston found himself at the offside of the footplate, looking through the glass at the long barrel of her boiler, the metals of the main line ahead bright with the gold of the setting sun, his hands on the steam brake and regulator—and nervous.

"When we're called on," said Harriet softly, close behind him, "be very gentle with her regulator, and only when you feel her wanting to move, release the brakes. We have a slight gradient against us, and rolling back is terribly bad form."

He nodded, now even more nervous.

"Junction home *off*," reported Benjamin.

"Now, Mr Staley," murmured Harriet.

Royston eased up the regulator very cautiously and felt the locomotive shiver, moving from resting on her brakes to being held back by them. He pushed the steam brake lever forward to its stop. *Mercury* began to move sedately towards the waiting points.

"A little more regulator," suggested Harriet's warm voice.

Mercury clattered over the points and towards the station.

"Starter *off*, advanced starter *off*," called Benjamin.

Royston confirmed the same, then felt the wool of Harriet's glove close over his hand, encouraging him to open the regulator further as she wound on cut-off. *Mercury* accelerated smoothly through the station and out through Peterborough's environs. Level crossings passed, and the signals remained for them. Then they were coasting through fields, the trees casting long shadows in the last of the sunlight.

"Give her what she wants, Mr Staley," encouraged Harriet.

Royston carefully drew the long regulator lever higher, and *Mercury* surged forward, the plates beneath his feet shivering with the power he had unleashed. With wonder at what he'd helped create, he watched the track ahead swiftly begin to rush towards him.

"Outer distant *off*," called Benjamin.

He saw it also, the green of its lamp already starting to show, and confirmed it back. Soon he saw the emerald glimmer of the inner home and called it first.

"You are in grave danger of breaching Rule 145, sir," said Harriet, her voice tantalisingly close to his ear. "We are at ninety-five and still making steam."

So fast so soon, and yet *Mercury*'s confidence was unabated!

"Would you take her, madam?"

"It might be better that I did, sir," she admitted, and they swapped places.

"Thank you," he said in her ear. She glanced at him and smiled, then looked back at the road. "Home *off*, starter *off*," she called.

COLTON GOT HIS turn at the regulator as they ran fast through the gathering dusk, and then just north of Stathern, with Harriet again at the regulator and *Mercury* slowing to a more temperate pace, they were turned off the main line for the branch to Nottingham, with Chale Bridge beyond.

It was then that Colton produced a generous hip flask of brandy from under his coat, took a nip for Her Majesty and then another for *Mercury*, and passed it on. The flask went hand to hand, the burnished silver glinting in the firebox glow as each present repeated the toasts.

ROYSTON SQUATTED BY *Mercury*'s firebox and peered into the fire. Even after an hour standing in the fitting shop, the coals still shimmered cherry red; it would be some time yet before it was truly safe to leave her to her own devices. On any other locomotive, they could have drawn the fire, but the presence of the coal walker precluded that. That would be the first improvement for *Mercury*'s progeny—a simple means to withdraw the walker from the firebox to allow normal fire management.

He stood, lifting an oil lamp to peer at the pressure gauge and sight glasses. The first stood high enough to operate the injectors, and the second was low but not intolerably so. He then paused to listen. The forge's strident steam-hammer temporarily at rest, the only sounds in the darkened fitting shop were soft ones from *Mercury*—the gentle hiss of steam escaping one of the many unions, the creak of the boiler, and the occasional small clatter of a clinker dropping into the ash pan. They were soothing sounds, and it was easy for his imagination to project onto this thing of metal a sense of contentment over its first day out on the rails.

Two chipped mugs appeared on the edge of the foot-plate, and then Harriet clambered up, for when Royston volunteered to tend the locomotive as the fire burnt down, she had declared she would stand watch also.

"I apologise for the delay." She stooped to offer him a steaming mug. "The forge wanted to hear all about the run."

"I would be disappointed if that was not so." He blew on the tea. "But what of the carriage forgings?"

"They proceed agreeably." Harriet placed her mug on the shelf above the firebox. "The forge-master is careworn, but not unconfident."

She shrugged off her heavy outdoor jacket and put it aside on the tender bench, then returned with her father's hip flask in hand and fortified her tea. She looked at Royston enquiringly and, when he nodded, tipped the flask generously over his mug. She then retreated with her mug to the tender bench and wrapped herself loosely in a blanket.

"Father is very content with *Mercury*."

"I believe we all are." Royston joined her on the bench, trusting the boiler to not suddenly misbehave.

Harriet sighed. "She is invigorating to drive."

Royston sipped his brandy-laced tea, remembering the heady sense of limitless power he'd experienced when *Mercury* was under his hands. "She most certainly is."

She shifted around into the corner of the bench. "Yet you seem thoughtful, sir."

Royston knew he was being studied. He glanced at Harriet's face, soft and sweet in the firebox glow. "I confess I am diverted by the brake trial."

"The inspector declared himself quite satisfied, sir."

"I too believe *Mercury* answered well."

"Yet at greater speed…?"

"Indeed." He nodded. "That is what preoccupies me. We might have seventy miles an hour more from her, and then the mile and three-quarters of today will become nearer six miles. More, in truth, once she has her carapace and wind drag is rendered less of a factor in deceleration."

"We shall at least be forewarned," she replied.

"I would wish the Challenge did not end in a terminus," he said bleakly.

"Come now," she said, "I will be most cautious. The others may assail the buffer stops at Paddington, but you may be sure that I shall not."

"You will be driving her in the Challenge then," Royston asked, not welcoming the answer.

"Of course. Whyever would I not?"

"Did you note the buffeting as we entered the tunnels today? The prospect of entering Box Tunnel distresses me; the buffeting will be violent at high speeds."

"Not so very—"

"And then there is the matter of braking," he said, cutting her off. "I warrant with prudence Paddington is not a danger, but what of an unexpected obstacle? A drunken carter might tarry on a level crossing perhaps. Six miles, Harriet; nothing on earth could prevent a violent collision."

She was silent now, yet his fears for her safety fed upon themselves.

"We cannot even hazard how well she will ride at truly high speed—she might leave the rails completely. Or the injectors might prove insufficient to maintain the water level when the fire is truly furious; the firebox crown could collapse."

With the locomotive becoming many small pieces in the instants afterwards, he added to himself with a shiver.

"What are you trying to say, sir?" Harriet's sudden chilliness was quite in contrast with *Mercury*'s steady warmth.

Royston had upset her again without meaning to. "I would not have you exposed to such dangers."

Now she became anything but chilly. "And pray why not, sir?" she said irritably. "I designed her. I built her. The risk is mine to assume."

"But you are—"

"I am what?" she demanded. "A frail creature, and it is a man's duty to safeguard me? Or rather, mollycoddle me into subservience? I am disappointed, sir. I would have hoped that the months we have worked together might have disabused you of such notions."

Royston scoffed. "That is not what I mean, madam." Her assumption was annoying, especially when he was more supportive of the Act of Entitlement than many.

"Then what *do* you mean, sir?" She glared at him with

the fury of a thousand fireboxes.

He took a deep breath. "I have the greatest admiration for your abilities as an engineer, Harriet, and think them the equal of any man, yet in this matter I am conflicted. On the one hand—"

She sighed in dramatic exasperation. "For once speak plain; I implore you."

Royston gazed into her anger and hated himself for occasioning it. He hesitated, yet how could he continue to dissemble? How could he keep his true feelings to himself any longer when his heart felt so pressured as to endanger as violent an explosion as he had just imagined of *Mercury*?

As if to underscore his dilemma, the forge steam-hammer again began its ponderous, monotonous heartbeat.

She awaited his response, impatience in the set of her jaw. "Well, sir?"

He looked to the fire's glow, calmed his thoughts, steeled his nerve, and then returned his attention to her.

"Harriet, I confess that I have the deepest affection for you and would not see the woman I regard with unreserved fondness exposed to mortal danger. My hand was also in *Mercury*'s design, so train me to her regulator that I might take her in your stead."

She stared at him, and then her face crumpled and tears ran down her cheeks, horrifying him. His declaration was clearly the last thing she had wanted to hear.

"I apologise, madam, but I speak from my heart," he said miserably. "I am more than willing to forfeit my life if that is what will keep you safe."

Her tears redoubled. "Would you have me alone, sir, mourning your loss for the rest of my life?"

"I… Harriet…" He stumbled, his thoughts in turmoil.

"I would rather go to eternity with you than be left without you. For you have my heart, and none may ever claim it from you."

FINALLY—AFTER ALL HER weeks of hope and disappointment, finally—Royston had declared his affection. Then in the same breath he offered the ghastly prospect of his demise! Harriet should have been elated but instead was terrified he would be foolish and headstrong, and inexperience and bravado would seal his fate.

Through her tears, she saw him abandon his mug, and then he drew her into his arms, comforting her against the serge of his overalls. "Then let me fire for you, my dearest Harriet," he said, his voice catching. "For whether God grants we reach Paddington or not, we shall remain together."

Harriet looked up at him then, and he bent his head, his lips tenderly kissing away her tears, his eyes full and moist as if, unbelievably, tears threatened him also.

"You shall, my wonderful Royston," she promised. "I would have it no other way."

His lips shifted to her other cheek, but then Harriet had the incontestable need to kiss him also, and she moved her head, seeking his lips with her own. All at once he was possessed by the same urgent desire, his embrace tightening, the pressure of his warm lips the sweetest balm to her soul. Clasping his broad shoulders, she gleefully welcomed his impatient tongue with her own. Immediately the worries and fears of the world receded, and it was only the two of them and the firebox glow.

Harriet could sense the warmth of the man she loved against her, and *Mercury*'s warmth bathing them, but soon fiercer, more needy warmth was filling her, a fire fanned by his lips. How unreasonable it was that he could affect her so swiftly and profoundly. Royston was twisting now, pressing her around to the bench behind her, and she willingly acceded, shuffling, drawing her feet onto the rough canvas and its meagre horsehair stuffing, and he was laying her down and stretching out beside her, lifting her head to his lips as she wrapped her arms gratefully about his body. Oh, how incontestably right this felt!

His free hand now slid from her waist towards her bosom, and she welcomed its approach, arching herself into him, the heel of her boot striking the bulkhead of the mostly depleted nearside water tank, setting up a soft, reverberant boom. Now his hand found her left breast, cupping it. Even with the many intervening layers of clothing, Harriet drew a sharp breath of pleasure, so welcome was his license. His fingers were kneading her softly now, and her breast swelled gladly at the attention, making Harriet rue the prudence of her corset, even this workaday one, delicately boned and lightly bound.

A needful recklessness consumed her as they continued to kiss, a wildness that welcomed his reaching for the buttons of her bodice and encouraged her to push the straps of his overalls free of his shoulders, the better to delight in the strength of his torso. He loosened her buttons, then his hand reclaimed her breast, and as they contested ownership with his lips, his fingers worked methodically down from her neck to the waist of her skirt.

Pausing only to unhook his arms from the straps of his overalls, his hand was assaying her confining corset. Harriet sensed it thwarted him, and she was no happier about it than he; beset by the needful excitement that coursed through her, she truly contemplated wantonly unlacing herself. His impatience outgrew her own, however, for he took a fierce grip upon the top of the offending undergarment and hauled it down, tightening the lacing but freeing her breast from imprisonment. Hungrily, he claimed her softness again, and Harriet whimpered in pleasure as his fingers brushed upon her nipple that challenged the soft lawn of her chemise.

Now he was kneading her softly, encouraging the pleasure that warmed and infuriated her and feeding the impatience that shimmered between her legs. There was impatience at her breast also, and she knew an inexplicable craving, driven by anything but maternal affection, for him to take suck. Once planted, the notion was undeniable, and she hooked her fingers under the neckline of her chemise and, uncaring of whether it tore, tugged it down, baring her breast, with her other hand encouraging his head there also. He resisted her for a meagre moment and then his lips found her nipple and closed about it, his tongue engaging a new, more sensitive opponent. Closing her eyes to the fire's glow, Harriet shivered and gasped, one set of fingers woven in his hair, the other clutching at his shirt in delighted intolerance of the pleasure his attentions brought.

HER HAND HAD displaced his at her breast, and for a moment

Royston thought he saw a distant signal shining baleful yellow, but then he'd heard the delicate sound of the fabric tearing, felt the hand on his shoulder impatiently pushing him towards the wondrous fullness of her bared breast, and he'd understood. Seeking out the nipple that so belittled his own, Royston tenderly closed his lips about it, thrilled at the response he evoked. The impassioned fever he'd once witnessed gather in a moonlit glade gathered here also, but whilst then it had disoriented him, now he rejoiced. It bound him and the woman he loved, who had professed her love to him, and it burnt fierce. It intoxicated him, and brought his need for her into a frenzy, pushing aside fears of discovery and any semblance of patience.

Expressing his exigent desire to her yielding breast, he hunted furiously for the hem of her skirt, found it, and slipped his hand under it. Discovering a delicate petticoat beneath the coarse serge, he drew them both up the sinful silkiness of her calves, and then higher to where her hidden skin gave way to loose fabric. He ran his hand higher, and sensed her thighs snatching at his fingers, just as her hand punished his shirt. Her thighs gave out then, and his hand grazed onto the base of her body, close up under the skirt tightened about her.

Unable to resist, he sent his hand burrowing where her legs met. He sensed them squeeze at his fingers and then ease, allowing his touch to the hallowed place they guarded, torrid and where the silk grew enticingly slick. Harriet gasped out loud then, and he felt her hips press up against his hand. Furiously banishing a sudden thought of steam injectors and their innermost workings, he tarried there, a stranger tentatively exploring an unfamiliar region, and that set her whimpering and rolling her head distractedly on the cheap canvas, not in refusal but in the heat of their conjoined fever. In it he read the pure green aspect of a home signal set for him, and with a clumsiness borne of need no longer capable of deferment, he shifted upon her. With a bright crash, china shattered.

WRIGGLING FLAT UPON the thin horsehair padding, Harriet heard the mug's destruction upon the footplate's unyielding iron but paid it no more than a moment's distress, for her thoughts raged with shameless desire tinged only a little with anxiety. There had even been an odd sense of relief when he'd dared assail her skirts, such was the fuming impatience hidden under them, needful of attention and anticipating his touch more even than her own, even if it meant he would know how shamefully ready she was for more than his touch. Now he was moving upon her, strong and powerful, resolute in his purpose, and she allowed herself a little fear but also trust that the intolerable hunger that burnt at the base of her belly would soon be sated.

Kneeling between her outstretched legs (and she still in her nail-shod work boots!), he was purposefully gathering up her skirts. He felt his hands on her drawers now, fruitlessly picking at the draw band. Should she intercede? There was a sudden flair of intolerant rage in his face, but then his fingers found the opening between the legs of her drawers and pulled it wide. There was the sound of more fabric tearing. Cool air caressed her intimately, but Royston was already moving purposefully forward, impatiently banishing his own clothing. She caught a fire-shadowed glimpse of his prodigious rearing piston, but even as Harriet cringed from her own metaphor, he was settling upon her and she felt something thick and impossibly unyielding within her underclothing. Closing her eyes, and biting her lip, she followed its blind probing, and then suddenly it lodged against where it was meant to be.

Harriet found herself counting the steam-hammer's beats. At three, there was sudden, irritable pressure and his shaft pushed into her, like a piston into a nicely oiled—No, please be gone, accursed metaphor!

She had been anticipating pain, yet there was none, just the sense of being awfully stretched by his bludgeoning thickness, a veritable driving fit between his flesh and her own (Heavens! Not another engineering metaphor). The thick presence drove deeper into her, and what had been needful felt entirely gorged. Yet there was a serene sense of completeness in joining with Royston in this greatest intimacy, and great accomplishment in proving her body had met the challenge of his disturbingly stirring lust. He was pulling back now, and then driving his firm shaft deep into her again, an action that Harriet discovered held unique delight. The action was leisurely repeated, as if Royston was working expansively (No!), and to her surprise Harriet found she was lifting her hips to meet his, offering light counter-stroke to his power stroke (No, and no again!).

ROYSTON HAD SEEN the anxious tension in her face as she

yielded her splendid body to the demands of his loins, yet now she seemed no longer anxious but absorbed, her eyes closed and her lips parted as she breathed quick and shallow. He drove once more into the unspeakable luxury of her liquid clasp, and knew joy as her one bared breast shivered in response, the darker nipple casting a long shadow on creamy fire-tinted softness.

He wanted this to last forever but knew that it could not. That damnable steam-hammer! It had him at its mercy, holding him to its half beat, to drive full into her one stroke, and slide from her on its next, and the pleasure that granted was too exquisite to allow pause, yet also too exquisite to last. One part of him was, however, impatient with staying the half beat, and demanded a doubling to the full beat. Royston resisted its call as long as his crumbling will allowed, desperate to savour the intoxicating delights Harriet had granted him, but soon the distant steam-hammer's beat became undeniable, and he drove faster, meeting each plunge of the hammer upon the heated metal with a plunge of his own into the silky tantalising warmth of Harriet's body.

She was sighing his name, and her hands clasped at his ribs, rocking him into her. His pleasure was gathering, and the steam-hammer became infuriatingly pedestrian. He abandoned it for the more strident counsel of his demanding member, driving as deep as he could into her with wilful abandon.

Suddenly Harriet was throwing her head back and forth, and her strong fingers bit into his flesh; again she gasped his name, and then let slip a pure high keen, her body arching up into his. He drove into her yet again, and her fluid warmth snatched at him, furiously demanding reward he could not help but provide. With a groan he drove once more, and with the unwanted thought of delivery and receiving cones and the fierce thread of steam and water leaping between them, collapsed on top of her, pinioned upon unconscionable pleasure.

His weight was full upon her, but she welcomed it, clasping him tenderly to her. "Oh, Royston," she murmured, suffused with satiation so perfect she was sure she glowed, and with the strongest affection for the man that had occasioned it.

"Harriet," he murmured, and the look of blissful contentment and fondness as he bent to tenderly kiss her brought a song of joy to her heart. His firm flesh remained within her, and that felt so right that she wriggled her hips up into his, profoundly wishing this moment could stretch until the final trumpet sounded.

"I love you," he murmured as his lips withdrew.

"And I love you," she readily returned. Daringly, she tightened her intimate muscles about him and felt his flesh yield begrudgingly to her grip.

They kissed again, and Harriet was content to simply hold him close and let her thoughts be warm and inconsequential. But then he moved subtly to ease his weight, and she shifted also to appease her muscles, and his flesh slipped from her, bringing subtle sadness.

"The boiler," she murmured, practicality imposing itself now the fury and its precious aftermath had passed.

"Great heavens!" he exclaimed with alarm and immediately struggled up, offering her a shadowy glimpse of his maleness drooping heavily before he dragged up his clothing. He swung from the bench and, indecorously clutching his loose overalls about his waist, stumbled to the boiler back plate. It was so comical a sight that Harriet could not help but laugh.

ROYSTON LIFTED THE lamp to the sight glass and breathed a sigh of relief. The water level had not quite vanished. He glanced at the pressure gauge and then opened the steam valve on the nearside injector. With pleasing immediacy, the injector broke into reassuring song.

He turned then. Harriet was sitting up, her skirts pushed down, grinning at him like a naughty schoolgirl as she tugged up her corset and quickly buttoned her bodice. He returned the grin and the secret it hid, shrugging his overalls into place and pulling his shirt straight.

"Are we respectable, sir?" Harriet asked over the injector's labour, buttoning her jacket.

He appraised her carefully. "I quite believe so, madam." Returning to the bench, he took the corner, the iron hard against his back, and she snuggled against him, her head upon his shoulder. Their hands clasped, they stared into the glowing coals at *Mercury*'s heart.

Royston did not care now if someone struggled up onto the footplate and discovered them gently familiar, not even if it were Colton himself. A darker thought did, however, intrude upon his contentment, and once there, demanded voice.

"Harriet?"

"Yes, dearest Royston?"

"I have been made aware that a person in the North is most attentive to you."

"Oh, heavens!" She did not groan, yet exasperation was clear in her body. "I am afraid that is true."

"Do you hold affection for the gentleman?" he said carefully, but with hope.

"Professor Barnet?" She laughed softly. "Gracious, none at all! I found him personable, yet never have I harboured an iota of romantic hope concerning him."

"Yet there was word of an engagement following the Challenge."

"*Engagement?*" she queried incredulously. "I do not ask for your source, sir, but you may be sure that he is misinformed." She thought for a moment, staring at the fire. "Professor Barnet has fallen prey to a great admiration of me, and I am sure I do not know when or how that arose. He wished to attend on me before Christmas, but I pressed him to delay until after the Challenge, not knowing what else to do."

"You might have disabused him of his notion," Royston suggested gently.

She was silent for a moment, but then spoke. "I now wish that I had, but at the time I was uncertain of your affection. I feared you would offer for my sister. If that had come to pass, my heart would have absolutely no wish to remain in Chale Bridge. Newcastle might have offered me a kinder future; it was certainly not one I was ready to dismiss."

Saddened to have been the cause of her fears, Royston squeezed her gently. "Lady Alicia's wishes in the matter are poorly veiled, but she was, I fear, headed for disappointment from the outset. My interest was only for you, dear Harriet; I would have made that plain sooner had I allowed the courage of my heart."

THE INJECTOR SONG stumbled, then spluttered, and then there came from it an impotent hiss and the splash of water on the stones under *Mercury*.

"The steam pressure has fallen too low," murmured Harriet.

Royston roused himself and closed the requisite valves, and the steady, mechanical rhythm from beyond the closed doors once again imposed itself. Harriet was immediately cast back to having Royston's body upon her own, driving her intemperate with his lust. Could she ever hear a steam-hammer again without blushing?

Having inspected the sight glasses, Royston crossed the footplate and stood before her.

"Has she taken sufficient to outlast her fire, sir?" Harriet asked.

"What?" he said, and then rallied. "Oh, undoubtedly; the level lies above the glass."

"That is agreeable."

He nodded absently and clasped her hands in his own.

"Bianca Colton was always eclipsed by Harriet Colton," he said. "But I would have her Harriet Colton no more." He stumbled to his knees and gazed up into her eyes. "Harriet, would you make my life perfect and consent to be my wife?"

She wished she could agree promptly, but disquiet nagged at her conscience. With dismay, she saw her hesitation deliver uncertainly and then crushing disappointment in his eyes, and she rushed to reply, awkward though the matter was.

"You are a decent and principled gentleman, sir," she said as kindly and earnestly as she could muster. "If you now feel obliged to offer for me because we… we ceded to our nature, then I must relieve you of that obligation and refuse."

He digested that in silence, then responded. "I do not act to safeguard your reputation, madam, for you have assured me most emphatically that it is your responsibility alone, and I allow you that prerogative. I *am*, however, under obligation to offer for you, for my heart demands it of me. My true wish is to have you as my wife."

"Then I accept your offer, sir," said Harriet joyfully, "for I would have no other husband but you."

She drew him to her and, with glad tears in her eyes, placed a seal upon her contract with her lips.

"I shall seek your father's permission tomorrow," he pledged, still clasping her hands. "I would tonight if the hour was not so late."

Harriet quickly thought that through and was uneasy. When Mother learnt that Harriet had quite upset her dreams for Bee, she would be furious. It might even be deemed worthy of a scene. Royston might be spared Mother's anger, but she would not and neither would Father, for Harriet was confident he would throw his lot in with his daughter. It was not the time for unpleasantness, not when she had to focus on the Challenge. Even if Mother grudgingly admitted defeat, she would insist on drawing Harriet away from *Mercury* to fulfil the necessary social obligations of an engagement.

"Would you be terribly upset if I wished we did not make known our engagement immediately, Royston? I am quite certain it could not but distract us from our work, and *Mercury* needs us both. The Challenge beckons."

"My troth pledged, I would not have you think me reticent of the niceties," he replied. "But I allow there is good reason to delay any declaration."

"I am convinced that winning the Challenge can only bring greater delight to the announcement," enthused Harriet.

"*If* we win," said Royston soberly. "That is by no means certain. As we strive with *Mercury*, you may be sure that Merthyr and Durham do also, and with equal assiduity."

Harriet withdrew her hands from his grasp to clasp his instead. "We win, Royston, and we shall always be together. We lose, and things may grow bitter, but that comfort can never be adulterated. Even if we both die in the attempt, we shall not be parted."

He nodded slowly, his eggshell blue eyes muted in solemn agreement.

"But winning… that would be the most agreeable," she suggested with a smile.

"I have every intent of fostering an agreeable conclusion, Harriet."

"Yes… yes, I am quite inclined to believe that, dear Royston," she replied, blushing.

14.

Distant On, Home Off

Harriet pounded up the threadbare risers of the servants' stairs, hoping to get to her bedchamber unseen. When she burst breathless into her room, Dimity was sitting by the fire, reading a small well-thumbed book.

"There you are, miss." Immediately she rose, slipping the book into a pocket of her apron. "And my, aren't you happy? I'm guessing the run went well."

Harriet closed the door carefully. "*Mercury* answered most satisfactorily, Dimity. But... but also, Royston has declared his affection for me!"

"See?" Her maid rushed forward and caught her in a hug. "I told you that you only needed to be patient."

"I see that now," admitted Harriet. "And you were right: Royston did vacillate for fear of rejection."

Dimity released her. "Well, I'm right happy for you, miss, but first things first. You need to bathe before bed, and it is already late."

"Do I look that disgraceful?" asked Harriet with sudden concern.

"No worse than after any other day out on the footplate, miss, but Lady Alicia would not be pleased if she saw you right now." Dimity gathered into her arms Harriet's night clothing.

Following Dimity to the bathing room at the end of the hall, Harriet reflected that Mother's disapproval of her appearance would be nothing compared to when the truth was out.

The benefit of success that Father proclaimed most often was never again to suffer the cramped indignity of a tin bath before the fire, all the fetching and carrying that entailed, and the no more than lukewarm profit. The bathing room was therefore something he took pride in, but could not help but occasionally attempt to improve. Thus the water controls at the end of the bath had evolved over the years into a fitter's nightmare. Valves and gauges proliferated, quite overshadowing the footplate of a locomotive. Indeed, several parts had originated in the works, Harriet recognising with ease the ejector valve of a Pennine, the sanding lever of a Cheviot, and the steam gauge of a Peak.

Dimity consulted the gauges, and then cautiously cracked open valves. Steaming water erupted furiously from openings in the bottom of the great boat of enamelled metal. The maid eyed developments carefully, tinkered with the valves, consulted the mercury, and then turned to Harriet. "Let's get you undressed then, miss," she said.

With awkward hesitation, Harriet undid her bodice.

Her maid gazed at her mistress and grinned. "Looks mostly coal dust," she said, addressing Harriet's skirt and coaxing it to fall. "Never you mind; that'll come out easy."

"I am afraid we grew rather diverted." Harriet blushed, turning to allow her maid to help her from her bodice.

"Nothing a little soap and water won't fix," said Dimity, unlacing her, "and no one need ever be the wiser."

Harriet knew that the ruinous state of her underclothing

must betray how truly transported she and Royston had become, yet oddly it did not trouble her, for she had an irrepressible desire to share her great news with Dimity, just as Dimity confided so readily with her.

Turning, she clasped her maid by the shoulders. "We grew *most* distracted," she murmured over the groan and rumble of the filling bath. "I… I lay with him, Dimity."

Dimity offered her a soft smile. "And judging from your expression, I'm hazarding you don't regret it."

"Oh, heavens no," sighed Harriet. "It was most, most splendid."

"I'm envious, miss, truly I am," said Dimity. "I wouldn't call my first time splendid to any degree. Needful, aye, but never splendid."

She tugged the corset up, and Harriet obediently lifted her arms.

Frowning at the small rip in Harriet's chemise, Dimity pulled free the knot securing Harriet's petticoat and had it fall with the skirt. "Ah," she murmured, with a discreet glance as she stooped to gather the clothing from the floor. "Someone *was* eager."

"I am afraid we had both grown *most* impatient," confessed Harriet, aware she should be ashamed, but finding no will for it.

She drew her chemise over her head as her maid closed the valves, and then, stepping from her drawers, she cautiously swung herself over the edge of the bath, and then sharply drew breath.

"Too hot, miss? I can add some cold," said Dimity and then frowned. "Well, possibly."

"No, it is not unwelcome. It has been a long day."

Dimity knelt to gather up Harriet's undergarments.

"Can you affect repairs?"

"The chemise, yes," pronounced Dimity. "It's not that much of a rip, and it could have been plain carelessness. The other...?" She shook her head in slow regret.

Harriet carefully knelt in the water. "I... I would not have them thrown out," she said in a small, timid voice.

Dimity grinned compassionately. "Never you fear, miss. I'll launder 'em and put 'em away safe. No one goes through your things but me."

Grateful, Harriet eased lower in the water. She suddenly winced.

"Sore, miss?"

"Rather decidedly," squeaked Harriet, forcing herself to bear the discomfort and settle right down.

"That'll pass in a day or so," advised Dimity, perching on the edge of the bath to free Harriet's hair from its pins.

"I shall take your word for it," said Harriet, but that the sting of the water was easing encouraged her.

The maid picked up a tin ewer, filled it from a spigot, and upended it over Harriet.

"Dimity?" Harriet closed her eyes against the soap her maid lavished upon her.

"Yes, miss?"

"I fear we were in no way... careful."

"Ah."

"It was rather distant from my thoughts to be honest," said Harriet, recalling the consuming passion, and shivering happily.

"Maybe Cook has a lemon," she heard her maid muse.

"A *lemon*?" queried Harriet. "I am most surprised to learn that could in any way be efficacious."

"You'd be surprised, miss," replied Dimity. "I'm sure it'll

work wonders on that smug grin of yours."

"Dimity!"

"Well, miss, something better had, or Lady Alicia will be down on you like a hod o' bricks. Never underestimate your mother, I say. I did, and don't I wish I hadn't."

"Is not that I may find myself in an awkward position a more pressing concern?" said Harriet tetchily.

"Oh, I very much doubt that will happen, miss," said Dimity, rinsing. "Your courses are around the full moon, just as mine, and it's a three-quarter moon tonight. I only get cautious when there's less than a half-moon in the sky."

Harriet frowned "I can hardly credit matters to be that simple."

"I had it from a wise woman, and I ain't a mum, am I, miss?" said Dimity. "Besides, even if you were unlucky, I'm sure Mr Staley would do the decent thing."

Harriet hesitated. "He has done more than that already. He has offered for me, and from his heart."

"Lor'!" gasped Dimity. Then, with marvel in her eyes, "Have you accepted him?"

"I have, but you must not tell a living soul. We wish to keep it to ourselves until the Challenge is run."

"My lips are sealed then, miss," Dimity assured her. She paused. "Congratulations."

"Thank you, Dimity. I have no idea what my marital arrangements may be as yet, but my wish is that you remain in my service."

"Gladly, miss," declared Dimity heartily.

"I also believe," ventured Harriet carefully, "that I might value a better understanding of… of being careful."

Dimity thought on that. "That I can do, miss, but I warn you I may have to be indelicate."

Harriet laughed. "I quite believe that I am greatly more prepared for that than I was this morning."

"Well then, miss, let's get you clean and dry and tucked up in bed, and then you can ask away."

That turned out to entail broadening the subject, two glasses, a fair portion of Harriet's port wine decanter, a good degree of blushing, and some stifling of immoderate giggles.

A SLEW OF charts and copious notes from the team in the dynamometer carriage were spread across Royston's desk as he attempted to quantify *Mercury*'s performance at the various speeds and the gradients she had faced the day before. A March shower beat upon the windowpanes, yet it being one of those days where the weather was capricious and changed moods by the minute, the trees along the Kearby road swayed in incongruous sunshine.

Harriet appeared at the doorway, a drawing rolled under her arm and the newspaper in the other. They looked at each other, and for a fleeting second Royston feared that yesterday evening had never occurred, that he had been deceived by a spiteful dream, but then she smiled, and with such shy uncertainty that he knew his memory could be trusted. "Harriet," he murmured.

"I do not believe it prudent to be so familiar, sir," she suggested softly. "Not where others might hear."

"You are of course quite correct," he said as quietly, and then in a normal tone, "What might I do for you, Miss Colton?"

"I thought you might be curious to know that *Mercury*'s excursion did not go unnoticed."

She offered him the *Birmingham Post*, folded open to an article.

"'Another great locomotive seen at Peterborough, which given the locale must be the Colton and Holm offering to the Challenge being subjected to trial,'" he read out loud.

"I am pleased the reporter could give no better description of *Mercury*," said Harriet.

"I also, although the interest shown is encouraging."

"Are you surprised, sir? Hardly a day goes by when there is not some mention of the Challenge in the newspaper, and Father quite despairs of the reporters that hound the gate."

"They are persistent."

Harriet nodded, but then hesitated. "There was something more I would trouble you with, Mr Staley."

"I am sure it shall be no trouble, madam. What might it be?"

"I was assisting the construction of the carapace and was affected by a curious notion, sir."

"Pray tell."

She came to his side of the desk and unrolled her drawing upon the dynamometer logs. Royston immediately recognised the schematic of the nose of the carapace. "As you see"—she indicated with a finger—"I have placed these large panels in the nose to allow access to *Mercury*'s..."

Royston, peering over the drawing, slipped her other hand beneath the desk, entwined his fingers with hers, and offered a heartfelt squeeze. A moment later, she squeezed back, then stared at the drawing for long moments.

"Where was I?" she murmured.

"*Mercury*'s access panels," he supplied.

"Oh yes. These give access to *Mercury*'s smoke-box door. I designed them to hinge outwards so the pressure of the wind would keep them firmly closed, the force being borne by these ledges."

"That appears to be quite satisfactory."

"Indeed. But what if they were hinged *inwards* and we could have them fall open from the footplate? Would not *Mercury*'s drag immediately increase?"

"You are suggesting we use them to supplement the braking arrangements." *Impressive.* "I would have to test the concept on the drying engine, but in principle it appears of great merit. How would you have them open?"

"I first considered a simple arrangement to draw locking bolts, but now I am convinced that steam rams will answer better. They would allow us to not only open the panels at will but also close them. One could even have the arrangements act in harmony with the main steam brakes."

"Do you believe we have time to put this in hand, madam?" Royston asked.

"Oh, certainly. It is by no means complex. I shall have the special projects shop work upon it; it is surely too late for Evans to do harm."

"I would hope it to be so. And I must to the model shop to have them make a modified model for testing."

"What of your current endeavours, sir?"

"I am certain they can withstand a little delay, Miss Colton," he said, and then hesitated. "Although there is one calculation that I would value your opinion upon."

"Truly, sir? It is you who is the academic designer, not I."

"Even so." He pulled over his day book and a pencil from the old Ellis Antrum speed-gauge dashpot that helped keep his desk tidy. On a page on which calculus spread unabated, in a small island amongst the flowing symbols, he briefly wrote.

"Ah," she said. "I believe that premise lacks its corollary." Claiming the pencil from his fingers, she bent forward and wrote with untidy haste beneath his inscription *I love you also.*

Dear Professor Barnet,

In the period following our last correspondence, I have grown gradually more disquieted by the prospect of renewing your acquaintance if it is to be in a romantic context. Do not read into my words, I pray, a slight upon your worthy self, but rather the curse of my own ambition.

I am aware from my time at the Institute that an important duty required of a person of your position is to attend the divers ceremonies and social gatherings that desire to be uplifted by the patronage of learned gentlemen. At such occasions, you would quite properly expect the attendance of your lady wife. If I were that lady, I fear I would often be unable to comply due to the pressures of my profession. Indeed I can imagine engineering engagements having me absent for weeks at a time. I can hardly imagine a distinguished person such as yourself finding this circumstance tolerable, and in time I am very much afraid we could make each other quite unhappy. Put simply, sir, I am convinced that our conflicting ambitions make us a profoundly unfortunate match.

I am certain that there are many young ladies in Carr Hill society who are perfectly charmed with your character, wit, and reputation. More than one I am sure would gladly receive your suit, bring joy to your life, and in every way be the wife you deserve.

Please believe me when I say that this has been a diffi-

cult letter for me to write, but I judge I act in both our best interests.

My regard for you and your work at the Institute remains unbounded, and I look forward to renewing your acquaintance at some occasion in the future.

Yours very truly,
Harriet Colton.

Harriet sighed deeply as she reread her final effort. It was more kind, yet surely no words were gentle enough to mask the unpleasantness of rejection. She wished she'd had greater courage in her convictions from the onset and not fostered in Barnet false hope.

Hating herself for hurting a perfectly decent gentleman, Harriet sealed the letter and addressed it.

THE SLEEK CARAPACE, dull and grey with coats of primer, hung in the shadows above *Mercury* from the overhead cranes. Royston was pacing back and forth along *Mercury*'s nearside flanks, peering up under the carapace as it was brought down inch by inch. He knew Harriet roamed on the offside, equally watchful for unexpected obstructions, both of them anxious that the efforts of their long days suffered no damage. The tender had already received its less complex cladding, faithfully continuing the cross-section of the carapace, with the carriages also due to receive the same treatment, albeit with accommodation for windows.

Just as the barrel of the boiler was half consumed by the descending carapace, Royston noticed Colton loitering in the background, bearing some long object swaddled in sacking. He was trying not to disturb the delicate operation, but pleasantly agitated also.

"Hold both and make fast," Royston called. "Miss Colton? Your father wishes a word."

Harriet appeared about the front buffer beam, which had been extended forward from *Mercury*'s frames with stout girders so as to be properly positioned at the tip of the carapace's tapered nose.

"Father?" she said, joining Royston and Colton.

Colton unwrapped his bundle. It contained *Mercury*'s nameplates, the bronze letters raised in a field of enamelled scarlet.

"I know Mr Staley's worried about anything catching the wind but… well, it wouldn't be right otherwise," he said.

"Of course she shall have her plates, sir," said Royston. "No locomotive should suffer being forbidden to bear her own name."

"Men, come see," called Harriet.

The fitters came over, and the nameplates passed reverently from hand to hand. *Mercury* had always had a name, but now she had a *name*. Now she was truly a locomotive.

"Have you decided upon her livery yet, Father?" ventured Harriet. Usually Colton and Holm locomotives were delivered in the customer's livery; with *Mercury*, they had free choice.

"Aye, I think I have," responded Colton. "Persian Blue, with crimson detailing. I think she'll look right handsome in that."

That brought a thoughtful consensus of nodding heads.

"And I'd like to make something of that long broad nose you've given her," continued Colton. "I'm wondering if the paint shop are up for putting *Mercury* himself upon it."

"If they are not, then perhaps the *petasos* or the *caduceus*," suggested Harriet.

Royston stared at the half-clad *Mercury* and drew inspiration from her. "No," he murmured to himself, then turned to Colton. "Might I offer a suggestion, sir?"

"Suggest away, sir."

Royston walked to the wall to where a chalked 27 harried them all. He found Benjamin's chalk and, further along the wall, sketched a simple figure. "This." He stepped away from his work. "In gold. And proudly proportioned."

"Oh! Her alchemistic symbol," exclaimed Harriet, and turned to her father. "I very much like this, Father. Is it not… inspiring?"

"More like intimidating, lass." Colton chuckled, yet Royston could see he also was attracted to the idea.

Encouraged, Royston grew a little wild. "I would have it upon the flank of her cab also, sir. Indeed, why should we not deck the entire train in her livery, and place her symbol on every carriage door?"

Colton laughed. "God, sir, if this does not make her go faster through pride alone, it will surely cause our competition to stumble." He turned to his daughter. "What do you think, Harriet?"

"I think it a perfectly insidious machination, and I approve wholeheartedly," announced Harriet with a broad smile. "She will look splendid."

"I HAVE NOT seen a letter for you from Professor Barnet," commented Lady Alicia.

Harriet looked up from her book. "Does that surprise you, Mother?"

Her mother smiled at her over her embroidery. "I happened to notice that you wrote to him last week. Given his sentiments for you, I would have imagined him eager to return the correspondence."

Harriet considered her options. She could gracefully dissemble, but later Mother would certainly know that she had, and then it would bring greater censure. Moreover, whilst Harriet felt no compunction over keeping secrets from her mother, she drew the line at outright lies. And what if Barnet appealed to her parents? That was how he had begun the sorry business, had he not?

"I imagine quite the opposite, Mother," she said, pretending to return to her book. "My letter bore my refutation of his attention."

"Pardon?" said Mother. "Did I hear you right, Harriet? You have *refused* him."

"Indeed. He is a good gentleman and I am sure his sentiments are genuine, but I have grown convinced that he would find a poor match in me."

"I hardly think that relevant, Harriet. It is his decision to make, not yours."

"But I would make it, and I have, Mother," said Harriet. "I would make him miserable, and that would make me sick with guilt."

"Why would you make him miserable, pray?"

"He needs a conventional wife who will reflect well on him in society and bring succour and comfort to his life. I can offer neither, for my profession must come first."

"I am sure I warned you of this dilemma, and you gave me then the tenuous example of Her Majesty. Now you acknowledge my wisdom, but choose to oppose it anyway," said Mother sadly. "You will rue your decision, Harriet. You are already twenty-three, and I am afraid every year will bring less hope of an offer. I beg you to reconsider your decision before you consign yourself to a life of loneliness."

"Loneliness only befalls a woman who refuses society, not because she has no husband. Besides, one should wed for happiness, not desperation. Dimity considers that—"

"Dimity is your *maid*, Harriet," snapped her mother. "It is not the place of a servant to offer an opinion, and you should certainly not encourage it."

"Actually, Mother, I rather value Dimity's opinion."

"Then I am afraid you are a fool." Mother sighed. "I fear you grow too familiar with your maid, Harriet. That is never wise. Positions must be maintained, or you encourage the taking of advantage."

"Dimity would not take advantage."

"Do not be so sure, Harriet."

"You do not trust her?"

"I never fully trust any servant," declared Mother. "It is a healthy attitude, and they respect you for it."

"Yet you trusted me to Dimity in Newcastle for four years."

"I was not at all at ease with that situation, but it was better than having you without anyone." She considered Harriet across the parlour hearth. "Perhaps it would be wise to find you another maid."

Harriet frowned. "I do not require a second maid."

"Do not be obtuse. I mean of course a maid to replace Dimity."

"That is not your decision to make, Mother. Dimity is in my employ, not that of the household. That is how matters were arranged when I went to Newcastle, and so they remain."

"In that case you had better instruct her that if she is to remain welcome in this household, she should be more respectful of its rules."

"Dimity is always respectful of the household."

"Then you are blind, Harriet. Bolsover relayed to me last week that Cook considered Dimity sluggish at her chores and appeared suffering from overindulgence. We cannot allow such behaviour, lest the malaise spreads."

"Perhaps it would be best then if she ceased to be a member of the household."

"At last some sense dawns." Mother snorted.

"I am sure I can find a suitable residence for lease in the village."

They gazed at each other, engaged in a silent battle of wills.

"I shall consider that an unreasonable threat and forget that it was made," said Mother. "I only request that you advise your servant to act with proper regard to her position."

Harriet realised with astonishment that she had won. "I promise that I shall, Mother," she said magnanimously.

"*Off,*" CALLED HARRIET and Royston together.

"Take us out, lass." Father leaned out the offside cab

door, as if he doubted the long sight panes moulded into *Mercury*'s sleek form.

Now the carapace was in position, the ambience of the footplate had completely changed. Locomotive footplates never provided a great deal of protection, and some companies even espoused austerity, avowing that only when assailed by the elements would drivers remain alert. Now Harriet was driving from… from, well, a *room*. It was complete with iron walls and windows and doors, and the curved roof swept back right over the tender.

Gathering speed towards Nottingham, she was struck by how much the whistle of the wind was muted and how *Mercury*'s own sounds were heightened—the staccato beat of her exhaust, the rumble and clack of her wheels upon the rail, and even the crackle and spit of the coals—and that with the footplate doors latched back to offer some relief from the firebox.

The run was the perfect repeat of *Mercury*'s first outing from Chale Bridge, saving that the usual man was at the Mallow Junction single-box and instead of being condescending was greatly admiring Harriet's charge, and that they made not one but two full braking trials.

In the first the nose panels were sealed shut; in the second the pressure on the rams was released as soon as the signal was given so that the panels fell open, increasing the drag of the air. To their delight, it shaved a full quarter of a mile off the stopping distance. Royston produced his slide rule and quickly declared that at 170 miles an hour, opening the panels would bring them to a stand a good mile earlier than would otherwise have been the case, a handsome dividend for so simple a contrivance.

Harriet was unashamedly proud of herself. She could see

that Royston was proud of her also, and that redoubled her contentment.

Oddly, the sensation of raw speed that had thrilled her on the first run was not so marked. There was no doubt that *Mercury* relished the pace, but the signals and stations rushing at her in the spectacle panes seemed oddly unreal, the enclosed footplate subtly distancing her from the outside world. The carapace also held in the heat from the boiler back plate with a vengeance, and even though the day was grey and misty, Harriet had no need of her pea jacket, and indeed wished she had dressed for summer. Royston suffered too, brushing away perspiration until his brow was black with coal dust.

"I do believe," he ventured as they ran north for Strathern Junction and the Nottingham branch, "we would do well to improve the cooling louvres."

"I am in agreement, sir," she replied. "The heat quite affects me. I can imagine growing truly insensible here at the footplate."

"I also, madam," he assured her, gazing at her with such perfect affection that her heart sighed happily.

The only other person who had not retreated from the footplate's heat was a hand from the test-car, who perched on the tender bench, completely unaware of its significance in their exchange. "I'll fetch water like, Miss Harriet," he offered. Setting aside his clipboard, he stumbled into the tender corridor. Royston gazed after him for several seconds, then scrambled over the coal walker.

With a glance down the rails to ensure no red lamps warned in the darkness, she came eagerly into Royston's arms. Despite the heat, their embrace was close and heartfelt as they snatched the moment to share the affection they had for each other.

By the time the hand lurched onto the footplate bearing mugs, Royston was back over the coal walker and at the sight glasses, and she had the regulator closed in anticipation of receiving the caution of the Strathearn outer distant.

So it had been for the past two weeks—acknowledging their love through look and subtle gesture and risking an embrace when the chance of discovery drew away for a few moments—with the works frenetic at the proximity of the Challenge, how rarely that happened!

MERCURY STOOD IN the cold of the fitting shop, her warmth palpable even through cladding and carapace and with steam softly hissing from underneath her. Her lower panels had been raised up as by lamplight they inspected the locomotive meticulously. Bearings and collars were checked for wear, rods for any sign of distress, lubricators for any evidence of misbehaving, and cylinder and valve gear for the integrity of their packing.

Satisfied, the small team of designers and fitters gathered at the nearside of the footplate.

"Everything appears to be quite satisfactory, Father," Harriet called up to Colton, who stood in the footplate door. "I believe we can let the men home."

Colton nodded, and the workmen drifted gratefully away.

"You need not stay either, sir," said Royston. "I shall wait up with her."

"And I," said Harriet. "Mr Staley and I need to discuss some minor modifications."

"Thank you both, but you stood watch after the last run. Ben and I shall take turn tonight."

"Are you sure, sir?" Royston reined in his disappointment.

"We are both quite determined to volunteer, sir," responded Colton. He then fished in his pocket. "Catch, lass," he said, and a coin spun, flickering in the lamplight. "I'm sure Mr Staley will be so kind as to escort you to The Just Swan for an ale or two. You both deserve it after being on footplate all afternoon."

"Mr Staley?" she asked, looking at him.

"I would be most honoured, madam."

"Would you allow me time to make myself befitting of society?"

He bowed to her. "I too need to make amends to my appearance."

"You do, sir," she said, smiling. "For otherwise I am certain gentle persons will flee your presence. You are at present quite demonic, I fear."

THEY WERE NOT in the toasty snug of The Just Swan but in the cold dampness of the farm gate beyond Royston's cottage, yet Harriet felt splendidly warm and alive. The desperate need for them to be alone together had finally been granted, and here on the hard steamer bench in the sympathetic darkness, they were furiously slaking a thirst not born of *Mercury*'s torrid footplate.

"Come inside," he coaxed. "I would have you warm, Harriet."

With a wry chuckle, she shook her head, yet welcomed the return of his lips and the gathering impertinence of his hands within her cloak.

"Come inside," he pleaded with her again a little time later.

"Royston, I cannot," she said, yet with a resolve weakened by his attentions. "I shall be missed."

"But you and I are at the inn," he murmured, planting a series of impermissibly sensuous kisses upon her neck. "You shall not be missed."

"But what of the steamer?" she replied with a sigh.

"It is late. If the lamps are extinguished, no one shall know it is here," he assured her, kneading her bosom gently and feeding a hunger that was all the more sharp for knowing what tonight must be denied. Temptation, however, was an insidious mistress.

"Oh, Royston, you would have me quite dishonest," she breathed with mock affront.

"I would, dearest Harriet," he murmured, "for only then can I make an honest woman of you."

His words swaddled the urgent need she had for him with most particular warmth. "Might… might I take warmth at your hearth, sir?" she enquired softly.

THE FLICKERING GLOW was not of the parlour fire for,

offering only modest protest, Harriet had allowed him to draw her up the dark narrow stairs, their ancient timbers griping noisily at their weight. Her cloak was cast over a chair. His shirt hung loose; her bodice draped off the narrow bed.

With a mischievous glint in her eye, Harriet, her corset splendidly slack, the fabric beneath slipped from a shoulder, drove him with main force onto his back and slid over him, the intoxicating curves of her bare breast swaying. With a hungry sigh her lips dived down and upon his, urging them to receive her tongue. Clasping her to him, he dared to slip his hands lower, and then wondered at the audacity of the finest bustle from Paris, that it might hope to augment such perfection.

Soon Harriet was rising over him, munificently offering her breast to his lips. Royston gladly accepted, and was gladder yet when she arched her head back and throatily mewled her contentment. The passion of her cry fed his own and made him unconscionably anxious to have her, and he began to gather up her skirts, an audacity to which Harriet seemed careless. Soon simple cotton separated him from her yielding warmth, and there a ribbon dangled. Of course he had to tug upon it, and felt a bow yield. Immediately, the confusion of before was resolved, and his next action obvious.

Encouraging her lips to his, Royston impressed his passion upon her, at the same time coaxing her to roll with him. To this, she was willing.

"Oh, Royston," she sighed, squirming to help him tug down the intimate cotton, "Please be careful."

"How so, my lady?" he asked. Had he hurt her before?

She blushed "You… you must not reach your pleasure

within me; I would not have myself in… in an awkward condition."

"Nor would I wish to be the agent of such embarrassment," he said, discarding the drawers. He chastened himself for not restraining himself before, but it proved hard to sustain with Harriet waiting for him, gazing at him with an expression shy and eager both. Fumbling with buttons, he drove his clothing down and swarmed upon her, entirely eager but with one part of him more eager, and into the welcoming cradle of her soft thighs. He fidgeted then, seeking the entrance to the matchless pleasure of her body, and she wriggled, helping his straining member find its mark. Then, unexpectedly, he sensed the threshold and twisted his hips, pressing himself into her splendid, silky warmth. Harriet gave a great sigh, and he felt her hips rock up into his, encouraging him deeper.

Now he was beginning to move within her, and her arms were about him, her hands firm upon his bare skin beneath his undershirt, drawing him to her as her hips encouraged each thrust. The clasp of her body was so perfectly enthralling, and augmented by her small whimpers of delight, that he found it hard to hold on to the promise he had made.

She sighed his name and then gave a soft cry, her body clasping at him; he realised he had brought on her pleasure, albeit gentler than before. Gauging the tension in his loins, Royston decided he dared to savour the pleasure she offered him a little longer. After a few moments she began again to offer counter-harmony, her strong grip shifting to his hips and urging him to a sterner, more forceful rhythm. That felt perilous, and driving hard into her, Royston fought to suppress the pleasure that was beginning to surge towards release. Suddenly though, Harriet drove her hips hard against his, squirmed, and then with her hands clutching at the counterpane, gave a wondrous series of wild cries, each emphasised by the jolt of her hips into his, her body clasping at his treacherously provoked shaft, as if encouraging it to bring forth ruin. With alarm, he struggled back, drawing himself from the dangerous delight of her body. His member shivered and pulsed in thwarted fury, and he feared it would erupt out of pure spite, but then it steadied to a sullen, frustrated tension.

"Oh, dearest Royston." Harriet sighed happily, struggling up to kiss him softly. "You are truly my laudanum, for you bring a splendid delirium upon me to which I shall gladly grow addicted."

"And I to you, dear Harriet," he murmured, "for the praise is truly reflected."

"You kept to your word?" she asked softly.

"I did, although it was no easy charge you laid upon me," he admitted wryly.

She settled back then, her legs curling about his in contentment, and then her expression grew shy. "I would... I would not deny you your pleasure outright, sir. Indeed, I greatly wish it for you."

She slid her hands between them and timidly found his incensed member. "Perhaps if I fashion a simulacrum," she pondered, curling the fingers of both hands loosely about his shaft, "it might commend itself to your..." And then she softly murmured two words of Greek.

Astounded once again by Harriet's natural ingenuity, and delighted that she so wished his pleasure that she could find it within to be so forward, Royston flexed his hips. The brush of her fingers pleased what had been offended, and he repeated the action. Soon he was driving urgently into the clasp of her fingers. With her gazing happily up at him, he felt his pleasure rise, and then as it claimed him, need satiated itself upon cambric and silk.

HARRIET WATCHED THE timid flames floating above the glowing coals in contented *dishabille*, with Royston's warmth curled against her, his arm about her protectively, his hand shielding her breast.

It had not been flattery when she spoke of an addiction to being in union with Royston. Tonight had been more splendid than the first time, with his lust encouraging her to pleasure *in infra* and then shockingly *in ultra*. And how pleasant it had been in his cosy garret, safe from discovery, her boots sitting by his under the kitchen range, as she wished they soon would every night.

She felt him stir slightly.

"I now would wish that you had pledged me to caution upon the footplate, Harriet," he murmured.

She blushed into the small fire. "No mischief ensued, I can assure you."

"I am glad of that. I shall remain faithful to that particular charge until we are properly wed."

That brought disquiet. "Would you be terribly offended if we take care even then, Royston?" she said cautiously.

He was silent for a few moments. "Of later years, I have considered my father with the expectation that I would be a father also one day, and prayed that I fulfil that duty as well as he."

"Do not misunderstand me, dearest Royston; I wish also for a family, but not at once." She clasped his hand. "Have I accepted your proposal under false pretences?"

His clasp tightened. "Not at all. You assure me of a family, and with that I am content. I am equally minded that greater things may lie before us that demand our attention first."

"God willing," murmured Harriet, finding a deep contentment in holding his hand to her breast.

"God willing," he echoed, and then sighed. "I accept my charge shall remain."

"Oh, Royston, we do not *always* have to be careful," she murmured.

"We do not?" he said.

"No… I would not want to introduce unfortunate metaphors, but it is like with a locomotive: the timing is all."

"Are you quite certain, Harriet?"

"I have so been led to believe," she allowed.

He thought on that. "Once we announce our engagement and it becomes respectable, I quite believe I shall approach a physician on the matter." His manner softened. "I prefer not to work by rule of thumb, madam."

"You would have the calculus of the thing, sir."

"Only in that it serves your wishes, dear Harriet."

She chuckled happily and held his hand closer, and they lapsed into a companionable silence.

"Acorn?" Royston said, and Harriet could sense he

frowned.

"I am sure I constructed *mighty* acorn," she said quickly. "Acorn is I fear the classical euphuism, but I apologise nonetheless."

"I am certain it is a nobler epithet than most," he encouraged. "Such terms are habitually infantile, base, or ludicrous."

"Ludicrous, sir?"

"I would not have you learn how my nurse referred to that part of me."

"You know that I shall now insist," she said teasingly.

He sighed. "George Hamilton-Gordon."

She suppressed the urge to giggle. "Was he not once prime minister?"

"He was. I later understood that Nurse never forgave him for having the realm into the Crimea."

She thought on why this figure of Royston's past might then have dubbed his childish part thus, and then could not help but laugh.

The cosy silence returned, and then his warm presence against her grew heavier.

"Sir, you doze."

He stirred. "I do, and for that I apologise."

"I should be leaving; I worry for the steamer," she said, "and for the pretence that has me here. I surely should be quitting The Just Swan."

"I fear that is true," he said sadly, and sat up.

They dressed quickly, Harriet for a moment entertaining leaving off her drawers for him to find, but then remembered he retained a housekeeper and quickly sought after them herself.

"You do not think your father suspects us?" suggested

Royston, leading her down the stair.

"I am sure he does not, Royston," she returned, "or he would not have encouraged us to ale together."

"That would have been in public," he countered. "He was most adamant we should not be alone with *Mercury*."

"You worry overmuch," chided Harriet, dropping before the range to put on her boots. "Father truly wished that duty for himself and for Benjamin. Their acquaintance was close well before Father met Mother. On occasion, he enjoys the chance to reminisce at length with Benjamin, and you may be sure that there was already contraband of fine whisky secreted aboard *Mercury*."

"You reassure me, madam," he said, and began to don his boots also.

"Come now, sir, I am quite capable of attending to the steamer myself," she protested.

"I am quite aware of that, but permit me a shred of honour, madam."

She placed her hand upon his shoulder and kissed him softly. "You have much more than a shred, my dearest Royston."

15.

Obstruction Danger

T HAT WEDNESDAY, WITH Benjamin's tally on the fitting shop wall at eighteen, was a dull day that could not make up its mind whether to brighten and dare to let the sun shine or descend into drizzle. Harriet was busy with the essential but monotonous business of drag-smoothing one of *Mercury*'s carriages, and Royston was analysing the charts from the second test run, when they were both asked to attend Colton immediately in his office.

"Do you think your father has suspicions?" he murmured as they walked through the cry of metal and bustle of the machining shop.

"I think not," she said. "I believe it more to be to discuss the reporting in the paper of our second trial and that of Merthyr." She frowned. "I do wish they had sent someone who could do better than 'long, sleek, and red.'"

"Their lack of locomotive engineering aids as much as it hinders, madam," replied Royston. "See how they reported the carapace; they thought it solely to mask *Mercury*'s details, and unsporting."

"Be sure that Merthyr and Durham will not dismiss it so lightly, sir."

"I would hope it is too late for them to reason it out and

offer mimicry, madam," he said. "And if our summons *does* relate to personal matters, be sure I shall at once assure your father of my intentions."

"I know you shall, my love, but it will bring dreadful disruption nevertheless. It would be quite unreasonable to ask Father to keep the confidence from Mother."

Royston considered Lady Alicia for a moment, and with apprehension. "Of course it would be, my lady."

Colton looked uncharacteristically grim behind his desk, but Bracewaite's presence relieved the immediate anxiety. The general manager, however, looked equally sombre.

"Heavens! What has happened Father?"

"It's our competition in Durham, Harriet," Colton said glumly. "There's been a dreadful accident."

"What sort of accident, sir?" Royston demanded. "On a test run, presumably?"

Colton fingered a telegraph flimsy in front of him. "The facts remain elusive, but yes, upon a test run, and not at excessive speed."

"Derailment?"

"Devastation, Mr Staley," intoned Bracewaite. "Pure devastation."

"Great God!" gasped Royston.

"All perished," said Colton sadly. "Pace and Professor Gyllson amongst them."

There was a knock on the door.

"Come," demanded Colton.

Patcham, the telegraph clerk, entered and placed another flimsy before Colton. He read it quickly.

"It's from Merthyr," he said. "The Board of Trade have summoned them to London. They ask if we have been summoned also."

"The Challenge," whimpered Harriet. "They are going to put an end to it."

Royston so wished he could comfort her.

"Now, lass, let's not jump to conclusions," Colton said sympathetically. He then addressed Patcham. "Make this to Merthyr: Anticipate imminent summons. Must save Challenge."

"Else all lose," said Royston.

"Aye, have that in also, Patcham," declared Colton.

Patcham scribbled and then presented his pad. Colton read, dipped a pen, and put his signature to the message.

"Damnation, Father," cried Harriet. "Can you imagine the correspondence to the papers now? It shall be Abbots Ripton writ large; I am certain the steamer lobby are transfixed with morbid glee."

"I'm sure they are," said Colton grimly. "They scent weakened prey."

THE LETTERS IN the Thursday papers were as belligerent to the Challenge as Harriet had feared. Some questioned the need for higher-speed trains at all, others the foolhardiness of pursuing the concepts, whilst others not unexpectedly argued that high-speed travel went against God's will, citing the disaster as clear evidence.

The catastrophe had happened just north of Darlington and blocked the main line to Edinburgh. It had occurred at three twenty-five in the morning, the sound of the explosion startling the small village of Brafferton awake. Harriet presumed the early hour had been chosen by the departed Pace and Gyllson to keep the details of *Spindler* (for so their locomotive had been named) as secret as possible, but now those secrets were laid bare on the front page of the newspaper—what was left of them in any case.

She and Royston pored over the images. The last carriage of the short train was amazingly still on the rails, and almost undamaged, but the next two were shattered and buckled against the tender, which itself was slewed across the track and on its side, the wheels torn from it. Of the locomotive, little but the frames and driving wheels remained remotely close to the track, the remainder, tubes and lagging and twisted metal, scattered for some distance along the cutting, with the paper reporting that several components had been found a full quarter of a mile distant.

Harriet gazed at the grim images, her thoughts growing morbid. This devastation could easily be wrought by *Mercury*, and the bodies still unaccounted for would include her own.

"Incredible!" exclaimed Royston, his finger upon the paper. "That has to be one of her driving wheels, yet the axle is sheared clean through."

"A potent event, to be sure," she replied, glad to have her thoughts drawn away from her own demise, "but is that in truth a driving wheel? It is large enough, but I see no accommodation for drive rods." She peered closer. "Indeed, the wheel bears no counter-weighting at all."

"Gracious, you are right!" said Royston. "But how can that be?"

"I am certain I do not know," she murmured, and then quickly scanned the images again. "And here is another mystery, sir: I cannot see debris remotely resembling her cylinders or valve gear."

For some seconds, Royston was silent. "Nor I, madam."

"I believe this demands our most assiduous attention," said Harriet. "Come, sir; the inspection bench of the machining shop has a powerful burning glass."

Enlarging the images with the burning glass did not, however, reveal the fate of critical components.

"Cylinder assemblies are such weighty items," said Harriet, perplexed. "I cannot believe they can have been thrown far."

"Yet absent they most certainly are, Miss Colton," replied Royston. "Perhaps *Spindler* had none?"

"Now that makes no sense at all."

"So I would also believe if she was not anticipated to be *experimental*."

"I suppose I have to allow that," said Harriet, "although it is a particularly vexing puzzle."

Royston continued to examine the paper. "It appears they also had thought of wind drag," he said with veiled disappointment. "See, Miss Colton? This piece of fairing has clearly been smoothed to ease passage."

"It looks highly tapered, however," she said. "As if part of a cone."

"That is not to be unexpected. Indeed, I myself contemplated fashioning *Mercury*'s nose thus."

Turning the page, he glanced cursorily through further images showing incidental damage. Suddenly, however, Royston brought the newspaper up to his face and then, frowning, thrust it under the burning glass. Harriet found herself looking at a dour villager, a large fragment of *Spindler* at his feet. The caption claimed it had fallen through his roof from the night sky.

"What, Miss Colton, is *that*," demanded Royston.

Harriet stared. "It is… it appears to have been the blade of a fan, sir," she said hesitantly. "One of prodigious size."

"But what purpose would it serve?" mused Royston.

They stared at the image for long seconds.

"Surely… surely they could not have seriously contemplated it as the means of impetus?" hazarded Royston.

"It would explain the lack of drive rods, sir," she said, yet with equal scepticism.

"There was report of the howl of the approaching train before the explosion," noted Royston thoughtfully. "Which I admit I considered merely dramatic license."

"That they almost reached Darlington through such agency suggests it is not so hare-brained a schema as first it might appear," said Harriet.

Royston grew thoughtful. "I had not considered it, but… air pressing upon air. There could well be invisible yet useful resistance."

"But… but they would still need cylinders to drive it."

"You are right, madam. I fear that mystery remains."

"I suspect the trick of it will emerge from the Board of Enquiry." Her thoughts turned to Father, who had left on the first train for London, summoned as expected to Whitehall.

As with the Abbots Ripton accident, a sense of forlorn loss descended on the works, although this time it was tinged with more immediacy. No one talked of it, but everyone expected the Board of Trade would order the Challenge abandoned, and no more discussion of supra-expresses. What of *Mercury* then? What then indeed, with the ascendancy of the great Railway Works of Colton and Holm?

Father was detained in London, and his telegrams were terse and offered no encouragement. His chair was still pointedly empty at dinner on the Friday night, and all Mother's attempts at conversation came to nothing, Harriet unable to shake off a creeping melancholy, only managing to infect her sister with the same.

She was in her room, failing to read Walter Scott, when there was a timid knock at the door. It proved to be Bianca, looking nervous and distraught.

"Goodness, what is wrong, Bee?" Harriet hastened to seat her sister by the fire and knelt beside her.

"I fear… I fear I have been greatly improvident, Harry," sniffed Bianca.

"How so, Bee?" asked Harriet, but already guessing the reason for Bianca's anguish. "Bee?" she prompted softly when her sister made no reply.

"Oh, Harry, it is the most dreadful secret, but I have been meeting with a gentleman."

"Oh my!" gasped Harriet. For Bianca's sake she hoped her surprise sounded genuine.

"I know," said Bianca miserably. "It is the height of foolishness, yet I could not help myself. It was all too thrilling, Harry, and the gentleman entranced me."

"It is wrong of me, but I find myself wondering how… intimate grew this acquaintance."

"It could not have more so were I his wife," said Bianca, then burst into tears.

Harry gathered Bee into her arms. "There, there, Bee,"

she soothed, rocking her sister gently. "But what has happened to bring on such sudden distress? Do you find yourself carrying his child?"

"I don't... I don't think so, Harry." Bianca sniffled. "He assured me that... that..."

Harriet made a discrete enquiry founded on an understanding newly acquired, and was reassured by the reply.

"Then what is the matter?" she enquired.

"I fear he is about to throw me over, Harry, and leave me ruined."

Harriet sighed and held Bianca close. What was inevitable was about to come true. Silently cursing Lord Harlow, she asked, "Why do you believe it so?"

"Our meetings... they are not so frequent. He makes fine excuse, but I fear them to be fabricated, for when I *am* with him, he seems different towards me—more circumspect," she said. "What am I to do, Harry?"

"Since you consider the gentleman lost, perhaps you should find excuses of your own and bring the *affaire* to a close before it is uncovered," suggested Harriet pragmatically. "The longer matters remain as they are, the greater the threat to your reputation, Bee."

"But I do not wish him lost, Harry," wailed her sister.

"Of course you do not," said Harriet gently, "but what we wish, we cannot always have."

"I feel so terrible," mumbled Bianca miserably. "First I am losing him, and now I am terribly afraid of losing you also. I could not abide that, Harry."

"You are not losing me." Harriet tried to sound amused by her sister's notion.

"You are stubborn, Harry. You insist on driving the Challenge," said Bianca, "and it will end in a horrid accident just as it did for those poor northern gentlemen."

"I trust *Mercury*, Bee," said Harriet. "She will keep me safe."

"And I trust her not a jot," stated her sister. "And nor does Mother and nor does Father."

"Now, Bee—"

"Oh, you do not see it, but I do. They are being awfully stoical, but they are both terrified you shall die in this foolishness. I jolly well hope the whole thing is called off as everyone in the paper wants and my Harry remains safe."

"I have to drive *Mercury*," said Harriet. "So much depends upon it."

"There you are being stubborn again," responded Bianca. "Can anything be worth your very life?"

"You are overwrought over your gentleman, Bee," said Harriet with a slight edge, "and grow histrionic."

"I am not. I would have him and you both, but if I must choose, I would have you safe, my sister," said Bianca, and clutched Harriet to her with fierce desperation.

FATHER RETURNED ON the Saturday evening by the nine o'clock train. Appearing tired, he greeted Mother, assured her that he had eaten, and then retired to be with his books. Harriet allowed him a little time alone, but soon the need to know the Board's decision, whether for good or ill, drove her to the library door.

"Ah, Harriet, I was expecting you," said Father from his armchair, a generous whisky at his side. "Come rest your legs. Help yourself to a glass first though."

Harriet did so and then perched nervously opposite him. "Well, Father, is it all off?" she asked, there seeming no kindness in delaying bad news.

"Oh, it is very much still on, lass," replied Father with a weary smile.

Harriet grinned in relief. "I am terribly glad; I feared that popular opinion would make the Board of Trade craven."

"They, like I, believe opposition to be more vociferous than popular," said Father. "Indeed Lord Clifton argued that the Challenge has provoked great interest, and many intend to travel to witness the event. He had ticket receipts to back him."

"Lord Clifton is an extremely astute man, Father."

"Aye, he is. But then Lord Harlow—"

"Lord Harlow? *He* was present?" She thought of her sister, and grew coldly wrathful.

"Naturally, Harriet. He has a significant stake in the Challenge; it was only right that he be invited."

"Even so, I am surprised he deigned to attend in person and not send that agent of his in his stead," muttered Harriet.

"Well, he came himself, Harriet, and I am glad of it. I discovered in the past few days that when it pleases him he's capable of the most persuasive rhetoric. He had the Board quite convinced that it would be highly against the interests of the realm to cancel the Challenge, for it would undermine confidence in our ability to lead the world."

"Goodness," said Harriet. "I had not considered it in such a patriotic light."

"Nor I confess had I," said Father. "In truth, I felt quite inferior in the meeting, as did I believe Perkins. It was Lords

Clifton and Harlow who carried the day."

"A queer alliance." Harriet sipped her port wine.

"Perhaps, although it did not seem so at the time," said Father. "In any case, Lord Harlow went further than simply quelling the Board's reservations. He argued that we should turn adversity to our hand and make the Challenge an even bolder declaration of Britain's prowess."

"How on earth does he suggest we do that?" asked Harriet suspiciously.

"Two contenders now remain, and two tracks lead to Paddington. He proposed to make it a pure race, the two locomotives starting side by side in Bristol."

"With one train running the wrong way upon the down line? Would the Great Western even allow it?"

"Sir Daniel was won over at once. The Board took more persuasion."

"But they agreed?"

Father nodded. "With a great number of stipulations— the brokering of which held me up so long in London. And the new arrangements must remain confidential until Lord Clifton makes the announcement next week."

"I understand, Father," said Harriet. "And did you hear anything of import concerning *Spindler*?"

"No more than that the usual enquiry must occur. For obvious reasons, they wish that done in double-quick time, however, although the nature of the locomotive is causing them issues."

"From what we saw of the wreck in the newspaper, Mr Staley and I thought her highly unusual."

"She was, but the Board prefer not to go into details."

Harriet paused. "Do you fear for my safety in this race, Father?"

Her father smiled sadly. "Of course I do, Harriet. What you attempt is not without considerable risk."

"Do you trust *Mercury?*"

"Implicitly," Father declared. "She's a Colton and Holm locomotive, and nothing in her design gives me pause. And I trust you also, Harriet. No, what worries me is something beyond our control."

Such as Royston's drunken carter, thought Harriet. "I intend to be as careful as I can, Father."

"I know that you will, lass, and that comforts me."

THE "DRYING ENGINE" was silent and cold, and the building that housed it dim, daylight penetrating solely through cracks in the doors.

"I shall miss you, Harriet," said Royston, holding her to him.

"I shall only be away for five or six days," she assured him. "Your days will be so hectic that you will not notice I am gone."

"I can hardly credit that."

"You shall, for in the interim you shall have my responsibilities as well as your own." She sighed then against his neck. "I too would rather not be away from you, but now Lord Harlow has," she twisted her lip in disdain, "saved the day, I must learn the road, and Benjamin also."

"You will be careful, will you not?"

"Of course, and Dimity will be with me," she replied. "Although I freely admit that shuttling back and forth from

Birmingham and Bristol and London on an open goods engine footplate day in and day out holds no appeal. I am sure I shall be thoroughly glad when I sign the Route Book in Swindon."

"Hasten back, my lady."

"I shall," she promised. "And you must not work all hours, dear Royston. I quite insist you take time to relax. I would not have a haggard wreck awaiting my return."

"I shall."

"Now kiss me," she said, "before people come looking for us."

It was a pleasant instruction to receive.

HARRIET HAD NOT been exaggerating about how busy the days were. There was the last of the carriages to complete and test, fine adjustments to be made to *Mercury*'s valve timing, various small modifications suggested by Colton to put in hand, and arrangements for the teams of men who would support her in Bristol and London to be detailed and finalised.

Royston was up and striding for the works with the rising of the sun and returned in darkness, only taking time to bolt down a supper that had waited overlong for him before retiring to his garret bedroom, now sweetly suffused with Harriet's erstwhile presence and stolen passion. On a couple of nights he never even got as far as the stairs, instead falling asleep at the kitchen table.

Yet for all that fell upon him, there was more than

enough time for his thoughts to turn to Harriet, wonder how she fared, and to miss her terribly.

On the Saturday he fulfilled his promise to her, leaving the works early to spend an all too pleasant evening in The Just Swan. The race had now been widely promoted, and his usual drinking companions insisted on quizzing him over the details and plying him with ale in exchange.

Later, when he admitted he would be actually riding *Mercury* in the race, they insisted—and less recognised faces also—on buying him the best Navy-strength rum to be had. Fortuitously, their covetous admiration extended to carrying him home and putting him to bed, at least that was what he thought had happened when he woke at the unconscionable hour of noon, with Matins long past and a steam-hammer at work inside his head.

HARRIET WAS GLAD to be home, her mission fulfilled, her signature recorded in the Route Book against the Great Western main line and the Birmingham to Swindon branch over that of Benjamin. Her weary contentment dissipated though when she saw the letter that awaited her at her writing table. She picked it up and with sorrow considered the meticulous handwriting and Newcastle postmark.

"No need to open it all at once, miss," counselled Dimity as she unpacked. "Leave it until you're ready for it."

"That will not make it go away, Dimity," said Harriet, "and I would rather not have a sword of Damocles hanging over me."

She picked up her gunmetal letter-opener and slit the envelope with the wyvern's serrated tail.

Dear Miss Colton,

Thank you for your letter of the twelfth inst. I must at once apologise for the tardiness of my reply, for alas before I had time to completely consider my response, a duty more pressing than personal correspondence claimed my time.

I have these last ten days been imprisoned (I suggest here no malfeasance on my part but the absorbing nature of my business) in Durham castle, a fine fourteenth-century structure, given over to the University College in 1837, and possessing a most genteel and accommodating Senior Common Room, the facilities of which by reason of my chair at the Institute I was allowed to enjoy.

The reason for my time in Durham (how fortuitous for my metaphor since I understand convicts so refer to their sentence!) was the disaster involving the locomotive of Professor Gyllson, God rest his soul. The Board of Trade's Inspectorate of Railways, apprehending the true novelty of his design, issued writ to various learned gentlemen to support the Enquiry of Accident, and I was greatly honoured to be included in this company.

I understand that the disaster has led to unreasonable disquiet in some quarters concerning locomotives of un-precedented haste. Cognisant of your attention to this subject and since the initial report of the enquiry shall be presented to Her Majesty's Government within the week, I feel myself only slightly negligent to my terms of attach-ment to the enquiry, a document of some twenty-seven clauses and an appendix, in assuring you that speed was not thought contributory to the unfortunate occurrence. The principal cause appears to be the use of an "air screw"

(I draw allusion to the motivating screws enjoyed by our Navy and Merchant Marine) to provide impulsion.

This assembly Professor Gyllson had arranged to a novel steam mill, the whole revolving at a fearsome rate, and it appears maintaining this arrangement in seemly order lay beyond the capability of current engineering practice. One need not imagine (in truth, one is recommended so to do to appreciate the calamity) the result of the rotational vigour of such an assembly running amok in proximity to a boiler operated at most generous pressure.

I trust this will quieten any concerns you may have over the fallacious arguments being presented in public debate.

Your most obedient servant,
Thaddeus Barnet, Professor of Heat.

P.S. I was greatly relieved by the sentiments that you so kindly intimated regarding an attachment between your gentle self and my person. You express most eloquently the substance of the reservations that metaphorically grew in my heart in the wake of reckless fervour. Perhaps it is better we had both fallen into the sun[1] after all!

P[2].S. Be assured that I would also most welcome within our mutual interest of engineering your renewed acquaintance.

P[3].S. If I do not place too great a confidence upon our current acquaintance, I might allow that motivated by your counsel, I find a gentlewoman of the locality appears most favourably deposed to my inadequate person!!

[1]Personal correspondence between Barnet T S J and Colton H R (Miss); 2nd December 1875

"Thank goodness!" exclaimed Harriet, and passed the pages over her shoulder to her maid to read.

"Well, that's a comfort," declared Dimity when she handed it back. "Although he took his good time getting to it."

"That he did not forget completely what he was writing about can be counted a small victory," chuckled Harriet. "He can be that absent-minded; it cannot be discounted."

"We didn't need to be reminded about the Navy, though I can't say an air screw sounds very satisfactory."

"Royston believes it potentially efficacious," allowed Harriet.

"Well, be sure to tell me if it is, miss."

Harriet frowned. "I am not sure quite how, but I do believe you are making an unseemly jest at the expense of poor Professor Barnet."

"Me, miss?" replied Dimity with apparent horror. "As if I would!"

"YOU ARE BEING ridiculous, Mr Staley."

"And I quite insist on being so, Miss Colton. Now look away, I pray."

Obediently, Harriet gazed across the turntable to where trees were budding vivid green in the first signs of spring. She heard the fitting shop doors rumbling back on their tracks.

"Now close your eyes... Turn around... And now open them!"

"Great heavens!" She clapped her hands in delighted wonder.

Mercury had cast off her drab grey and now was deep blue and magnificent, her richly polished paintwork glinting in the early April sunlight. Her buffer beam was regulation signal red, but that looked less out of place with the subtle accenting in a slighter deeper hue along her principal lines. Upon her broad sloping nose, proud and daunting, was the horned Venus, alchemistic symbol of *Mercury*, and as she walked closer, Harriet saw it repeated, smaller yet still proud, under the stained glass of the cab windows. *Mercury*'s tender was in the same livery, proudly inscribed upon it in the old gold of the symbols, "COLTON AND HOLM, CHALE BRIDGE."

"She looks so splendid, sir." Harriet sighed happily.

Royston chuckled. "On this side she does; the offside remains decidedly patchy. Another two days, the painters tell me."

"And the carriages?"

"For the most part done, and surely ready for Saturday."

"Saturday…" mused Harriet. "This time next week, the race will have been run."

Royston nodded, gazing at *Mercury*. He began to whistle softly.

"Nervous, sir?"

He smiled slightly awkwardly at her. "I am, and I believe that perfectly appropriate in the circumstances."

"I was not accusing you of weakness," she said teasingly, then looked at *Mercury* herself. "I freely admit to being nervous also."

"We shall overcome our disquiet together," he murmured. "But do you not yearn also to give *Mercury* her head and see what she is truly capable of?"

"Oh, I am most certainly anxious for that moment." Harriet sighed deeply.

ALL CHALE BRIDGE turned out that Saturday morning to wish *Mercury* luck as she set out for Bristol. Men, women, and children lined the fences of the works spur and for some distance down the main line. In the field by the Kearby road, the works band played martial airs, and there was a general welling of contained excitement under the bright spring skies.

The same young guard who had accompanied them on the trial runs was with them again. Until Birmingham, at least, when he would relinquish his charge to a Great Western colleague. Royston walked around the train with him. Everyone else was aboard—the entire Colton family and their necessary servants, Benjamin, and Carstairs. Apart from Harriet and Benjamin, the remainder would take the train from Bristol in the morning, to be at the finish line before the main line was closed to all traffic but the competitors.

"I'm going down to Didcot to watch you pass, sir," the guard, checking the tail lamps were properly secured.

"Why Didcot, pray?" asked Royston. The Works Excursion tomorrow was bound for Swindon.

"You're sure to be at full speed by Didcot, sir, and that's a sight I don't want to miss. One for the grandkids, eh?"

Royston, on the verge of offering the usual self-effacing

response, stopped himself. "It *is* one of those moments, is it not?"

"Certainly is, sir. History will be made tomorrow," the guard replied, peering between carriages. "Don't mind saying I've a few bob on you making Paddington first."

"You are unreasonably partisan, sir."

"If that means I'm soft on you, then nah, sir. I've *felt* what happens when you open that regulator. Never felt anything like it, me. My brass is safe."

"What... What are the odds?"

The guard sniffed. "A tad against you, but that's only on what's been reported of both test runs. No one has the real form because neither of you has gone full speed yet, but the Welsh lot have the more impressive locomotive." He grinned at Royston. "They did have, anyway."

They clambered up onto the footplate, and Royston took over duty at the boiler from Carstairs. Harriet smiled across at him.

The footplate had also been transformed. The copper of the boiler wall was now burnished. A pair of bronze snakes writhed about the regulator handle, the handle for the reversing mechanism was fashioned into a stylised, angular tortoise, a cockerel's head bravely rode the automatic brake valve, stern rams guarded the injector and ejector valves, and the alchemistic symbol was bold upon every gauge. Even the coal walker had acquired a frieze of *talaria*.

Benjamin leant from the cab, waved the works gates open, and then looked back along the train that extended so far into the works that it only just avoided fouling the traversing pit.

Over the sound of the band, St Catherine's began to leisurely toll ten o'clock. An expectant hush fell over those gathered.

"Right-away," announced Benjamin, spotting the guard's flag.

"Up advanced starter *on*," said Colton.

"Down outer home *on*," responded Harriet, and reached for the whistle cord.

Mercury made entreaty with the distant signal box.

"*Off*," said Colton, and then murmured, "Take us out, lass."

A ripple of excitement ran ahead of *Mercury* as Harriet had her ease forward onto the level crossing where the vicar of St Catherine's waited in full regalia, bible in hand. He placed his hand upon *Mercury*'s nearside buffer, and all present bowed their heads as the strong dreadful voice that poured hellfire and brimstone into all their Sundays asked the Lord's blessing upon the locomotive, those who attended her, and all who took train behind her. With rare reverence, *Mercury* deigned not to ruin the solemnity of the moment by lifting her safety valves.

The clergyman stepped back, and they were moving again, passing through the uplifted faces, hopeful parents, and excited children, through union flags loyally waved, and through a confusion of cries bestowing good wishes, safe home, and the best of luck.

Then they were passing the last stragglers, and safely swung across to the up road, Harriet opened the regulator. Royston gazed down the line, watching for signals and wondering of the morrow.

16.

Running Under Clear Signals

6th April 1876, Bristol

MERCURY HAD BACKED her train first into the magnificent hammer-beam-roofed train shed of Temple Meads. As her fitters fussed about her, Royston and Harriet stood at the cab door to watch their competitor set back beside them against the down platform, Father having won the toss.

Red Dragon, her carmine paintwork glistening in the sun, was longer and lower than *Mercury*. She had the same wheel configuration, although the wheels of her leading bogie were not that much smaller than her driving wheels, presumably to help balance her substantive cylinder assembly. Indeed, she bore on each side *two* cylinders arranged on a common piston rod, one not remarkably oversized, but the other of such diameter that only by narrowing and lengthening the boiler barrel did the locomotive remain within the loading gauge.

"She's a tandem compound, Royston," murmured Harriet with unwelcome wonder.

Royston grunted. "Prodigious connecting rods, I note."

"So should they be, given her arrangement. The thrust must be terrific, sir."

"As will be the hammer-blow upon the road, I fear," he said. "I hope she can maintain the rails, Harriet."

"I also," she assured him nervously. "Or if she cannot, then I hope we are in the lead."

"They appear unperturbed by wind drag," he said then.

Harriet nodded. *Red Dragon* was beautifully turned out yet, albeit on a greater scale, very conventional. Her black smoke box appeared bluff-fronted, although it did bear unusual vertical plates set a small distance from the boiler barrel. On these were mounted her nameplates, and if anyone could not read them, they would be prompted by the imposing sculpture of a dragon, wings spread defiantly, which the locomotive bore in front of its stout brass chimney.

"Clearly," murmured Harriet, "although the dragon is impressive."

"An apt observation, my lady, for it certainly should add impressive *drag on* to her." Royston chuckled and then, apparently dismissing the competition, turned to his boiler.

HARRIET WAS BESIDE *Mercury*, lowering the last of the access panels and carefully securing it, conscious throughout her final inspection of being watched from the footplate of *Red Dragon*.

Benjamin approached along the ballast, accompanied by their guard. The latter was every inch a seasoned railwayman, his uniform trim and spotless, his muttonchop sideburns grey and neatly barbered, and his face kind. Harriet's immediate thought was of a perfect grandfather, and if he were not a grandfather, grandchildren somewhere were missing out.

"Is everything in order, sir?" asked Harriet over the roar of *Red Dragon*'s safety valves.

"Perfectly, madam," said the guard. "I shall return to my station and test the automatic brake, and then you shall have my right-away."

"Thank you, sir."

The guard walked off, and Benjamin gazed at her with soft concern. "I'll see you in Paddington, Miss Harriet. The very best of luck, like!"

"Thank you, Benjamin." Harriet tried not to think of *Red Dragon* and her fearsome cylinders.

Benjamin then did something he had rarely done, and never since her twelfth birthday: he hugged her. "Be canny, lass," he demanded fiercely. "No taking o' risks, you hear?"

"I promise," she assured him quietly, aware of the so-familiar pipe smoke lingering on his overalls.

He released her then and walked down between the metals with the rest of the fitters, who all shouted last-minute encouragement back at her over what was now the combined roar of both locomotives' safety valves. She smiled and waved at them, then climbed up into *Mercury*'s cab.

"Guard will be testing the brakes momentarily," she called to Royston as she pulled across the handle that shuttered the footholds.

"Excellent. The station master has passed word they are signalling box-to-box back from Paddington that the lines are secured and everything is set for us."

They both knew how devilishly hot it would grow on the footplate, and had dressed accordingly. Royston looked particularly rakish and reminded her stirringly of a pirate of yore. He wore thin cotton trousers and a shirt unbuttoned at the collar, and about his brow he had wrapped a bandanna of silk in *Mercury*'s colours. He climbed over the coal walker to her side of the footplate, digging in his pocket.

"Take off your left glove, Harriet."

She did so, stripping off the well-worn leather driving glove. He claimed her hand, then slid a thin band over her ring finger.

"It was my grandmother's," he said. "Whatever happens to us, I would have it upon your hand."

Harriet lifted her hand and gazed at the ring. The gold bore a rose-cut emerald in a simple setting. Tears welled in her eyes. "I… I shall wear it with a singular joy, Royston, one that you alone can bring to me."

She hugged him to her, but then a prolonged shush and the vacuum gauge spinning down to atmospheric reminded them both of their responsibilities. With a final squeeze, Harriet released him and reached for the whistle cord to chirp acknowledgement to the guard, and Royston scrambled across to restore vacuum to the train pipe. He then leant from the cab, looking back for the guard's flag.

"That's the right-away," he told Harriet who was replacing her glove. "And the station master is coming down the ramp to act as starter."

Harriet watched the station master, sombre in frock coat and gleaming stovepipe hat, stride purposefully in front of *Mercury* and down between the tracks to a little distance ahead of the locomotives. He turned there and drew a heavy gold hunter from his waistcoat to hold it open on his hand.

"Five minutes to two," said Royston, who had his hunter out also.

"Five minutes," acknowledged Harriet, closing and

latching her cab door. She then shrugged off her jacket and laid it on the tender bench, where the "complete set of Lamps, a box of not less than twelve Detonators, two Red Flags, a Fire-bucket, and such tools as may be ordered by the Locomotive Superintendent" had been stowed. The paraphernalia had astounded Royston when she lugged them aboard, with the simple fire-bucket prompting a wry glance at the glowing maw of the firebox.

Now clad only in a summer-weight dress, she moved to the spectacle glass, checked the steam brakes, and then called to Royston to spin off the handbrakes on *Mercury*'s tender. Her hand seeking the comfort of the regulator, she gazed out of the spectacle glasses at the start of the 119 miles of metals that would bring them to Paddington—and tried not to think of the snorting *Red Dragon* beside her.

"Down inner home *off*," called Royston. "Up advanced starter *off*."

She repeated the calls, watching the signal arms drop one by one until none stood against them.

"One minute," Royston then called. He leant out and saluted—presumably in farewell to Benjamin and the fitters—and then, latching closed the nearside door, bent to the fire damper lever.

Harriet closed her eyes and muttered a quick, heartfelt prayer. When she reopened them, the station master was holding a green flag aloft in readiness, his eyes upon his watch. She was aware of her heart racing in anxiety as she watched him, and then suddenly the flag fell and was being waved with respectable restraint.

To the heavy thump of *Red Dragon*'s exhaust, Harriet opened the throttle; *Mercury* returned her more complex reply, then spun her wheels. With a curse, Harriet snapped the throttle closed and tried again more cautiously, and this time *Mercury* bit the metal and drew her train steadily from the platform after *Red Dragon*.

Harriet opened the regulator as quickly as she dared, but when to the booming salute of the local artillery regiment they crossed the Avon, the Welsh train already had half a train's lead on them and was still drawing steadily ahead, so that by the time *Mercury* dived into Broom Hill tunnel, barely three miles from Bristol, she followed *Red Dragon*'s tail-lights through the darkness.

The Great Western had imposed a line limit of one hundred miles an hour until three miles beyond Bath, and *Mercury* reached that by the five-mile mark. Given the adverse gradient she had to contend with, that was quite remarkable. Yet their rivals had stolen a three-quarters-of-a-mile lead, the tail of their train disappearing and reappearing as the line meandered up the Avon towards Bath, leaving only drifting smoke for *Mercury*.

The pleasant villas of Bath rushed past now, the fence crowded with people gleefully urging them on, but Harriet's thoughts were on the line ahead, and how it curved sharply with the river through the station.

"Hold on!" she yelled across the cab to Royston.

He looked up from crouching at the nearside injector, nodded, and braced himself between the vacuum brake stanchion and the spectacle glass, gazing forward.

Harriet knew from getting her route ticket that this was going to be a bad moment. Generously super-elevated, at fifty miles an hour the curve had been a smooth swing to the left, but challenging it at their present speed brought severe disquiet.

Now it was upon them, the station platforms not already

strewn with Welsh wreckage, but then *Red Dragon*'s weight had sensibly been concentrated lower than *Mercury*...

Mercury felt the curve, and then lurched and twitched uneasily through the station, her wheels emitting the most ghastly banshee scream. Harriet was suddenly glad they were on the right road, with less danger of jostling the platform itself. The locomotive settled, then easily rode the gentler reverse curve east.

It was then that Harriet spotted the tail of the opposing train, now more distant, and swore in hot indignation. Furiously, she beckoned Royston over the coal walker. "They are increasing their lead, and they have yet to reach the milepost," she yelled. "They cheat, sir."

He frowned. "Then we must not," he counselled loudly, "and bring fault upon their honour later; there cannot be a lack of witnesses." He retreated, leaving Harriet fuming.

Begrudgingly, however, she accepted the wisdom of his counsel and with impatience waited for the cursed milepost to flash past. "Now my girl," she murmured, "show us your true colours."

With grim determination, she drew up the regulator—and felt *Mercury* readily respond.

The meagre platforms of Box Halt were there and were gone, and they entered a short cutting that ended abruptly with Box Tunnel, its majestic, classically styled portal dwarfing even *Mercury*. The speed-gauge reading just below 120 miles an hour, with a sudden concussion the locomotive plunged into the darkness. Seconds later, they broke the existing speed record, but that brought poor comfort, for surely *Red Dragon* had already done so.

DIMITY STOOD IN the shadow of one of the columns supporting the cathedral-like transepts of Paddington, glad to be within the cordon of police but trying to remain unobtrusive amongst all these Lords and Sirs and Ladies. Veracity and Lillian, Lady Alicia's maid, stood with her, and they all gazed up at the train indicator board above the concourse, Dimity with creeping dismay.

The board had been adapted for the race and showed the two locomotives' last-telegraphed position and speed. A panel marked LEADS had hung after *Red Dragon*'s name since the off, and the latest updates gave her fifteen miles an hour over *Mercury*.

She looked across the concourse where three distinct groups had gathered. The largest was centred about the familiar Lord Clifton, who was puffing upon a cigar and watching the board in discourse with eminent friends and colleagues. A second smaller group were the Welsh gentlemen and their supporters, all smiles and affable bonhomie, and the third the Chale Bridge contingent of Mr Colton, Lord Harlow, Mr Bracewaite, Lady Alicia, Miss Bianca, the Mallows, and a weasel-like man she had heard said to be Lord Harlow's agent. There was no cheer in that group—except for that of Lord Harlow, dressed extravagantly in *Mercury*'s colours—but even at this distance Dimity thought his efforts to bolster spirits appeared forced.

An empty platform awaited the contestants, a gay silk ribbon stretched across each of the two adjoining tracks to greet the winner, which if the board was to be believed looked as if it would be the damnable *Red Dragon*.

IT WAS THE stuff of nightmares—lurching through the constricting darkness, assailed on all sides by the thunder of *Mercury*'s exhaust, the firebox urgent orange and making hellish the air, and Harriet's face macabre in its fiendish light.

Royston knelt to gauge the fire, flinching at its livid heat. Retreating, he urged the coal walker to maximum speed, then jumped over it to open the offside injector to full flow, knowing how rapacious for fuel and water *Mercury* must now become. Heavens, but it was hot!

His ears popped and the sunlight filled the cab. Coming up behind Harriet, he put a hand on her shoulder and gazed at the speed-gauge, the twin needles passing 145 miles an hour. He peered forwards as Corsham station flashed past, but there was not one sign of *Red Dragon*.

"Call the speed for me." He gave her a brief hug and then, the sight glasses needing his attention, jumped back across the coal walker to check. The boiler water level seemed steady, and he had the nearside injector only open partially.

"One hundred and fifty!"

They had taken *Mercury* to this speed before, albeit on the rollers of the test shed. Then the brake cooling had started to boil, putting an end to onerous testing. They were thus crossing into unknown territory. What if *Mercury* demanded water faster than the two injectors could provide? Starving the fire of air would bring that situation under control if he caught it soon enough, but more worrisome was the terrific stress on *Mercury*'s running gears. They had been designed for faster than this, but they were designs untested, and a sudden fracture in a rod could bring instant catastrophe.

"One hundred and *sixty*, Royston!" Harriet called, grinning.

He grinned back, yet thoughts of catastrophe lingered, and with a horrible premonition he turned to stare at the vacuum gauge. It read a comforting twenty-seven inches, and he breathed easier. The train was intact; they could have lost all the carriages to ruin in Box Tunnel and not been any the wiser, for even with the brakes on the tender locked up, with an open regulator *Mercury* might arrogantly ignore the drag.

With the open downs of Wiltshire flashing past, Royston checked his watch to find the time just shy of the quarter hour, and already Bristol lay twenty-odd miles behind then.

"One hundred and *seventy*!"

He opened his injector further, then crossed to Harriet.

"This is what we hoped from her." He gazed at the telegraph poles passing in a mesmerising flicker.

"But she still has more to give, my love," said Harriet.

Indeed, the needles, although slower, were still creeping higher.

"Where is… was that?" asked Royston, as a town passed in an incomprehensible blur of detail.

"Chippenham. Twenty-five miles out."

Sweating profusely, he ducked to check the fire, although that seemed a very meek term for it now, and then stood on the coal walker to check the boiler level, and then back to the tender, balancing himself against the roll and shake of their progress to peer at the water gauges. *Mercury* had consumed less than a sixth of the offside tank, and the nearside tank stood higher still. It boded well.

"One hundred and eighty and… and smoke!" cried Harriet excitedly. "Smoke! I can see their smoke."

Royston quickly came to her station. Seeing nothing, he blamed a hopeful imagination but then saw for himself the thin veil under which they sped. "They cannot be that far ahead of us then."

Harriet then cursed and spun on more cut-off.

"What is it?"

"Wheel slippage," she replied, frowning. "How curious that it happens now. We do not face a gradient—quite the contrary in fact. There: It is resolved."

The line meandered left and then right, to then run straight along the foot of a long lofty hill, its steep slopes fresh with sweet spring grass.

"There! That's them, Harriet!" he suddenly cried, spotting the rear of the *Red Dragon*'s train in the far distance.

"It is! I am sure we should have seen them prior to this," hazarded Harriet hopefully. "We… We must be catching up upon them."

Their quarry vanished as the line eased left, and then right, but as another town flashed by, *Red Dragon* came back into sight, and closer.

"We *are* catching up!" said Harriet gleefully. "And look, Royston: 190!"

His arm tightened about her waist in happiness.

THE REAR OF the opposing train was creeping tantalisingly

close, but Harriet had to divert her attention then to the speed-gauge needles, which had again spread apart in slippage, the driving wheels turning faster than the rail passed beneath them. A few more turns on the cut-off shepherded the engine needle back to that of the tender, now steady at 190. It was an inconceivable speed, the headlong rush in which everything passed, coupled perhaps with the heat, bringing unsettling dizziness.

Swindon could only be another six or seven miles— barely two minutes away for *Mercury*. Might they delight Pennydale's workforce by having the lead by then?

"Water?" Royston yelled across the cab, waving the caddy.

She nodded thankfully and swallowed. Goodness, how much the pirate Royston looked now, for he had his shirt unbuttoned to the waist and *wore nothing beneath!* His firm frame, gleaming with sweat, brought a sudden flurry of desire and the unbidden yearning to have him naked as a savage, along with the exquisitely keen awareness of having forsaken her corset this one day for fear of being rendered fully insensible by the heat.

Shaking the alluring image from her head, she returned her attention to the road, and took a long draught from the caddy. The water was lukewarm, yet very welcome.

The gap had closed enough between *Mercury* and the swaying end carriage of *Red Dragon* that she could make out its every detail.

"We have them," crowed Royston from his spectacle glass. "We must be doing twenty miles an hour more!"

"Greater than that, quite possibly," she yelled back as *Mercury* nosed past the tail of their rivals. Now the carriages were slipping past them steadily, and the trackside fences were a blur of excited onlookers. *Mercury* came up upon *Red Dragon* herself, steaming hard, her connecting rods but a shimmer of silver. With a brief roar the platforms of Swindon station shot past, and then the carmine expanse of the tender with its sombre black lettering of OWEN PERKINS, MERTHYR TYDFIL slid abreast of her.

Still caught in the romance of her swashbuckling Royston, Harriet flinched down, fearful that the opposing footplate, whilst incapable of boarding *Mercury*, might have prepared a broadside. But then they were passing their rival's defiant figurehead, a quivering frenzy in the oncoming hurricane, and *Red Dragon* was slipping behind them.

The Vale of the White Horse opened before them, and as the Wiltshire Canal flashed underneath, Harriet knew the gradient now gently favoured them, and would until Paddington. A clear road lay ahead of her, the signals dropped in salute. She glanced at the speed-gauge, fearful of slippage, but the needles remained together… and were slowly creeping up.

"Come quickly, my love," she demanded.

Royston hurdled the coal walker, and she pointed to the needles, now venturing beyond the flowing serifed numerals of 195.

"Might we actually…" she ventured.

"Oh, great heavens!" he exclaimed.

The ancient white horse slid into view, high on the hillside, galloping with them.

"COME ON, *MERCURY!*" screamed Dimity, beside herself with exhilaration and no longer caring a jot for being inconspicuous. She need not worry, for the broad terminus was filled with cries and cheers, and so much excitement ebbed and flowed through the fashionably dressed crowds that the police cordon feared for decorum and had grown stern.

Unseen hands worked behind the board and had already indicated that *Mercury* had gained superiority in speed, but as Swindon was simultaneously accorded to both locomotives, the LEADS board was stripped from *Red Dragon* and offered to *Mercury*. Dimity clutched Veracity to her and screamed in delight.

The moods in the two camps suffered a sudden reversal, and even over the hubbub Dimity could hear Lord Harlow's delighted laughter. She knew from her mistress that *Mercury* might never have been completed but for his patronage, and at that moment she could almost forgive the marquess for everything... she *almost* could.

Lord Clifton was talking animatedly with his second wife as the speed figures were drawn away and replaced. *Red Dragon*... 171 miles an hour... horrifying fast! Now they waited judgement on *Mercury,* but the board remained blank. The delay drew a hush over the cavernous space, all eyes upon where the figures should be.

"What's the matter?" asked Veracity worriedly.

"I don't know," replied Dimity, her blood running cold for her mistress.

There! A three... now a nought and a three... and then in prefix, a two...

The glass canopy shook to the thrilled roar of the crowd. Two hundred and three miles an hour! Dimity glanced at her camp just as Miss Bianca wavered and slumped, fortunately to be caught by Lord Harlow.

"Oh, Lor'!" exclaimed Veracity over the clamour, then hurried to her mistress while rummaging in her bag for smelling salts.

MERCURY HAD ASTOUNDED them both. The speed-gauge shivered, yet as they hugged in excited, disbelieving celebration, it remained determinedly above the vaulted mark. Every eighteen seconds brought them a mile closer to London, but now Royston was deeply worried. The injectors were faithfully maintaining the water level, but something was deeply amiss within the firebox itself.

He peered into it, squinting at the blinding yellow-white light, wishing for smoked glass, and whistling. This was no fire, but a maelstrom of heat. The coal walker still drew the small lump coal into its heart, but the coal was ablaze almost upon entering the firebox, the inner section of the walker was cherry red, and about it danced a furious white glow.

Surely flames spewed from *Mercury*'s chimney? He worried the walker would soften and fail, but more, he feared for the copper roof. It was amply covered with water from above, but could that alone keep it from growing weak before this inferno and yielding to the two-hundred-odd pounds per square inch of destruction it withheld?

He glanced at Harriet, straining forward to the spectacle glass, her hand curled upon the *caduceus*, her full lips parted in absorbed delight. He thought of heat calculus, and yearned for his slide rule rather than the precious few aide-memoirs he had stuffed into his pocket for the run. How much longer must the copper bear this hellfire before he could damp down? At this speed, a quarter of an hour perhaps—barely the duration of an amusing discourse. Surely an inch of copper could be patient that long?

Unless he had the relevant calculus wrong, a good portion of the firebox wall must be comfortably below its melt point, and there were always design margins that first must be eroded. He weighed the risk and decided that too much rode on *Mercury* making Paddington before *Red Dragon*.

"Farringdon Road," yelled Harriet. "Halfway."

He checked his watch. Twenty-six minutes had elapsed since the station master's flag had fallen. He checked the boiler level, found it had eased lower, and gave another turn on the feed-water to the injector on that side. While he waited to see if that reversed the decline in level, he staggered to the tender and the gauges there. The nearside water tank had dropped considerably—barely half the tank was left—but the offside stood at nearly two-thirds full. He frowned. That could not be right. It was the offside injector that was wide open, not the nearside one. By all things logical, the level in the nearside tank should have stood higher.

He checked the tank valves. The injector isolators were open, the cross-feed between the tanks was closed, and both the fill stopcocks screwed tight shut. Then he remembered the second set of stopcocks at the rear of the tender. Could the nearside one have worked itself open with all the vibration? It sounded unlikely, but he could think of no other explanation. He tapped Harriet on the shoulder.

"Going back for a moment." He pointed to the tender corridor.

Making adjustments to the cut-off, she nodded.

Royston lurched into the corridor, balancing himself with both hands. He emerged from darkness into the thin daylight of the connecting plates, and as he welcomed the chill of the wind curling under the tender carapace as it flared over the first carriage, he saw legs splayed upon the plating, clad in overalls.

Who was this? There was only he, Harriet, and the guard in his fine uniform aboard. He moved forward, confused, and then was stunned. Benjamin lay sprawled face down on the plates, a heavy spanner loose beside him, and by the offside stopcock knelt the guard, minus his hat, twisting the stopcock… open.

Royston rushed him. At the last moment the guard looked up, his eyes opening wide in shock as Royston, bare-chested and streaked with coal, a plundering marauder of the Carribee, fell upon him.

Royston dragged the heavier man by main force from the valve, brought his knee up in a way that would have quite shocked the Marquess of Queensberry, and threw the older man down on the shivering connecting plates. As the man groaned, Royston bent and spun closed the valve and then staggered across to the second valve upon the nearside. It was, as he'd feared, wide open.

He began to spin it closed but then had an irrational forewarning of dread. He dodged aside, and the spanner cracked against the tank wall, leaving a dent and bringing forth a dull boom from the tank over the roar of the passing air. Royston sprang up, in and under the guard as the spanner swooped again, catching him on the shoulder as he furiously drove the older man back.

The guard tripped over Benjamin, staggered, and then

Royston clawed his fingers into the guard's face and slammed his head back into the bulkhead. There was a fleeting look of confusion on the guard's face, then he crumpled into a heap.

Royston leapt across Benjamin and screwed the stopcock tight shut. He then knelt by Benjamin and rolled him over. There was a livid bruise spreading under his eye, but he was breathing. Drawing water from a test cock, Royston splashed it onto the ancient fitter's face and then shook him. Blearily, Benjamin's eyes opened, and Royston helped him to sit up against the tender tank bulkhead.

"Are you all right, sir?" he yelled anxiously.

Benjamin shook his head as if to clear it, then nodded. "Not so young as I thought, like, Mr Staley," he admitted, sadness in his eyes.

Royston retrieved the spanner and pressed it into Benjamin's hands. "Can you watch our guard, sir?"

"Aye, I can do that for you, and it will give me great pleasure if he stirs," roared Benjamin grimly. Royston made to rise, but then Benjamin grasped his hand urgently. "How does she answer, sir?"

Royston smiled. "We are travelling at just over two hundred miles an hour, Benjamin."

The old man gave a low whistle. "Now there's a thing, like. And to think I almost slept through it."

HARRIET GLANCED BACK occasionally. The moment Royston had promised seemed to stretch on and on, but just as she contemplated abandoning the regulator to check on the boiler, he staggered onto the footplate, clutching his shoulder, and immediately consulted the tender water gauges.

"What has happened, Royston?" she called. "Are you all right, my love?"

He went to the boiler glasses and then squatted, his face bright with the fury of the fire. Only then did he come to her. "How far have we to run?"

"Why, we have just passed Pangbourne," she replied. "Another forty miles or so."

Royston closed his eyes in thought. "All right." He bit his lip. "I think we will make it."

"Whatever do you mean?"

"We have lost at least a couple of thousand gallons of water," he said grimly. "And to sabotage, I'd wager."

"Sabotage, sir!"

"Look to your road, madam. It passes exceeding quick."

She did so, yet remained filled with horror. "But *sabotage*!"

"We always feared it, Harriet."

"An unwanted passenger?"

"We had an *unexpected* passenger, I grant." Royston clung to the door handle as *Mercury* thundered towards the metropolis. "But that may have saved us from retiring hurt from this race. No, the reprobate was our esteemed guard."

Harriet thought of the kindly grandfather. "*Was*, sir? Is he cast from the train?"

"No indeed, madam. He is currently insensible, watched over by Benjamin."

"*Benjamin*! How is he upon the train?"

"I confess I have no idea, my lady," said Royston. "Yet I

sense I should be glad of it. He'll have quite a story with which to regale us at Paddington."

"A curious one, I am sure," she replied.

"Excuse me, madam. The boiler demands my attention."

Harriet held her next thought until her pirate returned. "But what of Paddington, sir? When should we begin to check our impetus?"

Royston tugged a sweat-damp sheaf of paper from his pocket and, peeling one from it, made consultation. "We should allow six miles or more, Harriet."

"Or more?"

"I confess to not anticipating *Mercury* would answer so well, madam, and have not the nicest confidence in my calculations."

Harriet digested that. "Then I would have us take off speed at Hanwell; that will leave us more than seven miles of metals to come to a stand."

"That appears prudent, although I wished I knew how our Welsh friends fare."

"You believe they may have coaxed more speed from *Red Dragon*?"

"It cannot be completely ruled out, Harriet, and I fear we omitted to include any means of looking back for them," he said. "But let it be Hanwell, and pray *Red Dragon* was not showing false colours at Swindon. How long until we reach there?"

Maidenhead was approaching; during their brief conversation, *Mercury* had covered twelve miles. "Six or seven minutes at most, sir."

THE OFFSIDE WATER tank was three-quarters gone; the nearside even lower. What remained *should* be sufficient, yet he was anxious. Was it time to start placating the firebox, take the onslaught off the copper, and also slacken *Mercury's* thirst? They would need steam for the braking, but not as much as to maintain this gallop. Royston hesitated, then disengaged the dog gear that drove the first stage of the coal walker. The remainder he kept running for fear that the part in the firebox itself, once stilled, might fuse solid.

He waited another minute or so during which the fire seemed oblivious to the lack of fresh fuel, then bent to the lever to close the dampers. He hauled upon it, but found it stuck fast. Grasping it with both hands, he tried again yet to no avail. With a loud curse as dismally constructed as it was scandalous, he pitted all his strength against the lever, yet it refused to budge.

Alerted by his profanity, Harriet scrambled over the coal walker to him, lit by the incisive radiance of the firebox. For a moment he forgot the intransigent damper, for her perspiration-soaked bodice had grown lackadaisical of modesty, to which she appeared to have given it sole charge.

She knelt opposite him, clasping her hands on the damper lever by his, and as he hauled on it, she did as well, her features creased with effort. When that achieved nothing, they tried again. Abruptly, the lever yielded to their combined efforts, and the sound of the fire softened. She grinned in delight, her face close to his, and then neither of them could relinquish the damper lever. Harriet's eyes grew misty and fond, perfectly reflecting the affection he held for her, and ceding in a moment to a perfect madness that denied the precarious water situation and the imagined peril of the firebox roof, he was kissing her, and Harriet's lips pressed back upon his with eagerness, her tongue savage and needful.

Too soon she rose from him, her eyes sparkling and the negligence of her bodice complete. Acknowledging the silent revolt within his trousers with a wry, tolerant glance, she skipped across the coal walker. Taking a firm grip upon the *caduceus*, she gazed at Royston with serene contentment. She then peered forward, and her expression grew puzzled, and then anxious.

"We are past Hanwell, sir," she said, drawing the regulator closed, and winding desperately on the cut-off lever. "Bring the train pipe to twenty inches, and I would favour the nose panels open."

Royston leapt over the brake stanchion, eased the valve open, and watching the vacuum gauge sink, felt for the simple ebony lever that controlled the steam rams in the nose and twisted it flush against the roof.

The roar of *Mercury*'s exhaust had ceased with the closing of her regulator, but to the banshee cry of the passing air was added an uneasy grumble from ahead of them. By then Harriet had the motion into reverse and carefully drew up the regulator once again. *Mercury* lurched, and her exhaust sounded again, but now in a staccato coughing hiccup. She was slowing, and slowing quickly, making Royston grab for the stanchion as the locomotive tried to have him into the boiler back plate.

"One hundred and seventy," called Harriet. "And... sixty... and... fifty... and... forty..."

"Distant *on*," called Royston, clinging grimly to the stanchion.

"Outer *off*... and... thirty... and... twenty... and... ten," yelled Harriet, "and one hundred." She drew the regulator down and the deceleration eased.

Checking the boiler, he slowed the injector on his side, then unlatched and drew back the cab door, admitting a roar of blissfully chill air. Where was *Red Dragon?* Had they left her far behind, or by leaving her braking to the very last moment, did she rush to steal victory from *Mercury?* He dared a glance back but saw only their carriages and a plethora of excited faces.

"Fifteen inches in the train pipe, sir," she called.

He obeyed, closing the nose panels as he did so, and then crossed to her side. The speed-gauge read eighty miles an hour, and the buildings of London passed with peculiar lethargy.

"She is completely in hand," she said, taking off the regulator completely and letting the brakes of the train slow *Mercury*.

"That is most relieving." He peered down into the fire. It retained an ugly brightness, but the yellow-white vehemence had died away. He then checked the tender tank. The gauges still registered water, but precious little. Collecting Harriet's jacket from the tender bench, he took it to her.

With a look of thanks, she shrugged it on and, her hand quickly returning to the steam brake, buttoned it one-handed, her eyes on the confusion of signals challenging *Mercury*. She did, however, spare a moment to give his open shirt a questioning look.

He quickly began to make repairs himself while still listening for the thunder that would presage *Red Dragon* overreaching them.

"Paddington, sir!" Harriet exclaimed. He looked ahead to see Wyatt's familiar triple canopy and the crowded platforms beneath. Harriet drew on the whistle chain, and *Mercury* bayed her victory.

They slid in amongst the platforms, guided beside one that, if lacking quantity of welcome, made up for it in quality. Royston was, however, leaning from the nearside door, motioning to the fitters clustered on the ballast awaiting *Mercury* at the rails' end. He mimicked drinking and reached back to pound the tender tank. Carstairs immediately understood and called the men to the hoses lying at their feet.

To the strains of "See, the Conqu'ring Hero Comes!" *Mercury* parted the tricolour ribbon stretched across before her, and with a sigh of her steam brakes, came to a halt a few yards from the buffers. She rocked back on her springs, content.

17.

Drawing the Fire

T HE CAB SEEMED suddenly crowded. Royston was elucidating *Mercury*'s state of affairs to Carstairs, two fitters were at the stopcocks, and another two back through the tender to the controls there. Then Benjamin appeared from the tender corridor.

"Benjamin! Are you all right?"

"I'll live, Miss Harriet."

"But what were you doing on the train?"

"Well see, Miss Harriet, there was something 'bout yon guard your father did not care for, and neither did I. So we hatched it 'twixt us for me to keep an eye on him. I slipped on board at the last minute when everyone had their eyes on the locomotives."

"It appears your suspicions were well-founded."

Benjamin nodded. "He tried to leak on the vacuum brake first, but we'd brazed a stop valve into the guard's release pipe last night, and Blakes had that closed after the brake test. He seemed right flummoxed then. Tried to get at the pipe line between the carriages, but I knew they were well out of reach. Then he went to see what mischief he could do to *Mercury* herself."

"And that was when you called him out?"

Benjamin gave her a wry look. "Tried to leastways, miss."

Royston was peering out. "Your father and Lord Harlow appear to have been thoroughly congratulated, Miss Colton. I believe our presence is demanded on the platform."

Harriet tugged at her jacket and smoothed her skirts. "I must look a sight, Mr Staley."

"You are far more comely than I." He indicated his face and clothing, smudged and streaked with coal dust. "And it is not as if we are expected to appear as though we have just taken a gentle promenade along the terrace."

She made final adjustments, then nodded. He slid the door open, stepped onto the platform, and offered his hand for her to alight. Father, Lord Harlow, and two most eminent gentlemen awaited them, the ladies a discrete distance away.

"Lord Clifton, Sir Daniel? May I introduce my daughter Harriet, *Mercury*'s designer and driver," said Father. "And Mr Staley, her fireman and designer also."

Harriet curtsied and was sure Royston bowed. "It is a great pleasure to meet you, Lord Clifton. And you, Sir Daniel."

Lord Clifton, shorter than her had it not been for the magnificent stovepipe he wore, appraised her shrewdly, then with a smile, bowed slightly in the French style. "I believe it is I who should be the more pleased, madam, for this day not only have you driven to victory in my Challenge, but so gloriously that I feel a young man's prideful arguments for the broad gauge have finally been vindicated."

There was subtle applause, and Harriet knew she was blushing.

"Forty-seven minutes from Bristol to London!" exclaimed Sir Daniel delightedly. "Who could have imagined it?"

"As I laid out the line, Daniel, so I imagined it," said Lord Clifton matter-of-factly. "Although I feared never to see it proven."

They then heard an engine whistle over the commotion, approaching in a continual howl.

"Our other competitor approaches." Lord Clifton looked up the metals westward. "Ah, there she is."

"She approaches… too fast, Isambard," offered Sir Daniel, knowing Paddington well.

Even in the bright sunlight beyond the canopy, Harriet could see the brake blocks glowed cherry red. "She is in distress!"

Royston turned. "Save yourselves!" he bellowed at the Owen Perkins fitters on the metals awaiting their locomotive, which was lurching drunkenly through the complex point-work on the approaches. "She is coming into the stops!"

They scattered, vaulting onto the next platform to safety. Royston's cry animated the concourse also, the crowds scattering from *Red Dragon*'s reckless path.

Red Dragon ran fast amongst the platforms, but she was slowing, and for a moment it seemed she might stop in time. It was not to be, however. With a tortured splintering crash, she hit the buffers at some fifteen miles an hour, and the dragon on her prow took flight. Windows shattered in her carriages, and the first two after the tender overrode each other, buffers pitching up from the rail. Her mascot landed in the concourse and skittered to a stop, its nose ground into the flags.

The echoes of the crash died away, and then the crowd

surged and Her Majesty's Constabulary were hard pressed to contain the excitement. *Red Dragon*'s driver climbed shakily from the cab but immediately went forward to the cylinder assembly, where the frock-coated contingent from Merthyr soon gathered with him.

"Did they leave off braking until too late?" suggested Father.

"I can hardly countenance such negligence, Father," replied Harriet.

"I believe we are about to find out," noted Royston as two of the Welsh contingent approached angrily.

"Sabotage!" cried one of them into Father's face. "You sabotaged our locomotive!"

"That is a very serious accusation, Perkins," said Sir Daniel. "I demand immediate substantiation."

Perkins turned to him. "Our reversing gear was jammed with a wedge, Sir Daniel; we could barely apply any counter-steam at all."

"That you came back into Bristol without difficulty suggests you should be looking to your own fitters," said Harriet. "I am sure no one else approached your locomotive before the off."

"I am sure we shall discover such a fitter, madam," said Perkins. "One in the pay of Colton and Holm!"

"That is an outrageous lie!" Harriet cried.

Lord Harlow looked horrifyingly serious. "Perhaps, sir, you accuse others of what you yourself have done," he said to Perkins. "For who placed a certain Evan Evans in Pennydale Works?"

"I have never heard such nonsense, my lord," declared Perkins, "nor know of this man."

"Then what of our guard, who put our lives at risk—and

those of the public—by attempting to drain our tender tanks in full flight?" said Royston. "Is he then your man, sir?"

Sir Daniel turned to Royston. "Is this true, sir? Our guard? A Great Western man?"

"I take no pleasure in assuring you that you have my word upon it, Sir Daniel," said Royston. "I myself dragged him from the stopcocks. An ugly skirmish ensued in which I rendered him insensible."

"Really, Royston!" said Harriet in awe.

"I fear I had little choice, Miss Colton; he already had Benjamin laid out." Royston then turned to Perkins. "Do you deny the guard also?"

"I do—and vehemently, sir!"

"I am inclined," asserted Lord Clifton, lighting a cigar, "to believe all who stand here honourable."

"My lord?" said Lord Harlow with curiosity.

"I see a single hand at work in this foul business, one distant from where we stand who wished my Challenge to end in disaster," said Lord Clifton. "I commend this notion for your consideration, my lord and gentlemen."

"Isambard, as usual I believe you may be right," said Sir Daniel. He then addressed Father. "The guard remains in custody?"

Father looked to Harriet, and she glanced to Benjamin, standing at *Mercury*'s footplate door, who nodded softly. "He does," she assured everyone.

"Then I would have him handed *discreetly* to the police for questioning," said Sir Daniel. "I believe the severity of the charges he faces will loosen his tongue and yield the names of others worthy of the constabulary's investigations." He looked then to Father and Perkins. "Well, sirs, will you accept Lord Clifton's counsel? Will you as gentlemen make your peace?"

The two contestants looked at each other steadily, and then Perkins put out his hand. "I congratulate you on your victory, sir. No malign hand prevented our progress, only the indecorous ending of it; *Mercury* quite plainly showed us her heels."

Father accepted the hand and shook it. "As did *Red Dragon* out of Bristol, sir, when we thought the race yours."

Perkins and his companion bowed to Father and then the company, then withdrew sadly to inspect the damage to their locomotive.

Lord Harlow made a gesture, and Hackett was at his side. "Hackett, attend with the Owen Perkins gentlemen," he murmured.

"Yes, my lord." Hackett was as quickly gone.

"And now," declared Sir Daniel, "I would examine this locomotive of yours, Colton." He stepped to the footplate, but Benjamin blocked the way, grimly protective.

"Oh, Benjamin." Harriet laughed. "Do you not know this gentleman? This is Sir Daniel Gooch—*the* Daniel Gooch. I am certain he has been building locomotives quite as long as you, Benjamin."

Benjamin caught his forelock. "Then you're in need of my apology, Sir Daniel. Come aboard, and welcome!"

Lord Clifton puffed impulsively. "I think I shall join you, Daniel."

"You may if you promise not to insist on driving her, Isambard. We have so far averted major disaster today," responded Sir Daniel.

"Thirty years and more, and still you do not forgive me that?" said Lord Clifton sadly.

"*Those.*" Sir Daniel smiled. "And in all conscience, Isambard, no."

Harriet made to follow, but Royston claimed her hand. "No, Harriet." He turned with her to Father.

Harriet clasped Royston's hand tight, suddenly anxious, excited, and embarrassed all at once. *Must it be now, Royston? And here?* Yet where else, what other time could it be *more* right?

"Mr Colton," he said with a subtle bow, "may I have your consent to taking your daughter's hand in marriage?"

Father appeared astonishingly unflustered, but instead turned to Harriet. "Well, daughter, would you have him?" he asked fondly.

Disengaging her hand from Royston, she nervously stripped off her left glove; the emerald glinted in the sunlight streaming through the lofty glass.

"A brilliant answer," commented Lord Harlow, "as those you offer so often are."

Mother swooped in like a Valkyrie. "What is this, Harriet? Mr Staley has offered for you?"

"Royston has, Mother, and I have accepted," said Harriet apprehensively.

"Then I am most splendidly happy for you, dear," said Mother, and hugged her.

"He proposed on the footplate, like?" asked Father with a broad grin.

"Why, yes, he did, Father, before the race began," allowed Harriet truthfully.

Bianca rushed up and hugged Harriet. "Oh, Harry, this is wonderful," she said, tears in her eyes, holding Harriet at arms' length.

"Oh, dash it!" exclaimed Lord Harlow. He eased Bianca from Harriet, took her hands in his, and dropped to a knee. "My Venus, would you consent to becoming the Marchioness of Harlow and my wife?"

Now Bianca's tears were streaming free. "I will with all my heart, my Justin."

Lord Harlow stood and addressed Colton. "Do I have your consent in this matter, sir?"

Now Father did look surprised. "I…"

Mother whispered urgently in his ear.

Father's brow cleared, and he smiled fulsomely. "You have my daughter's consent, my lord, and now you have mine."

Lord Harlow kissed Bee with unsettling passion, but then Royston's lips were upon Harriet's own.

Mercury's safety valves lifted with a roar.

12th May 1877, Chale Bridge

SO HECTIC HAD the year been that it seemed to have sped by as swiftly as *Mercury*. Lectures had to be given to learned societies and their honours graciously accepted (an even more grandiose chalice from the Society of Professional Gentlewomen awaited Harriet at the next Christmas party). There had been an exhibition trip around the country with *Mercury*, and then trial runs back and forth between Bristol and London, now with excited passengers and distinguished guests riding the footplate (of whom Sir Daniel and Lord Clifton were the only ones to dress for circumstance rather than occasion). On each run more level crossings had become bridges, and the special signalling needed to combine the supra expresses with the slower traffic was nearly complete. All the while, the production class locomotives were always there to claim their time.

The police investigation into the sabotage had been thorough, through agents and other parties leading back to a certain Mr Mordecai Leyland, already facing charges of criminal negligence brought by the Board of Trade over the horrific catastrophes involving his steamers. It could not be proven whether he incited the sabotage alone or acted with the material support of the greater steamer lobby, but the latter was discreetly suspected. There were also lingering misgivings over whether the *Spindler* disaster had truly been an accident.

Harriet and Royston had wed the previous June at St Catherine's in Chale Bridge. The wedding breakfast was held in the grounds of Pennydale House, and the entire village was invited. When the newly-weds returned from a short honeymoon in Italy, they were regaled with tales of the search in the morning for those who had fallen asleep in a hedge or ditch on their way home.

Soon after their wedding, they attended the much grander nuptials in the private chapel of Kimstanton Castle, when Justin Dallory, fourth Marquess of Harlow, Earl of Kimstanton, Baron Ravensworth, took to wife a radiant Bianca Colton, and the wedding march (in truth, more a wedding earthquake) rang out, played by Hackett upon the Tannhäuser-Trapp Steam Pandemonium. And now, happily burbling in Veracity's arms and being doted over by both her grandmothers, was the three-week-old Lady Aurelia Margaret Beatrice Dallory.

They had all gathered at Pennydale Works in the warm May sunlight to name the first of the production class, ready to be delivered to the Great Western. She stood in steam on the works roads, her nameplate discretely veiled. Beside her stood *Mercury*, soon to travel with Harriet and Royston to the Americas to show the advantage of supra expresses on that great continent. Beyond *Mercury* stood *Red Dragon*, her mascot restored, booked with her crew to India for the same purpose.

The newly completed locomotive combined aspects of both parents. She had *Mercury*'s carapace, although with an even sleeker nose, with subtle fairings over her compounded cylinders. Other inherited traits were not so evident—*Mercury*'s centrifugal compensator, superior injectors, and mechanical stoker, *Red Dragon*'s constant speed mechanism and anti-slip gear. In the assembly shop two of her class followed her, the *Countess of Kimstanton*, three-quarters complete and the *Lady Clifton*, with frames and wheels, and recently united with her boiler.

The *Countess of Kimstanton* was a clever conceit. The Law of Succession dictated that Lady Aurelia was the Heir Assumptive of the marquess until a brother arrived, and thus could never claim the honorary title the locomotive bore. But that Lord Harlow had insisted upon the name sent a clear message as to where he stood on reform.

"How goes Merthyr with the racing steamers, Harlow?" asked Royston.

The marquess, wearing a golden frock coat and an extravagant top hat, grimaced and clutched his side tenderly. "Most encouragingly, although I confess I rolled the prototype again."

Bianca gave him a disapproving look.

"Oh, my dear," Lord Harlow said soothingly, "you know Hackett is most attentive to the safety of the design."

"It is a testament to his assiduousness that you are but

bruised, my lord," commented Harriet.

The general manager rushed up, looking harried.

"Is everything ready, Godfrey?" asked Father, Mother upon his arm.

"I quite believe so, Sam," replied Bracewaite.

Father turned to the dowager marchioness. "My lady, if you would do us the great honour of performing the naming."

"Of course, Sir Samuel." (For Father had been knighted for his great service to the realm, which had had Mother walking on air for two months at the very minimum.)

Lady Harlow stepped carefully forward to where a velvet rope hung. "It is with great pleasure, and in the fondest hope that she shall run fast, serve well, and keep all safe, I name this locomotive..." She tugged the rope, and the velvet fell from the nameplate. *"Cupid's Arrow."*

"T'were nearly *Mercury*'s name," murmured Father to Harriet, and gave her a broad wink.

The End

Author's Notes

I was inspired to write an alternative history novel having written several police comedies set in altered times. I was also inspired by my love of industrial archaeology, of which locomotive development is a large part.

This book could have been all about *Mercury*, however my partner encouraged me to introduce a strong romantic element and then helped me craft what I hope is a satisfying romance. In the writing, it quickly proved to introduce an agreeable equilibrium between the three protagonists, one of metal and two of mortal flesh.

Mercury Rising's late Victorian world differs substantially from history in three ways. To permit a romance of equals, I had Queen Victoria politely yet firmly press for the acceptance of women into professional circles. I had Brunel win the gauge war of the 1840s because I needed broad gauge's stability for "supra-expresses" to be at all practical within the engineering of the time. Finally, I extended Brunel's short life (he died at 53) to allow him to present the challenge on his 70th birthday. I reasoned that if he found true love with an imagined second wife, he'd lose the passion to work himself to death. The remainder of history I left alone. The Abbots Ripton accident occurs on its true date, the battle between road and rail was already joined, and the steam turbine not yet… *perfected*.

While most characters in the novel are fictional, Major-

General Hutchinson of Her Majesty's Inspectorate of Railways was a real and dedicated officer, and Sir Daniel Gooch, ten years younger than Brunel, lived until 1889. Similarly, places and institutions were invented for the story amongst those that are real. Brunel's Great Western Railway existed and prospered until it was nationalized in 1948, yet the London and Northern Railway exists only in my imagination. George Stephenson founded the Institute of Mechanical Engineers in Birmingham, but there was never a Stephenson Institute in his home city of Newcastle.

Researching *Mercury Rising* centred upon achieving a credible historical context, and then, from various locomotive design treatises in my library, crafting a preliminary design for *Mercury*. I refined this design by computer modelling of her performance on the track, including coal and water consumption, wind resistance, track gradients—and of course stopping her! I freely admit that for the sake of the narrative, I took liberties to what was truly practical, but the spirit of *Mercury's* design has a sound foundation.

To describe the Abbots Ripton disaster, I referred to the report of the court of inquiry published on the 21st January 1876.

The oddest research was into Victorian fireworks and their amateur manufacture—definitely don't do this at home!